Sarah,

Enjoy the

good to see you,

Rod

MOHAWK BROTHERHOOD

rcarr97350@aol.com

RODGER CARROLL

ISBN: 1453653643
ISBN-13: 9781453653647

To my parents, Vic and Alouise, R.I.P.

CHAPTER ONE

Terry Malloy conversed with dead men. Only the men who covered his back in Vietnam could he trust. How the hell did he get into this mess?

A sledge hammer pounded his skull. He had to stop drinking so much. Let's see. There was Thornton, that bald-headed, pig-tailed, asshole of a reporter. Terry sat up. A lightning bolt crackled in his head. He put his head in his hands. It didn't really matter. His beautiful daughter, Ella, was dead, killed in Iraq.

Anderson's voice sounded in his head. "You need to slow down on the booze, Hillbilly." His old squad leader scratched the shrapnel scar on his forehead.

Terry rubbed his temples. Jesus, his head hurt. "It will happen, Anderson, just like I told you. Someone will call them 'Nazis' before long, start accusing them of murder and torture, having more suicides and doing more drugs, just like they did to us."

Terry could almost feel Anderson's pat on the shoulder. "We're here, if you need us."

Terry threw off the bed covers, slowly placing both feet on the floor. The sledge hammer kept pounding. "We?"

Balancing himself unsteadily, Terry wobbled to his feet. He sat back down. The painted face of another squad member, an unsmiling Cochise, came into focus, a cigarette dangling from his lips. "Steady there, Malloy. *Que pasa, amigo?* You used to be a fighter, a survivor." He could almost smell Cochise's cigarette.

Terry laughed. He must still be drunk from the night before. Jesus, his head. His old squad could have kicked some ass around this town. He stopped smiling. Ella was dead and he was talking to ghosts.

Last spring, Terry had come home after hearing the hysterical wail of his wife's voice reverberating over the phone. Clarissa, collapsed on the sofa, gazed into the fireplace. A young army officer stood behind the sofa. The letter, the official notice of Ella's death, lay on the floor.

Alex, his eight-year-old grandson, stood at her side patting her shoulder, his curly hair bouncing up and down with his nodding head. "It's okay, Nana. Please don't cry. It's okay. She's in heaven with my dad. Don't cry, Nana."

Waiting for the body to be sent home was like climbing out of a dark abyss and spiraling down into a darker one. Terry and Clarissa hovered between a shadowy twilight of expectant mourning and the clear hope that some mistake had been made. The two of them walked trance-like through their daily routines, hoping and mourning, praying and crying. His wife asked the English Department to find someone else to teach her classes. After three days of friends expressing their sorrow, Terry went back to work. Clarissa would not leave the house.

They received the news that their golden-haired daughter's coffin would be flown into the local airport the next day. Terry went to work, but could not lift his hand to the blackboard. He leaned his head against the board and mumbled, "My dear daughter's dead."

One of the students, Laura Boatwright, took him by the hand and led him to his office. Two fellow professors, Rich Breedlove and Sarah Stableford, drove him home in silence.

When Ella was five or six years old, she had asked him how much he loved her. Terry playfully paraphrased the Latin poet Terence: "*Filiam meam magis quam oculos meos amo.* I love my daughter more than my eyes."

At Terry's house, Rich and Sarah helped him inside. When Sarah asked if he would be okay, Terry mumbled, "I wish I were blind."

Terry and Clarissa made it through the funeral. Afterward, when they were alone, Terry, seeking solace for himself, sought to comfort Clarissa. Wrapping his arms around her, he felt her stiff and unresponding. She pulled away.

Leaning against the fireplace, her rigid back to him, she spoke quietly. "You should have said more. You could have done more to stop her or change her mind. I told you that when she was only talking about joining the Army." A day later, Clarissa moved into the guest bedroom.

Terry stormed into the kitchen. "Clarissa, for goodness sake, what the hell are you doing?"

Clarissa folded towels on the kitchen table. She didn't raise her voice. "Every time I look at you, I'm reminded of Ella and what you could have done. If only you could have been more insistent. Why didn't you try harder, Terry?" Picking up the towels, Clarissa moved past him. Her caustic voice sounded from the hallway. "She was our *daughter*, our only child for God's sake!"

They struggled through to the end of Spring Semester. In the following days and weeks of summer, his wife's accusatory glances followed him around the house. The sleeping arrangements stayed the same. Occasionally, Terry reached out to Clarissa with a touch or a word. She either pulled away or refused to speak. He returned to his daily routine of running with Sarah Stableford at the school track in order to escape.

Escape was an illusion. During the summer, Terry and Clarissa shared Alex with his other set of grandparents, George and Peggy

Holland. In the quiet evenings, when the fireflies twinkled among the honeysuckle along the outfield fence, Terry attended Alex's baseball games. Clarissa seldom went. When Alex stayed with them she would help Alex dress for the game and wave good-bye. A smile caressed her lips, but there was no smile in her sad, green eyes.

Sometime during that summer, Clarissa decided that she needed to get away. Sitting at the kitchen table, she ran lethargic fingers through her red hair. "I've asked the department for time off this fall. After Alex begins school, I'm going to London and stay with my brother Harold. They've told me I could stay with them for as long as I wanted."

Terry retreated daily to the den with a glass of scotch. Conversations with Ella erupted in him like geysers, spewing guilt and regret into every corner of his soul. He sipped his scotch.

Ella's sparkling green eyes broke through his meditations. "Dad, I'm going to join. I'm twenty-seven years old, I'm an adult, and my country needs me."

"Your son needs you, too, Ella. Have you thought about him."

She jerked her head, flipping redish-blond hair back over her shoulder. Seeing his hesitation and wanting his approval, she took his rough hands in her slender ones. "Dad, please, I know what I'm doing. Gus and I made mistakes. We married too young and you know why. After he died in the wreck…I need to do this. I've made a mess of my life. Alex, you guys, and Gus' parents, are the only good things I've got. My job isn't going anywhere and I'm tired of college right now. You've often told me that Vietnam changed your life. Well, I'm ready for a change. You and Mom and George and Peggy can take care of Alex while I'm in basic training." Ella blinked back tears. "I'm feeling guilty enough about leaving him. Don't make it harder. I want you to be proud of me, Dad."

The painful reveries always ended with the realization that his daughter was dead, killed by a roadside bomb in a small, dusty village in Iraq. He sipped his scotch and sank into the leather lounger. The setting sun pierced the empty room. Shafts of light suspended moats of dust in a timeless abeyance. Outside of the light, shadows solidified around his broken heart. He closed his eyes and sipped his drink. "I'll always be proud of you, Ella."

Terry wanted to talk about the ache that tormented his heart, the blame that squeezed the air out of his lungs and stole his breath, the doubt that made him fear getting out of bed in the morning. Did he contribute to the death of his daughter? Should he have done more to convince her not to join the Army? Could he have suggested alternatives such as the Navy or Air Force? In his secret heart of hearts, he was proud she had joined. Proud that she wanted to serve her country. And now she was gone. What was the purpose of it all? He couldn't talk about any of it. Hearing the haunting echoes of possibilities passed over, forever gone, the yoke of guilt and regret weighed on his shoulders.

When he attempted to talk to Clarissa, she waved a despondent hand at him in dismissal. "I'm trying really hard not to detest you right now." She stood in the kitchen, shoulders slumped, her hollow voice lacking hope, vindictiveness, or anger. "I can't find it in myself to forgive you. I'm drained, Terry. I can't help you right now. I need to get away. Everything I see and touch reminds me of Ella. That's why I'm going to England. You have to sober up, deal with your own problems, and help George and Peggy take care of Alex. My only regret is leaving Alex. You should have done more, Terry."

Over the summer, Terry habitually retreated to the den, drinking and listening to the 30s and 40s music of Benny Goodman, Tommy Dorsey, and other big bands. He lived and functioned in the fog of culpability that he had fashioned for himself. Preparing for his fall history class, the needs of his grandson, and jogging daily with Sarah Stableford kept him from diving completely into a bottle of oblivion.

A week into the fall semester, the day before Clarissa left for London, he picked up Alex at school. Walking into the house, he found a man in his living room talking to Clarissa.

Her small hands clutched and released a handkerchief. She dabbed at her red eyes. "This is Greg Thornton, a reporter for the local paper. Mr. Thornton wants to do a story on Ella. I've been telling him about her."

Thornton stood, revealing a man of medium height and slender build with a slight paunch. He pinched his thin lips together, not smiling as he shook Terry's hand. Gray hair surrounded his bald head. A six inch pony tail sprouted out the back. "Everyone calls me, Thorn. We're doing a series of articles on the casualties of Iraq and Afghanistan, Professor Malloy. One of your colleagues, Rich Breedlove, suggested I come by and see you." The journalist reached into a brown pouch and took out several typewritten sheets enclosed in clear vinyl. He offered them to Terry. "Here are some that we've done. Your daughter will be the last."

Clarissa raised her small, oval face to Terry and the reporter. She held several photos of Ella in one of her tiny hands and proffered them to both her husband and Thornton, brushing the handkerchief at her eyes with the other hand. "I've been telling Mr. Thornton what a wonderful girl our Ella was."

The reporter sat back down and glanced at his notes. "I've got most of the background information I need for the article. Ella was killed in Nasser Wa Salaam. That's where the marines shot those three civilians, isn't it?"

Terry's stomach muscles tightened. "There was a question whether those guys were civilians or not, wasn't there? If I'm not mistaken, didn't they find weapons in their car? Anyway, that incident happened before Ella's unit got there. Ella was in the Army, not the Marines."

Flipping through his notebook, Thornton did not look up while Terry talked. "Nasser Wa Salaam is near Abu Ghraib. Was your daughter associated with Abu Ghraib?"

"Our daughter was in a Military Police unit, Mr. Thornton." Clarissa twisted her handkerchief in her hands. "She helped people, Iraqis, trying to rebuild their country. She certainly had nothing to do with Abu Ghraib."

"Weren't the people at Abu Ghraib in the Military Police?" Thornton said, slapping the writing tablet on his knee.

Terry, jaw clenched, willed himself to relax. "Yes, but the people at Abu Ghraib were National Guard, not regular Army. So, Ella was not in that Unit." Terry took his hands out of his pocket. "Mr. Thornton, what are these questions about?"

"I'm just trying to tie up loose ends. What did Ella think about the war? Do you mind answering? Also, I was wondering if you two wanted to say anything about the war in general. And before I leave, I would like to talk to her son, Alex, and perhaps get a photo of you three."

Terry hovered near Clarissa. "Ella was proud of what she was doing in Iraq, Mr. Thornton. Her unit volunteered to help Iraqi villagers clear ammunition that had been stored in school houses. The villagers were eager to get the schools started again. She helped clear and restart over twenty schools."

Thornton had an annoying habit of tapping his pen against different parts of his face. He finished writing and pummeled his bulbous nose with his pen. Leaning forward, the light shining off his bald head, he rested both elbows on his knees. "What did she feel about the kids that Americans killed?"

Clarissa stiffened. White knuckles gripped the couch.

Terry, his face growing hot, leaned forward. "What the hell do you mean by that?"

The reporter, thumping his pen against his rounded chin, crossed his legs and leaned back in the chair. He stopped thumping and waved both hands in front of him. "Don't get me wrong. I know Ella wasn't a fighter. Mrs. Malloy just said she was in a Military Police unit. I just...um...wondered if she saw any overt violence against Iraqi civilians by American troops. She seemed to be near some places, like Abu Ghraib and Nasser Wa Salaam, where some pretty bad things happened."

Terry clenched and unclenched his fist. "Accidents and atrocities happen in war, Mr. Thornton. Don't indict and convict our entire military, and the men and women serving, because of a few random acts of brutality."

He wanted to slam his fist into Thornton's cocky face. "What the hell does this have to do with Ella? To answer your question, Ella never said anything about Americans killing civilians. She did say that she went to a mass grave site where several thousand Iraqis were buried by Saddam Hussein. She said that many of them had been buried alive by that maniac."

Thornton stopped smacking his ear lobe with his pen. "Mr. Malloy, please, I don't know anything about the war. It's just that I've read different things written by others. Ella's nearness to Nasser Wa Salaam and Abu Ghraib is probably coincidental."

"Probably? I don't care what you've read. Ella's unit was helping small towns clear schools of ammunition, rebuilding power generators, installing sewage lines, and stuff like that. She sent us many pictures," Terry nodded to the pictures in Clarissa's hand, "of her surrounded by Iraqi women, children, and men." Terry grabbed a photo of Ella with smiling Iraqis. He tossed the photo toward the journalist. "Do these Iraqis look like they're being murdered by Americans."

Done scribbling, Thornton stuck his pen in his small mouth. "What do you two think of the war?"

Clarissa stared at the pictures of Ella. "We were afraid for her to go, but--"

"Mr. Thornton,"Terry snapped, "is this going to be in the paper?"

Thornton looked up from his writing pad, nodding.

Terry moved closer to the reporter. "Can't you just write a story about Ella without getting into the political crap." Balling his fist, the muscles in his body tensed. Then his shoulders drooped. The pent-up energy and anger drained from him like air from a punctured balloon. "We're grieving over the death of our daughter. Do you really want to use our grief so you can get some cheap quote from us about the political aspects of the war?"

Closing his writing pad, the reporter leaped to his feet. "I think I have enough to write a good article about Ella. I hope I didn't inconvenience or bother you too much."

Clarissa stood beside Terry. She stretched out a beckoning hand. "I'll go get Alex, Mr. Thornton. Here is the picture of Ella."

Walking past Terry, the newsman took the picture of Ella, leaving the one Terry had offered where it lay. He watched Clarissa leave and then pointing the pen at Terry, said, "Mrs. Malloy told me you were in Vietnam. Were you in combat?"

Terry's arms itched and he wanted to scratch them. "Yes, I was."

Thornton folded his arms. "This has nothing to do with Ella. You're a History Professor aren't you? What do you think about Senator Kerry's having testified nearly thirty years ago that American soldiers in Vietnam raped, murdered, and tortured hundreds of thousands of Vietnamese?"

Terry's mind jumped from Ella to his Vietnam service. This sonofabitch was trying to link Iraqi civilians being killed and Kerry's rape-and-torture testimony. Eyes narrowed, Terry clenched his jaw. Trembling, he tried to keep his voice calm. "People in my department, the History Department, are talking about the campaign and

Kerry's testimony and some group called the Swift Boat Vets. Kerry's senate testimony is old news. I haven't really kept up with all of the breaking events. We've been preoccupied with our daughter's death and we haven't watched a lot of TV or talked politics with anyone. Besides, all you have to do is watch any recent film about Vietnam. We're still being accused of that crap out in Hollywood."

Shrugging, the reporter slipped his pouch over one shoulder. A defiant note filled his voice. "You might think it's crap, but Kerry's not apologizing for it. The Swift Boat Vets have started running commercials on TV about the Senator's service and they may affect the campaign. Are you telling me that you haven't seen the ads?"

Shaking his head Terry felt the yoke weighing him down. "Please, say something nice about my daughter, Mr. Thornton." He stretched out a discouraged arm.

Clarissa appeared with Alex and introduced him to Thornton. After he shook Alex's hand, he pulled a camera from his pouch. Clarissa and Terry herded Alex between them. Thornton fiddled with his camera. "Alex is the first child of a vet I've run across in doing this series. How do you feel about your mother being killed, Alex? You must really miss her."

Terry stepped in front of Thornton, grabbing his arm. "Of course he misses her. How do you think he feels? He's heartbroken and so are we."

"Terry, for God's sake, stop."

Terry turned away from Thornton toward Clarissa. She held Alex's shoulders. Alex hugged Clarissa's waist.

Thornton, jerking free of Terry's grip, backed up, eyes wide. He fumbled with his camera. "All right, all right, calm down."

Alex buried himself under Clarissa's arm. One wide, green eye peeked at Terry. Clarissa backed up. One arm circled Alex's head.

She dabbed at her eyes with her handkerchief. "Terry, please! What are you doing?"

Jerking a thumb toward the front door, Terry fought to hold down his rage. "Get out!"

Thornton quivered like a bowl of jelly. He backed away from Terry, fumbling with the camera.

Terry gestured to the door. "I don't think we want any pictures made today."

Thornton's pouch, holding the writing pad, slapped against his thigh as he made his way to the door. He placed the camera cover on the lens and slipped it into his pouch. "The article will be in the paper the day after tomorrow."

Terry opened the door. "Mr. Thornton, if it's all the same to you, please don't print the article."

Thornton adjusted his rumpled shirt, tucked part of it back in his pants and wiped the sweat off his bald head. "The public has a right to know." He turned and left.

Terry slammed the door.

Clarissa stood in the living room, hugging Alex and eying Terry. As Terry walked past them, Clarissa pulled Alex to her and backed up. Alex's big green eyes never left his grandfather's face. Terry wanted to talk, but knew he would only rant about Thornton. Moreover, he didn't want to bring up Ella in front of Alex. Walking into the den, he poured scotch over ice. He turned on the stereo. Glenn Miller's "In The Mood" filled the room. He settled in his chair and closed his eyes. His pumping heart wanted to leap out of his chest. What did Thornton know about Vietnam or Iraq? Nothing. Man, it would have felt good to smack that bastard. He sipped his scotch. The filtered twilight slowly turned to gray. Clarissa, upstairs, thumped around in her bedroom, packing for London.

What would Anderson, his old squad leader have done? You would have done the same thing, wouldn't you? Anderson's thin face drifted into Terry's consciousness and his voice, filled with suppressed fury, echoed in Terry's head: "You're damn right I would've. You were too fucking nice."

Terry closed his eyes and let the scotch flow through his body. The familiar faces of his old squad drifted in and out of his thoughts. "It's about time you kicked back, Malloy," Cochise said. "You used to be a fighter. You used to have *cojones, compadre*."

Two other faces, Duffy and Brumsen, floated before his eyes. Duffy, the radio man, smiled. Brumsen's ivory teeth stood out against his black skin.

"The press will eventually treat Iraqi and Afghan vets like they did us, guys." Terry gulped his drink. "You're nothing but rapists and murderers in their eyes. Somehow, you became the enemy."

Brumsen's deep voice echoed around him. "Then you got to fight for us, Hillbilly."

Terry shook his head, smiling. "Don't call me 'Hillbilly', Brumsen."

As he staggered up the stairs to bed, Duffy's gentle tones resonated in his head. "When did you stop fighting, Malloy?"

Awake now, in the early morning hours, sitting on the bed, he knew that his fury at Thornton would abate. Passion needed to be sustained by an act of will. Thornton was not worth the energy. However, guilt sustained itself, nurtured and grown in the fertile silences and pauses of the soul. Ella was dead and he was talking to ghosts. He barely remembered coming upstairs. Last night, he had felt a righteous anger about the stupid encounter with the reporter. This morning it didn't matter. Ella was dead.

* * *

Staggering away from the bed, he looked up. Duffy stood in the doorway, his radio crackling with static. His left hand rested on an M-16, which rested on an ammunition pouch. His right hand held a radio receiver. Duffy's helmet, tilted back on his forehead, exposed his freckled face. He pointed the radio receiver at Terry. "It does matter. It matters now more than ever. We're all in this together."

Terry stumbled backward, gasping and reaching for the wall. His hand grasped vines and twisted them violently. He shoved them aside in disgust. "I hate these damn things. Always pulling at you and grabbing you."

Duffy chuckled and ran a towel through his red hair. Draping the towel around his slender neck, he waved a hand of resignation at Terry. "Don't fight it. The jungle breaks everybody."

Brumsen squeezed mosquito repellent onto a muscled arm. "You gotta learn to give a little, Malloy. You gotta shuck'n jive. Be cool, man, be patient. Can't get in a hurry when you're fooling with them vines or this jungle."

Anderson stepped through the foliage with the natural grace of an athlete, his movements cautious and quick. He cocked his head to one side, listening to the sounds and the silence of the jungle. His angry gray eyes never stopped searching, taking in the surrounding variety, the order and the disorder, of bushes, trees, vines, smells, and sounds. Crows feet stretched from his eyes back to his hairline. He was twenty-one years old.

Anderson scratched his aquiline nose. His square jaw had a day's worth of beard. He spoke with slow deliberation, a subterranean current of suppressed fury and violence surged and bubbled near the surface. "Okay, listen up, guys. We've got a VC base camp up ahead. First platoon found a latrine. The CO says the second platoon'll stay on the outside left of the four files and cover the left flank." Anderson paused. "Our squad'll pull point."

Placing the receiver of his radio in its cradle Duffy groaned, youthful features hidden in the shadows of his helmet. “So, we’re pulling point again.”

Breathing heavily in the heat, Anderson knelt. His thin body leaned against his rifle. The squad had been in the jungle since 7 that morning. Now 3 in the afternoon, rivulets of sweat created tracks through the grime on their faces. The company had broken up its base camp and was marching to a new one. Their rucksacks contained the paraphernalia of war and personal gear: claymore mines, mortar rounds, rockets, insect repellant, cigarettes, foot powder, paper and pen for letters home, socks, and hundreds of rounds of ammunition. Grenades, canteens, and ammunition pouches hung from their webbing. Each man carried eighty to ninety pounds of equipment in temperatures that easily reached one-hundred degrees Fahrenheit.

Slumping against his rucksack, every muscle in Terry’s body ached. The fluid-draining heat exorcized all energy. At every break, he lay somnolent, moving only when he had a purpose. The vampire jungle engulfed him, leeching strength.

All the companies of the battalion would rendezvous at the site of the new base camp. The firepower of a full battalion, three full companies, left little chance of being attacked. So, the night would be a little less stressful.

For the last two weeks, the routine had been the same. A base camp, which was really a landing zone for helicopters to bring in supplies, would be established. The companies and platoons of the battalion operated out of the base camp, patrolling the area around the LZ, the landing zone. After two or three days, the troops emptied the sandbags, filled in the foxholes, and marched to another LZ.

Taking off his helmet, Anderson scratched his streak of gray hair and the shrapnel scar that had caused it. “We’ve been lucky. This sector's been quiet for the last two weeks. With any luck, we won't meet any VC at this camp. Lewis, it's your turn to take the point."

The statement hung in the broiling air. Lewis dragged on his cigarette and blew the smoke out. "Okay."

Cochise flicked a cigarette into the foliage. His mohawk haircut made a dark gash across his scalp. One red and one yellow stripe covered each of his high, bronze cheek bones. "Lewis ain't ready for this situation and this kind of point, Anderson. I'll do it."

"No. Lewis has been with us for two weeks. He and Malloy have pulled point a couple of times each now. He knows the routine." Anderson's slender hands moved quickly to tighten a shoulder strap on his rucksack. "It's his turn in the rotation. Lewis takes the point. Dangerous situations're gonna come up. Now's as good a time as any to become a full member of the squad."

Terry secretly breathed a sigh of relief. The rotation was a battalion-wide system in which the lead of a file, the point, was interchanged at regular times during patrols and sweeps. Companies of men rotated the point, as well as platoons in the companies, down to squads in the platoons. The individual members of the squads were the lowest common denominator. As long as the rotation was kept at a reasonable pace, no one man, no one squad, no one platoon, or company felt as if it took on an undue burden. Every man shared the danger. Where the action started, point was the most dangerous spot in a dangerous environment; when your turn came, you pulled point and prayed. It was Terry's turn to carry the extra machine-gun ammo. He did not have to pull point through the camp.

Sweat coursed down their grim faces. The heat and steam pushed hot air into their scorched lungs with every breath. Brumsen exchanged glances with Duffy, their mouths tight slits drawn across gaunt faces. Duffy's gaze darted to Cochise, who shook his head. What was the intensity about? He threw a look at Lewis. Lewis was surely thinking the same thing. What was the big deal? They had both pulled point a couple of times. They now had some experience.

Both new to the squad, this was their first operation. During the last two weeks, Terry had even become bored at times. Lewis and he talked about it in whispers when the veterans weren't around. They took turns at point, along with everyone else, when the squad was in the point position in the file. They also took turns carrying the extra machine-gun ammunition for Brumsen's M-60. To Lewis and Terry, who had seen no combat, everything they had endured seemed to be a lot of work with no result, but not overly dangerous. They just needed to be cautious. They would be fine. Both were turning into good soldiers, handling the jobs given to them without complaint. So, why were the vets passing concerned looks?

"Lewis, this isn't the same jungle we've been walking through," Duffy said, scratching a mosquito bite on his slender neck. "This is a base camp. Charley has been around here and could be close by now."

Cochise wiped an ammunition clip on his shirt and slid it into his M—16. "Those bastards're here. *Puta madre que los pario!* I can smell'em!"

Massaging a tattoo of his girlfriend's name, Annabelle, on his massive forearm, Brumsen rubbed in insect repellent. "If Charley ain't here, there's some booby traps around here for sure."

"I can do this. I can do it," Lewis said, clicking the safety of his rifle on and off. He stared away into the vegetation and took a deep breath.

Brumsen massaged his other forearm with repellent. "Sure you can, Bro. You gotta be cool though."

The glow of Cochise's cigarette reflected in the red and yellow paint streaked across his narrow face. Smoke swirled around him. "You gotta be a little more careful now. Watch where you're steppin', and keep your eyes movin' all the time. Try to anticipate."

Anderson glanced at his watch. "And remember, if anything's out of the ordinary, anything's unnatural, just stop and call me up, or move back, or do any fucking thing you want to do, just be careful. You've heard this before."

Lewis chewed on a fingernail. "I'll be okay." He spat the fingernail out and began chewing another.

The word filtered down for the squads to saddle up. The jungle percolated with drowsy men shuffling into their rucksacks. Gulping water from their canteens, they examined their weapons and flipped them off safety. Like sleepy tigers, waking and preparing themselves for the hunt, the weary men yawned and stretched, readying.

Anderson's squad walked to the head of their file. None of them talked as they stepped through and around other silent men. Lewis and Anderson halted beside a disheveled, older sergeant.

The sergeant bent over to sweep leeches off his boots. He stepped on the leeches. "This's where the second platoon stopped. Taylor's squad is to your right, and beyond him is Williams and then Czplicki. We move out at 1515 hours, which is around five minutes from now. Let's synchronize." The sergeant slapped at a mosquito. "I'll be with the captain. Don't take any chances. If you guys see something, stop and radio back. We'll probably call in artillery on this camp anyway. Let's do it with no casualties."

Studying the foliage, Terry barely listened. The endless variety of the jungle and the difference between his Tennessee hills and this forbidding wilderness fascinated him. He followed Lewis. Neither spoke as they waited for the word to advance. The order of the squad was Lewis, Malloy, Brumsen, Anderson, Duffy, who carried the squad radio, and Cochise. Murmurs percolated from behind Terry and the words, "Move out," came off his lips at the same time he heard Cochise say it to Brumsen. Lewis looked back at him, smiled nervously, and winked. Terry gestured a thumbs-up.

Lewis took a stride forward and disappeared.

Terry clicked off the safety. Standing five feet from Lewis, he could not see him. Surrounded by vegetation, isolated and alone, he followed Lewis into the green fog.

The troops had a saying: *The jungle broke everyone.* No one fought it for long. With every step, lush fronds and plants grasped at him. Branches and leaves slapped him in the face, hitting and scratching his hands and arms. Terry constantly pushed vegetation away, only to have clinging vines and fronds reaching for him. Long, slender vines snaked down through the trees, falling on him at odd moments. He moved this frond away and caught that vine. He pulled at the vine grabbing for his rifle and felt his feet ensnared in soft, green tendrils. An army of leeches crawled up the tendrils coiling around his boots. Stomping his feet to knock them off, he brushed against the underside of a frond where ants nested. The ants gnawed and bit their way over Terry's hand and rushed up his elbow. He brushed the ants off without pausing. A lizard stared at him, forked tongue flicking in and out of its mouth. An incessant cacophony of birds and monkeys, cooing and chattering, added a counterpoint of life to the dank smell of layer upon layer of dead and rotting vegetation that permeated the boiling air.

Shafts of light penetrated the high, canopied growth, constructing a vaulted cathedral of vegetation, lighting up some of the jungle, but also darkening other parts by creating shadows everywhere. Moats of dust floated through the pillars of light upon unfelt whispers of air. Yellow and green birds twittered in the sunlight.

He pushed into and through this overwhelming tide of tropical vegetation. Expectant. Tense. The enemy might be close by. Fully cognizant of where he was and what he did, Terry pushed away a three-foot leaf and ducked cautiously under vines while stepping over a log.

Lewis appeared and dissolved within a billowing cloud of red smoke. Red pulp flew past Terry's head. Smoke billowed around him. He floated upon a wave, hearing nothing. He felt nothing as the wave overwhelmed him, floating, lifted upon the tidal wave of numbness and terror, then lying upon the ground. The hurricane roar of guns assaulted him. Smoke roiled everywhere. The acrid smell of gunpowder filled his nostrils. He lay on his back, listening.

Over the tsunami of explosions ripping at his body, and people screaming, came a sound he had never heard before and couldn't quite place. He rolled over onto his stomach. Lewis crawled toward him waving a red, pulpy something. One of Lewis's legs was not working right. It slowly turned red. Lewis' bulging eyes screamed at him. Terry scrabbled toward the eyes. The strange sound he had heard was not coming from Lewis's eyes but from Lewis's mouth, which contorted into a bloody orifice of pain, spewing blood. Terry crawled toward the screaming eyes. Vines pulled at his legs. Little puffs of smoke and dirt erupted around Lewis every time he screamed. The bullets went away. His eyes and mouth screamed again and again as the bullets came back. Lewis's body twitched and shook from the impact. Insistent vines tugged at Terry. He lunged toward the screaming eyes. The vines became hands grasping both his legs, pulling him over the log.

Finally safe behind the log, safe with the others, Duffy yelled at him to get down. Brumsen, grabbing the machine-gun ammunition, fired over the log at the same time. Cochise jumped through the undergrowth. Cochise and Anderson held lumps in their hands. They threw the lumps. The grenades exploded.

He could not hear Lewis anymore. Over the log lay a motionless pile of bloody clothes.

Duffy hit him on the head. "Stay down!"

Brumsen yelled for more ammo. Safe behind the log, Terry fumbled with the machine-gun ammunition. And then, quiet.

Brumsen poured water on the barrel of his machine gun. Duffy looked over the log, sighting down the barrel of his M-16. Terry peeked over the log. Blood stained the ground around Lewis's crumpled body. Fronds, leaves, and pieces of fronds still fell. Shredded leaves and branches lay over and around him. Beyond Lewis, Cochise and Anderson knelt and peered into the jungle. Both men shouldered their rifles; the smoking barrels pointed forward. Neither glanced at Lewis. Cochise, leaping ahead of Anderson, vanished.

Terry slumped behind the log. "Jesus."

Anderson yelled, "First squad…All clear!"

The various squad leaders shouted 'All clear.'

Duffy ran to Lewis. "Medic! Medic!"

Brumsen squatted in front of Terry, cradling the smoking machine gun.

"Jesus," Terry said.

Brumsen leaned his machine gun against the log. "You okay, Hillbilly? Better check yourself out, man, and make sure you ain't hurt. Can't believe you and me didn't get hit, bein' close and all."

Andersen came back to the log where the rest of the squad gathered. "Check him over, Brumsen; make sure he isn't going to die on us. What the hell were you doing when Duffy tried to pull you over the log, Malloy?"

A cloud of caustic smoke floated in the air. Terry shook uncontrollably. "Jesus."

"Take it easy and get a grip on yourself. Just sit there for a couple of minutes." Anderson shook his head, reached out, and patted Terry's shoulder.

"How long did the fight last?" Terry hugged himself, trying to stop shaking.

Duffy released the ammunition clip from his M-16, checked it, and slid it back into its slot. "Forty-five seconds, a minute at the most."

Terry clutched his rifle. Tremors coursed through him. "I was trying to crawl toward Lewis, I guess. I don't really know. I thought my legs were caught in vines."

Two medics knelt over Lewis's body. Terry did not know then that field medics hate to pronounce anyone dead in the field. Men who were probably already dead were bandaged and their air passages cleared with a plastic tube stuck down the throat. The medics placed no bandages on Lewis. His right arm was sheared off above the elbow. He had also been hit in the mid-section and legs. Shrapnel and bullets had penetrated every part of his body.

The medics took Lewis's poncho out of his rucksack and slid it under him to create a stretcher of sorts and also to cover him. When the helicopter came to pick up the body, it would be easier to lift and place in the lowered litter using the poncho. Men chopped a clearing big enough for the medevac to lower a stretcher.

"You couldn't have helped him," Anderson said, "but you almost got Duffy killed pulling away from him like you did. Bullets were poppin' all around you two while he tried to pull you back."

At a sign from Duffy, Anderson eased up and spoke gently. "You have to think and react out here, Malloy. If you don't, you're going to die. If you die, don't take anyone else with you except the fucking gooks."

Terry hung his head. "Sorry, Duffy."

"This was your first fire-fight. Be careful, Malloy," Duffy said, flipping the safety switch on his M-16. "When you start attracting attention to yourself and drawing fire, it tends to irritate the men near you." He slapped Terry on the back. Although his wide mouth stretched in a grin, his pale blue eyes held no humor.

Cochise returned, cradling his M-16 in the crook of his elbow. He glanced at Lewis and crossed himself. "We found the machine-gun position and one dead gook. I found a blood trail. Some guys in third squad'll follow it."

Brumsen, who had been rummaging in the bushes, appeared with the lower part of Lewis's arm. He laid it on Lewis's chest.

"Jesus." Terry's stomach lurched.

"Jesus ain't out here in this green hell," Brumsen said.

"Jesus's closer than you think," Duffy added.

A steel edge entered Anderson's voice. He wheeled on Duffy. "You've gotta be joking or out of your fucking mind to think there's a God in this world."

Duffy rested his M-16 on an ammunition pouch, blue eyes wide, questioning.

"I mean it. Take a look at Lewis over there and tell me there's a God." Anderson gulped water. He gestured toward Lewis with the canteen, clenching his jaws repeatedly. "I'm sick of this shit. The Bible says 'Don't kill' and all I want to do is get one chance at these bastards. I'll bring down some 'shalt nots' on their asses."

Terry pushed off the log, using his M-16 to stand. "Is it always like this? Is it always this bad?"

"This is pretty routine, as far as it goes," Brumsen said, wiping Lewis's blood off his hands onto his fatigues. "We walk through this rotten, smelly, piece-of-shit jungle, and when they want to, they blow a mine or an artillery shell on us and disappear into the green fog."

Anderson nodded toward Lewis's poncho-covered corpse. "One of these days, I'm gonna get even with these sons of bitches. I'm going to pay them back for every death, for every wound, for every fucking drop of blood."

Dark eyes narrowing, a smile played around the corners of Cochise's thin lips. "Payback is going to be fun, *amigo*."

Cochise's cold, coal-black eyes and painted face hypnotized Terry. He shivered. Jesus, what had he gotten into?

Now opening his eyes, Terry gripped the bed and glanced at the doorway. His hands shook. Duffy and the squad were gone. Holy shit, now he was *seeing* dead men. He sagged to the bed. He could have reached out and touched Duffy. Stop drinking! Staggering from the bedroom, Terry stumbled downstairs and poured two fingers of scotch. He sat down in his chair and, with a trembling hand, drank. At 6:30, he went upstairs and showered.

CHAPTER TWO

Terry and Clarissa dropped Alex at his school. Alex stood beside the car, adjusting his blue backpack.

Clarissa hugged Alex, her fingers running through his brown, curly hair. She wiped away her tears. "I'll be back in a month. Take care of Granddad."

"I love you, Grandma." Alex wrapped his arms around her waist.

"I'll see you this afternoon. Tonight, we eat pizza. Just us guys," Terry said, putting the car in gear.

On the road to the airport, Clarissa chilled the air with her silence. Staring straight ahead, she fidgeted with her seat belt.

How had they come to this? What road brought them here? It had to be more than Ella. They were so in love when they first courted, offering themselves to each other. The secret understanding each had with the other. Among a crowd, her delicate touch of his elbow used to send chills, promising possibilities, down his spine. Her knowing glances and seductive smiles elicited hot loins and weak knees. Now she sat there, cold and immovable.

Was it more than Ella? They had sought their own careers, neither asking too much of the other. How much love was in their marriage before Ella left? Old habits die hard, if they die at all. Two people drifting through life with a daughter and grandson who held them together. Was he just a habit that Clarissa was now willing to shed?

She had been emphatic about Ella's leaving. "If anything happens to her, I don't know what I'm going to do. I can't talk her out of it, Terry. You've been in war. For God's sake, tell her what she's getting into."

How do you tell someone about fear and panic and bodies flying apart? It can't be understood, only experienced. "I've told her how bad it can be, Clarissa. What more can I do? She's a grown woman. You need to realize that." What did he believe? He defended his daughter and her choices with Clarissa, then argued his wife's point of view with his daughter.

Clarissa's fist hit the table. "Goddammit, Terry. Stop defending her actions. Tell her she's being irresponsible. Tell her she needs to stay here and take care of Alex. Take a stand!"

Now with his white knuckles on the steering wheel, Terry moved down the on ramp of the expressway. "Clarissa, don't leave like this. Please talk to me." He flipped on a blinker and slid into traffic.

"I can't believe what you did yesterday," Clarissa said, pounding her small fist against her knee. Her voice shook with controlled anger. "A reporter is writing a story about your daughter and you toss him out. He may still do a story, but God knows what he'll say now."

Terry shifted lanes. "For God's sake, Clarissa, you heard the questions he was asking about Iraqi civilians being killed. Then he launched into a tirade against Vietnam veterans while you were upstairs. When he said those silly things to Alex, I couldn't stand it any longer."

Folding her arms across her chest, Clarissa shook her head. "I just wish you had thought before you acted so rashly. You scared the devil out of Alex and me. Plus, there's no telling what that reporter will say about Ella now.

"Terry, there's no easy way to say this. When I get back, I want a separation. I'm going to use the time in England to adjust to our being apart. I suggest you do the same. I'll file legal papers when I get back." She touched his arm. "I'm sorry, Terry."

Was Ella just the excuse that she felt she needed? How long had she been thinking about this? Maybe he'd been taking too many things for granted. When had they last been intimate? He laughed to himself. He couldn't remember. Why did she have to batter him with Ella's death and use that as an excuse?

Switching lanes, Terry cleared his throat. "To be honest, Clarissa, looking back, I should have seen it coming. I'm too exhausted to argue with you about it."

He took the exit to the local airport. Clarissa's connecting flight to Atlanta was leaving in forty-five minutes. Terry rolled her luggage to the check-in counter outside the airport. Clarissa gave the attendant her ticket.

With an early class to teach, they had agreed that Terry would say good-bye here at the baggage check-in. He took Clarissa by the shoulders. "I know this has been rough on you, but it's been hard on me, too. I'll try to drink less. I've been thinking I need to slow down. Would that help?"

Without looking at him, Clarissa snapped her purse shut and adjusted it on her arm. "It's too late, Terry. Ella's dead and I feel nothing. You're exhausted and so am I. "

Terry wrapped his arms around his wife. She made no effort to return his caress. Her lips brushed his cheek.

Clarissa took her boarding pass from the baggage attendant. "Take care of Alex. The next couple of days are teacher's planning days at Alex's school. He has those days off and you're supposed to take him over to George and Peggy's tomorrow morning. They're taking him to the mountains, I think. You need to call them. George is planning on taking him camping this weekend." She tapped the boarding pass against her cheek. Her eyes tearing, she squeezed Terry's arm and walked through the entrance without looking back.

Terry watched the entrance for several seconds after Clarissa had disappeared. The bitter smell of car and bus exhaust fumes assailed his senses and brought him back to reality. He walked to his car.

He needed to stop feeling sorry for himself. Maybe he could call the reporter and apologize. Several scenarios ran through his mind. Thornton would either laugh in his face or accept his apology. God, this had all been a strain. He was placing himself at the mercy of a man who probably thought he was a Nazi. What did that bastard know about war? Now, Thucydides knew what war was about. He was going to lecture on Thucydides and the war on Corcyra today. Shifting lanes down the interstate, he reviewed his lecture.

* * *

In class, Terry did not look at his notes. "In this war on the island of Corcyra, you'll notice the complete breakdown of all norms of behavior. All rules and values, all customs and traditions are turned upside down. Truths became lies, and lies became truths. Rational thought and rational norms of behavior became perverted. Brutality and judging motives became strengths. Gentleness and moderation became weaknesses." With his back to the class, Terry wrote 'Corcyra' on the board while he talked.

He turned to face the class. His old squad from Vietnam stood in the back. Stupefied, Terry stood silently. "What the h..." Jolting ramrod straight, he attempted to lift a hand that would point a finger at the men. Gasping for breath, he grabbed the table. The classroom whirled. They had been on operations in the jungle. Their green, jungle fatigues were torn and dirty. Sleeves rolled up to the elbows revealed crisscrossing scars caused by jungle thorns and vines. Canteens and ammunition pouches hung from their webbing. They held their weapons with the casual nonchalance of the soldier who knows no danger is present. All four squad members were there: Anderson, Cochise, Brumsen, and Duffy.

Brumsen cradled his M-60 machine gun in his arms like a baby. His huge nose spread all over his face. Beneath the nose, a grin revealed teeth that sparkled against his black skin. Bandoliers of machine-gun ammunition draped across both shoulders and crossed at his chest. He shook his head at Terry, stage-whispering in a playful voice, "What kind of bullshit is the Hillbilly throwing around now?"

The men in the squad laughed.

"Professor? Professor...?"

Students grinned at him, bemused at his abrupt silence. Others questioned with looks of concern. Still others waited patiently for him to speak.

His hand shook as he brought it to his mouth. He was losing his mind. Feeling dizzy, he lowered his head and steadied himself by leaning against the desk. When he looked up, the squad had disappeared. Jesus! Deal with it later! Deal with it later! How in the hell did he deal with dead men?

Gulping for air, Terry willed himself to swallow. He raised the hand he had attempted to point with, wiping his sweating forehead. He had thought about this part of his lecture on the trip back from the airport. Was the world and world events, past and future, always to point to Ella? Terry strained to keep his voice from cracking. "You have to remember that Thucydides's world was pagan. We see the Greek columns and read Plato, Aristotle, and Sophocles. We study Euclid and Pythagoras. However, don't be misled. No Judeo-Christian God temporized the brutality that the Greeks perpetrated upon each other; nevertheless, Herodotus says that, 'No one wants war. In peace, sons bury their fathers; in war, fathers bury their sons.' What can we extrapolate about all war from this statement?"

Silence. The students fidgeted.

"It states in shorter form what Thucydides was saying about the war on Corcyra. War turns the world upside-down. War perverts the natural order. Children should bury their parents. It's not natural for parents to bury their children." God, how could he say that without screaming Ella's name? His beautiful golden-haired Ella. He closed his eyes and then opened them. "No culture that has a claim to civilized behavior wants to see their children die. That's totally unnatural."

Terry glanced at his watch. It was early, but he didn't care. He needed to go talk to someone. He was cracking up. "For tomorrow, we read the Melian Dialogue. As you read this dialogue, remember what we discussed about Platonic Forms. Class dismissed."

Throwing their backpacks on their shoulders, most of the students filed out of the room.

"Professor Malloy, I need to talk to you about my term paper."

"Me, too, Dr. Malloy," another young man said.

"There's a sign-up sheet on my door. If you want to have a conference, pick one of the times that are available."

Laura Boatwright held out several sheets of paper. She pushed her glasses up on the bridge of her chiseled nose. "I have a question about the term paper, Dr. Malloy. I want to do something that continues what I did for you in the spring. Perhaps I can turn both papers into my senior thesis."

"Let's talk about it on the way back to my office, Laura," Terry said, taking the papers and studying them. "You can give me an idea of where you want to go with the paper and your thesis."

He nodded to two boys huddled together. With an exhausted hand, he motioned them forward. "What can I do for you two?"

The taller boy, Jonathan, whose blond hair parted in the middle and had a cowlick in the back, spoke while he stared at the floor. "We're having an information seminar, a teach-in, on Iraq in Hudson Hall. With all the Kerry stuff and the election, some of us on the formation committee have been talking. Would you like to speak to us about Iraq? Professor Horowitz said he would speak as a Korean War Vet. With the Kerry campaign and the Swift Boat Vets grabbing the headlines, the committee figured we could use someone who was in Vietnam. Maybe you could make some comparisons between Vietnam and Iraq. You know, tell us what Vietnam was like."

Still looking at the floor, Jonathan stuffed both hands in his jean pockets. "Everyone knows about your loss, Dr. Malloy. We weren't sure that you would want to talk about Iraq, or Vietnam. I volunteered to speak to you since I was in your class."

Terry chewed on his lip. Could he talk about Iraq and make any sense? Could he talk about Vietnam and make any sense of it? Men killing each other. Ella. He'd never hear her sweet voice again. He folded his arms across his chest and scratched both of his forearms. He had heard the question many times: "What was Vietnam like?" It conjured up images: a boot lying two feet away from a screaming, wounded soldier... his foot still in the boot; the mangled corpse of a dead VC who had a hand grenade go off near him...hardly recognizable as human; Lewis lying in his own blood with his severed arm on his chest; an alert, intelligent Vietnamese man, his intense eyes burning into Terry, his face showing surprise as he dropped the huge claymore mine...small red circles blooming on his chest, the three tiny bullet holes appearing so quickly...as he collapsed to the ground, dead.

* * *

The classroom wavered slightly. The air shimmered with waves of heat. Sweat dripped down his forehead and under his armpits. His irritated arms, cut by vines and thorns, bitten by bugs, begged to be scratched. Green fronds of the jungle reached for him, undulating gently to and fro. The musty stench of rotting vegetation permeated the hot air.

Terry swatted at the swarms of flies and mosquitos buzzing around his head. The stream on his left lurked in malignant stillness. Here and there, close to the bank, small tree branches and reeds surrounded by green scum poked upward through the stagnant water. Squadrons of darting bugs skimmed the surface, flitting in and out of the afternoon shadows and bright heat. A lone red and yellow bird sounded a melancholy twitter in the branches.

Somewhere close by, a fuck-you lizard called out to his brethren. Moving vegetation aside, Brumsen motioned him forward. He reached the spot where Brumsen had appeared. A trail led from the river into the jungle. Branches to his right swayed. He turned in that direction, away from the river. Keep off the trail. Mine! He moved forward. Ten feet further, the squad squatted around Anderson. Terry knelt on one knee.

"The trail is clear from here to the stream," Cochise whispered.

Sitting cross-legged, Anderson studied a map that rested in his lap. A long index finger tapped the map. Helmet tilted back on his head, he scratched the scar on his forehead and whispered coordinates into the radio. His M-16 and rucksack lay at his side. "This is Lima Victor, out." Handing the receiver back to Duffy, Anderson held a finger to his small mouth, light brown eyebrows narrrowed above gray eyes reflecting concern and concentration. "Cochise found a rope tied to a tree, trailing down the bank into the water. We think the gooks use the rope to help them climb up the bank."

Anderson reached into his rucksack and brought out two pouches, each holding a claymore mine. "We're setting the ambush up here tonight along the bank. You guys stay here. Cochise and I are going to set up claymores."

Anderson and Cochise moved back down the trail and disappeared into the jungle. Taking off their rucksacks, Duffy, Brumsen, and Terry fanned out in a semi-circle across the trail facing away from the river. Brumsen set up his machine gun on the trail with Duffy and Terry on each side of him. No one talked.

Big hands moving over the M-60 machine gun, Brumsen extended the two legs attached to the barrel and lowered the weapon to the ground. Lying down behind the gun, a massive hulk, he sighted the barrel down the path.

Terry, on Brumsen's right, brought out extra machine-gun ammunition. Three weeks had passed since Lewis's death. They seemed like three years. Except for two days respite at their base camp, the battalion had been in the jungle for the entire three weeks. A leech, sensing Terry's body heat, crawled on the ground toward him. He crushed it with his rifle butt. His company had been through two ambushes similar to the one that killed Lewis. Two soldiers dead and three wounded. The squad had not been near the explosions when they happened.

Nearby, monkeys swung through the trees with a raucous chatter. Yawning, swatting at mosquitoes, Terry glanced up in the trees but did not spot the monkeys. The red and yellow bird still cooed somewhere in the branches. He had to stay awake. His company and the others in the battalion moved from landing zone to landing zone. During the day, companies and platoons patrolled areas surrounding the LZ. At night, smaller squad-sized units crept into the jungle to ambush maneuvering Viet Cong patrols, which also maneuvered to ambush American patrols. Men running around in the jungle trying to kill each other. It was crazy.

Fading light filtered through the trees. A hand touched Terry's foot. Cochise, his painted face barely visible in the shadows, crouched behind them. Cochise's sinuous body uncoiled as he stood. Every muscle moved with deliberate purpose. Like a panther stalking prey, he disappeared down the darkening trail toward the river.

Crouching, Terry and the others followed.

Mosquitoes swarmed around them. Anderson met them at the river bank where the trail stopped. He motioned for Brumsen and Terry to follow. Pushing aside vegetation, with the river to his right, Terry scrambled along the bank.

Anderson halted and peered through the branches toward the river. "You two dig in here. Clear a field of fire for the machine gun to fire down into the water." Anderson took Terry's helmet off. He placed a grenade in the helmet and then pointed to it. "Put your grenades in here. Malloy, you'll be the grenade man. Don't pick up your weapon until you've thrown all of 'em.

"Clear some branches so Malloy can see where he's throwing," Anderson said, searching through the thick undergrowth. He knelt down. "You don't want 'em hittin' a limb and bouncing back. Any questions?"

"What happens if they don't come across the river?" Brumsen said, removing a taped grenade from his web gear. "What if they come down the same trail we were just on?" He picked at the tape.

Anderson's thin face broke into a grin. "Good question. Cochise is booby-trapping the trail with a couple of grenades. If they go off, it means the gooks are coming from the wrong fucking direction. We have two claymores set up on the bank directed at the river. There will be another claymore directed back down the trail just in case they come from that direction. I'm going to be on the trail tonight. If the grenades on the trail go, you guys get your asses to my position pronto. I'm not expecting anything or anyone until early morning, but you never know." He vanished into the jungle.

Terry and Brumsen cleared a field of fire for the machine gun. While Brumsen dug a depression for them to lie in, Terry studied the branches through which he would have to hurl grenades. He cut several small limbs with his machete. After considering his work, he chopped off two more. Satisfied, he sat down.

Brumsen lay behind the machine gun. "Why don't you get some Zs, Hillbilly. I'll watch til I get sleepy. Dig it, at 10 o'clock we go two hours on and two hours off til morning."

Nodding, Terry closed his eyes. He smiled. Brumsen had tagged him with the name as soon as he realized Terry came from Tennessee. "Hillbilly, when you and I get back in the world, I'm goin' to take you to my city, Washington Delta Charlie. DC and Baltimore are great places to party. You ain't gonna want to go back to the farm once I show you the city lights."

"Brumsen, I don't live on a farm. I live in Memphis." Terry raised both hands in frustration. "My grandfather and great-grandfather have farms that I visit. I don't live there."

"Malloy, you got hay coming out your ears." Brumsen laughed, white teeth showing ivory against his black skin.

Terry woke. Brumsen gripped his shoulder. The luminous dial on Terry's watch read eight o'clock. Lying prone on his stomach to sleep, he sat up and crossed his legs, laying the rifle in his lap. Brumsen, his head resting on his crossed arms, slept.

Through the limp branches, moonlight reflected from the surface of the stream. Flotillas of insects flashed through the moonlight across the pestilential water. Down the bank, a frog croaked, answered by another more distant frog. The screeching of two quarreling monkeys shattered the stillness. Terry shivered. His fatigues provided little warmth from the chill.

At 10 o'clock, Terry decided to take the first shift. The monkeys had calmed down. Obscuring clouds darkened the stream. The soft patter of rain plopped and dripped among the fronds. Just what he needed–boil during the day and freeze at night. His soaked fatigues clung to him. The big machine-gunner slept on, unaware of the drizzle. Moonlight pushed through the clouds, creating sparkles upon the water. A gathering mist crept down the river, swirling up the banks. Insects hummed and buzzed around him. How many leeches would he burn off tomorrow? At midnight, he gripped Brumsen's shoulder.

Terry woke to the sound of gunfire. Somewhere around the perimeter of the LZ, VC had run into American soldiers, either on ambush like his squad, or on a listening post. They might be probing the perimeter of the LZ. Heavy machine-gun fire intermingled with rifle fire. The crump, crump of mortar explosions cascaded upon each other. His watch read 1:30. He sat up. The firing stopped.

Brumsen lay behind his machine gun. An oozing mist, twinkling in the moonlight, slithered between the banks. Terry tapped Brumsen on the shoulder and pointed to himself, indicating that he would take over the watch.

Stay awake, Terry! He swatted at mosquitoes. Finding a leech on the back of his hand, he smashed it into the ground. Think about Mom and Dad. What day was it? If it were Sunday, Mom was cooking supper. He hoped the family was having roast beef and potatoes, green beans, perhaps some black-eyed peas. Dad was in his garden, maybe picking blackberries. Oh, man, a blackberry cobbler would taste so good. Three-fifty five, five more minutes and he would wake Brumsen. When was this night going to end?

Shrieking birds downstream broke the silence. An insect whirred in Terry's ear. Was the mist clearing? Terry's wet fatigues weighed upon him. Was that the opposite bank? He tried to remember the distance to the opposite bank. A moving shadow emerged from the haze of mist. Terry's muscles tightened. The shadow moved again, darkness blending with the darkness of the bank. Two shadows materialized out of the opposite bank, pushing through the chest-high river. Extended arms held rifles above the water.

Realizing he held his breath, Terry exhaled slowly. He gripped Brumsen's muscled shoulder and squeezed. Brumsen stirred. Another shadow emerged, then another. Brumsen propped himself on his elbows. The lead man was half-way across the stream. Blow the mines, Anderson! Jesus, another one! The next two men came together, hugging each other. A moan escaped from one of them. Wounded!

Push the detonator! Another man, holding a rifle over his head, slid into the stream, rifle high, and pushed forward. The foliage on Terry's right obscured the first man. Come on! Push the fucking detonator! Grabbing a grenade, he stood in a crouched position.

Two blasts rocked him back on his heels. Smoke roiled upon the water. Trees, repelled and attracted by the concussion, snapped to and fro. A blizzard of leaves swirled in the air. Spouts of water jumped up and down from claymore pellets and bullets ripping through the river and men. Someone screamed in Vietnamese. Pulling the grenade pin, Terry threw it into the maelstrom of smoke, leaves, and mist swirling upon the churning water. Stooping, he grabbed another grenade, pulled the pin, and threw it. A smoke-trailing flare arced from the jungle into the air, landing in the water. Brumsen shook as he fired his machine gun. Men, silhouetted against the light of the flare, struggled against the chest-high water. Green tracers sprouted from the river, fanning out through the foliage. Geysers of water and smoke erupted from the exploding grenades. Two more men screamed in Vietnamese. He launched another grenade straight at one of the men caught in the water. Another smoldering flair, trailing a comet's tail of smoke, arced toward the men trapped in the fury of the boiling river. Another geyser erupted. Ripples moved outward.

Bodies bobbed up and down on the undulating water. Terry shouldered his M-16.

Anderson's detached voice penetrated the jungle. "Cease fire. Stay where you are."

Silence settled upon the jungle like a shroud. A few leaves still spiraled earthward into the smoking river. The bodies in the river, arms flung outward, floated with a casual indifference. His heart pounded, attempting to burst through muscle and sinew. Brumsen tugged at his pants. Terry knelt.

The squad waited in silence for the coming light. The cacophony of screaming monkeys and chirping birds chattering to one another signaled a welcomed dawn. Anderson pushed vegetation aside and squatted beside them. "The Captain's sending two squads to relieve us. You guys stay cool til they get here, then we go back to the LZ."

"How's it feel to be on the payback end of this war, Malloy?" Anderson asked, glancing at the carnage in the river.

Bodies, dead fish, and parts of bodies hung suspended in the red-stained water. Red and yellow feathers floated beside a dead fish. Insects flitted and darted around the dead. Exultation surged through Terry. He was alive and those assholes were dead. "It feels good, it feels real good."

* * *

Someone touched his shoulder. "Professor, Professor."

The questioning gaze of Jonathan jolted him back to the present.

"Dr. Malloy, will you talk to the students? Will you be a part of the Iraq panel? Everyone is talking about the campaign, Kerry, and the Swift Boat Vets."

Terry gripped the desk behind him with both hands to stop them from shaking. Knees buckling, he leaned against the desk. His heart pounded. There was no jungle, no VC floating in the river.

Laura, her slender brown hand touching an arm, put her papers down on the desk. "Dr. Malloy, are you feeling all right?"

He exhaled. "I'm…I'm fine, Laura. I just felt a little woozy." He turned to Jonathan. "Like I said, I'll think about the panel. When is it?"

"Tomorrow night at 7:30."

CHAPTER THREE

Terry hurried out the door of the classroom. Laura followed a step behind, then walked beside him down the hallway.

Glancing over his shoulder, he sighed, relieved when he did not see the squad. Either he had a flashback or was going nuts. Maybe the flashback *was* the sign that he had lost his mind. Who was he fooling? This was more than a flashback! The squad was there, for Christ's sake! Keep talking and keep busy. "Laura, refresh my memory of your paper last spring in the Early Western Civilization course. After Ella, it's all hazy to me now. You did something on Thucydides didn't you?"

Terry was grateful for Laura's diverting presence. Her skin was almond colored. For some reason, he thought of her as delicate. Her hair was done in corn rows, which brought into prominence her chiseled features. She had high cheek bones, large eyes that promised intelligence and humor, and a small straight nose that hovered over petite, sensuous lips. A large blue ribbon with pink polka dots matched her pink blouse and blue dress. Her clipped voice and precise way of talking belied her Georgian roots.

"Yes, sir. Last spring, I did a comparison and contrast between the Athens of Pericles' Funeral Oration and the Athens of the Melian Dialogue. This semester, I want to compare and contrast Athens during the plague with the war in Corcyra in Book Three. In my thesis, I want to bring in the partisan politics in Athens, how divisive everything was toward the end of the war."

Laura had taken her first history class with him and then signed on for two more last year, one in the fall and one in the spring. In one of their discussions, Terry discovered her father had been in Vietnam. Eventually, Laura and her father had gone to lunch with him and both men found they enjoyed each other. Terry remembered Jim Boatwright shaking his hand and saying, "We vets have to stick together. Who else will talk to us? Who'll ever understand?" Jim and his wife had come to Ella's funeral. Laura was the youngest of four children. Keep talking! "How's your mom and dad?"

Laura's glasses had slid down her nose. She pushed them back up. "Mom's doing fine. Dad's architectural business is slow right now. He's beating the woods for clients. Dad said to say hi to you."

"Tell them I said hello also. Your idea for a paper sounds good. Let's see an outline of it and we'll go over it."

When they turned the final corner, he saw the Department Chairman, Jacob Horowitz, outside his office. Jacob's unlit pipe dangled from his lips. Seeing Terry, both his pipe and eyebrows shot up. He removed the pipe and raised both hands out from his side. "I can come back when you're done talking to this young lady."

"I think we're finished for now, Laura. I like your ideas. There should be enough there for a senior thesis in the winter."

Adjusting the straps of her backpack, Laura pushed the glasses back up her nose and smiled. "I'll start working on the outline."

Both men watched her disappear. Unlocking his door, Terry entered first and Jacob followed. Thank God for these diversions. He didn't want to think about what happened in the classroom. "Come in, Jake. Come in."

Jake ran a hand through wisps of white hair. A prominent set of bushy, white eyebrows went up and down above a pair of smiling brown eyes with crow's feet branching away from them. His eyebrows were famous. They moved up and down with every word that he spoke. The more animated he became (especially when talking about early American history), the faster the eyebrows moved. Students loved his lectures and had timed the up-and-down motion of his eyebrows at seventy-five a minute. He pointed his pipe at Terry. "Are you feeling all right? You don't look well."

"I honestly don't know, Jake," Terry said, crossing his arms and placing them on the desk. "I may be losing my mind. Clarissa left this morning for London. She wants a separation and maybe a divorce. I think of Ella all the time and I tossed a reporter out of my house yesterday. I'm sure my grandson thinks I'm nuts."

Adjusting himself in his seat, Jake's eyebrows shot up. "After I took over as Chairman of the Department, I stopped worrying about losing my mind. I figured if I wasn't carried out of here in a straight jacket before I retired, then I'm sane and everyone else is nuts."

Holding up his pipe and lighter, Jake asked permission to light up. Terry did not mind him smoking, but as a courtesy, he always asked. He puffed on his pipe and smoke billowed around the room. "Listen, I need to bring you up to date on the faculty meeting. Did you get the note I put in your mailbox."

"Holy crap, Jake," Terry said, slapping his forehead. "I forgot all about that damn meeting. I apologize. I've had a lot on my mind lately. I haven't looked at my mailbox for several days. With school starting for Alex and Clarissa's leaving, I haven't had time to catch my breath."

"Peace, Peace. We all know what you guys have been going through." Jake held up his pipe and waved it. "However, I wish you had been there to present your case. I have to tell you that Sarah did a lot of political maneuvering with the younger tenured faculty. She really wanted this young friend of hers to be hired and she pulled out all the stops."

"Jesus, Jake, you can't tell me that the faculty voted for this young lady, what's her name, Ashley Eberhardt, instead of Rovich."

Smoke belched from Jake's pipe, enclosing his head in a cloud. "Shoshonnah, she changed her name to Shoshonnah Sacagewea. She's made quite an impression around here."

A vision of a slightly pudgy Ashley Eberhardt, dressed as an Indian, prowling through the wilderness with a papoose on her back entered Terry's head. "Help me understand why a twenty-five-year-old, brand new Ph. D. named Ashley Eberhardt changed her name to Shoshonnah Sacagewea."

With eyebrows shooting up and down several times, Jake's chuckle ended in a slight cough. He tapped the pipe on his teeth. "Who the hell knows. The article in the *Times* said it had something to do with leading men to a better place. Sacagewea is her role model. I haven't talked to her about it in depth."

"Jesus, I thought I was nuts," Terry said, running a hand through his hair. "The only place that young lady could lead us is to the *Twilight Zone*."

Jake took his pipe from his mouth and shrugged. "Her interviews went well. Her paper caused quite a stir. I wish you had been here to help present a more mature point of view. There was a lot more talk about her paper than there was about the paper Rovich gave."

Terry clasped his hands behind his head and leaned back in his chair. "Her paper caused more talk because it was the most outrageous paper ever given on this campus: *Sir Thomas More: A Nazi for all Seasons*. My God, who can take this stuff seriously? When did the good guys become the bad guys?"

Clearing his throat, Jake relit his pipe. "Apparently a lot of people in our department take it seriously. And Sarah Stableford is leading the pack." Jakes's eyebrows went up and down as he puffed his pipe. "Our decision-making process was made more difficult, as you know, by our not having a lot of female faculty."

"You know as well as I do that the department has offered several jobs to women who've turned them down." Terry unclasped his hands, bringing them down on the desk in frustration. "You can't accuse us of discriminating against women when they won't accept our offers?"

Jake stood and put the pipe in his coat pocket. His gleaming eyes peered over his glasses. "Maybe we could move Northeastern Georgia State College closer to Atlanta. The big cities have so much more to offer. That would keep young single people here. Seriously, we have to consider the political ramifications of the hiring process. The reality is we've tried to hire more women and they haven't accepted. However, this department is still mostly male. Appearances are important. No one is going to look at what we tried to do. Moreover, there are monetary considerations. Rovich would have come in as full professor, who would demand a full salary. Dr. Sacagewea will be a fresh, assistant professor. She'll make a lot less than Rovich. That means more funds to spread around to the senior faculty. Besides button-holing the younger tenured faculty, Sarah pushed that idea to the senior faculty also. Anyway, it's been done."

"Did I hear someone mention my name?" Sarah Stableford stood in the doorway with her hands on her hips. She cocked her head to the side and her light-blue eyes laughed at both of the men. Blond hair fell around her shoulders. In her late thirties, she was tall, at least 5'8". Her high heels made her taller than most men. Her heels and short skirts emphasized her long slender legs. Despite their academic differences, she and Terry were good friends. Terry thought it due to the their shared Southern heritage. She came from Mississippi and he was born in Memphis. They jogged together every day when possible. Over the summer, Terry looked forward to their daily jogs.

"Yes, Terry and I were just talking about you and the faculty meeting." Jake's eyebrows hit third gear and laid rubber.

Terry, now standing, put his hands on the desk and leaned toward Sarah. "Hello, beautiful. I was wondering if what's her name, Tonto Goldstein, could channel Lewis and Clark for me."

The tall, blond beauty leaned against the door, laughing. She placed her hands behind her arched back, accentuating an ample bosom. She asked Jake, "Did you ask him if he could talk tomorrow night at the Iraq teach-in?"

"Oy, I forgot." Jake casually thumped his bald head with his hand. "Terry, I'm supposed to be a participant in the panel discussions this week. You know, the teach-ins on Iraq, the Environment, and Gay Rights. It's a good way to start the semester. But, I have to go into Atlanta. Some of the kids suggested you as an alternative. I think it would be good for them to hear what you have to say. As a matter of fact, I may miss all the panels. My mom is not doing well and I'm flying up to see her after my meeting in Atlanta tomorrow night."

"One or two of my students talked to me about it. I don't know if I can talk about Iraq yet, Jake."

Sarah spoke with an exaggerated Southern lilt. "Why mercy me, Mr. Terry, why don't y'all come? We can save you till last. You know, for dessert. If you don't feel like talking, you don't have to. It's such an exciting time. It's like the '60s all over again. Vietnam, My Lai, Abu Ghraib, Guantanamo. Think about it, Mr. Terry."

Terry grimaced. "I think you're stretching a bit to compare My Lai with Abu Ghraib."

"What's My Lai, *amigo*?"

Terry's knees buckled. His knuckles turned white against the desk top. Cochise sat in the chair Jake had vacated. His floppy hat twirled between his hands. Lines of red and yellow grease paint spread from both sides of his nose, under his dark eyes, around to his ears. The rest of his face, including the exposed parts of his neck, were painted black and green. A Mohawk strip of hair ran down the middle of his head. A half-smoked cigarette poked out from his ear. The black handle of a knife stuck out of the scabbard at the base of his neck. The dank smell of dead vegetation and unwashed bodies permeated the office.

Closing his eyes, Terry collapsed into his chair.

Sarah's hands touched his shoulder. "Terry, what's the matter?"

His eyes opened. Cochise's coal black eyes burned into him.

Handing Jake the coffee cup on Terry's desk, Sarah's voice lost its Southern accent. "Go get him some water, Jake. My God, Terry, you're sweating like a stuck pig and you're as white as a sheet."

They're going to smear my daughter like they smeared all the Vietnam Vets. They're going to call them butchers, and Nazis...

Eyes flashing, Cochise reached behind his head and drew the knife from its scabbard. "Then you have to fight." He slammed the knife point into the desk. Cochise's mouth contorted into a contemptible sneer. "You're a survivor, Malloy. When did you give up? Where's your *cojones*? Do you have a *platano* or not? What kinda fucking *hombre* have you become?"

Sarah dipped her handkerchief into the cup of water Jake held. The wet cloth caressed Terry's face and forehead. "Terry, never mind what I said. We can find someone else to be on the panel."

He pushed her hands away and held them, looking into her blue eyes. A hard edge came into his voice. "No, I changed my mind. I'll be there. I'll do it." He turned to see if Cochise approved. He had disappeared.

Jake stuck the pipe in his mouth. He talked around the pipe. "Are you sure you want to do it, Terry?"

"Yes, I'm sure."

"So be it," Jake said. "From your lips to God's ears."

Rich Breedlove's barrel chest and big-boned frame filled the doorway. His blue suit could not hide his athlete's build. A large wave of combed, black hair fanned out above a rather long face. His mustache turned down around the corners of his mouth, causing his face to have an abiding dour appearance. His grey eyes always seemed to contain either the look of the hunter or the hunted. They now shifted from Jake, to Sarah, to Terry. "What the hell's going on here? Terry, you okay? I've never seen Jake move so fast in my life."

Terry pushed Sarah's hands away from his face. "I'm fine, I'm fine. I just didn't get enough sleep last night. Clarissa left this morning for London and I've been busy. I just felt a bit woozy. I guess not eating doesn't help."

"I need to go prepare for my class." Jake squeezed through the doorway past Rich. "I'll see all of you at the party tonight."

Sarah maneuvered around the desk toward the doorway. "If you're okay, I've got some things to do." She hesitated. "You weren't at the track yesterday. Will you be there today?"

He shook his head. "I can't. Clarissa left for London today. I'm picking up Alex at school."

She nodded and touched Rich's arm. "Take care of Terry. I'll see you two tonight."

Rich smiled as he watched Sarah recede down the hallway. He moved gracefully into the office and filled the empty chair. "Man, what a woman. I've a date with her tonight for my party. I think she's finally coming around."

Rich was the departmental bachelor. Divorced nearly three years and in his early forties, he considered himself a lady's man. He had been seen with various female students at the local student hangouts. Rich threw one leg over another and propped a casual elbow on Terry's desk. "You coming tonight? I put an invitation in your mailbox. I assume you read it."

"I haven't looked in my mailbox in a couple of days. I can't come. Clarissa left today and I've got Alex till tomorrow morning when he goes to Gus' parents."

"Why don't you bring Alex?" Rich adjusted his tie. "The next couple of days are planning days for the teachers. The kids have got the day off. Diversity will be there with some of her friends."

Terry pulled at his lower lip. He had to get out of the office. "That's right. Clarissa told me that at the airport this morning. I'm supposed to take Alex over to George and Peggy's tomorrow morning. I think they're going to the mountains for the day. I'll ask Alex what he wants to do tonight. What are you doing with Diversity? I thought Joan kept her during the week."

Scowling, Rich pulled at his mustache. "Joan's got a new boyfriend. What with the students being out for the teacher planning days, he's taking her to the mountains for a long weekend. So, I've got Diversity." He looked at his watch. "I need to go. Look, if you feel up to it, bring Alex. He would enjoy being there. Diversity and I are going to show off our Portuguese Water Dog. We've been training him. Alex will have fun."

Bouncing out of the chair, Rich pushed his black hair out of his eyes. "It starts at 6. We eat around 7. Don't bring anything except yourself and Alex. One more thing, when was the last time you played golf?"

"I can't remember. Several months. Before Ella's... I've had other things to think about. The only exercise I've had is my runs with Sarah."

"Why don't you play with me tomorrow. You look like shit."

He didn't have a class tomorrow. Sitting here in the office, or at home, and looking at a computer screen held no appeal. Besides, he surely wouldn't run into the squad on the golf course. Terry rubbed his forehead. He was a mess, seeing and talking to ghosts. He inhaled and breathed out slowly. "I have to drop Alex at school. After that I could meet you at the course."

Rich slapped his thigh. "Terry, tomorrow is a teacher planning day. There is no school. I told you that. You just told me that you're taking Alex over to George and Peggy's tomorrow. Maybe Alex can spend the night with us. He and Diversity get along well."

Terry waved a tired hand at Rich. "I'm sorry, Rich. I'm just pre-occupied. Okay, I'll talk to Alex."

Rich's eyes narrowed in concern, wrinkling his forehead. "Terry, what's wrong. Is it Ella, or is there something else? You didn't treat my friend very well yesterday."

"Your friend? You know Thornton? That's right. He told me you suggested my name to him."

Rich sat back in the chair. "Yeah, he called me and wanted to know if I knew you. He needed some background information before he went to see you. He and I have been going to the same church for the last couple of months. We've been seeing a lot of each other working on different committees. He's the community advisor on our Transgender Issues Committee."

"Rich, can you call him and ask him not to print that article?" Terry asked, leaning against the desk. "He was acting funny yesterday and I may have been rude myself."

"Why don't you ask him? He's coming to the party tonight."

Terry scratched his head. "When did you start going to church?"

"It's a new church that's been drawing adherents for the last year or so around the country, The Unitarian Church of Universal Victimology," Rich said, crossing his legs. "I like the message of fighting the oppressors of mankind, the ones who control the energy and rape the environment for their own personal gain. The one's who make us all victims. What's more, one day even the oppressors will realize that they are victims."

"I've heard something about it. I just haven't paid too much attention to it because of what's happened. You live in very exclusive lakeside community, make tons of money, drive a nice car, and have great future in front of you. How the hell can you be a victim."

"It's all relative, Terry. Just because a person is successful, it doesn't mean he's not a victim," Rich said, standing. "We need to recognize whose side we're on–the victims of universal oppression or the oppressors. You need to wake up, Terry. You've been victimized and you don't even know it. When I realized that I'm not responsible for what's going on, it was like scales falling from my eyes. 'As the tree sheds its leaves, so you too can shed your guilt.'"

"Who said that?"

"Dr. Ayers, one of the co-founders of our church, or maybe it was Reverend Write. It was started in Chicago."

When Rich left, Terry checked his email. He deleted those he had no intention of answering. After staring at the screen for five minutes, he hurried out of the office, down the stairs, and into the parking lot.

Across the lot, girls and boys walked to and from classes. They leaned, as if into the wind, hunched over carrying backpacks. The fragrant aroma of Magnolia blossoms filled the September air. Sitting in his car, he finally realized where he wanted to go. Stopping on the way, he bought flowers at a supermarket.

At the cemetery, he took the folding chair out of his trunk and walked the short distance to Ella's grave. The stems of old flowers slept in the vase on the tombstone. Terry removed these and replaced them with the new ones. He picked up the water bottle near the base of the tomb, unscrewed it, and poured water into the vase.

He wiped the tears from his face. Once when Ella was fifteen, she had been reading the paper at breakfast, reddish blond hair done in a pony tail. A person who had been pronounced dead at the scene of an accident was later found to be alive when someone at the morgue saw an eyebrow or hand flutter. Ella had pointed a spoon at him, her mouth full of bananas and Corn Flakes. "Dad, if something like that happens to me, bury me with a phone in my coffin. If I wake up, I'll call you." She laughed and milk dribbled down her chin.

A soft, slow expiration of breath whispered beside him. Cigarette smoke filled his nostrils. The putrid odor of moldy vegetation surrounded him. A hand patted his shoulder. Cochise crouched next to him on one knee. He held his rifle by the barrel with the stock on the ground. Dragging on his cigarette again, he blew out the smoke. His helmet created shadows across his face. The black knife handle was visible behind his neck. Cochise stared at the gravestone. Cigarette smoke drifted from his nostrils. "She was a beautiful daughter wasn't she, Malloy?"

His chest tightening, Terry gulped for air.

Cochise took off his helmet, revealing his mohawk. The red and yellow stripes on his painted face glistened with sweat. Reaching into his helmet, he pulled out a picture of a dark-haired woman holding a smiling baby. "My boy's a grown man now." He glanced at the picture. "You're so lucky, Malloy, you saw your daughter grow up. You held her son, your grandson, in your arms. Terry, did you ever call my wife? Do you have a picture of my son? Do you know how he turned out? Do I have grandchildren? You should know these things. Children need their fathers, Malloy." He grabbed Terry's arm. "You were my *compadre*."

A weight pressed upon Terry's heart. He didn't need this now. His life was littered with a trail of dead friends. But what life isn't? The dead haunted him. His failures haunted him. Closing his eyes, he slumped back in the chair. "No, Cochise, I haven't seen or talked to your son."

"Your grandson, Alex, needs you. With you as a guide, he'll grow into a fine young man." Cochise flicked the cigarette away. "Why, Terry? What happened to you? You were a brave man. You always covered for us, *mi cuate*. The man I knew would have kept his *promesa*."

He turned to face his friend. Cochise had vanished. Life happened. Life, and the mundane things you waste a life on, happened. He lost momentum and faltered. The world dragged him away from who he was and who he wanted to be. He hid behind the pretentious titles of professor and doctor, writing papers that no one read, while the moments and possibilities ticked by. Life wasn't like a war. In war, he could separate the good people from the bad, friends from enemies.

Herodotus was right. In peace, children bury their parents. In war, parents bury their children. Why had he never called or tried to see their families? How many parents go to bed wondering how their children died? Did Ella suffer? Parents without children. Children without parents. Wives without husbands. It wasn't natural. Now he was one of them. I buried my child...I buried my child...a thumping sounded behind him.

* * *

"What the hell are you practicing with that knife for, Cochise?" Brumsen asked.

Eyes closed, Terry heard the whomp and thud of the knife striking a tree trunk. The dank smell of layers upon layers of decomposing vegetation, mingled with mold and mildew and unwashed men at work, assailed his senses. Thunk.

Thunk. Thunk. The repetitive sound of the knife hitting the tree floated, slow and rhythmic, through the stifling heat.

"You've been throwing that knife for thirty minutes," Brumsen said, wiping his oval face with a towel.

Grunting, Cochise pulled the knife out of the tree stump.

Terry, Duffy, and Brumsen lay beside the foxhole they had just finished. The battalion was establishing a new perimeter. All around them, men cut down trees, dug foxholes, and filled sandbags. The squad had finished its foxhole an hour before.

Putting back on his helmet, Brumsen grabbed his machine gun and laid it across his midsection. "Cochise, I mean it, Bro. What the frigging hell are you going to do with that knife?"

His helmet off, Cochise scratched his Mohawk strip with his knife. His high forehead wrinkled. "You never know, man. I hope I never have to use it, but if it comes down to it, I want to be ready. I can hit my target from twenty, twenty-five feet about ninety percent of the time."

Raising his muscular leg, Brumsen rested an elbow on his knee. "I tell you what, Bro, if you ever get close enough to Charlie to throw a knife at him, just take your M-16, step to one side, and shoot the sonofabitch as he runs past you. Then hack on him with that knife after he's dead. That's the only way that knife is gonna help you."

"What happens if I run out of ammo?"

"If you run out of ammo and Charlie's around, bend over and kiss your sweet ass good-bye, 'cause that knife ain't gonna kill but one of them mofos."

Terry and Duffy chuckled quietly. A helmet covered Duffy's face, protecting it from the sun.

"If it'd get me out of this jungle, I'd volunteer to knife fight Ho Chi Minh," Terry said.

"Listen to this hillbilly bellyache, would you?" Duffy said, voice muffled by his helmet. "You've been here for what, two months, and you think you're getting tired of the jungle. Give me a break."

"Hey, come on. I'm a combat vet."

Duffy stood and walked toward Cochise. "Yeah sure, you been in what, three or four, two-minute firefights, and you're a combat vet."

"Duffy, what the hell are you doing?" Brumsen said, extracting a can of oil from his rucksack. He poured the oil on a rag. "I can't believe you're really gonna try that knife throwing, too. Do you guys pay for your bullets or what? Dig it, you can get 'em free around here. My uncle don't mind if I use 'em because he's got plenty. Malloy, look at these guys."

Cochise gave Duffy his knife. "Okay, Duffy, take it by the handle and not by the blade. No, no, not like that, like this."

"It may be a good thing to learn,"Terry said.

Wiping an ammunition belt with the rag, Brumsen shook his head. "No way. I'm just gonna shoot the assholes about twenty times each with my M-60 and then these guys can hack on 'em with that–"

The thundering roar of an explosion rolled over the squad. Men ran to the sound. Someone screamed.

The entire squad stood. Duffy handed the knife back to Cochise. "Was that a 'fire-in-the-hole?'"

Terry put on his helmet. "That wasn't the demolition guys. There was no warning. When they blow something up, there's always a warning."

Everyone scrambled to put on helmets and check rifles. No one said anything. The wounded man screamed.

Anderson jogged toward the squad, jungle fatigues flapping around his slender frame. As always, he spoke in clipped tones of suppressed fury. "Get into the foxhole. Duffy, come with me and bring the radio. Charlie just snuck up to the edge of the jungle and set off a claymore right under our noses. He must've crawled right past the listening posts."

The squad jumped into the foxhole, a futile gesture. Charlie had set up the mine, retired into the jungle to a safe distance, and pressed the detonator. The VC were well away from the perimeter by now, the jungle covering their retreat.

They waited in the foxhole for ten minutes. Cochise slammed his knife into the dirt wall. Black eyebrows narrowed above flashing, dark eyes. "Same old bullshit. Jesus, would I like to get *mis manos* on those *bastardos*."

"Well, you're going to get your chance," Anderson replied from behind them.

They climbed out of the foxhole.

"What you mean, Dude?" Brumsen asked.

Anderson picked up his rucksack. "I mean that we're going to go after that shithead and kill him if we can. Start packing up and moving your gear out of the foxhole and back to the lieutenant's HQ. Someone else'll take this bunker for the night. We're leaving with Cziplicki's squad in an hour. Let's hurry, it'll be dark soon. We'll eat at the HQ before we go out."

Brumsen placed a bandolier of machine-gun ammunition around his broad shoulders. "I was afraid that was what you meant."

The squad dropped its gear at the communications bunker. They sat down, leaning against their rucksacks.

"Check your weapon, Malloy," Anderson said, giving Terry's shoulder a gentle squeeze. "I know you just did, but check it again."

"Come on, Cherry," Brumsen said, "get tight and get right."

"You assholes'll never let me forget that I'm the newest, will you?"

Anderson loaded a round into the M-79 grenade launcher underneath the barrel of his M-16. His small hands stroked the barrel. "You may be the newest, but you aren't cherry are you, Malloy?"

The men examined their weapons.

Cochise rummaged through his rucksack. "Malloy, loan me your cleaning rod."

"I agree with you, Cochise. I want to get these bastards. This friggin' routine never ever changes," Brumsen said, checking his machine-gun ammunition belt. Brumsen's pudgy fingers cradled the bullets. He brushed the belt with an oiled toothbrush, removing grime. "We move to a new LZ, dig new foxholes, and sweep the jungle for a day or two. Then we pack everything up and do the same thing somewhere else."

Placing a new battery in his radio, Duffy turned his freckled face toward the squad, consternation in his blue eyes. "It wouldn't be so bad, if we could just get our hands on Charlie every once in a while. What hacks me off are the constant mines and booby traps blowing up in our faces. Then Charlie's gone."

Handing his cleaning rod to Cochise, Terry rubbed the scars on his arm. "I want to walk on a path. The jungle skins me alive."

"The damn paths have more mines than the jungle, Malloy," said Anderson. "You know that. We have to go through the jungle. There's no other way."

Cigarette dangling from his mouth, Cochise pushed the cleaning rod down the barrel of his rifle. "I just want to fight the bastards. The constant mines get on my nerves too, Duffy. I'd rather go out on these *emboscadas* at night than pull point in that fucking jungle and let the gooks blow me away."

Anderson fed ammunition into a clip. "I feel the same way, guys. I'm putting targets on your backs every time I ask you to pull point."

Brumsen wiped the machine gun and the ammunition belt with an oiled cloth. "You're just doing your job, Anderson."

"Yeah, but the odds are against us," Anderson said, slamming the ammunition clip into his forty-five with the palm of his hand. "One of these days, one of those dink mines, booby traps, or wired artillery rounds is going to take one of us out, if not more. That ain't gonna be cool. That's why I like ambushes, too, Cochise." Anderson chambered a round into the pistol. "We have so much more mobility when we go out as a squad."

Terry taped the O-ring and cotter pin of a grenade. "The jungle at night is worse'n the jungle during the day. We're so alone out there. Five hundred yards from our perimeter at night might as well be five miles. If we get into trouble, we're up shit creek without a paddle."

Slipping the pistol into his holster, Anderson shook his head. "You're thinking too defensively, Malloy. Remember, Charlie can't see us at night any more than we can see him. I've picked up too many arms and legs. I want to get some payback on these fucking gooks."

"I wish you guys wouldn't call them gooks, dinks, and slopes." Duffy, taped his bayonet scabbard to his calf. "They're people. They have families, fathers and mothers, sons and daughters, just like us."

"Give us a fuckin' break, will you?" Anderson said, taping two magazine cartridges together. "You call them what you want, and I'll call them what I want. As far as I'm concerned, they're gooks." Anderson slid the ammunition-filled magazine into his M-16. It clicked into place.

Cochise, a cigarette dangling from his lips, pulled the cleaning rod out of his rifle. Smoke erupted from his nostrils. "I want them to be *muertos* gooks. The more widows we create, the sooner we can leave this shithole."

"Okay, here's the plan." Anderson put the tape in his rucksack. "After Cziplicki's squad leaves to set up their ambush, we'll follow them. Any Charlie that would sneak up to the perimeter of a battalion has to be one hard-core sonofabitch. That slope is out there somewhere watching the perimeter, waiting for us to send out a squad.

As a matter of fact, he expects us to send out a squad. Then later tonight, or first thing tomorrow morning, he hits the squad. I convinced the captain to let us go out after the first squad leaves. We'll set up along the same trail a hundred to a hundred and fifty yards from Czplicki's squad. Charlie expects the first squad. If he's not watching for us, we kill him. If he sees us, he hits us instead. Right now, we eat."

CHAPTER FOUR

Running down the sloping driveway toward Rich's house, Alex let out a whoop. The wooded lot, covered mostly by pines sprinkled with a few hickory, oak, and poplar trees, made the house invisible from the road. As Terry walked down the curving driveway, the lake behind the house shimmered in the late afternoon sun. His grandson disappeared around the corner of the house, brown, curly hair creating a flouncing halo around his head. A Beatle's song, "All We Need is Love," drifted toward Terry as did the sound of people talking and children laughing. A slight wind carried the dampness of the lake.

The deck of the house spread out above him. Stairs led up to it. Shadows cast by the deck darkened a door, which led to the downstairs of the house. A stack of split logs rested beside the door. Above, on the deck, people talked and laughed around a table that held drinks. Jake, puffing his pipe, stood by the grill with a spatula in hand. The burnt aroma of charcoal drifted on the bright summer air. The backyard, not as wooded as the front, allowed a good view of the lake. Scattered pines stood here and there. Twenty yards from Terry, a hummingbird fluttered in and out of the pink and white blossoms of a lone mimosa. Drooping willow trees grew along the edge of the water.

Several children stood on the pier with Rich. Rich's black Portuguese Water Dog, Carlo, hair cut similar to a poodle, bounced up and down around the group. Rich stepped to the edge of the pier and Carlo followed. He tossed what looked like a large bone into the lake. The dog jumped in, paddled on the water, and disappeared.

Dripping wet, Carlo pounced up the bank carrying the bone-shaped stick in its mouth. He shook himself vigorously. Running back onto the pier, he dropped it at Rich's feet. His daughter, Diversity, hurled it into the water again. Carlo, obediently, ran to the edge of the pier and dived without hesitation.

The group by the lake became harder to see as Terry walked up the stairs. The brilliant glare of the setting sun on the sparkling lake turned them all darker and indistinguishable. *"We all live in a yellow submarine"* flowed from speakers somewhere above.

Sarah, wearing a solid blue summer smock, blond hair flowing over her bare shoulders, stood with two men, who had their backs to him, and one woman he recognized as a teacher in the Biology Department. Waving to him, Sarah motioned him over.

One of the men talking to Sarah, wearing a blue Hawaiian shirt covered with parrots, had a familiar pony tail. Greg Thornton turned and saw Terry, nodding imperceptibly.

Barbara Jensen, the brunette standing beside Sarah, wore hip-hugging blue jeans. A short-sleeve-white shirt, tied in a knot below her breast, exposed a tanned stomach. A biologist, her large brown eyes expanded when he acknowledged her presence. She smiled, drawing attention to white teeth surrounded by small lips with an application of light pink lipstick. A square chin held a prominent dimple. A ruby glimmer came from a stud in her navel. An unrecognizable tattoo, next to her navel, peeked out of her jeans.

The thin man standing beside Thornton, Ralph Jefferson, taught English. His wavy red hair fell over a pair of large ears. Sipping his drink, he nodded to Terry. His Adam's apple, above the buttoned-down collar of his blue shirt, moved up and down his long neck.

Beyond this group, two women stood in the kitchen. One he recognized as Jake's wife, Gertrude.

"Why, Mr. Malloy, you're just the man we're looking for," Sarah said, pulling Terry to her side. Her voice held that exaggerated Southern lilt she did so well. A smile played around the corners of her full lips. "We've been talking about Senator Kerry and the Swift Boat Vets. Mr. Thornton has been telling us about the good old days when he protested the Vietnam War. It sounds like so much fun."

Thornton, drink in hand, turned his other hand palm upward with a shrug. He smiled broadly. "In some ways, it was the best time of my life. It seems like the whole world was turned upside down during that war. Long hair was bad, then long hair was good and crew cuts were for fascists. Dope was bad, then dope was good. Sexual morality was tighter than a virgin's you-know-what, and then skirt hems went up, panties came down, and everyone wanted to make love, not war. Man, what a time to be young."

Approaching the table, Terry poured a glass of red wine. He drank, sighed, and looked around. Brumsen stood towering behind Thornton, the M-60 machine-gun cradled in his muscled arms. A floppy field hat covered his forehead. A smile appeared below his big, flat nose. Brumsen winked. "What's the matter, Bro? You look tired."

Placing a hand on the table, Terry steadied himself.

"Yeah, who are these *hijos de putas*? What unit are they with?" Cochise's flashing dark eyes and painted face peered over Jefferson's shoulder.

"These guys aren't with any unit," Terry said, laughing. "These are the guys that talk a good war, but will only fight if it's Hitler they're fighting. They fight wars that have already been fought and the winner and the bad guys have been determined. They won't fight any wars in progress. These are the people that will fight to the last drop of *your* blood."

M-16 resting casually on his shoulder, Anderson appeared from behind Brumsen, thin face shadowed by his helmet. His gray eyes narrowed. The crows feet became more pronounced. "Tell them to go fuck themselves."

Terry's hand shook as he lifted the glass to his mouth and gulped. The squad vanished.

The quiet group around the table stared at him.

Thornton, wiping the sweat off his bald head with a napkin, smiled. "What's so funny?"

The warmth of the wine flowing down his throat felt good. He stared at the empty glass. His voice trembled. "Do you have any children, Mr. Thornton?"

Sarah touched his elbow. "Terry, he didn't mean anything."

"I'm okay, Sarah. I'm just asking a question."

"I've got two daughters and a son,"Thornton said, a cautious look in his hooded eyes. "Please, call me 'Thorn.' Everyone I irritate calls me 'Thorn'."

Terry poured himself more wine. He smiled, trying to keep a light tone in his voice. "I'm sure you've taught the 'goodness of drugs' to your children. Just as I'm positive you've told your daughters that making love is a lot of fun, also, especially when you're on drugs."

Laughing, Thorn wagged a slender finger at Terry. "You're trying to get a rise out of me. But you're not going to do it that easily. My daughters think I'm a straight-arrow prude. There's no way I'm going to tell them everything I did during the '60s."

Terry pointed his wine glass at Thornton. "Why not? Are you ashamed of what you did?"

Handing her empty glass to Terry, Sarah picked up a plate of cheese and crackers and offered them to everyone. "We all have our secrets and our secret selves. So, Thorn, you were active in the peace movement and Terry was a soldier. How exciting."

"The history professor and I were on opposite sides in the '60s." Thornton reached for a piece of cheese. "I hope we can be friends now." He stuffed the cheese in his mouth. "It wasn't all fun and games. I thought it was my duty. I was raised in a family that taught me to speak up for the people who can't speak up for themselves."

Jefferson crossed his freckled arms. His Adam's apple bobbed up and down. "I'm sure both you and Terry were doing your duty as you saw it."

Chewing vigorously, Thornton pointed a thin finger at Jefferson. A piece of cheese clung to the end of the finger. "It was more than duty for me. I can never be silent when it comes to the oppression of the little people who can't defend themselves. That's one of the reasons I became a journalist."

Rich slapped him on the back. "That's exactly why we asked you to write that article on UVAL. Because you stand up for the little guys. We know that you'll speak up for the animals that have no rights and can't defend themselves." The top two buttons of Rich's light blue guayabera were open, exposing a hairy chest and a gold necklace.

"What is UVAL?" Terry asked.

Barbara pushed her long, dark hair away from her slender neck. "It's a shadow group for people who don't like the idea of poor animals like pigs and cows being slaughtered. Thorn has agreed to write an article about it. The initials stand for 'United Vegetarian and Animal Lovers.' There are some pressing issues to be dealt with."

Rich removed his arm from Thorn's shoulders. "Right now the whole thing is *sub rosa*. There's a real underground movement on the internet about the formation of UVAL. All of the Veggie and Animal Rights bulletin boards are buzzing about it."

"What's the buzz about?" Terry asked. He reached for the bottle.

"The buzz is about trying to save the animals." Barbara handed her glass to Terry to be filled. "But, there's more than talk about the morality of slaughtering innocents. Now there are people *doing* something."

"Terry, you've been so out of touch." Sarah popped a piece of cheese in her mouth. "Let me bring you up to date. There are rumors, and more than rumors, about people saving animals that are to be slaughtered by the MEs, the meat eaters. It's just like the underground railroad back during and before the Civil War. Animals have been disappearing all over the nation, a pig here, a goat and cow there. Poof, they're gone without a trace."

"All the stories from the papers have been put up on the internet bulletin boards," Barbara said.

Terry sipped his newly filled glass. "You mean people are stealing other people's property, cows and such?"

Rich's gaze drifted down to Barbara's tattoo. "Animals have rights, too."

"What are they doing with the stolen animals."

"They're not being stolen, they're being freed." Barbara pulled her jeans up above her navel. "This is a real underground movement. It's rumored that there are several farms where the animals can roam free like nature intended them."

Resting a hand on Sarah's shoulder, Rich held his glass out to Terry. "We're waiting on Shoshonnah. She's supposed to be one of the leading members of ULVAL and they work, or supposedly work, with UVAL. Like I said, it's all kind of *sub rosa*."

Somewhere, Alex and Diversity were laughing.

Terry scratched his head. "Okay, I'll bite. What the hell is ULVAL?"

Barbara pushed her blue jeans down exposing her tattoo of two butterflies. "Dr. Sacagewea is one of the few outspoken members of 'United Lesbian Vegetarians and Animal Lovers.' It kind of has a super-secret membership. They work hand in glove with UVAL, but they only free the females of the species."

Coughing up his wine, Terry wiped it away from his nose. "Are you people out of your minds? You can't be serious?"

Thorn nodded, taking a drag off his cigarette. "I'm afraid they're very serious. Although I haven't met her, I've talked with Dr. Sacagewea. If you truly believe that animals have rights, and she does, then you have to believe that the females have rights as well as the males. It wasn't long ago that humans were forced to breed. If you were a female cow or sheep, how would you like to be forced to spend your life in pens breeding with males."

Terry would have turned away to talk to Jake, but he had taken the food downstairs to the children. Should he say anything to these people? Would they even care what he thought? Was this what Ella died for? "Saving female cows from breeding like animals seems unnatural. That's what they are, aren't they, animals?"

"Actually, it's quite natural." Barbara pulled up her jeans again. "As a biologist, I can tell you that at least ten to twenty percent of all animals are homosexual. So, if we can save one lesbian cow from being raped repeatedly, that would be worth the risk of jail. After all, if the men and women who risked their lives saving slaves can do it, so can we. People have to take a stand."

Catching Terry's gaze, Sarah's blue eyes gleamed with humor. She had shrugged off Rich's hand on her shoulder. "Just think, Terry, one hundred years from now, we could be the Harriet Beecher Stowe's of our generation."

Adam's apple bobbing up and down, Ralph Jefferson ran long, thin fingers through his thick red hair. "We're the vanguard. This is just the opening battle. It'll take a while, yet."

Sarah lifted her wine glass in a toast. "Here's to the new age."

"A new morality," Rich said, his arm now around Sarah's waist.

Rich turned to Terry. "Alex just told me he's coming on the camping trip that our church is sponsoring. Are you bringing him?"

What was he doing here? His daughter was dead and these people were stealing victimized, lesbian cows and pigs. Get drunk. The evening would be easier and the time would go faster. Terry grabbed the wine bottle. "No, Alex's other grandfather, George Holland, is taking him. How did George get mixed up with you guys and the Victimology stuff?"

Beads of sweat formed on Thorn's bald head. He lit another cigarette. "Someone probably invited him. I don't recall him being a member. It's not 'stuff,' Terry. Rich and I are both excited about the fervor that Victimology Theology is generating. Campuses all over the country have been seeing multitudes of college kids, professors, and others gathering together to proclaim their Victimhood.

Jake appeared out of the kitchen, a smoking pipe in his mouth and a drink in hand. "The kids are stuffing the soy burgers down their gullets. Did I hear someone mention Victimology Theology? I've read a little about it. Tell me what you guys do in your service. Do you read from the Bible or what?"

Thorn popped a cheese-loaded cracker into his wide mouth. "The first thing we do is meditate for about twenty minutes. We try to clear our minds, recognizing that we're not responsible. 'As the snake sheds his skin, so you too can shed your guilt.'"

White eyebrows moving swiftly, Jake suspended his pipe in midair. "That's an interesting analogy. Who said it and what is it that you're not guilty of?"

Terry was swimming upstream against a current that was taking him out to sea. He thought of Clarissa's call earlier in the afternoon. She had landed safely and the flight had been uneventful. Harold and Porter met her at Gatwick outside of London and she was now in their flat. They were going to the French Riviera next week. Then she spoke to Alex. He handed the phone back to his grandfather. "Don't hide in that bottle, Terry." A strained silence followed. She expected him to say something to acknowledge her comment. "Don't worry about me. I'll be all right." They said good-bye, but no 'I love you.' Divorce! It was hard for him to grasp.

Walking to the edge of the deck, he placed both hands on the rail. Carlo ran in and out of the long shadows of the pines chasing twinkling fireflies. A chorus of crickets sounded the death knell of the day and a croaking symphony of bull frogs signaled a new night. The yoke still pressed on his shoulders. Ella was dead and people were stealing female cows so they couldn't be raped. Everyone's a victim. What was he *doing* here?

A new set of hands grabbed the rail. The arms were cris-crossed with old and new cuts and sores from the jungle. The sleeves of his green fatigues were rolled up above the elbow. Black and green paint covered Anderson's thin face. The grim set of his thin lips were barely visible. His helmet, almost too big for his head, rested at an angle, the straps hanging loose. His deep-set gray eyes flashed anger. "Is this what you do now, stand around and listen to bullshit and feel sorry for yourself?"

The aroma of expensive perfume caressed the air around him. Sarah's hand touched his shoulder. "How's my hero doing?"

His wine glass was empty again. "I'm tired and old. I need a drink. How's my Dulcinea?"

"If you keep drinking like this, your Dulcinea's going to have to take you home. You won't even be able to see a windmill, much less charge at one. Come in for supper and sit by me. Rich wants me to sit by him, you can be my knight that rescues me from his clutches.

"You and Jake are from a by-gone era. The world is moving on. It's a new age, new values, Professor Malloy." A smile played around her lips. Her soft hands clutched his arm.

"Rich told me he had a date with you tonight. I think he's sweet on you."

As they entered the house, Sarah rolled her eyes. "Rich is sweet on anything that wears a skirt. He's going to find that I'm not the dating type. Besides, I tend to like old-fashioned men."

Terry sat between Ralph and Sarah. Ralph's Adam's apple moved in harmony with his chewing. "I have to say that you don't fit the profile I've built up of the average Vietnam Veteran. The publicity surrounding Kerry and those Swift Boat guys has swung the spotlight back on you all. If you combine it with all the TV documentaries, movies, and newspaper articles on atrocities you guys committed, that would seem to support what Kerry said in his senate testimony. But you look kind of average to me."

Sloshing wine around in his glass. Terry half-listened to Ralph and to the Beatles' song, "Money Can't Buy Me Love," which drifted through the house.

* * *

Scratching a bite on his freckled neck, Duffy turned the radio down. "I still think C-4 heats better than the heating tablets."

Brumsen shoveled ham and lima beans into his mouth. "I don't know, Duffy. I'm always afraid you're going to blow our asses away cooking with plastic explosive. It makes me nervous. But when you're eating a mess of ham and lima beans, who really gives a shit how you're cooking it."

Cochise held up a can. "*Esa es la neta*! That *is* the truth! If the C-4 doesn't blow us up, or the VC don't kill us, the ham and lima beans will do the job." Cochise pointed to the can. "This is definitely not my mother's cooking."

"Man, oh man, what I wouldn't give for some of my mother's chicken'n dumplings." Brumsen spooned in another mouthful.

Monkeys ranted outside the perimeter. Anderson bit down on peanut butter and bread. "Chicken and dumplings, my mother hardly ever cooked chicken and dumplings. What are they like?"

Brumsen and Terry looked at each other and both laughed.

"What fuckin' country were you raised in, Anderson?" Brumsen asked. "You've never eaten chicken'n dumplings?"

"Believe it or not, my mother's Italian," Anderson said. "I grew up eating tortellini, spaghetti, and ravioli."

Cochise wiped his hands on his pants leg. "Tortellini, what the hell kind of food is that? No wonder you're so mean and angry."

A chorus of birds had joined the cacophony of screeching monkeys. Brumsen positioned the C-ration can between his beefy legs. He clasped his hands behind his head. "I can see my mother now. She's standing at the counter next to the stove in her apron. The chicken has already been boiled and picked off the bone and it's in a pot on the stove. There's a huge ball of dough in her hand and flour all over the counter and all over her. I mean, she has flour up to her elbows. She has to wipe her face with the back of her hand, because there's flour caked all over her hands.

"She rolls and kneads that dough and sprinkles flour, rolls and kneads and sprinkles flour. Then she takes out a rolling pin and flattens it. After that, she cuts the dough into big thick dumplings and dumps them into the pot. Man, that's some fine eatin'."

"That's funny," Anderson said, smiling. He sat relaxed, rubbing his square jaw and chin. Green and black camouflage paint covered his high cheek bones and aquiline nose. The worry lines around his eyes had disappeared for the moment. "I can see my mother doing the same thing. Only, she's making ravioli. There's a big bag of semolina flour on the counter. She mixes the egg, water, and flour together and works the dough, kneading it back and forth. Sometimes my brothers and I help her."

"I didn't know you had brothers," Duffy said.

"Two. Anyway, my mom mixes the cheese together."

Placing the spoon in the can, Brumsen wiped his mouth with his sleeve. "Mix the cheeses? How many cheeses do you need?"

"You have two kinds of cheese, ricotta and mozzarella. You grate the cheese and mix them together with some greens, parsley I think, and some egg. She rolls out the dough like Brumsen's mom, but probably thinner. We, my brothers and I, stamped the round ravioli patterns from the dough. Half of each ravioli is filled with the cheese and egg. We used to fold them over for her. Then we crimped the edges of the half-moon shapes to seal them."

Anderson spread more peanut butter on his bread. "After we made about one hundred or so ravioli, my mom made noodles, or linguini, with the rest of the dough. We spread bed sheets over the dining room table and kitchen table. Then we spread out the noodles on the bed sheets, all over the house, so they could dry. The pasta was everywhere. There were noodles on the kitchen counter tops, on the tables, and even in the bedrooms. We pretended that the sheets draped over the tables were forts and hid under them. We did it on rainy days, and we played all day."

The odor of stale lima beans and ham hovered about the squad. Duffy stirred his C-ration can. Green and black paint covered his pug nose and freckles. "My mom used to cook dumplings, Brumsen. She mixed raisins into the dough. Then she sliced the dumplings and placed them in a big cast-iron skillet and simmered them in homemade butterscotch sauce. It makes my mouth water just to think about it. My brothers, sisters, and I used to run out in the fields around lunchtime and pick the sweet corn while those butterscotch dumplings were simmering. If you've never tasted the sweet corn in Iowa, you've really missed some 'fine eatin' as you and Malloy would say."

After swallowing, Duffy scraped food from his dimpled chin and wiped it on his fatigues. "We'd pick handfuls of corn, run back to the farmhouse, and shuck it by the pigpen, feeding the husks to the pigs. My mom cooked it for lunch."

"Duffy, if you guys lived in Texas, and were *Mexicanos*, you would have given the corn husks to your mom for tamales. Whenever we had a big party or celebration, the mothers would make tamales from the *masa*." Cochise leaned against sandbags. He used his finger to scrape out the last of his meal from the can. "My favorite dish was *mole con tamales*."

Brumsen rolled his eyes. "I'm afraid to ask what *masa* is."

"Cornmeal. You know, *maize*, you big, black *gringo*. When my mom made *mole con tamales*, she would use plantain leaves to roll the tamales, not corn husks. The *mole* was like a stew with either chicken or turkey. It was cooked in *salsa verde or salsa roja*. For you foreigners, that's green sauce or red sauce."

The squad chuckled quietly.

"When I married Maria," Cochise continued, "her family used to make a sweet meat, dessert biscuit called an *empanada*. You cook some meat and then mix it with raisins, sugar, and *pinon* nuts, pine nuts to you *gringos*. Then you stuff everything into a half-moon-shaped piece of dough and crimp it shut. Dip the dough into hot oil, cook it, and chow down." Cochise crossed his arms and sighed. "If I were eating it now, it would be close to Christmas."

Anderson looked at his watch. "Cziplicki's squad left ten minutes ago. Let's finish up and go kill that gook."

Anderson sat quietly on his haunches, biting into his bread and peanut butter. He stared silently at the adamantine wall of the jungle.

His rifle, an M-16 with an M-79 grenade launcher attached under the barrel, draped carelessly across his knee. He passed his bread and peanut butter to Brumsen, who wolfed it down. Anderson knelt on one knee, using his rifle for support. The squad, crouching behind him, watched and waited for him to give the signal. Turning to look at them, Anderson grinned, then vanished. The green whirlpool of the jungle drew the squad ineluctably into itself.

* * *

Terry, hands trembling, gulped his wine. Keep it light, keep it light. "There's one thing Senator Kerry, the newspapers, and the documentaries didn't tell you. We only murdered, raped, tortured, and smoked dope on Tuesdays and Thursdays. The other days we were just kids, who missed their homes and families. When we got lonely, which was often, we talked about our mothers and families. We talked about our wives and children, sisters, brothers, and girlfriends. On every day but Tuesdays and Thursdays, we were no different from other American soldiers in other wars." Feeling a slight pressure from Sarah squeezing his left knee, Terry grew silent and poked at the tuna.

He placed his fork on the plate and reached for the wine glass. "However, we went out in that fucking jungle day after day, week after week, year after year. Even when the war became unpopular, we went. The volunteers went. The draftees went. We huddled in that godforsaken wilderness, like all the other American soldiers in every other war, depending on no one but themselves. We got killed, shot, and maimed, but we still went.

"All of the guys I know who're Vietnam vets, once they stopped raping, torturing, smoking dope, and murdering people, came back and tried to earn enough money to get their kids through college. They're leading boring lives with other boring people, just like me.

The war became unpopular here in the States with the citizens and with the media. So, the men fighting the war became unpopular. Most, and I emphasize most, of the stuff published about Vietnam Veterans, either in film or print, or senate testimony, is bullshit added to bullshit."

Although the pressure on his knee had abated, Sarah's hand stayed where it was.

CHAPTER FIVE

Pushing peas onto her fork with a piece of bread, Sonya Jefferson's plump fingers grasped the bread as if it were a living wriggling worm. "We're trying to approach each child as if they're special. A lot of troubled kids out there are in a state of gender mutability. They really don't know if they want to be little boys or little girls."

Jake and Gertrude listened. Eyebrows breaking the sound barrier, Jake's unlit pipe moved up and down in rhythm to his brows. "And how exactly do you do that?"

Sonya dabbed a napkin at her lips. "In my fifth grade-class, for instance, I've started asking the boys to play girl roles in our plays and asking the girls to play boy roles. This reversal of roles gives those who are undergoing doubts about their gender to recognize cognitively that gender is mutable. They can deconstruct their old selves if they so desire."

Mouth open. Jake's pipe drooped. His eyebrows quivered slightly.

Gertrude's fork, piercing a hunk of tuna, hung suspended in mid-air. "And what are the results?"

Pouring himself more wine, Thornton waved a hand in the air. "Two of my best friends and I were real radicals back then. One is a big insurance executive now, lives in Connecticut. The other guy died of AIDS a few years ago. We used to go down to Harlem and help organize the blacks. They loved us."

"The men in Vietnam were American soldiers," Terry said, wiping a spot of wine on his shirt. "For the most part, they behaved honorably and distinguished themselves with their service, and most of them were volunteers. In other words, they acted like all the other American soldiers in all of our wars. There're a lot of myths fostered about Vietnam and Vietnam veterans that just aren't true. Of course, it doesn't help when you've a U.S. Senator testifying about rapists and murderers that he has no proof of, in front of a Senate Committee."

"I thought most of the soldiers in Vietnam were draftees." Ralph rubbed his pointed chin, then folded his bony arms across his chest.

The knife and fork rattled on Terry's plate as he shoved the dish from him. "The only service that took draftees for the most part was the Army. The Navy, Air Force, and Marines were all almost entirely volunteer. I don't have the exact figures, but I think a lot more volunteers were killed in combat than draftees. The ratio was two to one almost."

"Then," Ralph asked, "how do you account for My Lai?"

Sarah squeezed Terry's leg while she spoke to Mary Thornton across the table.

There it was. He'd be answering that question until the day he died. And the Iraqi vets would be answering questions about Abu Ghraib and about torture. "How do I explain My Lai? I can't explain it. My Lai was a tragedy. All I can say is that tragedies happen in war, and we do our best to prevent them from happening, but they happen anyway. I guarantee you that it was not a policy decision to kill those civilians."

Barbara, her mouth open, stared at Sarah as if she had just confessed to murder. "I can't believe you're pro-life. Tell me you're joking."

Sarah placed her glass on the table. Her blue eyes gazed calmly at Barbara. "I'm afraid that is where I part ways with my feminine sisters. I've managed to escape most of my poor Mississippi upbringing. But I have to admit that I'm pro-life." Long fingers twisted her hair as she held it away from her slender neck. Her high cheek bones and pale complexion indicated delicacy. Her firm jaw line and the determined set of her mouth pointed toward a solid bedrock of core beliefs.

"I've had this conversation with her before, Barbara," Rich said, slapping his napkin on the table. "I was adopted and I'm thankful that my natural mother," Rich smiled, "little slut that she was, decided not to have an abortion. But I still have to defend the right of women who want one."

Wiping his mouth, Ralph coughed. "It does seem that whenever I think of Vietnam Veterans, I think of My Lai and those dead women and children."

"War is brutal," Terry said. "It turns thinking upside down. Bad things appear good and good things appear bad. Take Dresden, for instance, or Hamburg, or Tokyo, for that matter."

"What have they got to do with My Lai?" Ralph asked. "Those are German and Japanese cities."

"When you think of World War Two, do you think of the thousands of civilians that were brutally killed by Allied bombs in those cities?"

Ralph crossed his arms. "No, I'm not much of a historian."

"They're good examples of reasoning in war gone astray. All of those cities were firebombed during World War II. The allies didn't just bomb industrial areas. Thousands of women, children, and old men were killed in each of those cities. This was done as a matter of policy, a matter of planning. In one night, Tokyo lost over hundred thousand people, mostly civilians, because of a *planned* attack using incendiary bombs on a city made of paper."

His forehead wrinkling, Ralph rubbed it vigorously. He extended his hands palms up. "But surely, these bombings helped to shorten that war."

Terry reached for a glass of water. "Are you saying that sometimes it's justifiable to kill women, children, and old men? Because I can assure you, that's what happened. Hundreds of thousands of innocent civilians, mostly women, children, and old men were killed as a policy, or part of a plan, to bring the greatest war to an end. Those cities had no strategic value whatsoever. It's funny, but no one seems to mention that when talking of World War II, or when talking about My Lai. Compared to the civilian deaths in World War II, Vietnam was a walk in the park. But everyone wants to talk about My Lai and how evil Vietnam Veterans are. You can bet the press didn't label the bomber pilots who flew in the Eighth Air Force 'baby-killers.'" Terry heard the bitterness in his voice.

"So tell me," Ralph asked, "what do you think? Should the people who bombed those cities be held accountable or should, at least, the planners?"

"People do crazy things in war," Terry said. "Like I said, things get turned upside-down. They forget morality. They forget goodness, fairness, all the things that we take for granted. When it comes to staying alive and surviving, all traditional ways of treating people are thrown out the window. A lot of a soldier's thinking is controlled by emotion. You know, fear and anger, and power. My example is an attempt to indicate that, not only individual soldiers and units, but cultures and societies can be led to incredible acts of brutality and destructiveness in the name of what is right or who is bad. In the end, I think that every individual has to come to grips with what he himself has done and for what he himself is responsible. Arguments have always been made to justify civilian casualties.

"In some instances, like Germany after the War, an entire culture needs to delve into its psyche. Sometimes institutional structures, such as the Joint Chiefs of Staff, need to do a little soul searching on the means they used to end a war. But the victors very seldom do any soul searching."

Duffy stood behind Barbara, his face darkened with camouflage paint. "We shouldn't have done it, Malloy."

Anderson appeared behind Thornton. He shook his field hat at Duffy. "We did what we had to do, Duffy. Don't pay any attention to him, Malloy."

"There were non-combatants there, Anderson," replied Duffy calmly.

Brumsen, behind Gertrude, adjusted the ammunition belts slung across his broad chest. "They were right in the middle of a combat zone."

Cochise towered over Jake. "It was war, Duffy. They shouldn't have been there."

* * *

The green fog surrounded Terry. He brushed an ant from his arm and wiped his brow. A vine fell across his face. The jungle shimmered with clarity in the late afternoon heat. He pushed hot air in and out of his lungs. Cochise, on point, proceeded with caution.

The occasional rest allowed Terry to get his bearings. Anderson pulled duty as slack behind Cochise on point. Duffy, with his radio, walked behind Anderson. Brumsen followed Duffy, and Terry brought up the rear. Cochise stopped every two minutes. They waited in the jungle, listening. The macabre, ululating chatter of the birds and monkeys echoed through the trees.

Swarming mosquitos and flies hummed and buzzed. Billowing spider webs of shade surged over the jungle floor. Ephemeral strands of sunlight flickered to and fro, ineffectively highlighting a tableau of whispering plants, shrubs, and trees.

Sweat trickled down Terry's brow and flowed into his eyes. He mopped his face with his towel. They waited. He swatted at the flies attacking his face.

Always cautious when on patrol, today Anderson slowed the tempo even more. "I want to go home one day."

With every pause, Terry, responsible for the rear, looked backward. Jesus, was he really going through this fucking jungle looking for someone to kill?

Something hit him in the back. Brumsen had thrown a small piece of wood at him. They talked as little as possible on patrol. Nothing was done that might give away their position. Brumsen stepped off into the jungle. Terry looked down to check his boots for leeches. Seeing none, he pushed aside the fronds and plunged forward.

Fifteen minutes later, they reached the bank of a small stream. The other ambush encamped two hundred yards upstream. A path ran beside the stream twenty-five to thirty yards from the bank. Each man knew his job. Anderson did not talk. He pointed men to different spots, and they hurriedly placed their assigned ordinance.

The sky and the jungle darkened. Terry grabbed a claymore mine and two flares from his rucksack. Anderson led Terry thirty yards down the trail to the left and pointed where to place the claymore. Anderson left to help Brumsen set up another mine on the other side of the ambush sight. Alone, Terry set up the flares that would guard the approach to the squad and the claymore.

Terry taped the flare to a small tree trunk four inches off the ground. He tied a wire to a sapling five feet away. He walked back to the tree that had the flare taped to it. Gently, he eased the cotter pin out of the flare. When the cotter pin was drawn out halfway, Terry took a deep breath. The flare, when ignited, could not only burn right through his skin but also possibly ruin the ambush.

He slipped the wire through the O-ring attached to the cotter pin. Keeping a little play in the wire, he secured it to the O-ring. The wire stretched across the space between the two trees four to six inches off the ground.

Anyone touching this was dead meat.

Moving closer to the path, he used the same technique for his second flare. The approach to the ambush was almost secure from his side. Terry walked back to the claymore he and Anderson had set up. He took a blasting cap out of his shirt pocket. Attaching the wire lying beside the claymore to the blasting cap, Terry inserted the cap into the mine. He breathed another sigh of relief.

Playing out the wire, he ran it back to where the squad arranged their ambush. Anderson watched him attach the wire to the electric handheld detonator. Terry signaled a thumbs-up. The flanks were secure. Anyone approaching the squad would have to do so on the trail, which was also mined. The entire procedure, performed in complete silence, had taken five minutes.

He laid out his poncho, sat down, and leaned against a tree. Anderson silently motioned up and down the path, indicating the kill zone. Terry nodded. The rest of the men, finished with their work, came in and sat down. Darkness fell across the jungle, caressing them. The waiting began.

There would be no food. No food meant no odors.

At almost seven o'clock in the evening, the location each member of the squad had chosen would be his for the night. Each would lie on his stomach or sit up, leaning against a tree or against his rucksack. That would be the extent of any movement.

Leeches crawled on branches above the squad. During the night, while the men slept, the leeches would either crawl to the men or drop down from their perches for their feast.

The watch schedules had been set before the men left the perimeter. For the rest of the night, they would wait. Anderson had the first watch until eleven o'clock. Brumsen watched from 11 until 12:30; Cochise from 12:30 until 2; Terry, the newest, from 2 until 3:30. Duffy stood guard between 3:30 and 5. He would wake the rest of the squad at 5.

The men slept next to each other in the order of their watch. No one had to move to awaken someone else. Everyone slept as much as he wanted until his watch.

Terry studied the rear area toward the stream, looking to both sides, then to his front noticing prominent trees and bushes that might stand out in the darkness. He lay down on his poncho, investigating his front one more time. The last thing he saw was Anderson fiddling with the squelch on the radio before he drifted off to sleep.

Cochise shook Terry, handing him the radio. Terry rubbed his eyes and looked at his watch. It was 2:05. Cochise took the two o'clock sit-rep call. Terry grabbed the phone connected to the radio. He nodded to Cochise, who lay his head on his folded arms and went to sleep.

The situation report, a sit-rep, came every half hour. Every ambush and listening post outside the perimeter at night was in constant radio contact with those inside the perimeter. Every ambush and listening post had a call sign. The squad's call sign was "Lima Victor." Every thirty minutes, all night long, someone inside the perimeter contacted the squad via radio and asked, "Lima Victor, what is your sit-rep?" in an audible whisper. Instead of talking, the soldier on duty answered by depressing the squelch button that stopped the radio static. One break of the static with the squelch button signaled that something was wrong. Twice indicated that every thing was normal.

Birds and monkeys clamored noisily. Terry listened and kept still. He leaned against the tree, gaze moving constantly over the terrain. Light reflecting from the stream made the jungle a little less impenetrable, leaving less strain on his eyes.

His head and neck moved constantly, gazing ahead, behind, and to both sides. It would be wonderful if they had a front and that was it. If they could only just attack people in front and not worry about the people behind and to the side.

"Lima Victor, what is your sit-rep? Over," came the whisper on the radio. Pressing the squelch button twice, he listened to the jungle and the slow breathing of the men. Leaning back against the tree, Terry yawned, shifting his M-16. *"Lima Victor, what is your sit-rep? Over."* After the next sit-rep, he woke Duffy. Duffy pushed up quickly on both elbows. He looked at his watch and took the radio.

Someone shook Terry. It was 5:05 by Terry's watch. He breathed a sigh of relief. No contact. In the darkness, they waited until whispers of gray penetrated the jungle foliage. The other men stirred. Cochise and Brumsen moved into the jungle to disarm the ordinance they had placed there the night before. Terry did the same.

Anderson had discussed what would happen this morning before they left the perimeter yesterday. He, Cochise, and Duffy were going to make contact with the other squad. Both squads would either go back into the perimeter, or they would make a sweep of the area. Terry hoped they would go back. But no one cared what he hoped.

When he returned with his claymore and flares, the men had gathered their gear. Anderson motioned for Brumsen and Terry to stay where they were. They watched the others disappear into the jungle. Duffy whispered into the radio, trying to raise the other squad.

More gray light crept through the foliage. After five minutes, Brumsen, barely more than a shadow, took out a small roll of toilet paper and pointed to it. Terry nodded. He must need to go bad, if he was going now. Brumsen crossed the trail and disappeared into the jungle with his machine gun resting on his shoulders.

With the dawn, the jungle banter of birds and monkeys increased. Terry squatted Vietnamese style, listening to the racket. He yawned. His M-16 lay across his lap. He smiled about Brumsen having to take a dump in the jungle.

The surrounding aspect of the jungle changed. The hairs on the back of his neck stood up. His stomach lurched. Sandaled feet stepped along the path, legs clad in black pajama pants? He lifted his M-16. Were there four feet or two? His M-16 made a soft click being switched to automatic.

The Vietnamese stopped and turned toward him. The man's left side faced Terry. The Vietnamese held a large, round, claymore mine, much bigger than the American claymore, on his shoulder with his left arm. The mine obscured the man's view to the left where Terry squatted. The Vietnamese slowly brought his right side around to Terry. The man's right hand held an AK-47.

* * *

A quagmire of plates, spoons, forks, food, and discarded napkins littered the table. Thornton threw his head back. His pony tail flopped to and fro. "I consider myself a soldier, fighting for the rights of women. I've declared war on those who want to take away those rights."

Sarah reverted to her Southern Belle voice. "But helpless, little infants have rights also don't they, Mr. Thornton? Surely, you realize that?"

Shoveling a fork-load of tuna into her mouth, Barbara waggled a finger at Sarah. "That's exactly our point, Sarah. They're not human at all. They have no rights. That's why we call them embryos and fetuses, for God's sake."

"Every fiber of my being tells me that they are ensouled creatures," Sarah said. "I guess it's a leftover from my religious upbringing."

A piece of tuna hung on one corner of Thorn's mouth. He wiped it away with his napkin. "That's why we are at war with you religious people. You want all of the rest of us to go along with what you believe. Let me remind you that this is a secular country. There is no God here. Your morality and your belief are simply that, *your* morality and *your* belief. Don't try to impose it on others. "

Sarah threw her hands up in exaggerated frustration. "But Mr. Thornton, I'm not a religious fanatic. I don't even go to church. And I don't know anything about Victimology Theology."

"Peace, peace. Oy! I've heard these arguments for thirty years," Jake said, waving his napkin like a peace flag. "No one ever changes his or her mind."

Gertrude placed both of her hands on the table. The gesture caught everyone's attention. "Down at this end of the table, we've been talking about gender mutability. It's funny how many new things they're finding to make kids unhappy. I wasn't mutable and I think I turned out okay. My mom and dad never had these problems with me or my brothers. You can bet when they were growing up before and during the Depression, her mother didn't have those problems, either."

"That depression generation," Thorn said, "the World War II generation, they were the greatest. They had their feet on solid ground. They had values and they knew what they believed. Thank God for them and their willingness to make those incredible sacrifices."

The heavy aroma of brewing coffee came from the kitchen. "My grandfather fought in World War II," Rich said, placing a bowl of cobbler on the table. "During the '30s, he helped support his family by shining shoes in Trenton. He did it from the time he was twelve until he was fifteen. You can't get kids to work like that anymore."

Holding a dessert plate in her large hand, Mary Thornton waited for cobbler. Her double chin shook as she pushed her fork through the peaches. "Thorn has started to idolize his father and his father's generation."

"What's wrong with a little hero worship?" Thorn asked, shrugging.

His wife laughed and poked a fork at her husband. "There's nothing wrong with loving your father, Thorn. I just remember that in the '60s your philosophy was 'Don't trust anyone over thirty.' As a matter of fact, you called your father a fascist pig, because he supported the Vietnam War. You absolutely despised him. Now you think he's the greatest thing since sliced bread.

"Moreover, I knew you back then. I have to say that the stories have gotten bigger and a lot more fantastic as the years go by. You weren't quite the big, anti-war demonstrator you say you were." Mary pulled at her earlobe.

Thornton laid his fork on his plate. "Mary, that's enough. People change."

"I know you, Greg Thornton. You spent a lot more time smoking pot than you did demonstrating."

"Mary, that's enough." Thornton wiped his forehead with his napkin. "I admit there were excesses during the '60s. I still think it was the best of times to live through."

"What about you, Terry?" Ralph asked. "Do you think the decade of the '60s was the best decade of the last half of the twentieth century?"

Everyone waited in silence.

"The only lasting thing my generation did in the '60s," Terry said, shaking his head, "was introduce drugs into our popular culture. We never realized that we would have to raise our kids in this culture. That's the sole accomplishment of my generation. I'm ashamed of it. We've done nothing else."

"Oh, come on, Terry," Thornton said. "We all got caught up in the sweep of events. We couldn't possibly see how things would turn out. We were young. Small things like drugs, that we should have noticed, we swept under the rug. We were too busy looking at the big picture. Everyone worried about the draft. Somehow, we just integrated the drugs, the sex, et cetera, into our normal way of looking at the world. It was a way of saying to our fathers, 'Your rules don't hold anymore. We're creating a new culture, a new morality, a new age, the Age of Aquarius.' I regret some of the excesses. I should never have called my parents and their generation fascists. Especially all of those who sacrificed their lives fighting Hitler. The ones who fought and died in World War II were the ones who really sacrificed for this country. Those guys were really committed."

Cochise, his jungle-fatigue jacket open to the waist, jerked a thumb toward Thornton. "That *hijo de puta* wouldn't know a sacrifice or a commitment if it kicked him in the *culo*."

The squad was arrayed in the living room. They looked expectantly at Terry.

Anderson rolled his eyes, shaking his head in furious disgust. "Malloy, why do you put up with this bullshit? You've killed better men than these guys. Take him outside and whip his ass!"

"What about Korea, and World War One, and yes, Vietnam, Thorn?" Terry asked.

"What about them?" Thorn retorted. "What do you mean?"

"I mean, once you're dead, you're dead. Soldiers who died fighting in those other wars sacrificed no less than the men who died in World War II."

Sarah held on to his elbow. "Terry."

"What the fuck would you know about commitment and sacrifice?" Terry snorted. "Mr. Radical Chic, who makes a living writing about other people's lives."

In the living room, the squad patiently waited for him. The weight on his shoulders pressed him into his chair. "I once knew and fought with men who would have sacrificed their lives for me. And I would have done the same for them. Have you ever had a relationship with men, with your brothers from the movement, like that? I forgot how incredible those men were. We should be ashamed of ourselves for what we, as a nation, have done to them and how we portray them."

Footsteps on the stairs heralded a herd of children exploding into the room. Diversity and Alex ran to Rich. "Dad, can Alex spend the night with us?"

CHAPTER SIX

The sledge hammers pounded on gongs inside Terry's head. Geez, why didn't he learn to slow down? Did he make a fool of himself last night? Terry sipped his coffee. The aroma and the steam from the mug signaled another day. Stupid bastards! United Veggies and Animal Lovers my ass! Gender mutability! God, what a world.

Did he jump on Thornton too hard? What a pompous ass. He should have jumped with both feet. What difference did it make? No one was going to listen. He didn't know why, but Thornton really set him off.

Terry held his head and tasted the black coffee. Thank God Alex spent the night at Rich's. He was definitely drinking too much. My Lai, My Lai! Sarah convinced him to let her take him home. "Please, Terry, if not because you're drinking too much, do it for my sake. I need to leave before I get trapped here with Rich saying good-byes to everyone from the front porch. It's just too domestic for me."

In the car, his simmering anger bubbled to the surface. His arm went up and down in short chopping motions for emphasis. "You have no idea what it's like to constantly be on the defensive. Stupid people believe anything. How many villages did you burn? How many innocent civilians did you kill? It's My Lai this and My Lai that, and 'the movie ads said it was 'Vietnam as it really was', so why should I believe you?' I want to scream, 'Because I was there, you stupid bastard!'"

Sarah made a left turn onto Terry's street. "The war has been over for almost thirty years. Why can't you let it rest?"

"That's just it. I can let it rest if everyone stopped assuming that I was sneaking around shooting women and children in their sleep. If the movies would stop portraying good men as insane dope addicts and killers, I could let it rest. If we didn't have a Vietnam vet Senator, who is a candidate for President, saying on tape that Americans killed, murdered, raped, and tortured thousands of Vietnamese, I could let it rest."

The lights of the car illuminated the driveway. Sarah said, "I've never thought much about Vietnam. It was almost over when I was born. Plus, there are more pressing, more current things for me to think about. I have to say that Thorn seems to live in the '60s." Sarah laughed. "If he mentioned 'the movement' to me one more time, I think I would have offered him some laxative."

Terry opened the car door. "Can't you see that these people are supposed to be intelligent college professors and professionals? They all have stories, or have heard stories, of how screwed up some guy was who came back from Vietnam. They really believe the wild stories some twenty-one-year-old, who was probably a postal clerk, told them thirty-five years ago. Regardless of whether they can verify the story or not. If these people, who are supposed to be reasonably skeptical, believe all the bullshit, then what does that say about the rest of the people in the country?

"Our culture sees what's on the TV, or in the movies, and they believe it. They actually believe some dickhead director's version of Vietnam and what he puts into a movie. These professors would be the first to question any authority, but let some Hollywood director make a movie about Vietnam, which has the most absurd crap in it that shows Americans at their worst, and they swallow it as fact, hook, line, and sinker."

"Terry, there's no need to yell at me. I'm your friend." Sarah pulled Terry to her and kissed him lightly on the lips. "You need to stop drinking so much."

Putting one leg out the car door and then bringing it back, Terry sighed. "I know you're my friend. But they're going to do the same thing to the soldiers in Iraq and Afghanistan. Any little incident will be blown out of proportion. They'll make movies that will show American troops raping and killing. When I think of them doing that to Ella, I get furious."

"I'm not even going to pretend to know what you feel about Ella, Terry, and the other soldiers that have lost their lives. All I can say is that I'm sorry you lost your daughter."

She studied herself in the mirror. "Most of these professors grew up in the '60s. It was the best time of their lives. You can't believe how boring it is to listen to a pot-bellied old poop talking about smoking dope when he was young. At least you're keeping yourself trim and handsome. I've never heard you bore anyone with what you did in Vietnam."

* * *

The coffee burned his lips. Maybe he should call Rich and cancel the golf. He was in no shape to play. Terry walked to the picture window. His car, Rich had to take him to his car after the golf. Could he stand Rich's antics on the golf course? Terry put down the coffee, rotated his back and bent over, stretching muscles. He needed the exercise. Exercise? He needed a psychiatrist, a 'physician of the soul.' He blew across the coffee. Would that cure the visions? What would cure the heartache? Ella would never exercise nor run nor breathe again.

The five-year-old Volvo station wagon turned into the driveway. Terry rushed through the kitchen, turned off the coffee, and went out the back door into the garage. Holding the coffee in one hand, he lifted his golf clubs onto his shoulder and walked down the drive to Rich's waiting car.

His grandson slumped next to Diversity in the back seat. Yawning, he rubbed the sleep out of his eyes and smiled. "Hey, Grandad!"

Rich helped Terry place his golf clubs in the trunk of the station wagon. "Do you have any clothes you want to bring for Alex?"

"Are you kidding. Alex has two wardrobes. One here at our house and one at his other grandparents. Once he outgrows them, we could go into the clothing business."

Alex unbuckled his seat belt and watched them from the back seat. Ella's big green eyes smiled at Terry. A sunburst of love enveloped him, exploding from his heart and suffusing warmth throughout his body. He opened the back door and hugged Alex. "Hiya, Alex. It's good to see you this morning, son. Did you have fun last night?"

"Yes, sir. We had a good time. Can Diversity come and play over at Nana and Poppop's?"

Running her slender fingers through her straight brown hair, Diversity turned away from the window. Her bright eyes looked at the back of her father's head. "That would be fun. Can I, Dad?"

The Volvo rolled out of the driveway and accelerated down the street. "Diversity, you know your mom would accuse me of dumping you off on another set of parents. All she's looking for is an excuse to tell everyone what kind of bad father I am."

Diversity folded her thin arms and stuck out her lower lip. "I won't have anyone to play with at the pool. I don't know anyone at your club."

Adjusting his seatbelt, Terry instructed Rich on how to get to Peggy and George's. "I'm sure George and Peggy wouldn't mind if Diversity spent the day with Alex."

"Diversity needs to stay with me. She'll have fun swimming at the pool. I've got a baby sitter who is going to meet us there. Maybe Alex could come with her?"

It was Terry's turn to smile and wave off Rich. "No, Peggy and George would fight you if you tried to take their only grandson away."

The newspaper landed on Terry's lap. "Have you read Thorn's article about Ella this morning?"

Terry did not reach for the paper. His hands fumbled nervously with the seat belt. "What does he say?"

"He says Ella is a beautiful young lady who was loved by her family and friends. What did you think he would say? You've got to stop thinking that Thorn is the enemy."

Did he think Thornton was the enemy? "Thornton and his ilk have been calling Vietnam vets names for years. Why should I trust that sonofa–" Terry glanced toward the children in the back seat. "Why should I trust him to say anything nice about anyone I know, especially these young soldiers who are in Iraq? Journalists lost my trust a long time ago. If it advanced his agenda, he'd turn on her in an instant."

Letting go of the steering wheel, Rich wagged his finger. "You got him wrong, old buddy. You have to get over that '60s mentality of yours that everybody is the enemy."

"It's kinda hard to get over it," Terry said, "when you have all that Kerry crap going on. Thornton even brought it up when he was interviewing us about Ella."

Rich glanced at Terry while turning the steering wheel. "That may just be him doing his job. You don't know him nor the Victimology Theology that we've embraced. Thorn sees you as a victim, Terry.

It's not your fault that Vietnam happened. You're not responsible for what you did. In pursuing stories, I bet Thorn would tell you that he's exposing the real oppressors, not you."

"Then tell him to go find the real oppressors and ask them the stupid questions."

After dropping Alex off, they drove quickly to Whispering Waters Country Club. Rich talked about his swing plane and follow through. He was in the middle of a monologue on timing when he turned into the parking lot.

Diversity held her father's hand. "Oh, Dad, the pool isn't even open yet." She looked around. "The baby sitter's not here either."

"That's okay, Sweetie. She'll be here soon. They'll open in about thirty minutes. You brought a book, didn't you? You can read while you wait."

"I have two books, Dad. But can I come with you? I can drive the cart."

Pulling his daughter to him, Rich hugged her. "Sweetie, you're going to get bored out there."

The child's brown eyes pleaded with Terry.

Clubs rattled together as Terry set his golf bag down. "Rich, I don't care if Diversity comes. I haven't played golf in months."

Rich, hugging Diversity, rolled his eyes. Eyebrows narrowed, he looked hard at Terry and shook his head slightly, making a shush movement with his mouth.

The little girl's small shoulders slumped. Her bag scrapped the ground as she pulled it after her.

Rich shook his head and gave Terry an abashed smile. "Diversity, come back here."

Swinging the bag up on her shoulders, she ran toward them, grinning.

Kneeling down, Rich held out his arms. "You forgot to give Dad a kiss, Darling. Give me some loving, baby."

Diversity stopped running. The smile disappeared. The blue bag dropped to the pavement. Diversity left it there as she walked back and pecked her father on the cheek.

"Now, have a good day at the pool. Daddy'll be back in no time and we'll have dinner together."

Both men watched the small child walk toward the pool. She did not look back.

Terry put his hands on his hips. If only he could see Ella one more time or spend the day with her. "Rich, why didn't you let her come. I haven't played golf in months and don't care. If I had Ella back, I wouldn't be here with you."

Rich patted Terry on the back. "She'll be okay once the sitter gets here and she has someone to play with. Besides, Diversity's not going to be joining the Army. I'll have plenty of time to spend with her."

Clinching his teeth, he choked back a response. That was the smart thing to do – teach your children not to take chances. Teach them that joining the armed services is for suckers. That was what most academics did. He gave a last look at Diversity's small form walking away and picked up his clubs.

A torrent of old memories overwhelmed him. He had just started work at the college and Ella was four years old. Clarissa was taking care of her and working on her dissertation. To make extra money, besides teaching his three history courses, he taught introductory English and History at the city's small technical school at night. That totaled five classes with five new lesson plans. He was also trying to write some journal articles based on his dissertation. For weeks, he only saw Ella on the weekends and sometimes not even then.

One Saturday morning as he sipped his coffee and read the paper, he heard her cry, "Daddy!" Ella ran to his arms, her pink nightgown with butterflies on it flowing behind her. She jumped into his lap and clung to him, her little arms barely reaching his broad shoulders. Finally, brushing her reddish-blond hair out of her green eyes, she looked up at him. "Daddy, where do you live now?" It was the last time he ever had two jobs.

"You better think about where you're living, Rich."

Rich smiled thinly with a questioning look in his eyes. "What? What the hell does that mean?"

* * *

The green of the fairways and the rich odor of newly mown grass energized Terry. He loosened and stretched on the practice tee. The sledgehammer in his head changed to a simple hammer beating against a brick wall. He watched Rich's slow rhythmic swing. The ball sailed majestically down the driving range with a faint leftward bend. Try to imitate it, you dumb bastard. Terry's ball kept veering to the right.

They drove the cart to the first tee. The sun had topped the trees. Down the fairway, the dew on the grass sparkled with sunlight. Rich breathed with exaggeration. "Man, smell that grass. I love this game."

Although Terry's first tee shot veered to the right, it stayed in bounds. He breathed a sigh of relief.

Rich fired his usual draw. Watching the ball, he posed with the club on his shoulder. Bringing the club down to his side, He turned to Terry with a smile. "I used my three wood since the hole is so short. That bitch'll hunt." In the cart, he tipped his hat back and smacked Terry's leg. "Let's go out there and spank some ass today."

Yanking his next shot to the left, Terry's ball landed fifty yards short of the green on the wrong side of the cart path. Rich's second shot landed on the green, five yards to the left of the flag. It took

Terry two more shots to reach the green. His three-putt gave him a score of seven.

Rich lined up his birdie putt while Terry played out. When he finally putted, the ball looped in and out of the hole, stopping six inches away. Rolling his eyes, Rich slapped his thigh. "You gotta give me some of that hole, baby."

On the next hole, a par five that dog-legged to the right, Terry pulled his shot to the left, landing in the rough.

"Don't worry, old timer. Your swing'll come back," Rich stalked to the tee box before Terry's ball had stopped. His tight golf shirt showed off his athletic form and fluid grace. Once again the ball sailed down the fairway with a slight draw. "I used my driver on this hole. That shot's a tit-kisser." He laughed at Terry's puzzled expression. "A tit-kisser – it opens up the hole."

The cell phone rang and Rich answered it. Listening briefly, he said, "Sure, Honey. We can do that."

Stuffing the phone in his back pocket, Rich jumped in the cart and accelerated down the fairway. "That was Diversity. She wants to watch a TV show tonight that her mom won't let her watch, Sluts on the Town. I tape it for her."

The breeze from the speeding cart felt good. Terry removed his cap to feel the wind. He wiped his forehead with his sleeves and put his cap back on when the cart stopped near his ball. "That show's a little too adult for an eleven-year-old isn't it?" He grabbed a club and walked toward his ball.

Rich, slouching in the cart, shook his head. "Nah, kids these days know twice as much as we did when we were their age."

Taking a practice swing, Terry set up to hit the ball. "What does Joan say about it? She can't be too happy. Besides, just because they know more stuff, it doesn't mean they should."

Draping one long leg over another, Rich shoved his cap back on his head. "What Joan doesn't know, doesn't bother her. It's a secret that Diversity and I share. It brings us closer together. It's a way of being a friend and not a parent."

Terry's club hit six inches behind his ball, spraying dirt everywhere. The ball did not move. His shoulder ached from the impact of the club with the ground.

Rich growled, "Keep your head down."

Keeping his head down, he swung more slowly. The ball sailed down the fairway, but landed in the rough again. Sitting down in the cart, Terry removed his cap. "Forget about Joan. Aren't you worried that your daughter's watching a show like that?"

The cart lurched to a halt near Rich's ball. "Terry, it's a new age. Everyone is growing up faster. The culture is changing. Who's to say Sluts on the Town shouldn't be watched or should be watched. I believe in giving children rights that they think they can handle. Diversity is mature enough to handle shows like Sluts. Besides, why should I make Diversity a sexual victim of our middle-class upbringing by laying a load of old-time outworn values and guilt on her?"

His blue eyes questioned Rich. "Are you talking about standards that we impart to our children? Surely you're not mixing that up with your Victimology crap."

Fondling his mustache, Rich studied his shot and picked a club. "I've eagled this hole twice." Rich's trim hips and legs shifted his weight with his smooth swing. The ball flew toward the green, hitting it and continuing to roll. "Stop, you stupid cunt."

Ramming his club into the bag, Rich jumped in the cart and sped down the fairway. "It's not crap, Terry. There's a lot of serious issues that our society needs to discuss. I think the best way to do it is through Victimology Theology."

"Good shot," Terry said.

Rich shook his head and smiled. "It's like when you're on a date. You gotta be able to see the hole clearly if you're going to score."

They played the rest of the front nine with Terry struggling to keep the ball in the fairway. Rich shot a thirty-nine with four bogies and one birdie. Every close miss of a putt brought out a, "Give me some of that hole, Baby."

They walked off the ninth green. Terry put his putter into his bag. "I've never understood how you talk like you do on the golf course and yell as loud as you can for women's rights. It's like I'm seeing two different people. The one at the college and the one when you're out here."

"I'm for women's rights and equality." Rich slammed his putter into the bag. "What's that got to do with my screaming cunt out here?"

Terry stretched his back before sitting down in the cart. He laughed. "Doesn't it seem hypocritical to use all the sexist language and then talk about women's equality?"

Steering the cart toward the tenth tee, Rich shrugged. "Why hypocritical? Whose morality are you using to judge me. There's a new age coming, Terry. We're riding the first wave. Your values don't exist in this world. You don't have to be the same person all the time. What you do in one setting doesn't have to jibe with what you do in another. This is the Clinton Age. The age when you can get Lewinskis in private and talk about women's oppression in public. It's the best of all possible worlds. The feminists love you and will fuck your brains out, if you give them half a chance. Especially these serious little college girls."

Terry pressed his lips together and shook his head. The cart stopped. He stepped out and moved toward the back.

Rich laughed. "All you have to do is mention oppression and Simone de Beauvoir, and these college girls flop over and spread their legs. For a single guy like me, it's heaven. And who's to say

I'm wrong. The little, middleclass whores are going to put out for someone, it might as well be me. My natural mother was probably someone just like them. They don't have a brain in their head." Rich's somber brown eyes studied Terry. He pulled at his mustache. "It's a game, Terry. Say the right thing, make the right moves, and you win the prize. It's every man for himself. Besides, Victimology Theology has helped me to see things a lot more clearly."

"How in the hell does Victimology Theology help explain 'Lewinskis in the coat closet'"?

Rich jumped out of the cart. "It's simply that I can't help the way I am because there are so many other factors that constitute my personality, my ego, the way I see the world. I can't possibly control all of them or be responsible for them. When Diversity gets bigger, I don't want her to look back, blaming me, and seeing herself as a victim of my oppression."

Terry slipped a hand in his pocket and pulled out a tee and ball. "Of course you can help who you are. You're responsible for what you believe and how you behave. And no matter what you do, it's still going to have an impact on Diversity."

Rich waved a hand in exasperation. "But that is typical victimology mentality. You think you're responsible for what you do because you don't know any better. It's called Bourgeois Victimology. You have to lose that kind of thinking."

Terry shook his head in disbelief. "You can't be serious."

"I'm deadly serious. There's Bourgeois Victimology, Lesbian and Gay Victimology, Black Victimology, Animal Victimology. You believe you got to where you are because of hard work. When really, you got to where you are because of factors that you couldn't control. You mistakenly believed there were choices when there really weren't any."

"Okay, okay, give me an example of Gay and Lesbian Victimology."

Rich rested both hands on the shaft of his club. "That's easy. Gay and lesbians in the past have always thought that they were responsible for their lifestyle choices. As a result, they've suffered tons of guilt. When really the choices are hard-wired in by nature. They're not responsible for their choices. It's all natural. So, they lose the choices, they lose the guilt."

A hawk flew overhead. They both watched it. "And Black people?"

Rich snapped and unsnapped his golf glove. "Black people aren't responsible because white people have been stepping on their necks for the last four hundred years."

Lifting both hands in frustration, Terry's shoulders sagged. "But what about black leaders in Africa who have been murdering their own people. And Arabs, who were enslaving Africans hundreds of years before whites ever thought about it."

Rich shook his head and smiled. "Black leaders in Africa have adopted behavior patterns of their colonial oppressors. They aren't responsible for what they do. It's like the Stockholm Syndrome. You begin to identify with your kidnappers. The colonialists kidnapped the countries they colonized."

"But, Rich, all kinds of people have been oppressing other people for thousands of years all over the world."

"That's right. Now you're getting it. The oppressors aren't responsible either, Terry. Remember, it's the Unitarian Church of *Universal* Victimology. No one is responsible for what they do. When everyone realizes that and forgives everyone, when the oppressor and the oppressed can meet on equal terms, that's the secular paradise that Victimology Theology is aiming for."

"So, what's this got to do with the way you treat women?"

"It's simple. I mentioned that there are various factors over which we have no control. Well, one of those factors is that some people can't help making themselves available for exploitation by others. I can't help exploiting those women who want to be exploited by men who pretend to care."

"So, it's not your fault. It's the women's or the student's."

"It's no one's fault. We're not searching to blame anyone. We're all just looking for love. It is what it is. Your thinking with the old standards. Lose them. It's liberating."

"Maybe I'm too old to understand."Terry knelt down and pushed the tee into the ground. Looking up, he saw the Vietnamese standing several feet away.

* * *

Heart pounding against his chest, he pulled the trigger. The gun was not attached to him. It seemed to belong to someone else as it erupted in smoke and flame. The Vietnamese man's eyes opened wide in surprise. The gun jumped in Terry's hands. Red dots appeared on the man's chest. A corona of red mist blossomed behind him. The red blooming on his shirt slowly expanded. The gun dropped to the ground. The mine tumbled off his left shoulder. His legs buckled.

Two other feet moved behind the collapsing Vietnamese, running into the jungle away from Terry. The M-60 roared as Brumsen yelled, "Mofo, mofo, mofo!"

The running Vietnamese, screaming, thrashed and staggered to and fro among the foliage. Terry stood on watery legs, pointing his rifle at the Vietnamese lying in a pile on the jungle trail. Mouth dry, heart pounding, he cautiously approached the man. His heart was going to explode.

"I can't even shit without these bastards trying to kill me!" Brumsen yelled to no one in particular. "I dream about the mofos and have nightmares about them. You'd think they'd let me shit in peace, goddammit."

Brumsen's words exploded among the vegetation. Terry tried to say something, but his mouth was too dry. He licked his lips. The Vietnamese lay still on the jungle trail, slumped across the huge claymore mine.

"Hillbilly, how you doing, man? You okay? Let me get my mofo pants up. Is that guy dead?" Branches and leaves rustled as he moved through the jungle. Terry caught sight of his helmet. A scream of pain came from Brumsen's area. "This no good motherfucker's still alive."

Terry touched the dead man with his boot. "My guy isn't."

The big machine gunner emerged from the jungle. "Your guy? Damn, I don't know why, but I figured you had missed that sonofabitch I shot."

"Why don't you guys put this conversation on a loud speaker?" Anderson said. "That way every friggin' VC in Vietnam'll hear you."

Cochise and Duffy came up behind Anderson. Both of them stared at the dead Vietnamese.

"Did either one of you think there might be other bad guys around?" Anderson turned to Duffy and Cochise. "You two go down the trail fifty yards or so and make sure everything is tight. Duffy, call the base and tell them we got two gooks."

"I'll tell them we shot two Vietnamese," Duffy said.

"All right, Duffy, whatever you want to say. Just do it."

They disappeared down the trail. Duffy spoke into the radio, "*Lima Lima,* this is *Lima Victor*, over."

Grabbing the dead Vietnamese by the hair, Anderson jerked him away from the mine.

Brumsen pointed a thumb over his shoulder. "We got another one back there about ten yards. Malloy killed this guy, and I shot the other one. He was still alive about two minutes ago. I really fucked up his legs. He isn't going anywhere. It looks like one of his knee caps is missing. He carried the tripod for this thing." Brumsen gestured to the circular claymore mine.

Reaching down to lift the claymore off the ground, Anderson grunted. "This thing weighs at least twenty-five pounds. It has to be two feet in diameter."

This was Terry's first close inspection of a Viet Cong claymore. American claymore mines weighed much less. They had the shape of a concave rectangle about five inches in height, eight inches in length, and two inches in thickness.

The wounded Vietnamese moaned. Anderson walked through the jungle, kneeling next to him. Terry and Brumsen followed. The VC glared at Anderson.

Anderson poked at the man's legs with his M-16. "You fucked up, didn't you, you little bastard?"

The man moaned, grimaced, and reached for his legs. The pajama pants on both legs were torn and bloody. The kneecap of his left leg was turned inside out, hanging on by a thread of skin.

Anderson kicked the man's leg. He screamed.

Motioning Brumsen to help him, Anderson grabbed one of the man's arms, and Brumsen the other. The wounded man's face contorted in pain. He screamed again as they dragged him to the trail next to his dead accomplice.

"Shut up, you bastard." Anderson pointed to the dead Vietnamese. "Malloy, strip and search that son of a bitch."

Anderson pulled off the wounded man's shirt, having no regard for the man's pain. A moan escaped from his lips and did not stop.

"Brumsen, take his pants off."

"Malloy, move it. Strip and search that guy."

Terry pulled off the dead man's pants. He reached for the pajama top and pulled. Blood oozed from the material onto his hands.

Another pair of hands reached down and tugged at the top also. "Let me help," Duffy said.

Cochise, standing behind Duffy, whistled. "Good shooting, Malloy. Way to go, man. What happened?"

"I'll tell you what didn't happen," Brumsen said. "We didn't throw no mofo knives at these bastards. Malloy shot that mofo. I shot this mofo."

"Okay, Brumsen, okay," Cochise said. "Knives aren't for everyone. I told you, man, this knife is only for emergencies."

"Well, I don't know what you call two gooks walking around in the jungle trying to turn your ass into shredded wheat with a fifty-pound claymore. As far as I'm concerned, these two assholes qualify as an emergency."

Cochise laughed. "Brumsen, I don't mean that."

While the squad talked, Anderson knelt down next to the wounded man and shook his head. He muttered to himself. Without a glance at anyone, he picked up his rifle and stood. Snapping the lever off safety, he pointed the rifle at the wounded man's head.

The man raised one arm. He shook his head. His eyes pleaded. He managed to yell three syllables in Vietnamese. Anderson pulled the trigger. The head bounced off the ground. A font of blood shot up from the temple and then subsided.

Duffy, Brumsen, and Cochise jumped. Duffy's shoulders slumped. His arms hung at his side. "Goddamn you, Anderson. Why'd you do that?"

Still looking at the man he had just killed, Anderson whispered, "You know why, Duffy. Don't ask stupid questions."

"It was completely unnecessary." Duffy held his arms away from his side and gestured toward the dead man. "He was wounded and no danger to us."

"What's unnecessary is your religious, ethical bullshit. There's no place for it in this jungle."

Cochise kicked the Vietnamese claymore with his foot. "Duffy, look at this mine, *amigo*. They were going to use it against us. There's no telling how many of our guys these *bastardos* have killed."

"He's right, Duffy," Brumsen said. "These guys got exactly what they deserved."

"If he had walked in and surrendered to us," Anderson said, "I can understand letting him live. But this asshole was trying to kill us. You're telling me now that he was shot, we should let him live. That's horseshit. These gooks aren't even human as far as I'm concerned."

Duffy's eyes flashed. He stepped forward toward Anderson, balling his hands into fists. "And what makes you think that we're any different than they are, if we act like this?"

Holding up his rifle, Anderson shook it in Duffy's face. "*This* makes me different! We're alive, and these sonsofbitches are dead. Trust me, they wouldn't have had any doubts or arguments about killing us."

"We have orders to bring in wounded for interrogation," Duffy shot back.

"Yeah, right," Anderson snorted. "Bring 'em in and let some dumb-ass Second Louie decorate himself with a bronze star for capturing a VC. I'm glad I shot this bastard."

Duffy said, "Everyone else has thrown in his two-bits, what do you say, Malloy?"

Anderson grabbed Duffy's shoulder. "This isn't a fucking democracy, Duffy. It's the army. I'm not taking any votes on killing these bastards. This is war. I'm fighting to win it. You can forget about morality and democracy shit. God, and the rest of all the good things you find back in the world aren't in this fuckin' world. In my world, these two dead gooks don't have any rights. If you don't like it, then get out of the fucking squad."

The two men glared at each other.

Pushing his helmet back on his head, Anderson took a deep breath. His shoulders slumped. Arms hanging by his side, he lifted a weary hand toward Duffy. "Look, Duffy, I need you, I didn't mean that last remark. Get on the radio and tell Czplicki that he needs to hurry. I need his squad to help us carry these guys back to the perimeter. Cochise, you and Brumsen cut down two poles. Let's load these guys on ponchos."

Duffy reached for the transmitter. Cochise and Brumsen grabbed machetes to cut down two trees for poles.

Anderson threw his poncho to Terry. "When we get back to base camp, we have to go into town and relax a little." He lifted a body. Terry slipped the poncho underneath.

"That's right. It's the beginning of Tet, isn't it," Cochise said, handing a pole to Anderson.

Terry snapped the buttons of the poncho around the pole. "What's Tet?"

"The Vietnamese New Year," Anderson said. "The first round is on me."

Five minutes later, Terry, leaning against a tree, stared at the two extended lumps underneath the ponchos. He stroked his M-16 casually. A bird chirped somewhere. Soft tendrils of sunlight filtered through the jungle, sending sparkles glancing off the stream. A breeze brushed high vines to and fro. Purple butterflies pounced here and there, dancing along the creek bed. Terry relaxed and closed his eyes.

* * *

"Terry, you going to hit the ball or look at it for the next couple of hours? Jesus, what's wrong with you?"

Terry shook his head. He took a breath and swung.

After Rich hit his ball, they returned to the cart.

"Like I was saying, Terry, when it comes to poon, everyone's on his own. It's a jungle out there."

CHAPTER SEVEN

Terry walked into the house through the garage. The remnants of the morning's perk sulked on the counter. Dust moats floated in the curtain-filtered sunlight. The stillness screamed at him. A fist encircled his heart, squeezing it. Was this to be his life? Play golf and listen to men talk nonsense? Go to parties and listen to nonsense? Had he been a sucker, living according to rules that no one gave a shit about? Sending his only child to die in a war that even he himself doubted? No, not sending her, but letting her go. To die, so Rich could screw little college girls and idiots could run around stealing cows and pigs. He needed a drink.

In the den, he grabbed Johnny Walker Black and poured. Sunlight sent sparkles into the pool of liquid gold. His hands shook and his mouth watered. Anticipation of the taste lurked beneath the swirling liquor. He looked into the glass. Ella's green eyes stared back. "Where do you live, Daddy?"

Terry stared at the glass. Where did he live? In this bottle, in this crazy world that seemed to have turned upside down? Get the gun and get it over with. Ella's eyes became Alex's. Where do you live, Granddad? What kind of a world would that child inherit? He wasn't a quitter. Gulping twice, he pushed the glass away.

In the kitchen, he grabbed the coffee pot and cleaned it. He pushed the button on the answering machine. Clarissa's voice filled the room. Terry inserted a new filter and grabbed the can of coffee off the shelf.

"Hello, guys. Alex, I sailed down the Thames today. You'll have to look on your map of England to see where it is. We visited a place called Greenwich. Ask your grandfather to tell you what happens there. Harold and Porter say 'Hello.' We are all well here. Tomorrow we're going to the Tower of London. I miss you, Alex, and love you. Terry, I received an email from Peggy telling me about the nice article Mr. Thornton wrote. I guess I overreacted the other day. I'm sorry." Pause. "I still haven't changed my mind about our relationship."

He poured water into the coffee machine and watched the coffee drip into the pot. The phone rang and he answered.

Sarah's voice came over the line. "Terry, how do you feel? Are you ready for tonight?"

"Tonight? Ready for what?"

"Don't tell me you've forgotten. The teach-in on Iraq is tonight at 8."

His stomach lurched. "Sarah, I forgot about it." What the hell did he know about Iraq? Could he speak without embarrassing himself?

"If you don't want to be on the panel you don't have to. I wondered what Jake was thinking when he asked you?"

"No, I'll speak. I just forgot."

"You really don't have to give a speech. It's a panel format. Each member will give an opening monologue and then the audience will ask questions. The panel can answer the question and respond to the answers of other members of the panel. That way we hope to generate a discussion."

He rubbed his unshaven face. "I don't care what the format is. I'll be there."

"I'm going to run. Do you want to meet me? I've missed you the last couple of days."

His watch said 2:30. He had time to run and come back and clean up for the panel. "I'll be there."

He went to the den. The golden glass of scotch sparkled. Where do you live, Terry? Taking two sips, rolling scotch around on his tongue, he shuddered as the liquid flowed down his throat.

Terry studied his unshaven, angular face in the mirror. Honest and open blue eyes stared back at him. The light brown hair had streaks of gray running through it. His square jaw, straight nose, and small mouth did not repel anyone at a first meeting. He kept in good shape, running as often as possible. There was no pudginess around the neck or eyes that he saw in so many of his colleagues. Only Clarissa knew that he boxed in the Golden Gloves as a teenager and had won a couple of championships. Thoughts and images of Sarah popped into his head, replacing Clarissa's face.

On the track, Sarah waved and pulled her left leg back against her buttocks, stretching it as much as she could. The red spandex halter accentuated her firm breasts. A blonde ponytail stuck out of her baseball cap. Tight red spandex pants hugged her hips and buttocks and clung to her slender thighs. She wore no make-up. "I always feel safer when I run with a man. I hope you don't mind coming over."

"Hello, beautiful." He felt sloppy standing next to her. His green tee-shirt fell outside of a pair of burgundy gym shorts that had the Northeastern Georgia logo of a tiger on it.

"Hello, good looking, yourself. You look ruggedly handsome today." Her smile showed two rows of gleaming teeth.

"I feel ruggedly grubby. Rich kicked my ass playing golf this morning." He examined her and whistled. "You look terrific."

"I feel terrific." She laughed and twirled on her toes.

Ella whirled around in her brown, desert fatigues. Her cap shaded her face. She saluted. "How do you like them, Dad? Is this what you wore in Vietnam?"

Watching his daughter spin about, Terry tried to hide his anxiety. "They look great, darling. No, we didn't wear any camouflage fatigues. They were just solid green jungle fatigues."

Ella fingered her name tag. "The first sergeant told me I could make E-3 after I go through training."

Terry shook his head. He stopped smiling. Sarah's grin disappeared. He put one foot in front of the other and jogged down the track. Ten feet behind him, Sarah's footsteps echoed his.

The run didn't take long. Terry walked back through the door at four o'clock, energized. He went to the den and inserted an Ella Fitzgerald CD into the player. Leaving the room with the CD blaring, he took off his shirt and walked upstairs, carrying a refilled glass of scotch. He had promised Sarah that he would go for a drink with the group when the panel discussion finished. Another boring evening.

The hot water from the shower invigorated him after his run. What was he going to say tonight. He didn't have a clue. Rebel without a clue? His whole life, he never had a clue. Steam rose from the sink. He pushed the brush around the shaving cup. Smearing the soap on his unshaven face, he dipped the brush, watching as the soap melted into the water. At least his hands had stopped shaking. He grabbed a hand towel and wiped the steam from the mirror. Creases and lines around the eyes had multiplied. Tired eyes stared at him. He looked like shit.

Reaching for his razor, his hand froze. A Vietnamese man stared back at him from the mirror. The man's black eyes bulged in terror. A slow dribble of blood came from a wound to his neck. Tongue protruding from his mouth, the hole in his neck widened and blood cascaded from it. A red froth of spittle and bubbles dripped from his lips.

* * *

Students drifted into the auditorium. Terry lounged in an uncomfortable plastic chair. His hands gripped each other. The knuckles stood out white against the brown table top. Young faces, some familiar, stared at him. They talked to their friends. Was he ever this young?

A shadow crossed the table in front of him. A strong body odor, of men working and sweating in the hot sun, surrounded him. A hand seized his shoulder. "Hey, Bro, you were the same age as these guys when you were in Vietnam with us."

The students continued to talk to each other. Sarah, wearing blue jeans and a white, short-sleeved shirt with button-down collars, talked with Rich. Only Terry heard Brumsen's voice. He looked up into Brumsen's calm, black eyes. "We never had a chance, did we?"

Brumsen shook his head. He knelt beside Terry's chair. "We almost made it. But that's okay. You have to make sure the men fighting now have a chance, Terry. Give them a chance to win or get them home."

"How? What the hell am I supposed to be able to do?"

"Are you ready?" Sarah smiled at him. "We've changed the format. I'm just going to ask you to give a brief statement on Iraq to begin. You can talk, if you want to. Then we're going to open it up for questions right away and just go with the dialogue."

Laura Boatwright entered and walked down the aisle, white ribbons in her hair reflecting the auditorium light and creating a contrast with her almond skin. Smiling, she waved a writing pad at Terry. He waved back. "Sarah, I still don't know what I'm doing here. What's your role in these shenanigans?"

Sarah, walking away, turned back. "I'm the master of ceremonies."

"What the hell am I supposed to say."

Shrugging, she turned her palms upward. "Say whatever you want. You're tenured."

Walking to the podium beside the panel's table, Sarah tapped on the microphone. "Let's get started. This is the first of three 'teach-ins' presented by the History Department that we're going to have in the next several days."

Sarah introduced the other three panel members, doling out praise with bits of information about their academic achievements. Besides Rich and the petite Barbara Jensen, Dr. Wanda Pollard taught anthropology. Terry had met her, but did not know her very well. She was a heavy woman with graying hair, a big nose, and a prominent mole on her chin. He had served on two or three committees with her and found her professional and diligent.

"Sitting in for Dr. Horowitz, is Dr. Malloy. Several students on the steering committee for these panels thought Dr. Malloy should be on this Iraq panel, since he is a Vietnam Veteran. He doesn't know it, but he will also take Dr. Horowitz's place on the other panels.

"I want to open the discussion by asking the panel to state briefly their overall views on the war in Iraq. We'll start with Doctor Pollard, then Doctors Breedlove, Jensen, and Malloy."

Dr. Pollard cleared her throat and fingered the black mole on her chin. "This is an illegal and unjust war..."

Terry stared out over the audience. He'd heard it all before.

Rich made a brief aside about the justified liberation of the oppressed women in Afghanistan from the Taliban. "Saddam, on the other hand, tried to bring his country into the twentieth century by freeing the women of Iraq from the shackles of an oppressive religion. When it comes to the oppression of women, I'll always be the first to fight for women's rights." Polite applause rippled through the audience. "What I really want to know is why do we always have to be the aggressor nation? That's why the rest of the world hates us."

Barbara mentioned the injustice of Abu Ghraib and Guantanamo, criticizing the current administration for grabbing power out of the hands of the people and circumventing the democratic process.

What was Alex doing now? He needed to pay more attention to his grandson. You're feeling sorry for yourself, Malloy. Why was everyone staring at him?

Expectant faces watched Terry. He drummed his fingers on the table top. Wiping his brow, he took a deep breath. "If we were fighting a war, I would support it. But we're not fighting a war." Murmurs rippled through the room. "In a war, you're supposed to kill people. In this war, we're trying *not* to kill people. You can't win a war like that. What we're doing is putting targets on the backs of our soldiers, giving them ridiculous rules of engagement, and telling people to shoot them. Then we refuse to kill people. Everyone on the panel except myself has suggested that we're losing the war. Why is that? We're losing because we refuse to kill people and our enemy kills everyone they want. Our enemy is fighting a war. They're killing everyone they deem it necessary to kill. They accept collateral damage. By that, I mean, the killing of civilians. If we want to win, we need to get beyond this idea of being nice and playing nice. We need to start killing people. If we can't accept collateral damage in attacking our enemy while supporting our soldiers, then we need to get out of Iraq and never fight another war."

No one spoke. Students moved and whispered. Rich held up his hand, waving it at Sarah. "I would like to respond."

Sarah, narrowed eyes focused on Terry, bit her lower lip. She nodded to Rich.

* * *

"His arm moved, Malloy," Cochise said, "did you see it?"

Terry sighted down the barrel of his M-16. "I saw it. Watch the corner where the other guy went, Cochise. I've got the guy in the street."

Moans floated down the street.

Cochise pressed the binoculars to his eyes. "Go ahead, you *hijo de puta*, call your *compadre*. Don't worry, Malloy, I've got the corner." Cochise lowered his binoculars and looked at his watch. "How long has that guy been out there? It seems like forever."

"Watch the corner, Cochise. It's only been five minutes."

"That was a great shot, Malloy."

Terry's cheek rested lightly on the stock of his M-16, his eyes accustomed to the bright light of afternoon. He did not want to glance away from the wounded man lying in the dusty street.

Anderson crawled over and through the collapsed wall. "Coming in."

Rifle in hand, Anderson scrabbled to Terry and Cochise. "When those guys took off from the corner, we saw nothing but blurs. Then they disappeared. The machine gun couldn't cover that side of the street."

"Don't worry, Anderson, Malloy got one of them." Cochise gave the binoculars to Anderson.

"I know, I've heard the moans." Anderson, the binoculars at his eyes, whistled. "Good shot, Malloy. That guy has to be one-twenty-five, one-hundred-fifty yards?"

"It's a better shot than you think. Malloy got him running."

"You guys watch the corner. His friend went around the corner. It's farther than you think and it wasn't as good as you think. I aimed for the guy's chest. The bullet hit him in the hip, maybe his side. Anyway, I shot three or four times trying to hit the bastard and finally got him. I was lucky. Save the back-slapping."

A beer sign creaked, swinging to and fro. Gusts sifted armies of dust up and down the street. A cry of pain floated upon the wind, echoing off the buildings.

"Go ahead, call your friend." Cochise took the binoculars from Anderson and looked through them.

"Watch the corner, Cochise,"Terry said.

"Which corner?" Anderson asked.

Cochise pointed. "See the building with the cigarette advertisement? That's where the other guy ran."

Terry wiped his brow with a rag. "I wish I had a scope. A scope would be great."

The man in the street moved his leg. Underneath him, blood turned the dust dark brown. An agonized cry wafted into the collapsed building where Terry, Cochise, and Anderson huddled.

"Come on, you bastard," Cochise said. "You've got no *cojones*, if you don't help your friend."

Duffy crawled through the wall. "Coming in." He crabbed over to the three men.

Dust fell on Terry and his rifle. "Don't bump me, guys. This roost isn't big enough for four of us."

"Is Brumsen by himself?" Anderson asked.

"Cziplicki's with Brumsen. He stopped by with his radioman. He wants to know how long you're going to wait before you finish that guy. He can be heard a couple of streets over." Duffy brought his hands up to cover his eyes and stared down the street

"We wait until we're sure the gook's *amigo* isn't waiting there for an *emboscada*. If he's still there, we're hoping he'll try to rescue him, so we can kill him."

Duffy brushed a fly from his pug nose. His pale blue eyes focused on the street. "Cziplicki told me they're calling this the Tet Offensive."

"Who is 'they'?" Terry kept his gaze on the street.

"The newspaper people and the people back in the world," Duffy answered.

Anderson removed his helmet and wiped his dusty forehead. An undercurrent of rage boiled up. "I don't give a shit what they call it, as long we can kill these shitheads."

"I don't see a lot of offense." Cochise narrowed his dark eyebrows and pursed his small mouth. "I've seen about twelve dead gooks."

Duffy scratched a red eyebrow. "You know how journalists are. They tend to exaggerate. Cziplicki's radioman told me that 'A' Company found thirty to forty civilians shot in the head."

Anderson scratched his wiry shoulder. He shook his head, mouth drawing downward. "What a kick in the ass. A bunch of gooks sneak into town, shoot forty civilians, and the press calls it an offensive."

Removing a clip from his ammo pouch, Duffy blew across the bullets. "Cziplicki said there're rumors about finding three or four thousand bodies of civilians in Hue. The NVA executed them."

"This is just like the jungle. The gooks don't want to fight here, either." Lowering the binoculars, Cochise rubbed and stretched his neck.

"If I'm going to fight, I'd rather fight here than in that crazy jungle," Terry said. "You can't see shit in the jungle."

"Where did you learn to shoot, Malloy?" Anderson asked.

Hot air and dust drifted through the group of men.

"I've been hunting rabbits and squirrels on my grandfather's farm since I was about ten. I had a twenty-two. But, when I was twelve, my dad let me use his Enfield to hunt deer."

Cochise's white knuckles gripped the dull blackness of the binoculars. "I see a rifle barrel."

Anderson's head swivelled toward the street. "Where?"

"It's sticking out from the corner, underneath the cigarette sign."

Duffy shook his head. "I can't believe we're leaving a wounded person out there in the street."

"You need to get over it. He's not a person, he's a fucking gook," Anderson said, taking the binoculars from Cochise. "That wounded 'person,' as you called him, more than likely helped kill those forty civilians they found." Anderson peered through the binoculars and handed them back to Cochise.

Terry peered down the barrel of his rifle. "No mercy."

"Get ready, Malloy," Cochise said. "I see some black pajamas and the rifle barrel. Come on, you sonofabitch. You got no *cajones* if you don't help your *compadre*."

"I take it back, Duffy," Anderson said. "He's not a gook. He's bait."

"There he is."

A man sprinted from the corner. A rifle hung from his back. The strap holding the rifle crossed his chest. The rifle bounced as he ran. He crouched down and lifted his wounded friend. Terry shot him as he stood, arms extended, holding the wounded man under the armpits. The man dropped his wounded comrade, clutched his stomach, staggering sideways. The next shot hit him in the chest. Every muscle in his body relaxed. The Vietnamese collapsed upon himself.

"Did you see that? I must've hit him in the heart with my second shot. I've seen deer collapse like that when they're hit in the heart." Terry turned and stared down the street. "My first shot was low again. I wish I had a scope."

Cochise patted Terry on the back. "Great shot, Malloy, *muy padre*." Taking the binoculars from his eyes, Cochise stared down the street at the two men. "You couldn't hide in the fucking jungle, could you?"

Anderson patted Duffy on the arm. "Okay, Duffy, go tell Cziplicki we're going to get those guys. I want him and Brumsen to come down here and cover us."

Lighting a cigarette, Cochise inhaled. "I guess they won't be blowing any mines in the jungle, will they?" Smoke drifted out of Cochise's mouth and nostrils. "You have to admit, the guy had *cojones*."

* * *

"And you know that would be wrong. Everyone here knows that." Rich, leaning forward with both hands on the table, sat down and crossed his muscular arms and legs.

"Whose morality are you using?" Terry spread his arms, shrugging in a questioning manner.

Unfolding his arms, Rich placed his hands on the back of his head. "I'm using the morality of our culture."

Terry seated himself also. "That's the morality of dead white men. This is a new age. Who are we to say what's right or wrong?"

Rich, eyebrows narrowed over a look of puzzlement, rested an elbow on the table. Pinching his lower lip, he pondered Terry.

Barbara raised her hand. Sarah recognized her. "Terry, even if we assumed that it was morally all right to kill civilians– which I'm not saying it is– we would be international pariahs. Other nations would hate us."

"How so, Barbara? Saddam Hussein killed several hundred thousand of his citizens and a lot of countries still traded and had relations with him. France, Germany, Russia, China, and every Muslim country except Iran. No one broke off relations with Iraq. Actually, a lot of these countries defended Iraq. We were supposed to have trade sanctions against Iraq and it appears that all those countries were disobeying the sanctions and trading with Saddam. Perhaps, if we start killing people, it would improve our foreign relations."

A wave of soft laughter swept through the student audience.

Rich licked his lips. Wiping his brow, he placed the napkin down on the table. "This is preposterous, Terry. You're making a mockery out of this panel. You know it's wrong and you're destroying any chance for dialogue."

At least half the audience had their hands up. Terry waved his hands at them. "It looks like I'm creating the opportunity *for* dialogue. Now, I want to know why you're forcing your morality on the rest of us? Who are you to tell me, or any of us, what's right and what's wrong?"

Rich smacked his forehead with the palm of his hand. "I'm not forcing any morality on anyone."

Terry smacked his forehead, copying Rich. Several students laughed. Two or three snickered. "Yes, you are. You keep telling me that what I'm suggesting is wrong. I'm telling you to stop being a Nazi. Don't force your morality on me or on the rest of these people for that matter. This is a new age, Rich. We don't force our morality on others."

More laughter and applause welled up from the students. Barbara and Rich whispered to each other.

Dr. Pollard shifted her sizeable weight, which drew everyone's attention toward her. "Who's to decide what's right or wrong? We have to go by the customs and the rules of war. That's the only way to determine how we are to act."

"Why not take a vote?" Terry said. "I'm sure everyone here favors a democratic solution. This is a new age. We can vote. Let's start here with this audience. Who here would favor a more lenient policy of collateral damage against communities that support terrorists?"

Sarah shouted into the microphone, "Hold it! Wait! We're here for a discussion, not a vote."

"But this is part of the discussion. Some of our panel have mentioned the backroom grabs for power and the wheeling and dealing of the current administration to subvert the democratic process." Terry drank from a glass of water. He was having fun. "I'm ready to stop that with a vote to accept a more lenient policy of collateral damage when dealing with terrorists."

Cheers erupted from the audience and chants of "Vote, Vote, Vote," broke out.

Rich, leaning back in his chair to see around Barbara, his hands balled into fists, spoke furtively to Terry through clenched teeth. "Malloy, I can't believe you've done this!"

Sarah rapped on the podium with her loafer. "Let's have a little decorum in the audience. This is a college. We're not going to have a vote here. Mr. Thornton has been waiting patiently to ask a question of the panel."

Thornton's bald head reflected light. He studied his notepad. "Dr. Malloy, your encouragement to accept 'collateral damage,' as you call it, has brought up the specter of Vietnam. As you know, Senator Kerry has criticized Vietnam Veterans like you for raping, murdering, and torturing hundreds of thousands of Vietnamese civilians. And now, here you are encouraging a policy of acceptance of civilian casualties. Do you really think this is a wise policy? Can't you see the difference between, say, World War II veterans, who are treated with respect, and Vietnam Veterans? Do you think this is because you're advocating the killing of civilians? Further, would you rather have the Iraqi vets treated like World War II Vets or like Vietnam vets?"

"The World War II generation were different from us in one respect," Terry said, running his hands through his hair. "They didn't mind killing civilians. It's remarkable that the left idolizes that generation." Terry held up his arms and wiggled his fingers to indicate quotes. He spoke ponderously to specify the weightiness of what he said. "'After suffering through a terrible economic depression, they defeated Hitler and stopped the spread of Fascism in Europe and Japan.' They defeated the fascist because they killed civilians by the hundreds of thousands. Did all those civilians support Hitler's and

Japan's policies? Probably not, but the greatest generation still killed them. They murdered civilians in Dresden, Hamburg, and Berlin. On one night in March of 1945, the Greatest Generation killed over 100,000 people, including women, children, and old men, when they firebombed Tokyo. Then they dropped atom bombs on two other cities, murdering, once again, thousands and thousands of old men, women, and children. Guess what? We won that war."

The students all stared at him, mesmerized. He had them.

"Now I've got a question for you, Mr. Thornton. We've all seen the burnt-out cities, the cities I just named– of World War II. Our destructive capabilities, as you know, were much greater in the Vietnam War. Given the level of civilian deaths in World War II, how many civilians do you think we killed in twelve years of bombing Hanoi?"

Thornton wiped his brow and sneered at Terry.

No one in the audience moved.

"I'm waiting for an answer, Mr. Thornton. If you don't know, say so. Do you know? This is not a trick question." Terry's clasped hands rested on the table top. He drank from his glass and poured more water into it. God, his mouth was dry.

Thornton beat his pen against his chin and managed to sneer at the same time. "No, I don't know. I would assume there were thousands of innocent civilians killed in Hanoi."

Wiping his nose with his handkerchief, Terry placed it back in his pocket. "Would anyone like to guess?"

Nervous movements of self-conscious people added to the weight of the silence.

"We never bombed Hanoi. We never bombed the major capital of our enemy. Nor did we bomb the major harbor, Haiphong. We were afraid of killing civilians and afraid of world opinion. Guess what? We lost that war. How can we make war, not bomb the capital city of our enemy, nor the major harbor, and expect to win?

"Mr. Thornton asked me why we esteem the greatest generation. They were led by men who didn't mind killing civilians. After World War II, we became concerned about not bombing. In Korea, we didn't bomb China. We fought Chinese troops for three years, lost 36,000 men, and never bombed China. Some people say we lost in Korea.

"In Vietnam, we dropped random bombs on individual targets, like dams and hydro electric plants. But we never bombed Hanoi and Haiphong. How are we going to win a war, when we don't bomb the capital of the country that we're fighting? Unfortunately, that policy got a lot of Americans killed. Now, we aren't bombing places like Falluja and Ramadi. Places where, again and again, our boys are getting killed." Terry raised his hand and jabbed a finger into the air in front of him. "Including my daughter, my little girl. And we refuse to bomb these places. Is there any surprise that people say we're losing this war too? Since 1950, we've sent men off to fight and we haven't supported them. I say, it's time we committed ourselves to waging war or we get our asses out of Iraq and Afghanistan! Don't send troops into places where we refuse to back them up!"

The students stood, laughing, applauding, and whistling.

Rich, Barbara, and Wanda Pollard traded glances. Rich stood, moving the chair away from him. He held up his hands and pressed them forward as if warding off the crowd. The students sat down. "This is a sad commentary on the times we live in. Isn't it time we showed which culture is better and keep the moral high ground? Are we going to sink to the same level as the people we're fighting?"

Leaning forward, Terry unclasped his hands, resting his elbows on the table. "This is elitist, racist nonsense. I can't believe that Professor Breedlove is comparing our culture to another culture and saying that we're better. This isn't a cultural or racial matter of who is better. The Muslims have a wonderful culture. So did the Germans and the Japanese. This is about war and killing people. Let's not stoop to racist and elitist tags that we're a better culture. Once again, all I'm saying is that we should kill the people we're at war with or we get out." Most of the audience applauded. Someone shouted, "Go, Dr. Malloy."

Barbara ran her fingers through her flowing, black hair as she stood. "We can't start killing civilians indiscriminately. People all over the world would hate us."

"But that's simply not true." Terry took another sip of water, soothing his parched throat. "I used Saddam as an example earlier. But the terrorists in Iraq are killing civilians by the thousands, and many nations support them. Other examples are Stalin and Mao. Those two are responsible for murdering *millions* of their own countrymen. Not only were they not hated, but even people in the United States supported them. Countries around the world supported them. Once again, maybe if we started killing more people, the countries that hate us now would love us. Another example is the one I just gave you of the 'Greatest Generation.' They killed civilians by the hundreds of thousands and people in this country fall over each other praising them and telling how great they are. I say we start imitating them. Instead of giving peace a chance, which obviously doesn't work, why don't we start killing more people like the 'Greatest Generation' did? Let's give war a chance. If the way the 'Greatest Generation' waged war is right, then it's right for us. If killing civilians is wrong, then it was wrong for the 'Greatest Generation.' Either they're the saviors of humanity or some of the biggest mass murderers in history. You can't have it both ways."

The students erupted in cheers. Rich leaned over and whispered loudly in Barbara's ear, "This is insane." Rich jumped up again. He pumped a fist in the air. "That's what we've been doing for the past three years. And we haven't gotten anywhere. We've used smart bombs and every kind of digital gadgetry known to man and we're not winning. Killing civilians would be another losing strategy."

"Smart bombs and smart people are all digital bullshit." Terry dismissed Rich with a wave of his hand. "If they're so smart, why aren't we winning the war? We're using smart bombs to minimize civilian casualties and we're losing the war. It's time we stopped using all of this smart crap and started killing people the old-fashioned way. Once again, if we don't want to do that, then let's get our asses out."

The auditorium exploded in cheers and clapping. Students stomped their feet and whistled.

Sarah held up her hand, calming the audience. She turned toward the panel. A smile played around her lips and eyes. "Professor Malloy, you'll have to watch your language."

Students sat down, smiling and talking. The auditorium buzzed.

"Killing civilians is a strategy for losers." Rich, sweating profusely, hammered the table. "The only way to achieve any type of victory, moral or otherwise, is to maintain a casualty-free battle zone."

"Rich, if killing civilians is a strategy for losers, then I guess the terrorists are losing and we're winning. Because, they're the ones killing civilians. Sometimes they murder hundreds in a week. So, I'm confused, are we winning or losing the war?"

Rich, looking at the audience, pointed a trembling finger at Terry. "He's twisting my words."

"The truth is, Rich, that the terrorists are winning because they kill as many civilians as they want. They're fighting a war. We're trying to limit casualties and we're losing. Either fight a war or get out."

"Thanks for ruining the discussion, Dr. Malloy," Rich said, sitting down.

"I'm saying what's on my mind. That's what these people came here to hear." Terry pointed at the audience.

Thornton continued to stand during and after the student outburst subsided. He thumped his ear with a pen held in one hand, writing pad in the other. He raised his voice to be heard over the murmuring students. "Professor Malloy, given the murderous outburst we've just heard, isn't it natural for us to assume that Senator Kerry was correct in stating that Vietnam Veterans murdered, tortured, and raped thousands of Vietnamese?"

Terry shifted his gaze from Thornton to the students, who held their collective breath in anticipation. He caught sight of Laura Boatwright writing in her tablet. The white ribbons in her hair shimmered in the subdued auditorium light. She caught his gaze and smiled, lifting her eyebrows in encouragement.

A conversation over lunch with Laura's father ran through his mind. Laura's caramel-colored skin made Jim Boatwright's look like dark chocolate. Jim had talked of his first firefight. "They ambushed us. I was so stunned, everything happened so fast, it was hard to give orders. You know how confusing everything becomes, bullets flying, people screaming in pain and anger, the noise and smoke. But I learned that you can't sit there and let the enemy take potshots at you. It was hard, but I had to get my men up and charge the ambush. It goes against their first, and natural, instinct, which is to duck and hide from the bullets. I realized that the longer we stayed there with our heads down, the harder it would be to get moving. Plus, it gave the enemy time to maneuver on us. So, I got up, grabbed other soldiers and pulled them to their feet, and ran toward the enemy, shooting and firing. The long and short of it was that we killed several North Vietnamese and a lot of them ran off, using the jungle for cover."

Everyone was waiting for him to speak. Say something! "When I was in Vietnam, I did my share of killing. I'm not going to lie. But I never did anything dishonorable. One night we ambushed several Vietcong crossing a river. We killed all of them. There must have been ten, eleven, I forget how many. It was a good payback. In war, you take and you take and you take. And then you get a chance to pay a little back. The next morning, before my squad returned to camp, we helped pull the bodies from the river. Two of the Vietnamese had no bullet holes or wounds. They had drowned in the water. There were footprints on the backs and shoulders of these men. During the firefight, they got pushed under in the panic and some of their own men stood on their backs to keep their own heads above the water. Men had stood on the backs and shoulders of other men to keep from drowning.

"Please keep in mind that I'm speaking as a Vietnam Vet. This is what Senator Kerry did to me and to all Vietnam Veterans. When it suited his purpose, he called us murderers and rapists. Now he calls us his band of brothers. He wants to bond with us. He's trying to climb on our shoulders one more time."

CHAPTER EIGHT

Merle Haggard's voice drifted, slow and lazy, through the bar, floating upon the general buzz of the establishment's youthful clientele. Terry lifted the margarita and let the cold liquid flow down his throat. He drained the glass and reached for the pitcher. The taste of the salt rimming the glass lingered in his mouth. "Well, that was interesting."

Sarah, Rich, and Barbara watched him intently as he poured each of them a drink.

He refilled his glass. "What?"

Rich, with raised eyebrows, reached for his mug and gulped quickly. He shook his head. "Interesting? All I can tell you is that you've offended about eighty percent of all the people over sixty. What were you thinking, calling the greatest generation baby killers."

Terry moved his glass around on the table. "I didn't call them baby killers. That's a very overused expression. Besides, it was in the form of an either/or statement."

Barbara waved to a group who sat at another table.

Shifting in her seat, Sarah pushed her empty glass toward Terry. Her eyes were bright with amusement. "It doesn't matter what you said. It's what people think you said."

"I can have one more drink." Rich waved the empty pitcher at a waitress. He looked at his watch. "Then I've got to go home and release the babysitter from bondage." He shook his head. "And challenging Thorn on his knowledge of the war..."

Barbara left the table to talk with students sitting at another table.

"I love a good margarita," Sarah said, licking her lips. "Wasn't one of his daughters in the audience?"

Terry waved to Laura. She sat with the group of students chatting with Barbara. "Whose daughter?"

Rich wiped his marguerita-stained moustache. "Great, embarrass a man in front of his children. Way to make friends, Terry, challenge a man on what he considers to be the halcyon days of his youth."

"I expected him to start talking about the movement and the '60s at any moment." Sarah ran her slender hands through her blond hair and shook her head. Yawning, she stretched her arms and smiled, studying Terry. "What is it with you '60s people. You guys have to let it go."

"It's hard to let something go, when your whole life is wrapped up in it." Terry stirred his drink. "If Thornton let his idea of Vietnam and the '60s go, it would mean he's lived a lie. That's the worst lie – the lie in the soul. People will fight to the death to keep that lie in the soul intact."

A student patted Terry on the shoulder. "That's the most awesome panel we've ever had, Dr. Malloy. Thank you."

Willie Nelson's voice drifted out of the juke box.

"Thornton didn't seem too interested in making friends with me," Terry said. "I didn't challenge him. As a teacher, it's my obligation to make people see things differently. After all, what we're trying to achieve is diversity and acceptance of different points of view. Aren't we?" Terry brooded. "Anyway, at least he has a daughter."

Sarah reached across the table and patted Terry's hand.

"People don't like their myths destroyed," Barbara said, having just returned. She hiccoughed.

"What was all that stuff about 'dead white men,' and 'a new age'?" Sarah asked, pushing her drink toward Terry for another refill. "Have I finally convinced you that you need to leave those outdated values behind?"

"I decided to pull what everyone else does." Terry motioned to the waitress, a tall girl with short black hair, and ordered a single malt scotch, neat. "Accuse anyone who disagrees with me of being a Nazi and use buzz words like 'dead white men' and 'new age.'"

The waitress's mouth snapped, chewing gum. "We've got the eighteen-year-old if you want it."

Terry nodded.

"It's a man thing," Barbara said. "These two guys went at each other like two bulls in a china shop."

"Barbara, I can't believe you're saying that." Rich, looking at his watch, pushed his chair back from the table. "I spoke because I disagreed with Terry. I mean, he was talking about killing civilians, for God's sake."

The scotch appeared in front of Terry. Letting the liquid roll across his tongue, he relaxed as it went down. "I was talking about war. People get killed in war. War turns everything upside down."

"Don't you understand." Rich pointed to Terry. "He called me a Nazi, for God's sake, in front of two hundred students. Me! Who's been on the front line fighting for women's rights, gay rights, and civil rights. It only takes one person to say it and then it gets repeated and all of a sudden I'm out of a job."

"Rich, I apologize for calling you a Nazi. You're a nice guy. I dig you, man." Terry walked around the table and grabbed Rich by the shoulders, hugging him.

Sarah sputtered and coughed up her drink. She grabbed a napkin and patted her shirt.

"And animal rights," Rich muttered. "I've fought for them. I've even tried to be a vegetarian once or twice. I need to go. The baby sitter has some school project tomorrow." He turned to Sarah. "Can you come out tonight?"

Burping, Sarah propped up her dimpled chin with one hand, using the other to fiddle with her glass. She shook her head. "I have to get up early tomorrow."

After Rich left, several students, including Laura, came over and asked Barbara, Sarah, and Terry to join them. Sarah said she needed to get home. She grabbed her purse and stood. "Call me tomorrow when you get up and we'll run."

Nodding, Terry sat down next to Laura with several students around him. This was what he lived for. The give and take with students kept him young.

A lanky student with crew-cut dark hair touched his shoulder. "What are you drinking, Professor?"

"Single malt scotch. The waitress knows which one."

"Dr. Malloy, we've been talking about movies." Laura slipped her arm through Terry's. "Oliver Stone's Platoon came up. I've been telling these guys that my dad hated that movie. What did you think about it?"

Terry took the drink from the lanky boy. "That's the one that all the news magazines promoted as 'Vietnam as it really was.' I didn't like it either. What disturbed me more is the attitude toward art that it promoted. You see, they're telling you that 'nature imitates art' rather than 'art imitates nature.'"

There was silence around the table. Johnny Cash's deep voice boomed across the room. Laura linked her hands around his arm and squeezed it. "Dr. Malloy, what does that mean?"

"It means that Hollywood is trying to convince you that, rather than the movie being like Vietnam, Vietnam is like the movie. Hollywood wants to replace one reality with another."

"Terry, I can't find my keys."

Terry turned to see Sarah standing behind them.

Barbara, across the table from Terry, hiccoughed. "I would offer to drive, but I was going to ask Terry to take me home."

"Come on, you two. I'll take you home." Terry stood, scooting his chair from the table.

Grimacing with annoyance, Laura tapped the table lightly in frustration. "Dr. Malloy, you just sat down."

"I need to get up tomorrow and work around the house." Terry reached in his pocket for his keys. "I better be on my way also."

Laura stood and hugged Terry. "I'll be by to see you soon. I've almost got my outline finished."

Barbara slid into the back seat and lay down. "Don't report me for not wearing a seat belt."

In the front, Sarah tilted the seat back, and closed her eyes. "To tell you the truth, I don't know if I should be driving either."

Terry asked Barbara for her address. When she didn't say anything, Sarah, with her eyes shut, told Terry where to go. Snores came from the back seat.

Reaching Barbara's house, Terry helped her out of the car.

Fumbling in her purse for her keys, Barbara staggered around the car and used the headlights to ransack her purse. Taking out her keys, she bowed into the headlights ceremoniously, her black hair falling over her face. "Thank you, one and all." Staggering backward, she turned and headed down her walkway to the front porch.

"Okay, beautiful, let's get you home." Terry backed out onto the street, put the car into gear, and sped down the road.

In the driveway, Sarah opened the door. Using the dome light of the car, she rummaged through her purse. "Look. Here're my keys. Isn't that strange? I thought I had lost them." She touched Terry's arm. "Help me into the house and I'll give you a drink."

"You would have made a great salesman. I'll take you up on that offer."

Handing Terry his scotch, Sarah sat beside him on the couch, patting his knee. "You were a wild man tonight. What got into you?"

"I just decided to say what I wanted to say. I'm tired of…I'm just tired."Terry felt the scotch hit his stomach and breathed a sigh of relief.

"When you told Rich you dug him it was too much." She rubbed Terry's leg. "Margaritas and wine can get a girl in trouble."

"They can when you're not with a man you can trust."Terry rolled the drink around on his tongue and swallowed.

"I'm not worried about trusting you. I'm worried that I can't trust myself." Sarah swirled her glass of wine. "I'm feeling some urges about you that I need to express. You're a vulnerable man tonight, Terry. You're vulnerable, tragic, and sad all at once. Your crying in the wilderness and you don't know if anyone is listening. I don't know if I should take advantage of you or not."

Pulling herself to him on the couch, her tongue flicked his ear then moved down his neck. "Somewhere along the way tonight, I told myself I needed some company. So, you're invited to stay if you want." She nibbled Terry's neck.

God, he didn't want to go home to that lonely house. He didn't need to see his ghosts. Sarah's hand rubbed his crotch. He had said what he had to say. There would be repercussions. What, he didn't know. Was that it? Was that all he had to say? Was he supposed to tremble in fear now. Fuck them. He had killed better men than Thornton.

Terry turned toward Sarah and drew her close. She came willingly. He lost himself in the soft taste and touch of her lips. Her tongue moved in and out of his mouth. He took her hand. Standing, he pulled her up. "No ghosts tonight."

Sarah glanced at him, a quizzical look in her eyes. "Let's fix up our drinks and go upstairs."

His hands trembled as he unbuttoned her blouse. Tongue probing her mouth, he unsnapped her bra and pulled her toward him. Soft breast pressed against his chest. His fingers caressed and played with her nipples. Their hunger for each other built. Her hot mouth and tongue ran up and down his neck. He dropped to his knees and unzipped her blue jeans. His tongue ran over her stomach as he pushed her gently back to the bed. He took off her pants, yanking them from around her ankles.

Moaning in anticipation, she pulled off her panties.

Kneeling in front of her, he spread her legs. Placing a hand on each knee, his fingertips roamed across both inner thighs. He moved forward into the 'V' of her legs, nibbling and caressing her thighs with his lips and tongue.

Groaning, she thrust her hips.

Kissing her stomach, he penetrated her with his fingers. The musty smell of sex filled the room. Her undulating hips surged upward onto his fingers. His tongue played along the edge of her mound and lips.

She grabbed his hair, drawing him to her.

Sarah muttered incoherently, draping both legs over his shoulders. His hands lifted and supported both buttocks. Her hands clutched his hair. He pushed his tongue into her. Her hips thrust forward again and again. "Fuck me. Please fuck me."

Taking her hips, he turned her over and pulled her off the bed. She bent over, supporting herself with her elbows. Her hips undulated in rhythmic circles. "I want you inside me *now!*"

Her hands grasped him, guiding him into her. Rotating hips met throbbing need and desire. Thrusting deeply into her several times, his hands grasped her hips and jerked her onto him. Grabbing her hair, he pulled her head up. Gasping, her back arched as she launched herself again and again upon him. Her hips surged, pushing backward. A "yes" escaped from her lips. "Ride me, Baby." He brought his hand down hard on her ass. Their bodies trembled and shuddered.

* * *

Terry jerked up with start, resting on his elbow. The strange room disoriented him. Moonlight through the window highlighted folds of the sheet covering Sarah's graceful body stretched out beside him. He turned on his side, slipped an arm around her, spooning his body around hers, enjoying the warmth and intimacy. Sarah grasped his hand, cupping it around her breast, murmuring softly. Her body molded itself to his.

He held up his arm to see his watch: 4:30. What was he doing? Clarissa, where the hell are you? Where do you live, Dad? Sarah moved slightly, shifting her body.

After the lovemaking, They had lain on the bed, heads on a single pillow, caressing each other. Sarah then suggested they take a shower, a mixture of wash cloths, soap, stroking, kissing, and laughter. Toweling off, Sarah, grinning, remarked on her red bottom, calling him an animal. Red faced, he shook his head. She put a finger to his lips. "Shhh… it was fun."

After the shower, they carried drinks to the bedroom. Pulling back the sheets, Sarah snuggled up to him. They were quiet, sipping their drinks. The rhythmic rise and fall of her chest told him she was asleep. Terry slipped the covers over both of them. They slept, legs and arms draped, both enjoying the comfort and warmth.

Around 2 in the morning, Terry felt the velvet touch of Sarah's hands. In the half twilight of dreamlike haziness and the moonbeam glow of the bedroom, he kissed her lips. She slid under him, wrapping her lissome legs around him.

Now, here he was awake for the second time tonight. He studied his watch again: 4:35. The vague sound of men laughing filtered through the house. Terry cocked his head. Brumson's bass voice boomed. Terry pulled on his pants. The sounds were coming from outside. Walking to the window, he peered into Sarah's wooded backyard. A soft rain pattered on the sill. Raising the window, men's voices and their laughter percolated from the woods. He glimpsed shadows moving and the unmistakable glow of cigarettes.

He hurried through the house to the kitchen and out the back door to the deck. Clouds darkened the yard. In the woods, hazy shadows of men sat on the ground.

Duffy's voice rose above the laughter. "I'm proud of it. I don't care if you guys laugh at me."

The voices and laughter proved comforting. Why had he ever worried about seeing these men? He could depend on these guys. Trembling, he walked down the deck stairs.

Cochise, squatting against a tree, puffed on a cigarette. "Duffy just told us that he's a virgin."

"Are they giving you a hard time, Duffy?" Terry asked.

Duffy, hands in pockets, gazing at the ground, kicked a rock. "Yeah, they are. But I don't care. I can take what they're giving out."

"Man, oh man, what I wouldn't give to be with my Annabelle now." Brumsen lay on his side, elbow on the ground and hand supporting his head. A twig dangled from his thick lips. "We talked about getting married, but my mom told me I needed to get a job first. You know, before I settled down and maybe started a family. I don't know what I would be doing now, if we had married."

"Me, too, Brumsen." Anderson walked from the shadows. Smoke from a cigarette drifted up his arm. "There was a girl named Janet that I thought I couldn't live without. God, she was beautiful. We went steady our junior and senior year of high school. After graduation, we still saw each other. She went off to college, and I stayed at home and went to work. I asked her to marry me, but she said she wanted to finish college first. That's when I joined the Army.

"I got a letter from a friend telling me she's engaged to some guy she met in college. The hell with it. I really hope she's happy wherever she is and whatever she's doing."

"Lucy and I have been going steady since the tenth grade," Duffy said. "She and I would date on Friday and Saturday nights and then go to confession afterwards.

"It wasn't like we did anything really bad. We just made out and necked and stuff like that. Sometimes, though, we got kinda excited, and either she or I'd have to stop it. After that, we'd spend a little bit longer in confession." Duffy looked into the woods, then up at the sky. "Man, if I could just hold her one more time, I would never let her go."

"Duffy, you and Brumsen are doing *lo correcto*." Cochise drew on his cigarette and closed his eyes. His warpaint gleamed from the glowing cigarette. "I know you have your doubts. Maria and I went to confession a couple of times when we were in high school. But, when you hold your *hijo* that your wife just placed in your arms, you'll know you made the right decision."

Brumsen lay on his back and clasped his huge, thick hands behind his head. "I just wish I knew more about what I wanted."

"I know that Lucy and I are doin' the right thing." Duffy stood and dusted off his jungle fatigues. "Eventually, we even stopped going to drive-in movies."

Anderson leaned against a tree and folded his arms. He scratched the scar on his forehead and smiled. "Janet and I could fog some windows at a drive-in ourselves. Those backseats just had too much room, didn't they, Duffy?"

Fireflies flickered in the woods. "What about you, Malloy?" Anderson asked. "Do you have a girl back home?"

"I didn't have too much experience with girls when I left for Vietnam." Terry, sitting on the ground, drew his knees to his chest and wrapped his arms around them. "No, I didn't have a girlfriend."

"When I came back, I went with several girls. Finally, I found the woman I wanted to marry. Her name is Clarissa. She's a beautiful woman, just like Annabelle, Lucy, Janet, and Maria are beautiful women. We had a great life together, but we kinda grew apart and we have a–" Terry choked. He swallowed and tried to breath. "We had a wonderful daughter." His voice cracked. "You guys never got that chance. I'm going to see my grandson grow up and become a man. That's an experience you'll never know. I've had so many tomorrows and you've had none."

Terry looked up expectantly, but the squad had disappeared. Crickets chirped. Moonlight filtered through the pines. A lingering odor of cigarette smoke hung in the air. Walking back to the porch, he hugged himself.

Sarah lay on the bed. She cuddled the haphazard sheet draped over her body. Should he go or stay? He wasn't afraid to go home, now. He wanted to see his friends, his buddies. The only buddies he had ever known.

Sarah turned on her back. Her eyes half-closed, she gazed up at Terry. "Get your ass back in bed." She rolled over on her side with her back to Terry.

Unsnapping his pants he let them drop to the floor. Shaping herself to his body, she reached around and patted his backside. "Good boy. Good boy."

* * *

"Hey, Malloy, wake up, man." Brumsen shook Terry on the shoulder. "Wake up and talk to me. I've something I wanna talk about."

Terry opened his eyes and looked up to see Brumsen looming over him. Brumsen's new mohawk haircut made him look wild and more intimidating than ever.

"Brumsen, we're shipping out tomorrow," Terry said, rubbing sleep from his eyes. "I want to rest while I'm able. Movin' to a new base camp is gonna be a bitch."

With no breeze, the oppressive heat combined with the cloying smell of damp canvas was only marginally alleviated by the raised flaps of the tent. Both men wore sweat-stained undershirts. Perspiration beaded their foreheads.

Brumsen's broad shoulders sagged. His arms drooped along his sides. He held a letter out toward Terry. "I know, but maybe you can help me. I got a letter from my sister. She's fussin' at me about the things I'm writin'. Check out this letter I wrote and see if it's as bad as she makes it out to be."

"You want me to do *what*?"

"You heard me. You have a year of college, don't you?"

Terry nodded.

"Anderson told me you helped him write a report. If that's true, you can help me," Brumsen continued, desperation in his voice. "I want you to check this letter and tell me if it's as bad as my sister Alicia says my other letters are. She says I'm scarin' my mother to death and I also need to clean up my language. I write what I feel. You know how little time we have to write these silly things, anyway."

Most of the guys felt that writing letters was a chore. They were in base camp for a very short time, one or two days at most. Tending to the necessities of their survival came first: rifles repaired or replaced, which meant hassles with the supply sergeant, clothing and shoes exchanged, ammunition stockpiled, canteens cleaned. Hygiene followed equipment: Hair cut, sores and abrasions tended, feet checked. The soldiers busied themselves, accomplishing many small, but necessary, tasks.

The men had two priorities: equipment preparation and relaxing. Relaxing meant drinking on base with friends or going into *Bien Hua* and drinking with the bar girls. Everything was done out of a sense of necessity. Writing letters home to parents or girlfriends was not a necessity. Cochise wanted to write to his wife, but married men had different priorities than single ones. To most, letters were the lowest priority.

Stalking in, Cochise shoved grenades and ammunition boxes off his bunk. They clattered when they hit the wooden floor. He took off his field cap, rubbing his hands over his newly cut mohawk. He held up a letter and a picture. "Maria sent me a letter and a new picture of our *hijo*."

Brumsen continued to urge his letter at Terry.

"Okay, Brumsen, what exactly do you want me to do?"

"Look at this letter I just wrote and tell me if I need to change it. My sister's in college now and she thinks she's educated. She's rakin' me over the coals about what I'm writin'."

Terry took the letter and read out loud:

Dear Mom and Alicia,

How are you? I hope everything is well. We just came out of the jungle and are resting at our base camp at Bien Hoa. VC activity has been heavy since the Tet Offensive. We were involved in several firefights on this patrol, but nothing we couldn't handle. As a matter of fact, we blew a couple of guys away.

"You can't say that to your mother, Brumsen. What in God's name is wrong with you?"

"Why not? It's the truth."

"Well, it's the truth, but do you really want to talk about the combat? Moms and dads don't want to hear that kind of stuff."

"He's right, Brumsen." Cochise, lighting a cigarette, looked up from his letter. "I don't tell Maria anything about the combat. She wants to hear about the jungle, helicopters, and you guys, but no combat. Your mother and sister don't want to hear about it either."

Terry stroked his chin, his brow knitted. "Why don't we say that '*fighting has been sporadic*' and let it go at that."

"Sporadic? What the hell kind of language is that to use for your mom?"

"It means 'not often' and it will make her feel better."

"Trust Malloy, Brumsen," Cochise said.

"I knew you guys'd help. You just can't beat a college education. That's why I've been fussin' with my little sister to stay in school."

Duffy entered the tent, carrying a box of radio batteries. He placed them on his bunk. Bald stripes ran down each side of his head and a bright red mohawk brush ran down the center. "Cochise, if you want to go to confession, you better get over to the chapel. The line is short right now."

Terry continued reading:

When we arrived at our base camp, we heard that we would be moving to a place called Dak To. It is along the Cambodian border, a couple of hundred miles north of where we are right now. I have also heard that it is in the mountains. I hope it will be cooler there than it is here.

Mama, I haven't had a lot of time to go to church. I try to go whenever I can, but there are not a lot of opportunities when we are in the jungle.

"Why don't you just lie about it, Brumsen?" Terry asked. "What harm could it do? You know it will make her feel better."

"I don't like lying to Mama."

Cochise grabbed his knife and scabbard. "Brumsen, you got to listen to Malloy, *mi cuate*. You think your mama and sister want to hear about the leeches and mosquitoes and being tired all the time and not sleeping at night? You think they want to hear about all of us getting jungle rot on our feet because we haven't had a chance, or have been too tired, to take our boots off for three weeks? They certainly don't want to hear about anyone dying or getting shot. Trust us, the best thing you can do is lie to 'em. Tell your mama you're going to church, man. You gotta lie for her. It will make her feel better."

Terry chewed on a pen. "Let's see:" *Since I last wrote to you, I have been going to church quite often. The pastor is a fine fellow and all the guys like him a lot. The other day he gave a wonderful sermon on 'Romans 11:32.' Everyone in my squad thought it was a terrific sermon. Don't worry about me, Mama. The men with me are really terrific fellows, and they watch out for me.*

Brumsen snorted and reached for the letter.

Terry jerked the letter away. "Look Brumsen, what would you rather have? Do you want your mama and sister to worry about you all the time and lose sleep over you, or do you want them to at least think that you're safe and in a good place? The way I see it, there's nothing they can do to help us, and we can do a lot to ease their worrying. Am I right, Cochise?"

"Fuckin' 'A.' Maria has enough to worry about. She's going to college part-time, working part-time, and raising my little *Julio*. If she knew what I was doing, it'd drive her *loco*."

"While I don't think lying to your mama's a good idea," Duffy said, rubbing his freckled face, "I think Malloy's right, Brumsen. Why make them worry any more than necessary?"

Terry read on:

I have been thinking about going back to school when I get out of the service. I know that will make you happy. The GI Bill will help pay for it. Vietnam has changed me. I really want to make something of my life.

Alicia, stay in school and study hard. Do not let anything get in your way. I don't know who this Harold guy is that you have been writing about, but you keep your mind on your homework. You tell Harold that if he touches you, I am coming home with my friends, and we will beat the ever loving shit out of him.

"Brumsen, why do you want to antagonize your sister? Has she done anything that might make her deserve a comment like that? The way you talk about her being on the honor roll and being the valedictorian of her high school class, I thought you trusted her. Why do you want to talk about beating the shit out of her boyfriend? He's probably a nice guy."

Brumsen clenched and unclenched his monstrous hands, lightening bolts shooting out of his eyes. "She certainly doesn't mind antagonizing me, telling me my letters stink. Besides, I want to talk about beating the living shit out of him because that's exactly what I'm going to do, if that bastard touches her. That is, if I don't kill the sonofabitch."

Cochise threw his cigarette out of the tent. "I can understand that, Bro. If someone touched *mi hermanita,* I'd kill 'em, too."

"Oh great, Cochise. Why don't you throw oil on the fire. I thought you were staying in the service, Brumsen?"

"I still may stay in the service." Brumsen glanced at each of them in turn. "If I do, I want to be an officer. Being an enlisted man sucks big time. Going to college is the only way I can become an officer."

Everyone nodded.

"You got that right," Duffy said.

"Okay, guys, maybe we can salvage this in a way that won't get Brumsen's sister acting defensively or being mad at us." Terry studied the letter. "Why not say something like this..."

I am doing my best to make you both proud of me, and I have done nothing that I am ashamed of or that would make you ashamed of me. Alicia, you have to be strong and help Mama while I am away. Take pride in what you are doing. You are the first in our family to go to college. Don't let your mother down. I love you and Mama dearly, and I brag about you all the time to the guys in my squad. I am very proud of you, little sister. Some of the guys here worry about their girlfriends and sisters and what they are doing. I know that you would never do anything that would make me less proud of you.

"Man, that'll lay a guilt trip on her," Cochise said. "You'd make a good priest, Malloy."

"Ministers, Cochise, my family has ministers."

Terry finished:

Mama, I talked to the financial officer here. He said I am sending everything I am able. They are not paying me very much. Privates first class do not make a lot of money. You two keep praying for me. I love you both very much.

Your loving son and brother,
Guy Edmond

Brumsen and Terry were lost in thought.

"Hey, guys, you want to see the picture of my wife and son?" Cochise handed the picture to Terry. "Just handle the edges."

Cochise's wife wore a white blouse, which made her glistening, black hair even darker. Sensuous eyes looked at Terry. A smile disclosed perfect white teeth. Cochise's son sat on her lap and smiled.

"He's a very handsome boy, Cochise, and your wife's beautiful," Terry said.

Brumsen peered over Terry's shoulder. "He's really grown since the last picture."

"What does Maria have to say, Cochise? Is she doing okay?" Duffy asked.

"Since we're sharing letters, I'll read you some of what Maria wrote to me:"

My dearest, beloved Senor,

First, let me tell you the good news about your little sister. She has won an award at her school for being an outstanding fifth-grade student. Your mother and I went to the school and watched the principal give plaques to

Marguerite, and several other students. Then they lit candles and inducted them into the Honor Society.Your mother and I were crying, we were so happy. Marguerite looked beautiful, and you would have been very proud of her.

"Looks like the women in our families got all the brains, Cochise," Brumsen said.

Cochise's eyes were moist. "She's a very smart kid."

"Keep on reading, Cochise," Duffy said.

I told your mother that I was going to write you. She wants you to know that she says prayers for you every day at church. She asked God to hold you in his arms and bring you back safely to her. She is writing a letter, and you should receive it soon.Your father told me to tell you he loves you and will send a note with your mother's letter.

Brumsen wiped his nose. "Mamas do a heap of praying, don't they?"

My schoolwork is doing fine. I sometimes get discouraged when I think of two more years before I become a nurse. It is really difficult with my job at the grocery store.Your mother helps a lot. I don't know what I would do without our mothers to help me with our little Julio. When I get really down I look at your picture and I think about what you must be enduring. I tell myself to be brave, because my Senor is brave.

I see things on the television and I get scared for you. Sometimes when I go to bed at night, I take our son to bed with me and hold him close. It makes you seem a little closer to me.Then I pray to God to look over you and protect you and let no harm come to you. I go to sleep with your name on my lips. I send your name out of my window and up to heaven. I am sure that God hears your name coming, and I know in my heart that He will bring you home to me.

Your beautiful son is walking all over the house.Your mother and I can barely keep up with him. He is beginning to talk a little. I hold a picture of you in front of him and say the word 'Daddy' over and over. I think he said 'Daddy' the other night while looking at your picture.

Please, Jorge, do not take any chances. Do your job and let the other men do theirs, but please don't take any unnecessary risks. I remember what my mother told me when my father was killed in Korea. She cried herself to sleep for years. Even now, she misses him so much. I came in the other day and I actually think she was talking to a picture of him that is above our fireplace. I don't want to live with the memory of you. I want to live with you.

I grew up without a father to look after me and protect me. I don't want that to happen to our son. You need to take him to baseball games and play pitch with him. You need to be there by my side when he says his prayers at night. I do not remember my father ever tucking me in at night or giving me a good-night kiss. I want little Julio to feel his dad's arms around him and hear his dad's voice say 'I love you.' Let's see our son graduate from high school. Your son needs his father, and I need my husband. I want to grow old with you, and we can watch our son grow into a strong, brave man like his father.

I love you and can't wait to feel your warm body next to.......

Cochise paused and looked up. Silence filled the tent for several moments. Cochise looked intently at Brumsen, Terry, and Duffy. "I want you guys to swear to me that if anything happens to me, you'll find my son and tell him what kind of man his father was."

The tent was silent.

Duffy spoke. "Nothing's going to happen to you, Cochise. You're too mean to die."

"Cut the shit, Duffy. Sometimes I think I'll get out of this god-forsaken hellhole, and then other times I get really scared and think maybe I won't make it. I'm not afraid of dying. I'm afraid I'll never see my wife and son again. If I don't make it out, I want you guys to swear to me that you'll tell my son what kind of man I was, and tell my wife that I died with her name and his name on my lips."

A long pause followed.

"This is some serious shit that we're talking about now," Brumsen said. "Why don't we all swear that if anything happens to any of us, we'll all try our best to see the families of the guys who didn't make it."

"Great idea," Duffy said.

Terry and Cochise agreed.

"We need to write our addresses and phone numbers on sheets of paper." Terry opened his footlocker. "I know that if I died, my mom and dad would want to know how. I also want'em to meet you guys."

Duffy lifted radio batteries out of the box and placed them on his cot. "Anderson will want to get in on this. He'll be here in about an hour. Let's write duplicates of our addresses and numbers and wait for him. Then it will be official."

Cochise handed paper to everyone. "Put your name, address, and phone number on your sheet and pass it to the next guy. Then put your name and address on the next sheet as it comes to you."

"Let's make an extra sheet for Anderson," Brumsen said.

When they were done, Cochise walked out of the tent. At the flaps, he stopped and held up the knife. "You never know when we may need this."

Brumsen dismantled his machine gun.

"After listening to you guys," Terry said, taking paper and pencil out of the footlocker, "I think I need to write a letter to my parents."

Dear Mom and Dad,

We are back at our base camp now. You would not recognize me. I have written to you about the guys in my squad. One of the guys, Cochise, always wears a mohawk haircut. Everyone in the squad now has a mohawk. For laughs, we painted our faces last night to see how they would look. We all are going to start putting on war paint when we go on operations. In my next letter, I will enclose a picture of all of us with our war paint and mohawks.

My unit is leaving this area of Vietnam and heading to the Cambodian border to a place called Dak To.

He thought back to the day before, when the squad walked from the chow hall at noon. Anderson had been waiting for them, sitting on Terry's cot. The lines around his unsmiling, gray eyes were deeper. He was not too bothered. Anderson was always worried or angry about something.

"I've some information about where we're going," Anderson said. "You can take it for what it's worth. I got it from the lieutenant, who got it from the captain, who got it from God knows where." Anderson adjusted the .45 caliber pistol at his side. "The North Vietnamese are infiltrating troops in large numbers across the Cambodian border. *Dak To* is situated on a major infiltration route. We're being sent there to stop the infiltration."

Everyone is talking about this move. It appears that there will be North Vietnamese troops around Dak To. Anderson tells us that the nature of the fighting will change. I told you earlier how frustrating it is to not be able to get at the VC the way we want. They hit us at rare and opportune moments and never stay to engage in big battles. We get really angry, because we never have a chance to face the enemy in a decisive engagement. Anderson is constantly talking about payback and getting even. Some of the other guys talk the same way. I understand their feelings completely. Watch a couple of body bags being lifted onto a helicopter, or several of your wounded buddies being medevaced out, and you will feel the same way.

His lips compressed, Anderson pulled a folded map from a pocket. "The Vietnamese have been fighting in that region for decades. The lieutenant said that we can expect to see a lot of bunker complexes hidden in the jungle and embedded into the sides of mountains. We're going to be in a world of shit when we start operations up there."

Jungle fighting is nothing like I thought it would be. Nothing could have prepared me for it. You can read all the Caesar, Homer, and Virgil that you want. You can listen to stories about the Somme and Verdun, about Iwo Jima and the Chosin Reservoir, but you have to face combat for yourself to discover what it is really like.

Duffy said, "We have to stick together and cover each other's asses."

This move to Dak To may finally give us a chance to do some real payback. We all hope so. Please, please, do not worry about me. You have to remember that none of us want to risk our lives any more than necessary. Moreover, we have a very serious edge in firepower. With our tanks, helicopters, artillery, jets, and bombers, there is little chance that we could ever be overrun or that the North Vietnamese will engage in any serious battle.

Unfolding a map, Anderson placed it on the bunk.

Duffy looked at the map and whistled. "Look at the friggin' mountains and valleys."

"You can say that again. This is rugged, mountainous terrain." Anderson tapped the map with a finger. "The lieutenant says that the Vietnamese have been fighting in the Central Highlands for at least a hundred years, maybe more. France was the last country to have soldiers fight there.

"This move is a result of that stupid Tet Offensive last month," Anderson said, bringing out a pencil. "We have to stop them from coming into the country. The NVA uses these valleys as a staging area." He pointed at the valleys with his pencil. "The North Vietnamese ship troops and supplies across the Cambodian border and into Vietnam here. The highlands are perfect to protect the NVA movement. The small paths and trails, and even bigger speed trails, are well hidden by the thick triple-canopied jungle."

Cochise flicked ash from his cigarette. "In other words, we just think we've been in jungle."

"Absolutely," Anderson said. "The terrain is perfect to hide their movement. Our job is to stop them. We're going to interdict them.

Plus, the monsoon season will begin in about a month or so. That's just one more misery to add on."

Brumsen, chewing on a toothpick, stood with his arms folded. He took the toothpick out of his mouth. "It's funny, the map only has numbers on it. It tells us how steep the slopes are and how high the mountains are. It doesn't tell us about the jungle itself that we'll be slithering through and humping over during the monsoons. It doesn't show us all the men Anderson says have died there, either. These are just numbers on a map indicating distance and height."

Duffy nodded, staring at the map. "That's all we are. We're numbers at the end of a vast pipeline extending from the edge of California to the coast of Vietnam. Numbers are infinite. If we get killed or wounded, the pipeline will pour out someone who'll replace us."

"The only people who will give a shit are our families and ourselves," Anderson added.

I am glad you keep me in your prayers. I try to get to Sunday service as much as I can. Several of us have started a Bible study group, which we attend when we are in base camp. We heard a very good sermon on Paul's letter to the Romans last Sunday.

I love you all,
Terry

P.S. I am now the official counter for the squad. This is a chore that no one wants, but someone has to do it. When we move through the jungle, we need to know exactly where we are at any given time. This is especially true when we call in artillery. The maps are divided into grids of one thousand meters each. If we don't know where we are, then we can't call in any support, if we get into trouble. You will be glad to know that one hundred and thirty of my paces are equal to one hundred meters.

CHAPTER NINE

Terry woke to the salty-sweet aroma of bacon frying. Adultery! What was he doing? No, wait. He was separated and may be divorced soon. Worry about it later. Who gave a shit. No, don't say that. Go into the kitchen and stop it right now? Why stop it?

Sarah, her back to Terry, stood over the stove, flipping bacon with a fork. She turned and held out her arms. The sleeves of her blue terrycloth bathrobe bunched around both elbows. He embraced her.

Sarah speared a piece of bacon with her fork and placed it on a dish. "How guilty are you feeling?"

Terry picked up the strip of hot bacon and nibbled. "It's weighing on me. I have to admit it. But seeing you, I want more."

Licking the bacon grease from her fingers, Sarah turned with one finger in her mouth. "Guilt or sex?"

Rubbing his grizzled chin, he sat down. "How can you have one without the other? How about you?"

Sarah, still holding the fork, walked the small distance from the stove to the table. Her robe had slipped open, revealing cleavage. She grabbed Terry's hair in both hands and pulled his head to her breast. "You '60s fogies are a little more hung up than my generation. You may have smoked dope and let your hair grow long, but you've got as many hang-ups as your parents."

The warmth and softness of her breast felt wonderful. He slipped a hand inside her robe and rubbed the inside of her thigh. "It's a little too early for an anthropological study, young lady. I just asked how you felt about last night."

Pulling his head up, she kissed his lips. Then she wrapped her bathrobe around her and tied the cord. "Sorry, it's my area. Twentieth Century Political and Social Movements. You know that." Sarah opened the refrigerator and held up orange juice. "I feel great, but I'm not married. How do you like your eggs?"

Terry poured coffee into the cup stationed near the coffee maker. "Clarissa has told me she wants a divorce. Over medium, but in front of other people, scrambled." He sipped his coffee. "No one can stand watching someone else eat eggs."

She slipped bread into the toaster. "I didn't know it had gotten that bad. Go get the paper for me. It's in the driveway."

He buttoned his shirt and walked out. Looking around to see if anyone was outside, he shook his head, smiling at himself. She was right. He was just a hung-up love child of the '60s. The flower children were selling and buying insurance and real estate and watching the market rise, just like their Vietnam-veteran brothers. The drug culture they started had overwhelmed them. Did they do the right thing by their children, opening up more chances for sex, more chances for drugs? Guilt, guilt, guilt. The shock of moving from middle earth to the suburbs and facing responsibilities was too much for them. His generation never grew up. A quiet Saturday morning. Was anyone watching? Wrong question. Did anyone give a shit? Mea culpa! Sarah nailed it. This would kill Clarissa. But Clarissa wanted a divorce.

Picking up the paper, he studied it while walking back to the house. Soldiers killed in Iraq, a lurch in his stomach, sadness overwhelmed him. He couldn't read it. Election news, boring. Don't read it!

NGSC Professor: 'Greatest Generation are murderers.'

Professor Terrence Malloy, a history professor at Northeastern Georgia State College, shocked many in his audience last night with a backhanded compliment to the generation that fought World War II. "The generation that fought World War II was willing to kill people to win. Until we realize that war is not something you can do in half measures, we will continue to lose just as we are doing in Iraq."

Malloy spoke at a panel on the Iraq War on the NGSC campus last night. Rich Breedlove, another history professor on the panel, was cautious in criticizing his colleague. "He could have been a little more circumspect in using terms like 'mass murderers' when referring to the generation that saved the world from facism."

Many of the students attending last night enjoyed the debate. Professor Malloy's opinion was clearly the favorite with the cheering students. Only a few students disagreed with the professor. Gerald Jones, an economics major, "couldn't believe" what he was hearing. "I felt like he was mocking the sacrifice of the men who fought in World

See page 3, Killing civilians was the policy

Sarah, placing a plate of bacon, eggs, and toast on the table, stopped smiling when she saw Terry's face.

"I have to be honest." He threw the paper on the table. "I thought Thorn was going to rip me to pieces in this morning's paper."

Her slim hand picked up the paper. When she opened it to read inside, she looked up. Tapping the back of the chair, she said, "Sit down and eat before it gets cold. It's a fair article."

Terry picked up a piece of bacon and nibbled.

She finished reading just as the phone rang. Sarah looked at the caller ID window. "It's Rich," she said, knitting her brow.

Sarah leaned against the counter, holding the phone to her ear. "Hello." She grabbed a piece of bacon from the table. "I just read the article. I thought Thorn was very fair and that's what I told Terry."

Sitting down, Sarah reached for the bacon. "What do you mean there's another article? If you have it there read it to me. Terry came over to give me a ride to my car. I'll put it on the speaker phone." Sarah looked at Terry. "The Atlanta paper had a reporter there last night. Rich said it's brutal."

Rich's voice came over the speaker. "Well, the headline is 'Innocents slaughtered by Greatest Generation.'"

Terry pushed the eggs away, put his elbows on his knees, and clutched at his hair. "Holy shit."

"That's just the beginning," Rich said. "'In a stunning justification of the Iraq War, that left many in the audience feeling that they had been stabbed in the back, Terrence Malloy, a history professor at Northeastern Georgia State College, said the World War II generation killed women and children by the hundreds of thousands. Malloy dropped the bombshell during a panel on the Iraq War at the NGSC campus last night. One angry faculty member who did not want to be identified, said, 'We don't need fascists mocking the men and women who destroyed Hitler's armies and the Japanese Empire.'"

Rich paused. "Terry, they mention Ella in the article."

Terry nodded. Sarah said, "Go ahead and read it, Rich."

"Dr. Malloy's daughter was part of the Military Police Unit that ran Abu Ghraib. Before Malloy's daughter was killed in action in a fire-fight against Insurgents, it was rumored that she was under investigation for torturing and mistreating prisoners."

She switched off the speaker phone.

Where was his anger from last night? Weariness seeped into him. If he could only crawl into bed and pull up the covers. He couldn't fight these battles anymore. Why did they have to bring Ella into the damn article?

A movement caught his eye. Duffy stood behind Sarah, holding a canteen. The radio antenna waved behind him. Green and black camouflage paint glistened on his face. He gulped water from the canteen. A flicker of a smile played around his lips. "Anger comes from the outside. Outside factors change. Guilt is self-generating. It comes from the person you expect yourself to be." Duffy's light blue eyes held Terry's gaze. "We shouldn't have done it, Malloy."

"He brought me home last night and said he would pick me up to get my car. It's a long story, Rich. I didn't need to call you. Terry was there. He took Barbara home, too. We all had too much to drink. We'll meet you for lunch and then get my car. Yes, Terry, too. Rich, he's our friend, he needs help. What?" Sarah smiled at Terry. "I like him, even if he's an old coot."

She hung up the phone. "Rich is a little too possessive. Terry, go home and shave, or change, or do something. Then come back and pick me ... No, wait. Rich is driving me nuts." She ran her fingers through her blond hair, shuddered, and hugged herself, trembling. "Take a shower with me. Then we'll go to your house and you can shave. You look like shit."

Why was everyone telling him he looked like shit? "Sarah, I don't know about this. What am I doing here? I'm married. Heading for divorce, but still married. Plus, I'm twenty years older than you. You're only ten years older than Ella, for God's sake. Rich has you crawling out of your skin. So, you want to screw me? Let's be friends. Tell Rich you want to be friends. I don't need this complication."

The bathrobe dropped from Sarah's shoulders to the floor. Teasing fingers toyed with both nipples. She took his hand and moved it against her stomach and pubic hair while her other hand massaged his groin. "Women like men to chase after them. Please, you old coot, let's take a shower."

Terry shut his eyes. Arousal and desire surged in him like lava through a volcano.

She brought his hand to her lips and kissed his fingers. Still holding his crotch with her other hand and walking backward, she led him through the kitchen door. "I know I'm a bad girl. Maybe I need another spanking?"

On the way to the restaurant to meet Rich and Diversity, Terry pondered last night's panel discussion. "One thing I can't figure out. Why aren't you upset with what I said? You're just like Rich, if not more so."

Sarah adjusted herself in the seat, moving the seat belt around her shoulder. She wore faded blue jeans and a light blue sweater. She fingered the pearl necklace around her neck. "One answer might be because I know that we've won. My side is kicking ass in the public schools, the private colleges, and the public colleges. The culture war is over. There are not many bastions of conservatism on campus anywhere. All but one TV network is in our pocket and ninety-nine percent of the newspapers bend over and say 'kick me' to any liberal with an idea. You've lost. You just don't know it and neither does Rich. I've got what I wanted with Shoshonnah coming here. She's about as far out there as you can get and she's coming to a Southern campus. If conservative Southern schools are hiring people like her, think about who other schools across the nation are hiring."

Terry shook his head and snorted. A rueful smile played across his mouth. "So you decided to have an affair with me because I'm a loser? You really know how to make a guy feel good. What's the other option?"

Sarah laughed, speaking in her Southern-belle voice. "The other option is that I'm part of a vast Confederate conspiracy that has been weakening the moral fabric of the United States since the Civil War. The more insanity we can introduce into the culture, the weaker it gets."

He parked next to Rich in the restaurant lot. Sarah opened her door and placed a long leg outside. "Women like the embattled loser.

The noble hero makes a gallant, last stand. That's why most Civil War novels have Southern men as the main characters. I've felt sorry for you over the last few months. That's true. I know Ella's loss was heartrending. But, I've always thought you were a special person. You're a dying breed, Terry."

Rich and Diversity waved to them from his table. He wore fall colors – dark brown wool pants, a black turtleneck, and a light brown jacket. Diversity wore blue jeans and a purple and gold sweatshirt with the NGSC Tigers logo on it.

After they ordered, Rich unwrapped his implement-filled napkin. He lined up his knife, fork, and spoon beside each other. "I've been thinking that this is a win-win situation for us. The right gets accused of blaspheming the older generation by trying to justify the Iraq war on the backs of the World War II generation. And our side gets to say that our forces in Iraq are murdering women and children. It's poetic."

Spreading his napkin across his knees, Terry shook his head in exasperation. "What do you mean, your side. I'm not on anyone's side. And I'm not the 'right.' I'm Terry Malloy. I wasn't justifying anyone's war. I simply said that we need to fight a war or get out. You know that. The Atlanta paper slanted it and misinterpreted the whole talk. I can't believe you think this is a win. What about the truth? If this is a win, then the truth lost. Just tell what I said and let's talk about it."

The waitress, a blonde woman with grey roots and a stained apron, placed glasses of orange juice on the table.

"You may not be fighting a war, but Sarah and I are. This is a new age." Rich gulped his orange juice. "You can't be that naive, Terry. The press is our ally, not yours. It doesn't matter what you said. It's what they said you said that forms reality."

Terry clenched his napkin. His jaw tightened. The muscles in his arms and shoulders tensed. "Goddammit! I don't have allies, don't expect them, and don't want them. I do expect a little decency about my daughter. That paper had no right to bring her into this. Don't talk to me about war. You don't know what you're talking about. Whatever happened to civil discourse where people exchanged ideas?"

The waitress set the food on the table.

Pushing her dark hair out of her bright, brown eyes, Diversity attacked her hamburger. "Dad, when are we going to the zoo?"

"We promised Diversity we'd go to the Atlanta Zoo, want to come?" Sarah chewed on a small bite of her hamburger.

Smiling, Terry felt the tension ease out of him. "No, I'm going home and shoot myself."

Sarah swallowed her food. "Terry, don't talk like that, even if you're joking."

"Well, Diversity, what animals do you hope to see today?" Terry asked.

"I like the lions and tigers. They're so graceful."

Terry remembered a nine-or ten-year-old Ella coming into the den with a book full of dinosaur pictures. Her reddish-blonde hair fell over her shoulders. Jumping onto his lap, she opened the book to a Triceratops. "This is my favorite one. What's your favorite one?"

"Do I have to have a favorite one. Can't I just like them all?"

Making a no-nonsense face, her green eyes flashed. Ella shut her book, wagging a finger at him. "No, Daddy, you have to choose."

Sarah and Diversity left the table to go to the restroom.

Leaning back in the chair, Rich clasped his hands behind his back. "You're in a bit of a jam, Terry." Rich smirked, nodding his head. His eyes laughed at Terry. Raising his eyebrows several times, he said. "Yep, you're in deep shit."

Terry shrugged. "I don't care what they print about me. I just wish they would leave Ella alone and print what I really say."

"I think you're going to be in a tight spot around campus for a while. You better head for the hills." Rich held out his cup for the waitress to pour more coffee.

"If you think I'd run from these people, you really don't know me. Trust me, I've been in tight spots before."

* * *

Cochise slapped the side of the teak tree. His scabbard and knife handle stuck out from behind his slender neck. "They're hardwoods."

The squad rested at the top of a mountain ridge around the base of the huge tree. Up high on the ridge, the thinning jungle made the rain worse. The triple-canopy of jungle lessened the downpour, wrapping the men in a thick blanket of foliage protecting them from the deluge of the monsoon. An appreciation for the kindness of the indifferent jungle escaped them: in the jungle blanket itself, the dangers lay.

It had been a hectic month since the squad had moved into the central highlands along the Cambodian border. The entire battalion flew into *Dak To* and set up its base camp. Afterward, the companies boarded helicopters and dropped into the jungle. After two weeks of what the brass had called familiarization maneuvers, the exhausted men emerged from the jungle for a two-day respite. Their gear in good order, the men lifted into the jungle again.

The battalion pursued a North Vietnamese infantry division that had come across the Cambodian border within the last month. Contact had been light. Throughout the first weeks, the big battle that the higher ups looked for failed to materialize. The battalion pushed from one valley to the next. The men went up mountains and down mountains. Sometimes the battalion split into companies and went around a mountain. At other times, the soldiers airlifted into a valley and after two days of sweeps, flew out.

A point man for one of the files discovered the bunkers by accident when he fell into a ditch that connected them. Duffy, listening to his radio, heard the officers talking about finding a base camp. He passed the news to the squad. "It's a big one."

The squad relaxed and spread out among the gnarled roots of the teak tree.

Duffy pressed the receiver to his ear. "It's a bunker complex, not a base camp. "He motioned to Anderson and handed him the receiver. "The lieutenant wants to speak to all the squad leaders."

Taking Duffy with him, Anderson left. When the two came back, he addressed the squad. "We're gonna have to go through the complex, search it, and then destroy it. The two companies that were point today will set up a perimeter around the bunkers. Our company and Delta company will search and destroy the bunkers. There may be tunnels."

Cochise put his thin lips together and whistled. At first, no one in the squad saw it. The men walked through the perimeter of soldiers set up around the complex. The bunker was there, growing right out of the jungle.

Brumsen knelt and peered through the gun aperture. "Man, oh man. They really blend in, don't they?"

It was several feet deep and about six feet wide. Brown and green logs protruded from the ground on both sides of it. These logs supported longer logs, tied together with rope, used as a roof. Thick mounds of dirt covered the sides and roof, giving the bunker additional protection. Vegetation of all kinds grew out of the dirt, camouflaging the entire thing. A trench, deep enough to hide a man or men, ran from the back of the bunker up the hill.

Lowering themselves into it, Terry and Duffy examined the aperture. They stuck their rifles through and swiveled them back and forth, sighting down the mountainside.

"We would be in a world of hurt trying to take this place," Duffy said.

The lower vegetation in front of the bunker had been cleared. Lower limbs, branches of trees, and all of the small brush within two feet of the ground had been cut for at least thirty yards in front of it. The clearing was cone-shaped, with the bunker at the apex.

"We need to hurry, guys," Anderson said. "There're two lines of bunkers above this line. The captain wants the ones assigned to us destroyed by tonight. They'll be back here a week after we leave." Kneeling, Anderson gave Terry a bar of C-4 plastic explosive. "This entire system will be back in operation within a month. If you don't believe me, think about the constant work it must take to keep the jungle clear for the fields of fire. That should give you an idea of how often they come here."

"I can smell the *bastardos*. They're close." Cochise handed a blasting cap to Duffy. "*Puta madre que los pario!* They're real close."

The battalion spent the night on Hill 875. Anderson's squad went on an ambush. The downpour continued. Although the battalion was on a fifty-percent alert status, no unit reported any contact that night. The next morning, the exhausted battalion marched down the valley toward Hill 1036. The men hacked their way through the fronds and vines while slogging and slipping on the muddy jungle floor. Terry's company encountered heavy fire three hours later. A mine exploded along their front. Rocket-propelled grenades landed among the men. A ten minute firefight ensued. The squad's platoon attempted a flanking movement. The firing diminished. The NVA vanished. The platoon rejoined the file and the battalion moved forward.

The NVA ambushed the lead elements again two hours before dark. A repetition of the earlier fight that morning ensued. The NVA detonated a mine. RPGs burst among the men. A firefight developed. The enemy disappeared into the jungle.

Duffy took the receiver from his ear. "It looks like we're stopping for the night. They're talking about pushing up Hill 1036 tomorrow."

Rain dripped off Cochise's floppy field hat. Hollow eyes reflected exhaustion and frustration. His hand cupped a cigarette, keeping it dry from the rain. Smoke billowed around him. "This is the same kind of crap that we went through down south. They blow a mine and then skedaddle."

Brumsen leaned his machine gun against a tree. He removed the helmet, revealing his mohawk. "I think they have a union."

"A union?" Terry asked, opening a C-ration can.

"Yeah, they have a union." Brumsen attached a P-38 can opener to a can of ham and lima beans. His pudgy fingers worked the can opener around the top. "It's like the maid service my mom works for. I'm sorry, but we don't do windows. It's the same thing here. I'm sorry, Sir. We only do claymores and booby traps. We don't do battles, they're not cool. If it's battles you dig, you have to talk to the forty-ninth division."

Anderson took a can out of his rucksack. It had holes punched around the bottom. He placed a small ball of C-4 in the makeshift stove. Shielding the stove from the rain, he touched the plastic explosive with his cigarette. It burst into flames. "They know better than to fight us. They can't. Victor Charlie and the NVA don't have the resources to fight us. Every time they engage us in a fixed battle, we eat them up."

Brumsen placed his newly opened can on his own stove. "They seem like pretty good fighters to me."

"Me, too," Terry said.

"They're good fighters." Steam rose from the can as Anderson stirred the food with a plastic spoon. "I didn't say they weren't. I just said they didn't want to fight us in a big battle. We outgun them, and our men are just as good as theirs. After all, we have airplanes, helicopters, and artillery."

"I'd hate to go up against them in those bunkers." Duffy drank from his canteen.

"That'd be *muy fuerte*, man, very, very tough."

Knitting his brow, Anderson tasted his meal. He took out a small packet of salt and sprinkled it on the still cooking food, stirring and tasting. "If they decided to fight us, it would be in a situation and terrain like this. You know, where they have a definite defensive advantage. I'd hate to fight against them in these bunkers."

The battalion dug in for the night as the deluge continued. The squad dug its fox hole in the perimeter. It filled with rain as they were digging. The bottom became a swamp. The roof was almost complete when they were told they had ambush duty again that night.

The men stared at the bunker. Their soaked jungle fatigues clung to their rucksack-weighted shoulders. With a half-hearted effort, Terry gripped his rucksack, adjusting it. "I hope someone makes good use of it."

Cochise touched a lit cigarette to a leach embedded in his arm. The leach withdrew. He knocked it off and stepped on it. Blood ran down his arm from where the leach had been. "I got a bad feeling about this valley. I'm telling you, I can smell 'em."

The NVA probed the lines that night in several places. Small fights erupted around the perimeter. No one slept, neither the men in the perimeter nor the men on ambush.

The squad made no contact and slogged into the perimeter in the morning with drooped shoulders and haggard, unshaven faces. Their sunken eyes reflected weariness. The battalion moved out before anyone could eat breakfast.

Brumsen brushed his teeth while walking. "I should at least have the time to brush my teeth. I have moss growing on them."

Around noon, the point company, A Company, engaged with the enemy and was pinned down in one of the many draws leading up Hill 1036. C Company relieved pressure on A Company by supporting its flank. Both companies fought their way up the hill. The North Vietnamese, rather than hit and run as they usually did, dug in, fighting for every inch of ground. D Company took up a position on C Company's flank. All three companies pushed forward in a coordinated assault.

The squad's company, Bravo, drawing rear guard duty because of its role as point company the day before, heard only the noise of the battle. The impenetrable jungle hid its secrets. Individual small-arms fire rolled down the valley. As the fighting developed, a crescendo of explosions echoed from the direction of the hill. A cascading wall of sound rippled to and fro along the company front. Duffy, attempting to interpret what happened, listened to the battle on the radio and relayed the various excited calls and orders to the squad.

"They're pushing up the hill," he told the attentive squad. The thunderous sounds of battle reverberated around them, growing and diminishing in volume. "Oh, shit. They've run into bunkers."

The jungle around the squad erupted with explosions. Duffy's helmet flew through the air. Everyone hugged the volcanic, grumbling ground, which rumbled with thunderous detonations. Anderson appeared, yelling to be heard. Terry watched Anderson's mouth moving, but could not hear him. The earth trembled as a wall of shells walked its way through the jungle. Shells burst in the treetops and on the ground, blowing trees, shrubs, plants, and animals into the air. Wounded men screamed.

A tree behind Anderson shattered. The explosion spewed whistling metal and splintered wood. Anderson tumbled, sprawling to the ground. Terry attempted to push himself into the ground. The curtain of shells passed over them. A storm of leaves and fronds mingled with the smoke and the pungent odor of exploded munitions. Terry, numb from the concussive impact of the mortar shells, tried to stand.

Anderson staggered to his feet. He yanked Duffy into a crouch position, slapping him on the back. "Move! Get the fuck outa here!" Soldiers, carrying wounded men, ran through the jungle. "Let's go, Malloy, get your ass up!"

The shelling slackened as Terry's company carried its equipment and wounded closer to the hill. An officer stood in the middle of men who were chopping down trees. Anderson hurried over to the officer. Speaking, he motioned a direction and turned to another squad leader.

Gunfire and detonations came from the front in the direction of Hill 1036. Occasional blasts of mortar shells continued to tear up the jungle behind B Company. Terry ducked and flinched as the explosions reverberated through the jungle. Besides the rain, pieces of fronds, leaves, and wood continued to descend from the sky.

Anderson yelled over the sounds of battle, blinking his long eyelashes against the smoke and debris, "We have to form a perimeter to protect the LZ these guys are cutting. They're moving casualties down from the mountain, and they'll need to be evacuated. The medevacs are on their way."

The squad dug in at the bottom of the hill. The battalion commander, surprised at this sudden resistance, decided to pull back his troops on the hill. While the companies evacuated the wounded to the aid station, he called in air power and artillery to soften up the NVA in their bunkers.

Called away, Anderson took Duffy with him. A deep rumble came from the hill as artillery fell on the enemy positions. Terry smiled along with the other men. Cochise and Brumsen dug the foxhole. Terry filled the sandbags with mud and dirt.

After the shelling ended, full-throated, roaring jets flew over the squad's position. Diving on the hill, the jets dropped napalm and high-explosive shells onto the enemy bunkers. With the cessation of noise from the jets, Terry expected the assault to continue. An ominous silence fell over the hill. Only the moans and screams of the wounded drifted through the jungle.

Carrying a water canister, Duffy and Anderson ran in a crouch to the squad's foxhole. Terry handed his empty canteens to Duffy, who held them while Anderson poured. A corner of Anderson's mouth turned sarcastically downward. He shook his head. His eyes flashed angrily. "One of the fucking hot-shot pilots hit our lines with rockets. They killed some of the guys in Charlie Company."

Duffy's small hands gripped the canteen under the pouring water. "Give the pilots a break, Anderson. Can you imagine how hard it must be picking out a spot in this crap going three or four hundred miles an hour?"

Anderson stopped pouring. He slammed the can to the ground, staring at Duffy with narrowed, angry eyes. His small mouth a grim slit in his face, he spat out words. "No, I can't, but I can see dead Americans killed by our side. So if you don't mind, give me the chance to be pissed.

"Anyway, we don't have time for this." Anderson lifted the water can and poured. "I got some news from the lieutenant. It seems that this afternoon, when we were coming down the valley, a reinforced Long Range Reconnaissance Patrol of fourteen men was helicoptered into the next valley. The recon patrol was part of our overall bullshit plan to completely eliminate the presence of the North Vietnamese from these connecting hills and valleys."

Cochise handed his canteens to Duffy. "You're talking about a L.R.R.P. Team, a Lurp team?"

"The choppers dropped the Lurp team off without a hitch," Anderson continued, pouring water. "The team radioed that its LZ was clear. They jumped into the jungle to establish a camp for the night. The next-to-last radio call said that they had found a high-speed trail and were going to set up their camp somewhere near the trail.

"No one's heard from them since their last radio transmission." Anderson set down the water can. Small face overshadowed by his helmet, he blinked weary gray eyes at the men. He gestured futilely with one hand. "The Lurp team reported they were under fire. They attempted to coordinate artillery around their position. Helicopter flights over the general vicinity have been unable to pick up any sign of the patrol. That's not surprising, given how thick this jungle is."

Taking a drink from his canteen, Anderson screwed the cap back on. "Three different units are being sent into the neighboring valley to look for the team. They're sending units into each end of the valley. HQ's asked for one squad from each company to help find these guys. The captain volunteered us. We're gonna be taken back up this valley and dropped a little ways below the ridge line, and we're goin' over the ridge smack into the middle of the valley. All three patrols, including us, have a specific area to cover. We need to find the lost recon team."

"This is a blessing in disguise." Duffy wiped rain from his camouflaged face, scratching his pug nose. "One of the companies'll come down off the hill later tonight. Bravo Company will replace it and go into the fight tomorrow morning."

"They aren't gonna be able to get all the wounded out of here tonight," Anderson added. "We're stayin' here and helpin' take care of the wounded at the aid station."

Bravo replaced the men of Alpha one platoon and foxhole at a time. The men of A company trudged down the hill, shuffling quietly through the growing darkness, rain, and mud. They carried the remaining wounded with them. The wounded on the stretchers attempted to keep a stoic silence. Occasionally, a cry of pain escaped as weary stretcher bearers stumbled and staggered through the jungle darkness over the soft, muddy ground, trying to find the aid station. It was pitch dark by the time platoons of Alpha and Bravo finished.

At the aid station, the men helped the medics and tried to comfort the wounded. Brumsen and Anderson had taken two water cans each and left. They came back several times and picked up fresh cans to resupply the battle-weary men of Alpha Company guarding the perimeter.

While Duffy was giving water to various men on their stretchers, Terry and Cochise held ponchos for the medics. Like a tent the poncho allowed the medic to use a flashlight to see in the darkness, also protecting them from the rain. Throughout the night Terry sat with wounded men, holding their hands and adjusting their bodies to more comfortable positions.

One boy Terry helped had lost his foot in the rocket attack by the jets. He drifted into and out of delirium. Occasionally, when the delirium eased its grip, he would check to make sure that he still held his boot. The boot, with the toe and heel torn off, had the remainder of the foot inside of it.

He grabbed Terry's arm. The boy's hand trembled from weakness due to loss of blood. "Don't let them take my foot away. I ain't leaving it in this goddamn place." During the night, he awoke to lay the same charge upon the medics. While Terry assured him that the boot would leave on the helicopter, the medics checked his IV and leg tourniquet.

Terry held a poncho over another soldier with leg and arm wounds while a medic tended to him. "I need a cigarette, man. Is there any way I can light up?"

The medic tied off a bandage wrapped around one arm. The wounded man's hands were both wrapped in bloody gauze. "We're short of personal cigarette holders at the moment, Mac."

When he came out from under the poncho, the medic told Terry to take a break. Terry bit his lip, kneeling by the man. "Where are your cigarettes?"

The man moved one of his bandaged hands. "They're in my pocket."

Jerking the poncho over himself and the man, he retrieved cigarettes and matches from the pocket. Inserting a cigarette into the man's mouth, he lit it. "What's your name?"

The wounded soldier inhaled and exhaled smoke. "Talarico, what's yours?"

"Malloy." He took the cigarette from Talarico's lips. "How did you get hit?"

Talarico inhaled again. "It was bad up there. The worst I've ever seen. After A company made contact, the word came down that my company would go up next to support their flank. I'm in Charlie Company. After we came up and laid down some fire power, the NVA withdrew like they usually do."

Terry held the cigarette. Talarico blew smoke slowly out of his mouth. He relaxed a little. "Man, you have no idea how good that feels. Anyway, we got on line and started heading up the hill when the world exploded around us. I guess we had gone thirty yards when they detonated several mines along our front. After that, we started receiving fire, all kinds of fire, from everywhere.

"I mean, there was machine-gun fire, RPG rounds, rifle fire, and grenades." He paused to puff on his cigarette. "They threw everything they had at us. I shot a guy coming out of a spider hole, then had to take cover from sniper fire. The snipers must have shot four or five guys before we realized where the shots were coming from. There was just so much fucking noise, no one could think. I heard someone yell, 'Snipers! and everyone started shooting into the tree tops. One guy fell out of a tree and hung from a rope after he was shot. I mean, those sonsofbitches are hardcore. Get me another cig out, would ya, Malloy?"

"Sure."

"After we got the snipers, we advanced into the machine-gun fire again. You know, leap frogging by squads, supporting each other with covering fire. It was a good advance. We were suppressing fire. That's when we hit the bunkers. They laid down fire six inches off the ground. The NVA claymores had cleared some of the jungle because of their explosions. I still couldn't see where the fire was coming from. They're very well concealed. That's when the North Vietnamese charged us."

Terry's eyes widened and his eyebrows shot up. "The NVA *charged* your position?"

Talarico fidgeted and tried to move his arm. "Malloy, scratch my shoulder, would you." Terry scratched. "No shit, they came running out of the jungle and scared the crap out of us." He exhaled smoke. "There were about twenty of them. I think they had trouble picking us up. You know, the jungle being so thick and all. Anyway, we got all of them, and they only wounded one guy. It was crazy. I couldn't figure out why they were charging from protected bunkers. I guess they thought we would retreat or run. Maybe their officers wanted to test us. It was a waste of good men. I still can't figure it out."

Stubbing the cigarette into the ground, Terry threw off the poncho. "It's not like them to fight like this."

"When we were withdrawing to get away from the artillery and jets that were being called in, some wise-ass gook fires an RPG at us. I was the only guy wounded. I guess I'm lucky. At least, I'm getting away from this crap for a while. I definitely don't want to face those bunkers again. Thanks for the help, Malloy."

The jungle night and rain were refreshing and almost cool after being under the poncho. Anderson, talking to Cochise, motioned for him.

"Malloy, you and Cochise get some rest. We have a long day tomorrow. The chopper will be here early. If the medics need you, they'll wake you."

The next morning the helicopter descended like an angel of mercy and lifted the squad away from the carnage about to begin again on the sloping jungle-covered sides of Hill 1036.

While the squad headed to its drop-off point, Anderson spoke to the men over the roar of the helicopter engine and the continuous whomp-whomp of the blades. "If any of these recon guys are alive, they probably wish they were dead. That's exactly what we should expect to find when and if we reach them. All we have is a coordinate on a map that tells us where their LZ was. The team could be a couple of hundred yards from the last coordinates they reported, or they may be a thousand yards from there. We simply don't know. The only way to find out is to get men in there. You guys know as well as I do how hard it is to find anything in this green shit. Once we leave the helicopter, it's important to stay in our ambush routine."

CHAPTER TEN

Sweeping the shards of glass into piles, Terry stabbed the floor with the broom. Bending over, he shoved the broken glass into the dust pan. The fist-size rock sat on the coffee table, king of its domain, a billboard to anyone entering the living room. The two words, 'fuck you,' prominently displayed.

He turned off the light and switched on the flashlight. The remaining shards, lurking on the wooden floor, glittered in the beam. Kneeling, he began to pick up individual sparkling glass fragments in the dark.

Crap, right through his living room window. This was a perfect end. The entire day was a disaster. After lunch with Rich and Sarah, he returned home to the phone ringing. He should have known this would happen. Why couldn't he just keep his mouth shut. God, what a painful call!

Clarissa's panicked voice flooded the room. "I've gotten email from several people. Please tell me it isn't true what they've said about Ella. What did you say last night?"

Exasperated, he waved his arms to an empty room. "It didn't happen the way the Atlanta papers told it. I was simply using World War II as an example of a well-run war."

"I can't take this! I need to rest over here and not worry about you, over there."

"What can I do to prevent some asshole reporter from misconstruing what I said? I haven't done anything but present facts."

"Just think about me before you say anything to reporters. Do you know how helpless I feel?"

"How helpless *you* feel? I'm not going to sit back and let someone steamroll me, Clarissa. If they want a fight, they'll get one."

"If you're not going to think of me," Clarissa sobbed, "think of Ella."

He pounded the kitchen counter with his fist. "Goddammit, I *am* thinking of Ella! I'm thinking of how to stop kids like Ella from getting killed! That's all I was trying to do!" Terry took a breath. "Clarissa, let's not scream at each other. There's no reason for this. Look, I'll explain my motives in an email."

Clarissa hung up with a whispered, "I just can't take this."

He waved the beam around the floor one last time. *She* can't take it?

Terry did not have time to brood after Clarissa's call. The phone rang again.

"Hello"

A country twang penetrated the room. "You stupid commie sumbitch. What the fuck do you know about World War II or History. You Vietnam guys are all losers. It's just like a loser to criticize the only heroes we have." The line went dead.

Turning on the living room light, laying the flashlight on the table, he collapsed into the couch. The comforting soft leather enveloped him.

The phone calls from the two reporters were the last straw. Both conversations were in the same vein. What have you got against World War II vets?

Speaking slowly, Terry explained, "That's not what I said. The reporter misunderstood my remarks."

"What about your daughter? How long was she at Abu Ghraib?"

Terry's fist tightened around the phone. He bit his lip. Stay calm. Stay calm. "She wasn't *at* Abu Ghraib. She was in the same general area, but–"

"Then what's she being investigated for?"

"She's *not* being investigated. She was in the Army–"

The questions came rapid fire, the reporter not seeming to care what he said. "A faculty member, who doesn't want to be identified, said you're hiding something. Are you hiding something?"

"Goddammit, I'm not hiding anything. She was in the Army... not the national guard."

"We're going to find the truth, Mr. Malloy. We always do."

He slammed the phone back on the receiver. Then he took it off the receiver and slammed it on the kitchen counter. Jesus, why couldn't he keep his mouth shut? Just go along with everyone. Acquiesce to all the bullshit.

A shrill sound came from the phone. Terry let the wail continue, leaving the phone off the receiver. Yanking his cell phone from his pocket, he turned it off. He had plenty of things to do today. There were lecture notes to go over. There were a few early term-paper outlines he could peruse. There was work around the house. Finally, if everything was caught up, he would jog. How had he become the bad guy? Why were they pursuing *him*? He turned his back on the shrill phone and walked from the kitchen.

The rock turned as Terry tossed it through the air. Catching the rock, he flipped it back into the air. The 'fuck you' appeared and reappeared as the rock turned. Fuck me. Light beams played through the busted window. Standing in a crouch, Terry turned off the light. Clutching the rock, he stood next to the window, hidden from view.

A car door slammed. Peeking around the curtain, he relaxed. The grip on the rock loosened.

Sarah hurried up the walkway toward the front door. Stopping in front of the picture window, she shook her head.

"How do you like the new air-conditioning system I had installed?"

"I can't believe someone would do this," she said, gesturing toward the window.

Terry flipped on the lights and walked back to the window. He tossed the rock into the air. "They installed it for free. No charge."

Stepping up on the porch, she entered the house in a pink, sleeveless, cashmere shell with a matching open-stitch cardigan fastened with a single jeweled button. Her grey, pleated, full skirt swirled around her as she turned to shut the door. "I need a drink."

"You know where the wine is." He pointed toward the dining room. "Grab a bottle and I'll open it. I'm going to pour a little scotch for myself. I deserve it."

"You deserve it? I've spent the whole day with Diversity and Rich. I'd promised them I would go to the zoo today, then dinner. Although, the food was good and Diversity is the sweetest kid."

Sarah carried a bottle of Cabernet into the kitchen. "Where's your corkscrew?"

They walked back into the living room and sat on the couch. Benny Goodman's "Sing, Sing, Sing," blared from the speakers. Sarah picked up the rock and studied it.

The whiskey slid down Terry's throat. "Sarah, what are you doing here?"

Sarah smiled without opening her mouth. Intentionally playing the coquettish Southern Belle, her words dripped from her lips. "Why mercy me, Terry Malloy. Can't a girl, who's been calling you all the live-long day and getting nothing but a busy signal, come over and see how you're doing?"

Terry rolled the scotch around and swallowed. The tension seeped out of him. "You shouldn't be here." Terry looked at his watch. "It's eleven o'clock. Go home. Go to Rich's."

Sarah held the wine up to the light and rolled it in her glass. She talked in her normal voice. "This is good. What year is this? He invited me to stay with him tonight. I told him I wouldn't do it even with Diversity out of the house. He said that Joan's boyfriend stays when she has Diversity with her. So, Diversity was used to those types of arrangements."

"And what did you say." Terry yawned. It had been a long day.

"That's when I told him about us."

Terry's eyes widened. His eyebrows shot up. "Terrific! What exactly did you say?"

"I told him that you and I went to my place last night and fucked like wild Indians."

He exhaled a long suspiration of air. "Terrific! What did he say?"

"At first he didn't say anything. He seemed to sink into the couch and got that hunted look in his eyes. Then he told me that you and I weren't responsible for what we did, we're victims of our middle class-repressed-sex upbringing. If we were amenable, he said you and he could share me."

Fingers drumming on knees, he said, "Terrific. What did you say?"

Sarah swallowed her wine. A glimmer of a smile played around her lips. "Well, I told him that fucking like wild Indians wasn't exactly what the middle class did. Then I told him I would think about it. But I didn't think that you would be modern enough to break free of your bourgeois standards. So, it's going to be your fault if we don't have a *menage a trois*."

The warm glow of the liquor suffused his body. He smiled for the first time today. Throwing his head back and slapping his knees, he laughed. "Terrific!"

A hand lingered on his inner thigh. Then a second hand moved up the other thigh and pushed his legs apart. Terry opened his eyes. Sarah, on her knees in front of him, caressed his thighs and groin. "Just how tired are you, Mr. Terry?" Unexpected energy exploded in him as Sarah's hands moved over him.

She unfastened his belt. "I had so much fun with you last night and this morning." Sliding the zipper down, her hand rested on his groin. "Do you know how hard it is for a professional woman my age to find a real man in this town?" Her soft lips and tongue slid along his stomach as she pulled his underwear past his knees.

* * *

Sarah's urgent hands gripped Terry's arm. She shook him. "Terry, wake up. There are people outside. I think Thornton is one of them."

He sat up. "You're kidding."

She stood and walked to the window, wearing one of Terry's long-sleeved white shirts. Her long, bare legs made quick strides across the room. Peeking through the blinds, she smacked a fist into her thigh. "Damn. I wish I were kidding. I heard several car doors slamming about fifteen minutes ago. They seem to have taken up station outside your house. One of them has a TV camera."

Throwing off the covers, he slid on his underwear and walked toward the bathroom, yawning and stretching. "Let's put some coffee on and think about this."

Sarah grabbed her panty hose off the floor and draped them over a chair. Her pink shell and sweater, bra, and skirt lay on the chair. "Shit, why didn't I change clothes last night before I came over here."

"Ella has a lot of jeans in her room. Help yourself," Terry said. He walked out of the bathroom and reached for his pants. "I can't for the life of me think of what they could be doing out there for… oops…

the phone is still off the hook. I bet they've called and can't get an answer."

* * *

Steam rose from the coffee mugs. Terry tasted his and blew across the top of the cup.

Sarah placed her cup on the table.

He reached across the table and patted Sarah's hand. "I'm sorry you're going to be dragged into this."

She held her cup with both hands. "I don't need a lecture. I'm a grown woman, not a victim. You didn't seem to mind last night."

A blur, a hummingbird feeding at the window, caught his attention. "Ella and I put that feeder up years ago. It's time I started thinking about taking it down for the winter. They need to go further south. It gets too cold for them here. I'll get Alex to help me." He yawned and took one more sip of coffee. "I can't stay here the rest of my life."

Terry, in a NGSC sweat shirt, walked out the front door and down the driveway. Three other reporters stood beside Thornton. A dark haired-woman held a microphone. She was followed by a cameraman. The camera had a big 5 on the side of it. "It's too early in the morning. Don't you guys have a union? What the hell are you doing here? Surely, there are more important things to cover?"

The three reporters laughed.

Terry ignored Thorn, who did not smile. The man holding the camera aimed it at him.

One reporter with red hair and freckles caught Terry's eye. "Do you have any comment on what the governor said about you yesterday?"

He stooped and picked up his newspaper. "So, that's why you're here. I haven't been watching TV or reading the papers. What did Billy Bob say?"

The red head looked at his writing pad and read: "They should review the tenure stipulations for leftist teachers like you. If you don't love the country then what are you doing here?"

"Governor Billy Bob said I was a leftist? Look, guys, this is all a mistake. I didn't say the World War II generation was bad. My father was in World War II and so were most of my uncles. I have the deepest respect for those guys. If I've offended anyone, I apologize."

The woman reporter spoke into the microphone as she addressed Terry. "We have an English Professor, Dr. Ralph Jefferson, who says you said that very thing at a dinner with him the night before. Actually, he supported what you had to say. Dr. Jefferson said that it was about time we talked about our oppressive, militaristic policies of the past. He wrote an editorial. It's in your local paper and the Atlanta paper this morning. Would you like to comment on that?"

He scratched his head. "What? Look, I don't know what Dr. Jefferson said, but I don't remember saying anything like that."

The last reporter, a stocky man of medium height, pointed stubby fingers at Terry. "So, you're saying that an English Professor, who supports you, is lying?"

Terry tucked the paper under his arm and turned toward his house. "I need to go read Jefferson's column. I think we're making a mountain out of a molehill. Once again, I apologize if what I said has been misinterpreted or misconstrued. I can't make it any clearer than that."

The reporters followed him. The female reporter stuck the microphone in his face. "What about your daughter and Abu Ghraib, Dr. Malloy? Why is she under investigation?"

The woman's green eyes reminded him of Ella's. Don't react angrily. That was what they were looking for. "Did you know that you have pretty eyes. Has anyone ever told you that?" The woman smiled, caught off guard by the question. "I think any routine investigation by you guys will expose that story for what it is, a piece of shoddy journalism that should not have happened. Eventually the facts will be told."

The reporters moved up the driveway, following him. "I'll have to ask you to stay off my property. Remember, I'm a Vietnam vet, I may go berserk and shoot someone." The reporters backed up. He laughed and shook his head.

"Dr. Malloy, did you know that a leading left-wing blog, The Daily Rant, has called you a hero for speaking out!" Thorn shouted. "Other blogs are saying you were right to accuse the Greatest Generation of mass murder. They say you are a new beacon of hope."

Terry threw his hands in a questioning gesture and laughed. "This is a hoot. I went from a pariah who was a war monger to anti-establishment hero in one day? I'm a hero of the left? Don't you guys understand how everyone is being jerked around. There's no civil discourse any more. Everyone is taking sides and it's all a game of gotcha."

The reporter with the pudgy fingers yelled, "Was your daughter in any of the photos? There's rumors that there are photos of her at the prison."

* * *

Distant crumps of explosions and rolling thunderous booms of bombs indicated the ongoing battle they had gratefully left that morning. Three separate flights of jets passed over, making a run on the bunkers and enemy troops dug into Hill 1036.

The men all would rather be doing what they were doing than be absorbed into the blind, impersonal maelstrom of the ongoing battle for the Hill. No one wanted to crawl and claw up the steep sides of the mountain, which had been turned to mush by the monsoon rains; however, the alternative of scrabbling up the side of another mountain and attacking entrenched troops in bunkers was much worse.

Walking on flat ground was hard enough, as wet as it was. Going up the steep ridge, the men took one step and slid back two. Mud and dead vegetable matter clung to the soles of their boots, making traction difficult. It felt like ice skating backward downhill.

The ninety some-odd pounds they carried in their rucksacks constantly pulled them backward. The squad members leaned forward into the slope of the ridge to balance themselves between the pull of gravity and their own upward momentum. Grabbing a branch or vine was an act of faith. Terry glimpsed the vine in Brumsen's hand as Brumsen careened out of the foliage into him. They flew through the air like bowling pins, then fell and slid five yards farther down the incline in a tumbled tangle of vines, leaves, and mud.

The rest of the squad slid carefully back down the hill to where Brumsen and Terry straightened out their gear. Terry wore one belt of M-60 ammunition strapped around him. He looked forlornly at the mud-covered shells.

"Fuck 'em," Anderson whispered. "We have enough ammo to kill an infantry regiment. Toss 'em."

Terry and Brumsen brushed vines and leaves off their fatigues. They wiped mud from their pants, then wiped their muddy hands on their fatigue jackets. Eventually, the never-ending rain would wash the fatigues clean.

Reaching into a pocket, Cochise brought out insect repellent. "Hold still, Brumsen." He sprayed insect repellent on a leach. The three-inch sucker withdrew from Brumsen's neck, leaving a trail of blood. Cochise slapped the slimy monster off and crushed it with his boot.

"Both of you guys slid through the mud assholes over elbows," Duffy whispered. He looked at Anderson. "Do they have time to check for leeches?"

"We can do it later." Anderson jerked his head toward the dull sound of explosions coming from farther up the valley. "We need to find that Lurp team as fast as possible."

"What are you doing, Malloy?" Duffy whispered.

"Checkin' for broken bones."

Anderson smiled. "Ain't nothin' broken, you peckerheaded hill-billy."

Terry grinned. "I can always hope, can't I?"

Everyone chuckled. Anderson held up his hand for silence. He motioned the squad to gather around him. "Remember, we need to maintain noise discipline once we reach the top of the ridge. If Charlie or the NVA had heard us, we'd be dead now. Let's consider ourselves lucky and tighten up. Cochise, take the point."

Thirty minutes later, the squad emerged from the foliage atop the ridge. Faces drawn and tight, the men squatted at the edge of the jungle, listening to the rain. The saddle of the crest covered an expanse of approximately two-hundred yards. Once they cleared the ridge with its rocky outcroppings and waist-high grass, the vegetation would begin again.

While they crossed the ridge, the thin foliage offered a brief respite from the jungle. They pushed into the green fog. The deluge abruptly stopped. The sun appeared. Terry knew the cessation of rain would help the jets and choppers delivering their payloads; nevertheless, the lack of rain was no comfort to the men.

Steam rose from the jungle floor. A palpable heat weighed upon the men. Terry struggled through the steaming jungle air and vegetation. His shoulder straps cut into him, the dull pain and soreness gnawing. The dank, moist cauldron of the jungle boiled the air, searing Terry's lungs with every intake of breath. Rivulets of sweat ran down his face, armpits, and body. Rain-soaked jungle fatigues dried and grew damp again within thirty minutes.

The group endured silently. The only response to a complaint would have been, "Tough shit, drive on." The men experienced nothing that the rest had not. The silent bond of common suffering and shared hardship molded them into a cohesive unit, depending upon and trusting each other for the survival of the group. They moved with caution and patient effort, choosing the path of least resistance against the tentacled, grasping jungle. Monkeys, sailing from one limb to the next, screeched at them while bright birds trilled messages to one another.

Going down the mountain, the men slid through the slick mud and vegetable goo of the jungle floor. The urgency of reaching the Long Range Recon Patrol pressed upon them. No one wanted to fall or slip and make a noise. The tension between the necessity of completing their task and maintaining cautious awareness weighed upon all of them. One mistake could mean their death, a fact that floated in and out of their consciousness with every step they took.

"Remember, guys," Anderson had said, "we need to hurry slowly."

Terry inched down the trail. The jungle rot on his feet, which had developed with the rainy season, made every footfall painful. He winced as he put his weight on his front foot and pushed into the ooze of the jungle floor. His foot, mired in the mud, made a soft, sucking sound as he pulled it out again. He slid forward, balancing his weight as well as he could, pushing one foot and then the other into the ooze, descending into the fungal, vegetable muck. The rain started again. The rolling thunder of bombs striking Hill 1036 grew faint.

The rain had been constant, with occasional bursts of sunshine to heat things up to unbearable. The jungle shredded the men's tattered fatigues as they walked. Jungle rot gnawed at their feet. They had taken their boots off twice in two weeks. Terry's feet looked like wrinkled prunes. The skin peeled off in layers, the last time he took off his socks. The flesh of his bleeding feet peeled away with the tattered socks. The pain had been excruciating. It was the last time he wore socks. The combined smell of his feet and body was nauseating. It would not take the equivalent of a North Vietnamese Daniel Boone to find them. He had broached this fact to the squad.

"Don't worry," Brumsen said. "Those guys are just as miserable and smelly as we are. Actually, we smell like the jungle. We blend in very nicely with this dump."

The foliage increased as they descended into the valley. Anderson said they would head right for the high-speed trail, which, he assumed, ran all the way down the valley floor. The trail, a road built right through the jungle, was used to move troops, trucks, and other types of equipment that the small trails could not accommodate. The incredible amount of activity in the area was the sole reason for the trail. It would not be visible from the air, because of the thickness of the jungle and also because the North Vietnamese made every effort to conceal it by placing a canopy of jungle vines, branches, and growth over it.

"In other words," Anderson said, "it's a tunnel right through the middle of the jungle."

Terry followed Brumsen silently down the mountainside through the layers of vegetation. No foothold was secure. The enemy was close. Shoulders tense, he inched forward.

A week before, Cochise told Anderson that he wanted to pull point all the time. Terry assumed the job of the rear guard. He carried extra ammunition for Brumsen. In addition to his duty of counting, he was the assistant machine-gunner.

Anderson did not argue with Cochise. He simply nodded, and that had been that. They all felt better and more confident with Cochise doing point duty. Terry was the logical choice to be a "tail-end Charlie." He guarded against anyone following the squad by occasionally stopping and waiting thirty seconds.

The squad progressed down the mountain slope, slow and deliberate. Pushing away the frond in front of him, Brumsen held his arm up for Terry to stop. His huge brown finger went to his lips.

Terry, immobile, grew attentive. The soft patter of the rain, of which he had not been aware, were explosions beating against his floppy hat. The water created multiple sounds, cascading through the green umbrella of the jungle. Birds called and whistled to one another. His heart pounded against his chest. He licked his dry lips and attempted to swallow.

Faintly, ever so faintly, he heard a series of whacks. As Brumsen and Terry both lowered themselves to their haunches, Terry heard the high-pitched, sharp, staccato sounds of Vietnamese drifting through the jungle. A voice was saying, *"Den day,"* or something like it. Then, *"Den do di,"* floated around the leaves. A conversation ensued with indistinguishable words. Closer, so close.

Two voices? Twelve? A dull, thumping sound of something hitting something penetrated the silence. Terry wrinkled his brow. He'd heard the sound before. They were chopping wood. Chopping wood, just like the squad did.

Anderson came into view below Brumsen. Crows feet around the tense eyes very pronounced, Anderson made quick gestures for him and Brumsen to follow him.

Did his fear show?

The squad traveled at a right angle to the direction it had been going. Instead of down the slope, the men went along the side of the mountain, away from the voices, parallel to the valley floor. No one made a sound. The conversation and cutting floated up to them. They had gone about two hundred yards when he found the squad crouching, facing down the mountainside. The voices could no longer be heard.

Anderson gestured forward, along the side of the mountain parallel to the jungle floor in the same direction they had been moving. He held his finger to his lips. The first priority was to find the ambushed men and to avoid all contact with the enemy until this was done. After traveling sideways along the mountain for another two hundred yards, the squad stopped again.

Duffy wiped his forehead with his jungle hat and smiled at Terry. His calm, youthful demeanor hid behind a mohawk haircut and camouflage paint. He had painted a scowl with the green and black paint. His bright red eyebrows and red mohawk were as red as the red line of paint stretching across both sides of his face to his ears.

They all looked ferocious with their war paint and mohawks. Terry's heart stopped pounding. After he heard the voices, his feet stopped hurting. Now the insistent pain of his feet gnawed at him once again. Strained eyes staring out from his floppy hat, Brumsen raised a hand to his chest and patted it. Terry smiled, and nodded, as did Duffy. A crease of a smile lingered on Anderson's gaunt face. Cochise, standing, looked down the mountain, staring into the jungle.

Pulling out his map, Anderson laid it on the ground and motioned for everyone to circle around him. Water beaded on the map's plastic cover. A red line marked the center of the valley, indicating the location of the high-speed trail. An 'X' on the map indicated where the Lurp squad had been dropped. Spreading out from the 'X' was a circle for the estimated distance the Lurp team could have traveled.

The lost squad had found the speed trail. Then members of the squad tried to radio in their coordinates while under attack. Anderson narrowed his search within the circle, not more than thirty to sixty yards from the trail. Laying a compass on the map, he studied both. He pointed to the map with his pencil a little to the south of the red line indicating the trail. "Thirty minutes."

Once again, the rain let up. Cochise vanished down the mountainside. At the trail, Anderson knelt down on one knee next to Cochise and motioned for the rest to come forward. An eight-foot swath sliced through the jungle. The trail ran as far as Terry could see in both directions. Boughs from both sides arched over and concealed it.

Ruts lined the trail. Its relatively clean sides indicated that it must be tended often to keep it precise. With the triple-canopy jungle surrounding them, including the tall teak trees that kept the aircraft from coming lower, the trail was invisible from the air. The rain started again.

The little group moved closer together. In the stillness of the jungle, the drip and patter of rain flowed down through the jungle canopy. Anderson, with a sigh, stood and walked back fifteen yards from the trail. He took out his map. Anderson and Cochise studied their compasses. The direction agreed upon, Cochise led the way.

This part Terry dreaded. Please no dead Americans. Shoving against the tide of vegetation, he pushed the thoughts of the recon unit out of his mind and concentrated on the present. There was nothing he could do for the them. His heart beat faster. Even with all of the rain, his mouth was dry. The plan was to go a certain measured distance along the trail and then go deeper into the jungle and come back in the opposite direction. In this way, Anderson felt they would eventually find the squad within the boundaries he had prescribed.

Thirty minutes. Forty-five minutes. Brumsen crouched. Terry did, also. From the direction of the trail, came Vietnamese voices. They grew louder. The Vietnamese were talking casually and seemed to be in no particular hurry. Terry could be no more than thirty to forty feet from them. They must be on the speed trail.

A voice penetrated the silence. *"Lam viec do sau nay cung duoc."*

Then another, *"Tao se nhanh len."* This voice was closer than the first.

The first voice, *"Nhanh len!"*

Terry sensed someone in the jungle to his left. A voice that sounded like a pistol shot exploded with exasperation. *"Dung co lo!"*

The man who spoke could be no more than five feet from them. Grunting sounded. He was taking a shit! Terry reached for his bayonet strapped to his calf. He gently drew it out of its scabbard. Brumsen watched Terry, not moving. Terry's white knuckles gripped the bayonet handle.

The Vietnamese grunted and stood. A jet thundered overhead, then another. The Vietnamese muttered, *"Do ma may!"* The voice was going away from Terry toward the trail. Someone laughed and said, *"Do ngu!"*

Terry released his breath. He slowly breathed in air and relaxed his grip on the bayonet. His body limp, he nodded to Brumsen, who turned and signaled to Duffy and Anderson. Brumsen looked back at Terry with a thumbs up and stepped into the jungle.

The small group of soldiers traveled silently and quickly for an hour. Then they turned at a right angle away from the trail. This was where they'd start back. The rain, which had stopped, began again. Rather than fifteen yards, they were now about fifty yards from the trail. Terry felt safer. Too much traffic!

As the men continued their travel back in the direction they had come, Terry counted the time in raindrops. The incessant drum beat of the water, the repetitive sameness of the rain dripping from the constant, endless supply of plants, leaves, and trees, numbed his senses.

The natural loam and fungal smells of the jungle, permeated with the sweet stink of rotting plants, changed. A dank overlay of putrescence crowded out the normal vegetative smells. Brumsen stuck his hand in the air for Terry to stop. They sidled off away from the trail and at a slight angle from the direction they had been going. The rotten odor grew stronger. A loud buzzing increased in volume. Terry came upon the backs of the men in the squad. He walked around Duffy and saw why they had stopped.

They had found the recon team.

CHAPTER ELEVEN

Terry threw the paper down on the kitchen table.

"Alex's other grandmother, Peggy, just called." Sarah stood by the phone. "The phone started ringing as soon as I put it back on the receiver. George has been throwing up all night and wants you to take Alex camping."

"That's the Universal Psychobabble Victimology Bullshit Camp, isn't it? The one they were talking about the other night." He rolled his eyes and put his head in his hands. "Rich and Thorn will be there. Exactly what I need, to go camping with a bunch of loons."

"You'll be going with your grandson. Plus, it might do you good to get away from all this." Sarah poured them more coffee.

Terry pointed toward the paper. "Jefferson has a column in there and in the Atlanta paper supporting me and my criticizing of the Greatest Generation. Read it for me while I call George and Peggy back."

* * *

..."And so, as Professor Malloy said, 'it's time we stopped worshiping that generation of mass murderers who killed so many innocent German and Japanese civilians.'"

He blew out a gust of air, shaking his head. "My father is turning over in his grave right now."

"You're my hero. I think you've started a neo-left movement composed of those people who don't want to worship at the shrine of World War II."

Smiling, he cocked his head to one side and cut his blue eyes at her. "Don't start with me. I told George that I would pick up Alex around 11:30. You, I, and he are going to lunch. Then I'm heading to the camp with Alex. But first, come over here and sit on my lap."

* * *

Alex held his glass with two hands, sipping his soft drink quickly through the straw. His large green eyes wide with wonder at the hubbub of the restaurant. "Diversity told me that you have to have a lantern of some kind. It gets dark. We can't see in our tent if we don't have a lantern."

Terry looked at his watch. Sarah came through the entrance and he waved at her. "Don't worry. Grandpa George gave me everything I need to camp this weekend."

Sitting in the booth next to Alex, Sarah hugged him. Her arm stayed around his shoulder. "You're having a rough time, aren't you? One grandmother is out of the country and then one of your grandfathers gets sick. So, are you guys ready for camping?"

Alex, snuggling under Sarah's shoulder, smiled and nodded. His brown curls fell across his forehead, shading his green eyes for an instant. He pushed his hair back from his face. "Yes ma'am. My grandpa George is sick. He's a good camper."

"What about Grandpa Terry? Isn't he a good camper?"

"Grandpa Terry doesn't like to camp out."

Terry's forehead furrowed. He drew his eyebrows down in mock consternation. "Now wait a minute. I'm being accused unjustly. Your Grandpa George was always willing to take you out. It's true that I'm not fond of camping, but I would have taken you if Grandpa George had not been so willing."

She questioned Terry with her eyes. "How come you don't like to camp? Vietnam?"

Terry, sipping his coffee, nodded. "But you know what, Alex. I come from an old line of squirrel barkers. I can assure you that we knew how to hunt and camp out."

Sarah's and Alex's eyes were question marks.

"Don't tell me that you guys don't know about barking squirrels."

They shook their heads.

"Well, it all started with my great-grandfather. At least that's who I heard it from. He told me he used to bark squirrels."

The waitress came over and they ordered.

"What's that mean, Grandpa?"

"Your great-great-great-grandfather, Jesse Malloy, I think he was born around 1861, when he was a boy, hunted squirrels with a very big rifle. It was called a musket. It shot a big shell called a musket ball."

Terry rubbed his chin, musing to himself. "I think it was fifty-eight caliber. Well anyway, if he hit the squirrel with the musket ball, it blew the squirrel to pieces. So, he shot at the branch below the squirrel. Pieces of the branch, bark and all, flew up and knocked the squirrel out of the tree. That's how you bark squirrels."

Alex's green eyes widened. "What happened when the squirrel hit the ground?"

"Good question, Alex." Sarah drank from her water glass. "That's what I want to know. What happened when the squirrel hit the ground?"

Terry unfolded his napkin and placed it on his lap. "Well, see, there's more to barking squirrels than just knocking them out of a tree with a well-aimed shot. You also need a good barked-squirrel bagger. It doesn't matter how well you shoot if your bagger's no good."

Shaking her blond hair to and fro, Sarah laughed. "Okay, Alex, it's my turn. What's a bagger?"

Terry shrugged. "It's the guy who held the bag of course. You can't let the squirrel hit the ground 'cause he might be conscious and take off. So, the bag man..." Terry moved his arms resting on the table to allow the waitress to set his food down. "So, the bag man had to be ready to catch the squirrel. Now this is not as easy as it seems. You have to remember that the squirrel is jumping around in that tree. The shooter is following him with his rifle. The bagger is running around on the ground following the squirrel from one branch to another." He paused to spread mustard on his hamburger. "That Jesse was really good at barking, the best barker in all of Gibson County, Tennessee. His brother, Buck, was the best bagger in Gibson, Crockett, and Malloy Counties. You have to remember that once you bark the squirrel, he doesn't just drop straight down.

"Jesse could bark 'em fifty, sixty feet up. That's a lot of branches to hit on the way down. So, the bagger really didn't know which way the barked squirrel was going to bounce.

"One time, Papa Jesse told me he barked one about sixty feet up. That squirrel started ricocheting from limb to limb on the way down. Buck was running around the tree with his bag. Now Buck had a natural instinct for barked, bouncing squirrels. When the squirrel was about half-way down, he ran around to the other side of the tree. Sure 'nough, the squirrel bounced and ricocheted from one limb to the other and wound up falling right into Buck's bag. Papa Jesse said it was the best job of readin'and baggin' a barked, bouncing squirrel he'd ever seen."

Sarah, her blue eyes smiling over her napkin, took Alex's hand. "What do you think, Alex? I think your grandfather knows how to camp. Anyone who comes from a family with a long tradition of squirrel barking and bagging has to know a lot about camping."

Wolfing down the last of his french fries, Alex wiped ketchup from his mouth.

"I wish Papa could have met you, Alex. He hunted with us until he was ninety or ninety-one. He couldn't walk very well, so he only hunted doves. Still, he was a pretty good shot at ninety. Your great-great-grandfather, we called him Grandpa Terrence, told me some stories about hunting wild boar with Papa when he was a boy about your age."

"What's a wild boar?" Alex reached for the apple pie.

"Boars are wild pigs that live in the woods. They have big teeth called tusks. There was one boar, called 'Old Snort,' who terrorized livestock and destroyed crops for miles around. If all the stories about him were true, Snort had been shot by every farmer in Gibson and Crockett County. One day, when Granddad was about your age, he and Papa found a newborn calf that had been killed and half eaten. There were wild pig tracks around the calf. Your great-great-grandad went to fetch his papa's rifle and the two of them followed the boar tracks into the woods. Grandad could hear some pigs rooting in a thicket. He stood behind Papa, who had just shouldered his rifle, when Old Snort barreled out of the thicket, snorting and squealing, running right at them. That big old boar was no more than fifty feet from them and running faster than greased lightning. The boar looked like a small tornado heading straight for Papa and Grandpa Terrence. Fire shot from his nostrils. His bloody tusks looked like they were two feet long. Sparks and dirt swirled around his feet. He was a blur coming down the trail. Remember that Papa only had one shot. Grandad said everything happened at once. Papa fired. The boar tumbled end over end, tusks over tail, and fell dead at their feet. Calf's blood still dripped from his tusks. Steam and smoke rose from Snort's nose for ten minutes after he died."

Alex sat with his mouth open, apple pie dripping from it. "Wow. What do you think Papa was thinking? Was he scared?"

"Granddad said he stood paralyzed for about ten minutes, rooted to the ground." Terry closed Alex's mouth. "I can't remember about Papa, but as a father, he was probably more worried about protecting his son than he was about getting hurt. When crunch time comes, a man worries about defending his family, before he worries about himself. You'll understand when you're a father and I'm an old great-granddad."

They walked out of the restaurant with Sarah's hand tussling Alex's hair. She stooped and kissed him on the cheek. He hugged her. "Have a good time with your grandfather."

Sarah kissed Terry. "I have to go to a charity concert this week. I want you to go with me. We also have another teach-in when you get back."

"You have a date for the concert. But, I'm through with teach-ins."

His cell phone rang while he shut the door. It was George, Alex's other grandfather. "Terry, you left a knife that you were supposed to take. If you haven't left town yet, you can stop by here and pick it up."

"Thanks George, but my house is closer. I've got a couple of knives there."

As he stepped up the walkway to the front porch, a movement caught Terry's eye. He gripped Alex's shoulder. Duffy knelt over the body of an American soldier. He pulled the dogtags from the man. The soldier's left arm was missing and the left side of his blackened face had no jaw. The white bone of the missing arm contrasted with the dark ground blackened further with the soldier's blood.

Terry left Alex watching TV while he went to the attic to look for a knife.

* * *

Some of the dead men were lying in grotesque poses of rigor. The man closest to the silent group lay on his back. His hand rested in a small, water-filled hole. The face and head had been punctured and torn by fragments from an explosive device, probably a grenade. An insect flew into the hole where the man's nose should have been. An M-16 lay under him.

Terry imagined the grenade floating softly and quickly through the air. The soldier, lying on the ground, fired blindly into the jungle, not knowing where or at whom he was shooting. He never saw the grenade as the deadly arc of its trajectory drew it through the fronds and leaves, ever closer to the unsuspecting soldier. He may have noticed some movement as the grenade plopped softly on the ground, its fuse hissing. The frightened soldier fired his weapon. The din of the gunfire would have hidden all sound. Hopfully, the explosion had killed him instantly.

Moving in a crouch to the dead man, Anderson grabbed the dog tags around his neck and yanked. The chain holding the tags broke. A blanket of insects billowed into the air with the sudden movement of the dead man's body. He held up the tags and chain and moved them in a circle. The meaning was clear. The men groped through the pestilential swarm to remove the dog tags from the dead.

Waving away bugs from his face, Terry stood over a man who lay face down with one arm underneath him. He rolled the soldier over, reached for the dog tags, quickly jerking his hand back. The soldier's lower jaw had been shot away. A centipede, eight inches in length, curled upon the soldier's uncaring face. Revulsed, Terry tore the dog tags from the man's throat. He took the tags from another man, whose leg and arm bones pierced the skin and jutted out at angles from the body.

The bloody rags of the dead soldiers' uniforms hummed and moved, alive with black pests hovering and crawling over them, disturbed by the passage of living men through their feast. Terry finished, and still in a crouch, stepped over to the group that had congregated around three bodies. These men were centered behind and separated from the solid line of dead men whose positions defined a semicircle of defense.

Everyone stood silently. Anderson, jaw clenched, stared at the three bodies. His cold gray eyes were narrow slits with worry lines stretching back into his hairline. The men's hands had been tied behind their backs. Each had wounds in his arms or legs. Each also had been shot in the head. Black blood pooled at their heads where bugs darted to and fro. A few vermin rested in the pools of blood. Anderson took the tags from each man. Buzzing insects and the patter of the rain were the only sounds.

Anderson motioned to Cochise to take the point. The rain beat incessantly upon all of them in torrents.

As they hurried from the scene of carnage, Terry pictured the three dead men fighting with their squad until all the rest were dead. Maybe the three of them had been knocked unconscious by explosions. Maybe they had passed out from loss of blood. Perhaps they had simply run out of ammunition. He pictured the North Vietnamese troops walking among the members of the squad. There might have been a groan from one of them, a movement by another. Perhaps another just surrendered. An NVA noncom must have ordered his troops to tie up the Americans that were alive and drag them to the center of the ambush sight. Were the Americans conscious when the NVA soldiers dragged them? Did they scream out in pain?

Making sure that the dead men and the men alive had been searched for all available documents, had the NVA noncom looked at the wounded men and decided that they should die? Were their deaths a given, and no decision necessary? Were the men killed one by one? What did the last two feel as they realized that they were going to be shot? What did the last one think as the rifle barrel swung silently toward him?

Images of the dead squad and the three executed men overwhelmed Terry. His heart, beating fast, wanted to explode from his chest. Heat radiated from his face and chest. A sinking sensation gripped his stomach. Okay, he was afraid, but also furious. He lost track of time and how long they had been hurrying away from the slaughter. You have to give yourself up. You're going to die. Take as many with you as you can. No mercy, no surrender.

Stepping around a teak tree, he came upon the squad huddled together and squatting. Brumsen, who had arrived just before he did, still settled on his haunches, steadying himself with his M-60. Anderson studied his map, keeping it balanced on one knee while holding the radio receiver with the other hand. Cochise, who had a map and a compass also, examined both. Duffy knelt beside Anderson, who talked quietly into the receiver, telling battalion HQ that the recon team had been found.

"It's too dangerous to be picked up on this side of the ridge, Sir. The helicopter would have to hover at least a hundred feet above the ground. There are gooks all over the place. We'll walk out and join the battalion tomorrow." After listening to the radio for several seconds, Anderson added a final, "Yes, Sir."

Terry's watch read four o'clock.

"How many claymores do you guys have?" Anderson whispered.

Each man held up two fingers, except for Brumsen, who held up one. Brumsen carried extra ammunition for his machine gun and was not expected to carry other extra equipment. Terry was surprised that he had the one mine.

"We're going to get some of these bastards. It's payback time."

Faces grim, eyes hard, they nodded in unison. Duffy ran his fingers through his mohawk. He wiped away the incessant, ever-present water from his painted face. Anderson and Cochise, holding compasses, studied their respective maps.

"A compass heading of zero-three-zero ought to do it," Anderson said. "That should take us to where we heard the guys working on the bunkers. We'll get a little closer to the bunker complex and wait for them to leave."

Perusing his compass, Cochise set off through the jungle. The men walked silently for an hour. When they finally stopped, Anderson held up both hands with his fingers spread, indicating ten. They were ten minutes from the complex. Anderson patted Cochise on the shoulder and indicated a direction to move. He spread both palms outward, telling the remaining three that he wanted them to stay where they were.

The three squatted and formed a defensive triangle facing outward. Terry concentrated on the jungle to his immediate front. Minutes passed. The three of them said not a word. Then Terry felt rather than heard someone coming through the foliage. Cochise motioned for them to follow him.

The four moved silently and quickly to Anderson. He drew a circle in the air with his hands. The squad formed a defensive circle, each man kneeling or lying down, facing outward. Terry's watch said 6:15. The squad took their claymores, in carrying pouches, out of their rucksacks. With Anderson leading, they walked in a crouch no more than a hundred yards. Terry stood at the edge of what appeared to be a small clearing.

Could the squad hear his heartbeat? He tried to swallow. His mouth was dry. Taking a deep breath, he squatted and surveyed the scene in front of him. The squad faced the up slope of what apparently would be the killing zone for one of the bunkers in the complex. The zone was actually a cone-shaped area with the bunker at the apex. Tree stumps, cut low and jutting from the ground, dotted the area. Bushes and shrubs formed a random pattern. Terry's gaze roamed across the killing zone to the bunker at the apex. Only the sides of the bunker were complete, with several logs stacked on each side of a large hole in the ground. Dirt that no doubt came from the hole covered the outside of the logs. To the left of the bunker, another bunker stood partially hidden, partially finished. Another killing zone fanned out from that bunker and interlocked with the zone in front of them.

Anderson examined the ground at the edge of the clearing. "These guys are wearing boots, so keep yours on." He slipped into the clearing, the rest of the squad following him.

They hustled to the first bunker and studied the clearing, looking back down the hill. The men stood at the apex of the killing zone. From here, the Vietnamese in the bunker could lay down deadly fire in a fan-shaped pattern. A path entered the jungle ten feet to the left of where they had been standing when they first saw the bunker.

Behind the bunker stood a hootch about six feet high, composed of a flat, thatched floor three feet off of the ground, an angled roof, and four supporting poles. There were no sides. Brumsen reached underneath the floor, removing a shovel from the shadows. Several more implements remained there as well. A bag of rice, weighing at least a hundred pounds, lay on the floor of the hootch. No one spoke.

After several seconds of silence, Anderson motioned Terry to follow and walked back down the length of the clearing, no more than fifteen yards. He pointed to two trees, ten feet apart, at the spot where they had come upon the fire zone and close to the footpath. Indicating a spot five feet off the ground, he pointed to both trees.

Taping a claymore to the first tree, Terry inserted the blasting cap with the detonator wire attached. Then he went to the second tree, repeating the process. He backed away and surveyed his work. The mines were hidden by overhanging branches. He returned to the squad.

Kneeling in the bunker, Cochise prepared a grenade booby trap. He held a pointed stake a foot and a half long and one inch in diameter. Finished taping a grenade to the dull end of the stake, he inserted the stake into the mud floor of the bunker as close to the corner as he could manage. Duffy's head poked occasionally out of the next bunker. After the stick had been secured in the dirt, Cochise picked up a second of the same height and forced it into the corner opposite the grenade. He shoved the stick into the ground easily. At least the rain'd done some good and softened the ground.

Cochise attached a wire to the second stick and strung it across the bunker, slipping it through the O-ring of the grenade. Pulling the O-ring attached to the cotter pin, he slowly drew the cotter pin from the grenade. The cotter pin held the handle on the grenade. When the cotter pin was pulled, the handle would come off and light the fuse. The fuse lasted four to six seconds. Terry held his breath while Cochise slid the cotter pin as far out as he dared. Tying the wire as taught as possible, Cochise cautiously placed small fronds over the two stakes. He carefully climbed out of the bunker, smiled at Terry, and gave him a thumbs up.

Down the hill from Cochise's bunker, Duffy finished his task. From the cone's apex, Duffy's bunker lay about twenty-five feet to the right and slightly lower than Cochise's. To the left of the original bunker, and outside of the cone of fire, an implacable, green wall of vegetation stood sentinel.

Anderson walked from the jungle on the left, carrying fronds. He waved Cochise and Terry over to him. "See if Duffy needs help," Anderson said to Cochise. He gave fronds to Terry and pointed to where the squad had come out of the jungle. "Spread them out to cover our tracks. It doesn't have to be perfect. There won't be a lot of light when they get here tomorrow."

Ten minutes elapsed from the time Anderson had taken Terry to set up his claymores. Terry laid out his fronds and joined the men at the jungle's edge. The men entered the vegetation. Brumsen appeared, sitting down with his machine gun across his lap. Placed in a row beside him were six detonators, wired to six mines strung out somewhere near the bunker complex. Darkness settled over the jungle like a funeral shroud.

Anderson placed two sticks in the ground and whispered, "Bunker and hootch." He pushed in six small sticks all in a row. Four of the sticks were to the left of the bunker stick and below it. Two of them were to the right and slightly above the bunker stick even with the hootch. "Claymores." Anderson placed two more sticks at right angles to the six claymore sticks, creating a reverse L. These were the two that Terry had wired. "We blow the claymores after the grenades explode that I booby-trapped in the tools. We blow these six first. Malloy and Duffy blow their two claymores asap after ours. Then, we shoot whoever is standing or whoever is alive. I really don't think anyone will be left, but we'll see. More than likely, the bastards that are left will jump into the bunkers." He looked at Duffy and Cochise and smiled. "Are the bunkers ready?" They barely moved their heads.

The squad sat for several seconds, lost in thought. Cochise's floppy hat rested on his head at a rakish angle. He knelt on one knee, leaning on his rifle. His knife, resting in its scabbard, protruded from his collar. The small group gazed reflectively at the sticks, wiping at the rain plopping softly on their heads.

With a stroke of his hand, Anderson swept the upright stakes aside. "Tomorrow, we pay a little back."

CHAPTER TWELVE

"Okay, Alex, hold the rod steady and let me guide it through this loop. There you go. Good job."

The tent was beginning to take shape. They had carried it from the car to the campground. The camp coordinator told them where to place it. A gust of wind blew the tent over Alex's head. He peeled it away from his face.

A small voice behind them shouted, "Alex, hey, Alex!" Both Rich and Diversity wore bright yellow t-shirts. The t-shirts had 'Victim Empowerment' printed across the chest. Rich carried a bag. Diversity left Rich and ran toward them.

"Hiya, Diversity."

Reaching into the bag as he approached, Rich handed a yellow t-shirt to both of them.

"Alex, Mr. Thornton is going to hike up Spook Mountain." Diversity, breathless from running, paused in her eruption of words to gasp several times. "He says we all have to leave at the same time. He doesn't want any stragglers to follow him up the mountain. If we're going to go, we have to be at the trail in five minutes. You have to wear that t-shirt so you can be seen."

Fixing Terry with a malignant stare, Rich remained silent. He clenched and unclenched his hands, arm muscles tensing.

"Go ahead, Alex, Rich and I can finish setting up the tent."

The two children vanished down the slope.

"It's been a long time since I've been camping, Rich. Give me a hand."

The two men worked in silence for ten minutes. Finally finished, they stepped back and looked at the tent. The tree-covered hills surrounding the site rose up to meet the vast dome of the sky. Birds chirped and whistled to one another. A gentle breeze moved the leaves of the trees, disturbed the tent flaps, and caressed the faces of the two men.

Tugging on his mustache while chewing on his lip, Rich made a sweeping gesture with one hand. "This is a terrific campsite. The woods and trails are truly beautiful. It's even possible to see a deer or two; no game wilder than a deer though. The cats and bears were chased up into the mountains years ago. We really don't have to worry about any big dangers. We teach the kids to be cautious about where they go. We don't want them wandering too far from camp and getting lost. But we're also encouraging them to be bold. It's a fine line. We don't want to instill a victim mentality, but we want them to use common sense."

Terry picked up Alex's back pack and tossed it into the tent. "Doesn't every parent try to instill common sense? It seems like your trying to choreograph things a little too much. You need a little spontaneity, don't you?"

"That's true," Rich said, eyebrows raised. "I guess. But as I was saying, you shouldn't be afraid of the woods. There's really no danger lurking. Just be careful how far you wander."

"Rich, if you have something to say, say it. Stop talking about the fucking woods. Sarah told me that she talked to you last night."

"If you wanted to fuck Sarah, why the hell didn't you say so?"

"It just happened spontaneously." Terry shrugged, extending his hands palms up. "It wasn't planned. We were drinking."

"Right! What I don't understand is why the hell everything has to happen to me?" Rich put his hands in his pockets, scuffing the ground with his shoe. His voice dripped with sarcasm. "Why can't I get lucky sometime? Do you know how hard it is to get twenty-year-olds to go to bed with you?"

"You need to grow up and think about where you live and how you live." Terry threw a sleeping bag into the tent. "You're forty-something and chasing after college girls, for God's sake."

"I just want to know one thing. How long have you two been fucking each other?" Rich said, sneering and yanking on his moustache. "This has been going on since you guys started running together hasn't it? Clarissa found out and that's why she left. Even through losing your daughter, you guys kept it up."

He moved fast, surprising Rich. Grabbing his t-shirt, Terry shook him. His voice was a whisper, almost a hiss. "If you ever mention my daughter again, you sonofabitch, I'll cut your fucking throat."

Eyes wide, Rich backed up, stumbling, prying Terry's hand from his shirt. "You're a little past your prime to be making threats like that, old man." Raising a muscled arm, he glanced at his watch and jerked a thumb over his shoulder toward the community house. "I have to get back. There's going to be a meeting at 2 to discuss our 'empowerment' game. All the dads, you included, are asked to come, if you think you're man enough to play." His arms swung freely from his muscled chest, head cocked slightly upward. "We'll take this up later. Don't think that I'm going to take this shit from you or her."

His receding form disappeared among the tents, which filled a sizeable clearing, inclining downward, toward the community house. The house was the last structure before the woods. The upward slope stopped at the edge of the woods forty yards above Terry. A few men congregated in small groups, shaking hands, renewing acquaintances. Terry threw the other sleeping bag into the tent. He picked up the yellow t-shirt and tossed it into the tent. He needed a drink. Thank God he brought a flask of scotch. As he turned away from the tent, movement in the woods caught his eye. Glancing toward the woods, he saw nothing.

Sitting on a picnic table bench, feeling the warm glow of the whiskey in his belly, Terry acknowledged a few of the silent men in yellow shirts who made eye contact. What in the hell was he doing here? It seemed like a good idea when Sarah talked him into it. Perhaps when these jerk-offs were playing the 'empowerment game,' he could hide in his tent and drink.

A red-haired man to his left tapped him on the arm. Terry had noticed him when he sat down because he was wearing black and green tiger-striped jungle fatigues and jungle boots. "Aren't you the History guy who's been in the papers, the World War II guy?"

Terry bowed his head. Holy shit, he was never going to get away from that crap. He wiped his mouth. There was nothing here that would quench his thirst. "I'm afraid so. Do me a favor and don't talk about it. Do you mind? I just want to be with my grandson and get away from it."

The man extended a hand attached to a muscled arm covered with red hair. "I understand. Listen, I respect you for standing up to the powers, man. I think we're all looking for a little centeredness out here. My name's Herb."

He introduced himself and turned toward Rich, standing in front of the group, gesturing for silence.

Rich ran fingers through his thick black hair. "We have a good crowd for our first camp-out and I want to thank all of you for coming. Our special guest is Herb Simmons. He's from Atlanta and owns and runs a business called 'Empowerment.' Herb is an outdoorsman who likes to help others help themselves. Besides being the president of the NCA, the National Counselors Association, he's a member of a paintball team that came in second place this year in the National Paintball competitions. Major corporations use his business to foster a sense of community and centeredness in their organizations when they come to his empowerment camp. Thorn and I have both participated in his paintball and other self-motivational games that he uses. We've learned a lot about self-empowerment from him. Listen to him and learn."

Polite applause greeted Herb when he stood up next to Terry and waved gently to the audience. "As you can see, I'm standing in the center of this meeting, not at the front. We all need to leave our egos at the entrance and find a way to center ourselves within ourselves and with each other. As you all know, that is the best way to build a harmonious community.

"The game we're going to play today is called 'Indians.' We discussed various types of community-building games. There are plenty of adult games we could play, but they would be boring for the kids. Indian's a game that the fathers and the children can play together. We'll all put on war paint and the kids will hunt for the dads in the woods around here. The father with the least amount of paintball splotches at the end wins the title of Big Chief."

A bald-headed man with dark moustache and goatee held up his hand. "Did you say paintball splotches? Are we going to be shooting each other with paintball guns?"

"Only the children will have the guns. The fathers will be trying to hide from the children and each other."

The bald headed man shook his head. "My child doesn't know how to shoot a paintball gun."

"Donald, relax," Rich said. "Thorn is teaching the kids about paintball guns up on Spook Mountain. That's why they went on the hike."

Herb put his hands on his hips and rocked back and forth on the heels of his boots. "I've had some experience in the woods. I've taught many survival camps with the idea of self-empowerment behind it. You would be surprised how much your confidence increases, how much empowerment you have, when you learn survival skills that can help you in the woods or in the workplace.

"I've done this game about four times with kids and the children love it. Everyone wears feathers and puts on war paint.

The boys and girls are going to be on teams with specifically colored paint in their paintball guns to signify the team identity. Your goal is to avoid being hit with the paint balls. The team with the most splotches on any father is the winner of that Dad."

Another man with a brown birthmark on one cheek and bad acne on the other raised his hand. "So, the kids can shoot us more than once? Don't these paintballs hurt when they hit you?"

"We've modified the paintball guns so they won't have as much impact power as the ones we use in competition. Plus, you're going to be well protected by the clothing and goggles we pass out."

Raising his hand, another man who had pudgy jowls and a thatch of thick blond hair, asked, "How is this helpful for engendering a sense of community?"

"The Indians were the first victims in this country," Rich said, tapping an index finger into the palm of his hand. "We're planning on having a discussion tonight about how Europeans invaded this land and took it from the Indians. The best way to understand Victimology is to learn what it feels like to be hunted and on the outside. This is a role-reversal strategy. The children are the ones with the power. As adults, we forget how our parents injected their beliefs into us and then we in turn project our beliefs into our children. We do this by power. This forced inheriting of the past has to stop. We have to overthrow that kind of mentality if we're going to build a guilt-free future for our children. Remember, do you want your child blaming you for all their hang-ups when they get older? Do you want that guilt to be laid at your doorstep? Would you rather be remembered as a nagging parent or as a friend. This will be a game to the kids, Arnold, but it should be, and will be, a lesson for all of the adults."

Several men voiced agreement. The pudgy man with the jelly jowls stroked his chin and nodded also.

* * *

Stretching and yawning, Thorn adjusted the drooping feather in his headband. "We just want the boys and girls to have fun. The one thing we don't want is for a child to get lost or hurt going too far afield looking for you guys. So, don't go beyond the boundaries marked with the yellow ribbons. That's one of the reasons we're going to put the kids into teams." He gestured behind him at the kids shooting paintball guns at targets. "Herb has a little more to say. After that, the children will come over and we'll help each other put on our war paint."

A thin man who was all joints, knees, and elbows held up his hand by moving his shoulder first, then his elbow, and then his wrist. "What other reasons do you have for having teams?"

"That's a good question, Marvin." Thorn straightened his feather again. "We have to remember that parents are a team against their powerless children. This is one more way to help us learn and remember that we were all child victims at one time, being imbued with philosophies and attitudes that take a long time to overcome. This will be especially true when these kids become teenagers. I hope you all remember this camp-out when your children start telling you how embarrassing you are and defying you."

Herb took the microphone from Thorn. His tiger-striped jungle fatigues accentuated his muscled chest. Splotches of green and black paint covered his face. A floppy jungle hat, which had a feather stuck in one of the air holes, concealed his eyes. Several leafy branches were tied to his arms and legs. "Okay, men, we want to have as much fun as possible and also not make it too easy for the kids to hit us with those guns.

He patted his chest and pants. "One thing I've learned about sneaking through the woods is that you have to make sure you're well concealed. In this game and in life, there are people who find joy and power in teaming up on other people. We're trying to make everyone realize how childish that attitude is."

Taking his jungle cap from his head, Herb wiped his brow. The feather floated to the ground. He bent with agile grace to scoop it up. "We have some secondhand army camouflage outfits you guys can use." He pointed to a pile of green pants, shirts and goggles. "That is, if you didn't bring your own like I did."

"You guys can climb trees if you want." He placed his cap on his expansive head and his massive hands on his hips. "But that's usually the first place the kids look. Try not to leave traces like broken branches or footprints." Herb gestured to the branches on his arms. "I like to use branches to conceal myself. It works well for us when our team goes to paintball competitions."

Rich and Thorn handed out Indian headbands with feathers on them. Each father received two headbands, one for himself and one for his child. Thorn raised his hand for silence. "It's time for the kids to come over and paint your faces. Then you need to head for the hills. You'll know the hunt is on when you hear the children yelling. Remember, it's every man for himself."

The boys and girls, laughing and joking, boiled around their fathers like foam on a wave. They smeared paint on their fathers, each child an avalanche of sound and laughter.

"Granddad, this is going to be so much fun." Alex dipped his fingers into a bowl of black paint and streaked Terry's face. "Should your face look like Mr. Simmons?"

"It doesn't matter too much." Terry hugged his grandson.

"Yes, it does. Diversity says her dad has done this before with Mr. Simmons and that she's going to win. I'm on her team."

"Then, by all means, do it like Diversity says."

Stopping in front of them, Thorn held faded fatigues draped over his arms. Measuring Terry, he lifted pants from one arm and a shirt from the other. "I think these'll do."

Terry placed his feathered headband on his head and reached for the clothes.

"You'll look like a real warrior now," Thorn said.

"You look great, Granddad."

As he put on his fatigues, a movement of a bush in the tree line caught his eye. Metal flashed as the sunlight struck it. A rocket-propelled grenade, an RPG, streaked out of the wood line and soared over Terry's head.

"Granddad, stay still."

"Okay, men," Herb said, "let's move out."

"I love you and I'm so proud of you." He enveloped his grandson in a bear hug.

"Run, Granddaddy, run." Alex pushed him away.

On his way to the tree line, Terry stopped by the tent. Rummaging through his sleeping bag, he drew out a package. He peeled off the duct tape and tore through the brown paper. Unwrapping the cloth, he caressed Cochise's knife and scabbard.

He entered the woods with the other men. The fathers, feathers stuck in their headbands, waved to each other as they split up. Terry trotted down a path that headed away from Spook Mountain. He exited the trail and knelt behind a tree. Whoops and howls of the feral children floated upon the air.

Somewhere to his left, the slight popping sound of paintball guns fluttered through the trees. A dad yelled. The patter of the guns and the squealing of children sounded again. The hunt for the fathers had begun.

Behind him, leaves rustled. A massive hand grabbed his shoulder. "Malloy, where've you been, man?" Brumsen asked. "We've been looking for you."

* * *

Anderson took the first watch as usual. Terry went to sleep immediately. Brumsen shook him awake.

Thank God, the rain had stopped.

Leaning against a tree, he heard the soft breathing of the sleeping men. His gaze slowly digested the jungle around him.

How did he feel? How should he feel? They'd definitely see action tomorrow.

A fuck-you lizard, Brumsen and Duffy said they were birds, Terry and Cochise said they were lizards, interrupted his thoughts. The mournful cry of the bird/lizard sounded just like it was saying, "Fffuuuuuccccccckkkkk yyoooouuuuuuuuuuuuuu!" He grinned. That was exactly what he wanted to say to this country and the people in it who wanted to kill him. The entire squad felt that way. The war was personal to all of them. Men were trying to kill them, and the group wanted to return the favor.

The vision of the men with their hands tied behind their backs, the dark pools of blood around their heads made deep-seated anger stir within. He was nervous, a little scared, but not quaking in his boots.

Duffy moved slightly, his hand shook. All of the men, tired from the events of the day, slept easily.

As he stood guard among the sleeping men, a sudden clarity of thought struck him. He trusted these men with his life. That was why he could sleep so soundly. They put the same responsibility and trust for their lives into his hands. Terry was not overwhelmed at the thought. He had an obligation to these men. He was prepared to shoulder that burden. He felt different; good and whole with a new sense of determination and purpose that he had never felt before. He had a role in this outfit. These were his friends. He could depend on them. They could depend on him. He knew who the enemy was. Everything was clear. Four fourty-five. *Fifteen minutes!*

The dark shadows of the jungle would not lift for another forty-five to sixty minutes.

"It's a good simple plan. We kill these sonsofbitches before they know what happened. Remember guys," Anderson said to him and Duffy, "set off your mines with ours. Then I want you to go to the trail and make sure no one escapes down that way. It's only natural that someone might try to take the one safe route they came by. For the most part, they'll stop thinking when bullets start flying. Brumsen, Cochise, and I'll finish off everyone around the bunker."

He could die or be wounded tomorrow. After finding the recon squad this morning, he would never be taken prisoner. The men had talked at times about that possibility, whether they would allow themselves to be taken. As an argument, it had been worthwhile to have the conversation.

"No fucking way," Cochise said. "They ain't never taking me prisoner."

Fingers of his other hand touching his pursed lips, Duffy tightened his grip.

Soft, subdued voices seeped through the jungle. Terry felt the early morning presence of the waking jungle more than at any other time. Perhaps because he'd survived another night. The splendor of the color, the cacophonous sounds of birds, monkeys, and insects, the fresh scents of new green growth mingled with the putrid smells of decomposing plants, presented an alien landscape into and through which he wandered with awe and trepidation. Every morning was a blessing. Hearing the subdued voices of the Vietnamese, he knew that they too were grateful to be alive in this majestic and deadly wilderness. They, too, had survived another night.

Terry sensed the nearness of the Vietnamese. He felt their presence. An icy coldness gripped him. He shivered and yawned.

"Tao doi bung roi. Tao muon an."

Another voice: *"May muon an them nua khong?"*

Soft laughter: "*E, Cai nay ngon thiet*!"

The men walked past them, up the slope toward the bunker.

Terry unconsciously gripped his bayonet in his boot. For what seemed like hours, they knelt frozen, not breathing.

More talking. There must be hundreds of them! The soft Vietnamese voices diminished.

Duffy let out a long breath. He reached for a detonator. Terry took the other one. In the clearing, the Vietnamese murmured quietly. The distance dissipated and muted their voices. A small bug crawled across a leaf in front of him. Come on! The insect flew off. Duffy brushed away a mosquito. Gnats and mosquitos hovered in the air around them. Come on!

Two, almost simultaneous, explosions tore through the fabric of the jungle. Grenades! Then six consecutive explosions, louder than the first two, ripped through the jungle foliage. *Claymores!* A primordial scream penetrated through the thunderclap. The scream ran up Terry's spine as he and Duffy pressed their detonators and felt the explosive reverberation of the claymores.

The concussion wave of the claymores swept over them. Terry's ears were ringing. Riding the crest of the storm, like foam upon the surf, screams and moans came from the clearing.

Duffy ran toward the path. Terry followed. Smoke billowed and roiled through the vegetation, obscuring the path and the surrounding jungle. Both men glided at a fast walk. The air was silver with spent powder and permeated by the sharp smells of smoke, gunpowder, and a descending blizzard of vegetation.

Gunfire erupted from the clearing. Anderson's calm voice said, "Shoot 'em all. Some are still moving."

Then Cochise said, "I'll check the bunkers."

A mournful, soft voice whispered from their right, *"Cu u toi vo i. Tao khong hieu. Tao khong hieu."* Both of them stopped on the path, five feet from the clearing.

Crouching and swinging their rifles to the right, they faced in the direction of the pleading voice. Duffy signaled with his left hand. He wanted Terry to go up the trail and then into the jungle in the direction of the voice. Duffy gestured that he would go into the jungle where he was.

Making sure his weapon was on automatic, Terry crept up the trail and into the jungle. He lost Duffy immediately. *"Cu u toi vo i,"* the voice gasped again. It came from his right, toward Duffy. He could hear Brumsen talking to Cochise while the two walked around the clearing. The gun shots stopped. The moans and screams ceased.

"Malloy, over here."

He walked ten feet to his right and forward, toward Duffy's voice. Pushing the jungle aside, he saw Duffy's back. The Vietnamese lay on the ground in front of Duffy. The man's black eyes were big and fearful. He moaned softly as he looked into their eyes. The Vietnamese bled from head wounds and one of his legs was torn open. He had probably run about as far as he could before his leg collapsed.

"Duffy, Malloy," Anderson called. "Hey, you guys; let's go. Let's haul ass."

The wounded Vietnamese was on his back pushing himself away from them. Duffy's shoulders sagged. The fatigue lines deepened around his mournful eyes. He shouldered his rifle, his lips a tight scar.

Terry brought his M-16 to bear on the wounded man. They both opened fire at the same time. The Vietnamese's body jerked as each bullet struck it. They searched the man's pockets. Nothing. Neither said a word as they both turned and walked toward the clearing.

Emerging from the jungle, Cochise and Anderson knelt over the unfinished bunker. Brumsen checked the bodies lying on the ground. "Leave the sonofabitch in the hole, Cochise," Anderson said. "Whether he fell into it after he was wounded, or he jumped, it was the last thing he ever did."

Duffy said, "Look at how well dressed these guys are."

Holding several Vietnamese pouches, Brumsen placed them in his rucksack. "Yeah, they're North Vietnamese regulars, all right."

"This is a good *embuscada*. Whoever they are, they're *muertos* now. *Puta madre...*"

Terry counted bodies. "There're nine men. I thought there must have been thirty or forty of them as they went by me."

Two bodies lay at his feet. Both had small blood spots on their chests and backs where they had been hit by the BBs from the claymores. Pools of blood formed halos around their heads.

"The tenth guy's in this bunker here." Cochise pointed toward the bunker.

Terry glanced where Cochise had set his grenade booby trap the evening before. The man's head, with blood soaked hair, sprinkled with brain matter and white bone, lay against the corner of the bunker.

"Let's get going, guys. Cochise, take the point. Terry, take the rear. Start counting. We've been here ten minutes. We need to haul ass. Get us out of this valley, Cochise."

"A valley of death," Duffy whispered.

CHAPTER THIRTEEN

The enthusiatic screams and whoops of children echoed through the trees and leaves, as did the booming bellows of their fleet-footed fathers.

Rich, his goggles askew, ran down the trail. One side of his head was blue. His jacket was a splash of red, yellow and blue paintball splotches. The popping sounds of the paintball guns grew louder as the shrieking children came down the trail.

"You guys go shoot someone else," Rich said, hiding behind a tree. "Those things hurt. At least give me time to fix my goggles."

Diversity led a team of youngsters that included Alex. When she heard her father, she stopped and put her fingers to her lips and gestured for them to spread out. "Okay, Dad, we'll let you put your goggles on." She held up a feather. "We've got your feather that you dropped, if you want it."

"No, you can keep the feather." Rich adjusted his goggles. He pushed his featherless headband farther up on his paint-covered forehead.

Alex pointed with his paintball gun, jerking it back and forth through the air. "There he is!"

The gun exploded. Diversity's blue glob of paint struck the limb above Rich's head, splattering the tree and him with bluish muck. "Get him!"

"You little monsters!" He ducked and ran down the trail. Eyebrows steepling, eyes wide, he looked back over his shoulder as another paintball sailed past his head.

The children's laughter and howls grew fainter as the team disappeared down the trail.

With Cochise's knife, Terry scrapped a small pit the size of his body out of the soft brown earth. He had pushed aside the damp leaves from the shaded ground. Black beetles scurried to and fro and an earth worm wiggled as fast as possible to burrow into the ground. From his vantage point, five yards from a 'V' in the trail, he could see in both directions. His feet pointed down a slight slope.

Two limbs of a worm-infested tree stretched out before him. He had adjusted the limbs slightly so that they angled away from his body, forming a V. He pushed moist leaves left and right up against the two sections of the decaying tree. Scrapping the ground, he pushed dirt behind him. With his feet on the downhill slope, he was only concerned with hiding his upper body. Hearing two men talking, he lay down and covered himself with moist, decaying leaves, using his arms in an angel-wing motion to cover his back. A beetle crawled across his neck and into his hair.

Thorn appeared up the trail, whispering to someone behind him. Breathing with labor, he stopped. His clothes had paint splotches on them. "I didn't think they would gang up the way they did. I thought they would stay apart in teams."

In his tiger-striped fatigues, Herb appeared over Thorn's shoulder. "Well, if you think about it. It makes sense for them to work in a pack rather than apart. That Diversity's a clever little girl. Rather than one team against the other, they're combing the woods together."

The two men walked by and disappeared up the trail. A minute later the screams and hoots of the children along with the sound of paintball guns being fired came from their direction.

"Here's two of 'em," a high-pitched voice screamed.

Thorn and Herb scrambled back down the trail. Something blurred and red whizzed by their heads, spattering on a tree. Herb pushed Thorn from behind. "Run, dammit, run."

They ran past Terry, Thorn leading the way. "I don't know if I can take this."

"Shut up and run. Do ya think this is a game?"

Five seconds later, shouting children stampeded down the trail. Slowing down, they mobbed where the trail turned. Other running children ran into the ones in front of them. A brown-headed girl, around ten years old with a pony tail, pitched forward down the slope losing her paintball gun in the process. The gun slid into leaves in front of Terry.

By the time she stood and brushed off the leaves, the other children had disappeared down the trail. Sobbing, she searched the ground. Staring frantically at the empty trail, she ran off. "My gun, I've lost my gun! Come back."

Taking the paintball gun, Terry slid back into his position. Talking men, breathing hard, came toward him. Herb dragged Thorn with him. "Come on, you tub of lard. I thought you told me you were in shape." Moving past Terry down the trail, Herb stopped to adjust the branches adorning his arms for camouflage.

The paintball hit Thorn on the back of the head, knocking his feather off. He bent over reaching for it. Another splotch of blue paint covered his ass. "Crap!" He rubbed his rear end, smearing paint on his hands. "You know, I'm thinking I deserve this. It's what I get for being white and smug."

Herb's head rocked as a paintball splattered the side of his face. "Holy shit! Let's get the fuck outa here." He turned to look from where the shot had come. His head rocked back as if he had been hit by a two by four. Blue paint covered his face and goggles. He coughed and gagged, spitting blue paint out of his mouth. He grabbed for his floppy jungle hat falling to the ground. Another paintball hit him on top of his head. "Godammit! Wait a minute! This isn't fair!"

"Come on! Be a man!" Thorn grabbed him by the arm. "We have to learn what the people of the world think of white people." They hurried up the path. Thorn dragged a stumbling Herb, who wiped paint from his goggles.

"Fuck the people of the world." Herb tripped and scrambled up the trail. Disappearing into the woods, Terry heard children hollering, ignited by the howls of Herb and Thorn.

The roars of young, feral children, energized by the hunt, reverberated through the woods. Lying prone behind a tree, he felt, rather than saw bodies moving past him. Terry fingered the hilt of Cochise's knife. Goddamn! This was fun!

When the children went past, men murmured. Terry crawled toward them. *Slow, Terry, slow!* Rocks, pebbles and twigs dug into his chest and stomach. These guys are making a lot of noise. Distinguishing three voices, one of whom was Rich, he shouldered his paintball gun and crawled forward.

A blond-haired man, leaning against a tree, made desperate gestures to wipe his hands with leaves. His camouflage fatigues were covered with paint splotches. "The impact of those damn things hurt. What the hell are we doing out here turning our kids into hooligans?"

A black man with a beard, lying on his stomach, studied the woods. He put his fingers to his lips. "You need to be quiet. The little assholes are shooting everyone. So, just sit there and be quiet."

Studying the woods also, Rich rubbed paint off his face with his sleeve. With goggles in hand, he turned to the blond-haired man, pointing the goggles at him. "We're trying to show what it's like if you have no power. How would you like to be a tool, a minority with no power, in the world you live in."

The blond-haired man swatted at a fly. "Aren't we as a society trying to address these inequities? What the hell am I doing out here getting my ass blasted off by my own child. I'm trying to teach her to be good. But this stupid exercise seems to have turned them into *Lord of the Flies* Nazis. It's insane."

The black man sat up. He rubbed leaves out of his beard. He hissed, "Fuck this! If you guys can't keep your mouths shut, I'm outa here. Don't you understand they're going to pound us when they find us. What the hell am I doing out here anyway? Do you see any white on my ass. No, you don't, 'cause I'm black. The only thing you see on my ass are red and blue patches. They were slammed there by crazy-ass little white kids going through the woods shooting at me, a black man. I'm black and I'm nothing but a moving target for white children. How fucked up is that?"

The paintball splattered against Rich's head. "Shit!" Blinking one blue-stained eyelid, he nervously put on his goggles while attempting to stand. The second paintball hit him squarely in the face smearing the goggles. Rich lost his balance and fell against the tree.

The black man with the beard ran into the woods, shouting as he went, "I told you white assholes to shut the fuck up!"

The blond-haired man, still on his knees, crawled toward an unseen Terry. Two paintballs smacked him, one on his head and another on the shoulder. Screaming, "Ow, ow!," he turned and crawled into the woods.

Rich, placing the goggles over his blue head, managed to stand up. He stretched his arms in front of him and staggered forward into the woods. "I can't see! I can't see!"

Children ran from every direction toward the bellowing Rich. As he stumbled from tree to tree, the pop, pop of paintball guns, his howling, and the laughter of children resounded in the woods.

Terry, placing the gun under a bush, walked empty handed toward the laughter. Tapping a blond-headed girl on the shoulder, he raised his hands. "What's your name?"

She wheeled and pointed her gun at him. "Gloria."

He leaned over, brushing dirt from his pants. "Well, Gloria, I surrender." A green paint ball splattered on the top of his head. He stood instinctively and two more hit him on his chest.

Gloria cupped one hand to her mouth. "Hey guys, over here I've got one!"

Laughing as the children ran toward him through the trees, he held up his hands again. "Don't shoot, I surrender."

As the paintballs thudded against his body, Terry covered his face, laughing. "No fair! I surrender! I surrender!"

It started as a rivulet, then changed to a stream, and then a raging river. The cries of the feral fathers reverberated through the woods. "Don't shoot! I surrender! I give up!"

* * *

For reasons that seemed to the enlisted men of any army as predictable as whims from Mount Olympus, the North Vietnamese decided to fight for Hill 1036. Terry heard about the battle from a medic at the battalion aid station.

As Terry's squad lifted out to search for the Lurp team, the second day of the battle began with bomb-laden jets making their approaches on the first bunker complex of the mountain. The American soldiers huddled in their hastily dug foxholes. The jets roared out of the cloud cover and thundered over the terrified soldiers. The GIs cringed as the explosions of the one-thousand-pound and five-hundred-pound bombs rocked the mountain in devastating tornadoes of shrapnel and sound. The bitter smell of cordite rolled down upon the men, along with the smoke of the bombs, and covered the mountain with a soft morning mist.

Big, black, two-engine bombers swooped in above the tree tops. The jets dropped big, black, tumbling bombs that bounced along the ground, exploded, and sent a cascade of roiling flame across the mountain side. In their bunkers, the North Vietnamese screamed as they burned and died while the napalm clung like a leech to whatever it touched. The jungle leaves and limbs evaporated under the blast-furnace force of the bombs. A forward air controller flew high above the battle. Through the burning jungle, he spotted trenches that connected the lower bunkers to the bunkers above them. NVA soldiers ran through the trenches filling the newly bombed, death-filled bunkers with new troops.

An artillery barrage, lasting for thirty minutes, struck the mountain. The American commander gave the orders to advance. The men making the assault abandoned hope of a quick victory, and the men defending the bunkers knew they were going to die on the mountain. Fire erupted from the NVA bunkers and a crescendo of sound engulfed the mountainside. Two thousand men shot at one another, screamed, maimed, and killed each other. The NVA met the American troops with small arms and heavy machine-gun fire. Rocket-propelled grenades burst in the trees. Snipers fired at the Americans from the trees left standing. Enemy troops shot from hidden spider holes when the men went by them.

The Americans, advancing into the fire as if into a driving rain, countered with their own machine gun, small-arms fire, and forty-millimeter M-79 grenade launchers. Wounded men crawled forward over dead men.

Eardrums burst from the explosions. The wall of sound made it difficult for squads to communicate with each other and their platoon leaders. The platoon leaders could not hear their company commanders. Platoons and squads became isolated from one another, but fought with fury and only one goal: push forward and kill the enemy.

Within an hour and a half of the initiation of the assault, the collapse of the first bunker complex was imminent. A squad using a seventy-millimeter recoilless rifle enveloped a flank. Hurling grenades and screaming, the five men ran firing into the trenches of the bunker complex. Three out of the five men in the squad were wounded, but the weakened position gave an opening to the other troops watching, and they began to roll up the first line of bunkers.

Helicopters flew in to suppress fire coming from farther up the mountain. One of the gunships made a pass from the wrong direction. A tongue of flame from its mini-guns uncoiled and licked the side of the hill. The bullets cut a swath through the headquarters area of a platoon, killing a medic and a staff sergeant and wounding two privates and one corporal. Enraged by the news, the commanding officer of the battalion ordered all helicopters except medevacs to vacate the area.

Sensing a change in the firepower that had been raining down and keeping his troops huddled in their bunkers, the NVA commander ordered two platoons to retake the bunkers that had been lost. Boiling out of their own bunkers and trenches like cockroaches, the NVA swarmed down on the lost line of bunkers. Closing within grenade-throwing range, both sides fought fiercely and bitterly, giving no quarter and asking for none. Men bled to death from holes made by grenade fragments and bullet wounds. Men died calling out in English and Vietnamese for their mothers, wives, and girlfriends. They died from bayonet wounds and shock. Men forgot their wives and their homes and fought like wild beasts for a little piece of real estate and for each other.

The battle raged for the rest of the day. By nightfall, the Americans were well beyond the first line of bunkers. Looking up from their newly won positions as night fell, many of the men could see and hear fresh NVA troops moving into positions above them.

The next morning, when the medevacs and supply helicopters received fire on their approaches to the battalion headquarter's LZ, the troops knew they were surrounded. The helicopter pilots, both medevacs and supply, flew supplies in and took wounded troops out. At first, they battled only the heavy, intermittent downpours of the monsoon and the gusts of wind that came with them. With the advent of the withering fire directed toward them as they approached the LZ, only volunteers crewed the medical helicopters and supply ships. These were held up after a Huey supply helicopter fell flaming from the sky.

While Terry's squad prepared to ambush the work detail, a platoon of NVA attacked battalion headquarters and the aid station attached to it. Two NVA sappers, carrying demolition charges, managed to get inside the perimeter. They threw satchel charges among the wounded, killing six men. The wounded men themselves shot the two sappers.

A volunteer crew picked up Anderson's squad and lifted it and supplies to the battalion on the morning of the third day, three hours after they had ambushed the NVA at the bunker site. A low layer of clouds hung over the valley. The helicopter descended through the clouds and rain, going down for what seemed to the men like hours.

When the helicopter shot out of the bottom of the clouds, everyone caught his breath. The helicopter hurtled through the air, skimming the teak trees, mountains, and jungle no more than one hundred and fifty feet from the ground. The pilot plunged out of the clouds between two ridges that were higher than the helicopter. Five hundred yards from the landing zone, green tracers zoomed up at them. The helicopter rattled with the impact of the bullets. The squad grabbed for whatever handhold it could manage as the helicopter, closing in on the LZ, bobbed and weaved. A rocket-propelled grenade, trailing smoke, traced a parabola through the sky as it rocketed toward them and descended back into the jungle.

Poncho-wrapped dead lined the landing zone. Brumsen whistled when he saw them as the helicopter flared for a landing. No one talked as they disembarked from the helicopter. Walking wounded, carrying two stretchers, ducked under the whirling blades to the Huey transport, laying the stretchers on the floor of the chopper. The walking wounded scrambled onto the ship. The squad helped load the stretchers and the wounded. They placed the stretchers as carefully as possible on the helicopter. The ship carried troops and supplies and was not equipped to carry wounded men on stretchers.

The heavily laden helicopter lifted and spun around. It slowly ascended toward the cloud cover. The motor strained, rotor blades whirling furiously with their load. Bright green rounds sailed past the ship tracing slow-motion arcs across the cloud-covered sky. Two smoke-trailing rocket-propelled grenades whispered by the Huey and then arced back into the jungle. The helicopter disappeared into the fog and clouds.

Anderson left the squad to find an officer. The rest of the men went to the medical station to help with the wounded as best they could. Duffy and Cochise gave water to those who could drink. Terry and Brumsen rearranged stretchers for the medics. Critical cases received priority. The dead, wrapped in their ponchos, could wait.

Sounds of battle came down from the hill. The irregular firing was cautious and probing. The morning's push up the hill had not yet started. The troops waited for another air strike and artillery bombardment. Anderson walked over to the aid tent and called the squad together. The camouflage paint smeared with the grime on their faces. Wet fatigues clung to their bodies.

"We're going out later this afternoon," Anderson said. "The big guys want to find out where all the NVA are coming from. They're sending out several recon patrols toward the Cambodian border. The first battalion is being choppered in on the other side of the mountain. They're going to set up a blocking force to keep reinforcements from reaching the NVA dug in up there." He jerked a thumb at the mountain. "We're now attached to recon. The captain said to tell you guys 'well done' on finding the squad and also getting those guys this morning."

The squad, exhausted, showed no emotion at Anderson's words. The thought of going out again fazed no one.

"Right now," Anderson said, "we're attached to the medical teams here. They want us to go up the mountain and, if possible, carry any wounded down. With the fog, the rain, and the low cloud cover, plus the NVA shooting at the choppers, the medevacs and supply ships haven't wanted to land. But we need to get all the wounded down here so they can get out when, and if, the ships can land. Plus, the air support's been put on hold because of this stinking soup hanging over us."

"This is one fuck-up of a battle." Cochise stomped a cigarette into the mud.

"So what else is new?" Duffy asked.

Terry glanced in the direction of Hill 1036. The jungle obscured his view, but he had seen the hill when he flew into the landing zone. Napalm scars slashed across parts of the mountain. Oases of jungle mingled with black patches of cleared space where bombs had struck. In the cleared areas, uprooted trees lay helter-skelter across a moonscape. Some of the trees were shattered and destroyed by bombs. Others, blown completely out of the ground, still had their root systems attached in huge balls of dirt. A few trees, stripped bare of leaves, still survived in the blast areas. Forlorn sentinels, their naked limbs reached upward into an uncaring sky. Smoke rose here and there from burning trees.

The men turned toward the mountain. They put on their web gear, picked up their weapons, and walked toward the base of the hill.

Brumsen took a twig out of his mouth. "You know, the NVA are digging in a little deeper up there, getting ready for today's assault."

Anderson talked with a medic. He turned to the men. "There's an aid station about halfway up the mountain. We're going up there first to see if anyone needs help. We may have to come back here with wounded or go farther up to the line. It just depends on what we find when we reach the aid station."

Rain pelted them. Terry shivered as the drops washed over him. They formed a file and marched up the mountainside. The first body they saw wasn't really a body, but the lower torso of an NVA trooper. Entrails spilled out of the open cavity. Even in the rain, insects crawled over the entrails and flew through the stench. There were more bodies and body parts of NVA soldiers. One NVA soldier's frozen arms were reaching toward the sky. No head was attached to the body. The bloated bodies putrified quickly in the heat and dampness of the jungle. The rancid stench, the smell of death, permeated everything. Mixed in among the bodies were various weapons, rifle stocks, helmets, bandages, all types of equipment that make up the detritus and waste of warfare.

The squad soon reached the aid station, which was also a company headquarters. A lean, unshaven captain talked on the radio. Anderson and his stood in the middle of the clearing. Two soldiers, sitting in the mud and rain, stared at them out of vacant, exhausted eyes. Their helmets accentuated the thinness of their unshaven faces. M-16s rested on their laps. Mud caked their torn clothes.

While Anderson talked to the captain, the rest of them stood quietly or looked for places to sit. The officer pointed to something up the mountain, giving directions. The conversation ended. The captain left with the two tired GIs.

"There's going to be an artillery barrage in about thirty minutes," Anderson said, gathering the squad around him. "Then they assault the hill again. Because of the fog, the rain and cloud cover, we'll get no aerial support until it clears. One of the platoons lost its platoon leader, and the captain can't raise them on his radio. He assumes that the radio that was on the command net was knocked out. We have to go tell them to expect the artillery bombardment and to be prepared to assault the next line of bunkers after the arty's passed."

They trekked up the hill, over the scarred ground. The equipment that littered the hill offered more obstacles than the jungle. Canteens, ammo pouches, rucksacks, helmets, bloody bandages, and food cartons lay scattered everywhere. Besides the holes dug for protection, craters had been gouged out of the ground by artillery, bombs, and grenades. Trees and limbs of trees lay here and there. Two NVA corpses slumped half in and half out of a hole. Water collected around the bottom of the foxhole and over the dead men's boots. Insects crawled into an empty eye socket.

The squad climbed over and under trees and around craters. The men maintained a steady direction upward. Boots caked with mud, they crept and slid carefully around water-filled holes and stumps of trees. As they moved farther up the mountain, they crouched lower. The squad finally reached a line of men huddled behind trees, in bunkers, or simply lying in the muddy, water-filled foxholes created by explosions.

Anderson said quietly, "We're looking for second platoon, C company."

"You found it," one of the men said, not turning around.

"Who's in charge?" Anderson shifted his M-16 from one hand to the other.

All of the men in the line gazed up the hill. The man Anderson addressed turned to face him. His name tag read Jones. He rubbed his grizzled chin and then spoke in a slow Southern drawl. "Lieutenant Castilla was, but he was hit yesterday. Then Sergeant Borowski got it. Smitty's in charge now. He's the squad leader of the next squad over." Jones cocked his elbow and flicked his thumb to the right.

A loud cry of pain, from farther up the hill, pierced the jungle.

"What the fuck is that?" Cochise asked.

"You mean 'Who the fuck is that?'" one of the men said.

Again they heard the moaning, and then, "Help me. Help me. I hurt."

"You got a fucking man out there?" Anderson's gray eyes narrowed into slits, the crow's feet at his temples becoming more pronounced

"Talk to Smitty," Jones said.

While the squad darted through the forsaken landscape to find Smitty, the wounded man yelled again, "Please, someone help me."

Fifteen yards farther, they came upon the next group of men. "Where the fuck's Smitty?" Anderson asked.

A gaunt man stood in a crouch and crept back to Anderson. The man, jaw bulging from a wad of tobacco, knelt. A brown stream of liquid squirted from his mouth, and a small rivulet ran down his chin. "I'm Smitty."

"What the fuck are you doing leaving a man out there?"

Smitty wiped tobacco juice from his chin. "Fuck you, Bud. We got two men wounded trying to find that guy earlier this morning. We had to evacuate one of them and almost got more wounded rescuing those two. He started up about two and a half hours ago. He's not from our platoon. We don't know who he is. The goddamned NVA let our guys get into the jungle about fifty yards out and then opened up on them. He might be a fucking NVA, for all we know."

Sitting on his haunches and using a tree for cover, Anderson looked beyond the line of American bunkers. "They're going to drop artillery out there in about thirty minutes or so. We need to make sure he isn't one of our guys."

"Okay, Bud. Help yourself. If it's worth anything, the guy isn't directly in front of us. My guys covered a lot of ground out there before they got hit and we think he's further over to the left, maybe about fifty or seventy-five yards out."

Smitty looked at the squad and then back at Anderson. "Leave your machine gunner here. He can help us cover you."

"Screw you. I go where he goes." Brumsen nodded toward Anderson.

"He's right, Brumsen," Anderson said. "You can't carry that thing out there and you can help us by laying down some fire. Malloy, you stay with Brumsen." Anderson turned to Cochise and Duffy. "You guys don't have to go, but I can't leave that guy out there without trying to get him."

Cochise stiffened. His head came up, a snake about to strike. "I go with you, *compadre*. Let's go get that guy."

Duffy said, "I feel the same way. Let's get that guy and get the hell off this mountain."

Smitty pointed to a fallen tree to his left. The root system, still attached and balled with dirt, caused it to slant toward the ground in the direction that Anderson and the squad had come. Two soldiers were using the hole where the root system had been as a foxhole. "That tree is a good place for the machine gun. You can place the M-60 under the trunk of the tree and use the branches for cover.

"Davis, go tell the boys down there we're gonna try to get that sonofabitch again and to give us support when the shit starts," Smitty said.

They moved the machine-gun under the trunk. Smitty brought over an entrenching tool and tossed it to Terry. The shovel sank into the ground. Terry scooped out a shovelful of mud. "This is like fighting in a fucking swamp. The more you dig, the more bogged down you get."

"Help me," came the siren cry again. The squad looked up the mountain in the direction of the voice.

Duffy took off his radio and checked his M-16. "Let's go, before I get too frigging scared."

"Smitty, can you make a stretcher with a poncho, just in case we find the guy?" Anderson turned to Cochise and Duffy. "Follow me at five-yard intervals. You know the drill, no bunching up. When I move to a different cover, Cochise, you move to the place I vacate. Duffy, you follow Cochise."

Rifle in one hand, Anderson moved up the mountain in a low crouch and jumped into a hole about ten yards out. A wall of jungle loomed over him. Directly in front, the jungle had been shattered by explosions. He jumped out of his crater, racing to the left and quickly disappeared into another. Cochise darted forward as Anderson left his first cover. Anderson rose again, and Cochise followed with Duffy behind him. All three vanished into the jungle. Brumsen and Terry waited, straining to hear or see anything.

"I'm hurt," came the haunting, plaintive voice.

Two minutes later, machine gun and small-arms fire burst from the NVA positions hidden by the jungle. A rocket-propelled grenade sailed out of the jungle and exploded in the trees left standing around Smitty's men. Green tracers shot out of the jungle, clipping branches above the men. Anderson and Duffy sprinted out of the brush above and to the left of Terry and Brumsen. They dragged an American soldier under his armpits.

Terry pointed in the direction from which the RPG had come. Brumsen's M-60 roared next to his ear. The tracer rounds disappeared into the jungle as he prepared another box of machine-gun ammunition. Bullets threw up small mushrooms of mud and dirt around the two running men hauling the wounded with them. Green tracer rounds sailed over the heads of the three men as they stumbled and lurched toward the American lines. The man they dragged screamed.

Cochise ran out of the brush several yards behind them. He turned, dropped to one knee, and fired. Spraying the area to his front, he squeezed off short bursts. A tree limb near his head disintegrated from the impact of bullets. Duffy and Anderson disappeared into a hole and drew the yelling, wounded man, with them. Slamming another magazine into his weapon, Cochise fell behind a log and continued to fire. Several American forty-caliber grenades, from M-79 grenade launchers, flew over Cochise's head and exploded in the jungle beyond him.

Two NVA soldiers ran out of the woods toward Cochise, firing. Every American gun fixed on the two men. Red tracer rounds tore through them. Bright red spots appeared on their shirts and a halo of red spray erupted from their backs. The two Vietnamese hung suspended in air as their forward momentum faltered, the bullets killing them and keeping them up at the same time. Two men from the American lines scrabbled toward Anderson and Duffy. Cochise crawled back down the hill using the log as a cover.

The two soldiers grabbed the wounded man and dragged him back to their lines. Anderson and Duffy fired into the jungle above Cochise, who clawed his way toward them. Bullets broke the sound barrier over Terry's head, snapping through the leaves and branches. Impacting bullets threw dirt up around Cochise, Duffy, and

Anderson. Cochise neared the hole of his squad mates. Duffy jumped out of the hole. He ran in a crouch to the American lines. Anderson continued to fire. Cochise slid into the shell crater.

Two RPG's sailed toward Anderson and Cochise. One fell short, exploding, and the other passed three feet over their heads, exploding between them and the American lines. Cochise lurched out of the hole, zig-zagging toward the line of foxholes, half crawling, half running. Five seconds later, Anderson followed. Another RPG landed on the hole he had left. The explosion knocked Anderson forward and down. He slid several feet through the mud. Brumsen stopped firing. Terry stopped breathing. Anderson crawled forward through the mud. Hands reached out to pull him to safety. Terry unpacked another box of M-60 ammunition. The firing subsided.

Ducking under the log, Duffy tapped Terry and Brumsen. "We need to get out of here. That guy's hurt bad. He's been shot in the lungs. He's gonna die, if we don't get him to the aid station."

While Brumsen and Terry crabbed from under the tree trunk, Duffy came back with the poncho stretcher that Smitty's men had made. Duffy, handing the stretcher to Terry, grabbed his rucksack-radio, and with a practiced flair, placed it on his back. "Let's go."

The three men headed toward the first group of soldiers they had come upon. Smitty stood with Anderson and a medic. Terry lay the stretcher down beside the wounded man whose name tag read Brigman. Brigman's face contorted with pain.

Cochise watched the medic unwrap a bandage. "Can't you give him some morphine or something?"

The medic wrapped the bandage around the compress on the wounded man's chest. "I ran outa morphine yesterday. If he needs it, they'll give it to him down at the aid station." Tying off the bandage, he gazed at his work with tired, resigned eyes. "You guys need to get this man down the mountain as fast as you can."

"Oh man, it hurts." Brigman moaned and clutched at his chest.

The medic took the stretcher from Duffy. "Lift him up and slide the stretcher under him."

Brigman screamed.

The squad each grabbed a limb of the stretcher and lifted it. Anderson walked down the hill carrying their rifles.

They slid several times on the wet ground. The men tried to be as careful and as considerate as possible. Brigman groaned all the way down. Brumsen slipped into a shell hole and nearly dropped the wounded man. The sudden lurch of the stretcher drew a scream of pain. His lips frothed with bloody bubbles. Reaching the aid station, the exhausted men dropped to the ground.

Medics cut away the blood-stained bandages and examined the wound. "If we don't get him outa here soon he's going to die. He's two bullet holes in his chest. We have a medevac chopper, carrying supplies, that's coming in about ten minutes. The medevacs and the supply choppers still won't risk coming in. You can't blame them. The choppers are getting turned into Swiss cheese when they land and take off. The one coming in now has all volunteers on it. The battalion will have to give them a party when this crap is over."

A medic pointed to Brigman. "He'll go out along with these two guys here." The medic gestured toward two men who lay on stretchers. Bloody bandages covered their arms and legs. One had a bandage over his eyes. "You guys can help load them on the chopper. We're really shorthanded."

The men, except for Duffy, lay prone on the mud-covered ground. Duffy picked up a canteen and gave water to the wounded men around him. Within five minutes, a medic told them to get ready for the chopper. Terry and Brumsen picked up Brigman's stretcher.

A medic took his hand and held it. "You're going home now." The wounded man smiled, but said nothing.

Duffy and Cochise carried another stretcher. Anderson and another medic held a third. Three wounded men who could walk stood with them. They had won the right to ride out on this chopper by tossing a coin with several others of the walking wounded.

Detonations quickly followed the whooshing of shells going over their heads. The mountain churned and boiled. Peering into the mist, fog, and low clouds, Terry listened for the whomp-whomp of the helicopter. He could not hear it over the artillery bombardment on the mountain. Four hundred yards out, the helicopter burst out of the cloud bank one hundred feet off the ground. Descending gradually toward them through the rain, its blades stroked a silent circle. Green tracers rushed out of the jungle upward toward the helicopter as it darted to and fro like a giant, flying insect. A smoking RPG round shot out of the jungle, flew by the helicopter, then plummeted earthward.

The growling of the helicopter engines drowned out everything, even the sound of the artillery bursting upon the mountain. The helicopter, big red crosses on its sides, flared and settled gently upon the ground. Bullet holes peppered the crosses.

The men in the ship tossed out supplies to waiting troops before it had settled to the ground. When the ship was empty, the squad, ducking under the spinning blades, hurried forward and passed the stretchers to the helicopter crewmen. Although the men tried to be as gentle as possible with the wounded men, the groans from the three stretchers were clearly audible. The helicopter medic strapped the wounded men into the stretchers.

The helicopter lifted and turned, ready to begin its flight out. It nosed down and pushed forward, gradually lifting above the jungle as it cleared the perimeter. The roar of its straining engines faded.

"Andale, hombre, andale!"

Tracers again darted out of the jungle. Several RPGs ascended toward the bobbing and weaving ship.

"Go, Bro!"

The ship's tail boom lurched to the right. The sound of an explosion followed a puff of smoke near the rear rotor blade.

The helicopter, still climbing, disappeared into the cloud bank. A bright flame erupted from the clouds. The burning, spinning ship reappeared, flames shooting out of the engine. The fire-enveloped wreckage of the helicopter gyrated as it plummeted, the red crosses on its sides appearing and reappearing as it spun. Men, arms waving wildly, plunged from the chopper. A smoking stretcher sailed from the spinning helicopter, tumbling end over end. A cauldron of fire and smoke billowed from the jungle.

"Goddamn this fucking war! Goddamn those sonsofbitches!"

"We aren't going to make it out of here alive, are we?"

"Let's get our gear squared away. We'll be leaving in about an hour."

As they walked away from the aid station, artillery shells continued to slam into the cloud-shrouded mountain.

CHAPTER FOURTEEN

After the showers and a lot of scrubbing by the fathers, the camp met to discuss what they had learned. Diversity, with a glowering look from Rich, spoke for her team. "I've learned how much fun it is to shoot someone, especially my dad." All of the children laughed, heads bobbing up and down in unison.

One father, with a shock full of bushy hair afro-style, waved his hand until Thorn recognized him. "Ron, do you have something to say."

Ron pointed a finger for emphasis. "I'll tell you what I learned. It's a lot better to surrender than it is keep fighting." He ran slender fingers through his black hair, shaking his head.

Diversity said, "It's no fun when the adults surrender, Mr. Haselton."

"Diversity, now you know how parents feel when they tell their kids that they can't do something." Rich put his hands on his hips. "It's fun to have the power. And the fathers know how children feel when the parents boss them around. Mr. Malloy had to ruin everything when he surrendered."

"I'm sorry, guys. I chickened out,"Terry said, laughing and shrugging. "No one else had to surrender. I didn't like getting shot with those paint balls. Gloria scared me. What can I say."

Ron shook his head. He had one arm crossed in front of him rubbing a sore shoulder. "No, Terry, thank God someone did what I, and apparently every other parent, wanted to do."

"I think we'll change the format for next year." Herb, one hand across his chest, rubbed his chin with the other. "I don't know yet what it will be, but it'll be changed."

After the awards ceremony, such as it was, everyone shook Terry's hand and patted him on the back. Alex jumped up and down with glee. Finally, the kids and fathers drifted off into various groups.

A softball game was organized on an unused part of the campground. The fathers played against their children. Terry played center field for two innings while his grandson played second base. Alex made several good fielding plays and had two hits that made it through the infield. Most of the fathers fell down at least once chasing grounders and flies. Every son and daughter managed to get a hit, reach base, and score. It was a joy for Terry to watch Alex play so well. The game finally broke up after the fifth inning. The children won the game fifteen to three.

Grandfather and grandson sauntered back to their tent. Alex picked up rocks and threw them. Terry placed a hand on Alex's shoulder. "We still have cookies that Sarah made. You can take them on your hike this evening."

After supper, they gathered at the communal house for the hiking party. They waved good-bye to each other, as the group of several adults and children hiked up Spook Mountain. The group wound their way between the tents. When they disappeared, Terry walked into the tree line. In the woods, he found a small clearing and sat down under a hickory tree. Kids playing frisbee called to one another.

A gentle breeze stirred the leaves and limbs. He closed his eyes and listened to the chirping of the birds.

A father and daughter walked into the clearing, binoculars strapped around their necks. They stared at Terry. The father, a balding man named Irving, who wore a brace, rubbed his hand through his daughter's curly, shoulder length black hair. "I hope we didn't disturb you. My daughter and I are birders."

Terry sat up from the hickory tree, twisting his cramped back. "Actually, I was sitting here listening to the birds. You're not bothering me at all. As a matter of fact, I just heard a hawk."

Irving held his binoculars in one hand and propelled his daughter with the other. "We're venturing further into the woods." His raven-haired daughter waved.

He leaned back against the hickory tree and closed his eyes. Men moved around him. A hand touched his arm. "You seem sad, Malloy," Duffy said.

Terry opened his eyes. Duffy knelt on one knee, supporting himself with his M-16. The radio antenna waved behind his head.

"I am sad, Duffy. I've been sad for a while, actually."

"What are you feeling sad for, Bro?" Brumsen asked, easing his large frame down beside him.

"I lost my daughter. I lost my wife. I'm not the person I used to be."

Anderson ran a hand through his mohawk and rested his arm on his M-16, supported by an ammunition pouch. His other hand held a floppy hat by his side. "No one stays the same. Everyone changes."

"You guys haven't changed. You will never change for me. You'll always be young men, handsome and strong. You gave so much of yourselves. You lost all of your tomorrows." He looked at each of them. "I've missed you guys so much. Now that I've lost my daughter, I know how much your mothers and fathers have missed you, too."

Beyond Brumsen, Cochise sat with his knees drawn up to his chest. His jungle hat tilted at an angle on his head.

Terry said, "I can't imagine what your wife and son went through, Cochise."

"An *hijo* needs his padre, *mi cuate*."

Terry's hand kneaded his brow. "Yes, he does. A boy also needs to have a hero for a father and hear how brave his father was. But your sons and wives and girlfriends, mothers and fathers have heard a lot of bad things about all of you. In the movies and press, we've been portrayed as drug users, rapists, murderers, and homeless bums. The nation seems to have accepted myths about you that mock you as soldiers and mock your sacrifices."

"I have a hard time believing that my mom and dad would think anything like that about me." Duffy scratched his mohawk, consternation in his eyes. "I know Lucy wouldn't."

"My family wouldn't believe that about me, *either*," Brumsen snapped. "As a matter of fact, if my momma heard someone saying those things about me, she'd get awfully riled up."

"No American mom or dad would believe that about their sons," Anderson added. "That's complete bullshit."

"They're right, Malloy." Cochise raised to a squatting position. "You know that Maria's told my son what kind of man I was. She wouldn't believe what some bullshit journalist wrote or what some filmmaker and actors created."

Terry said, "We might hope that they wouldn't believe it, but it seems that the media myth has become the reality."

A falling leaf fluttered and whirled from side to side. The hawk's screech could be heard, faint and far away.

Thorn stood at the edge of the clearing. "Did I hear you talking to someone?"

"Thorn, what the hell are you doing here?"

"To tell the truth, I really hesitated to come." Thorn took off his baseball cap and walked into the clearing. "I didn't want to interfere with you and your grandson."

"He went on that hike. They're going up the mountain."

"I know. I saw him leave and I saw you walk into the woods. If you had been with your grandson, I wouldn't have bothered you. I felt bad about the two nights we've met. We always seem to get into confrontations."

Shrugging, Terry gestured for Thorn to come and sit down. "I may have been a little belligerent or defensive in getting my point across."

Standing, Thorn smacked his hat against his ear. His bald head reflected the evening sunlight. "My wife, who seems to be in the habit of pointing out my faults, tells me I've a way of goading people sometimes. After I saw you this morning, I had to examine my own motives for saying what I did at Rich's party. I owe you an apology, too."

"Sit down, Thorn."

Thorn tossed his hat to the ground in front of Terry. "I think I was trying to goad you a little the other night, Terry. You know, needle you a little bit, by calling you a baby-killer and by talking about World War Two. I half-listened to your conversation with Jeff while arguing with Sarah."

"Why would my conversation cause you to goad me?"

"I spent a lot of my youth believing that the Vietnam War was the worst mistake our country ever made. I still believe that. It's hard to listen to someone like you, who was on the opposite side of the trenches, talk about the war without my saying anything.

"I agree with Cochise. If I'm down to my last bullet," Anderson said, "I use it on me."

The squad had been silent, pondering the idea of being captured. Now, he knew. If captured, he'd be executed, like those poor bastards in the recon squad. Resolve coiled in him like a snake. If surrender wasn't a possibility, then he'd die fighting. He gazed upward at the dark canopy of the jungle and closed his eyes. Please, God, let me die quickly, if it has to happen. His watch said 5:00. Soft drops of new rain plopped on the leaves. Making sure Duffy was awake, Terry turned to wake the others.

The men stared at each other until the darkness lifted a little. Brumsen drank from his canteen. Cochise checked his knife. Duffy fiddled with the radio. Terry checked his M-16 as Brumsen examined his machine gun. The men took turns relieving themselves. They ate quickly, not heating the food, and buried the C-ration cans. Finally, Anderson nodded to Duffy and Terry. "Good luck."

The two of them disappeared into the green. They edged around the clearing to the trees that held his mines. He checked the blasting cap and connection of wire attached to one. Duffy did the same with the other. Trailing the wire from the mines, both moved back into the jungle. Terry counted fifty steps before they stopped, at least twenty feet from the path.

They attached the detonators to the wires. His feet throbbed. He had not thought of them for several hours.

What would his parents be doing? His mother was probably reading the Bible, preparing the lesson for her Sunday School class. His father was just coming home from work, changing to work in his garden before supper. He longed to see them again.

The jungle changed to a dull gray. Though not yet day, night had vanished. Duffy cocked his head and touched his shoulder.

You represent everything my youth doesn't. It irks me that you have no doubts about Vietnam."

"Who said I have no doubts about Vietnam. Any thinking adult should have doubts about all wars." Terry picked up a branch and twisted it in his hands. "Do you think I liked being shot at? Do you believe I enjoy thinking about the fifty-eight thousand men that were killed in Vietnam? But, I'm human. I get pissed by your insulting good soldiers who did their duty. When you start off by calling me a baby-killer, it's difficult to treat you seriously. That's why Kerry's hard to take. If you want to have a serious conversation about Vietnam, let's do it without the ridiculous name calling. It's bad enough fighting all the Vietnam stereotypes the media proffers. To listen to a reasonably intelligent person hammer at the same stereotypes, it's hard to take."

Thorn drummed fingers on his chin. "What good can be accomplished by ravaging a country by war? How can you justify all the civilian casualties?"

Anderson appeared behind Thorn. *Who killed any civilians?*

We've become the bad guys, Anderson. We always have to explain and justify ourselves. We're like no other American soldier. I'll be answering questions like this until the day I die. I'm constantly on the defensive.

"Are you okay?"

"I was just wondering if vets from the World Wars and Korea had to justify themselves like this. What civilian casualties are you talking about, Thorn? Are you talking about the slaughter of two million Cambodians by the Khymer Rouge, or the mere murder of two-hundred thousand South Vietnamese after we left? You can chalk up the butchering of a couple hundred thousand or so South Vietnamese to the usual communist purge that takes place after they'd conquered a country. Neither of those two holocausts would have happened if we had stayed, and our being there delayed it."

"What would have been the price in young, American boys, if we had stayed, Terry?" Thorn exhaled and breathed deeply. "How long would it have taken?"

"That's a good question. I don't know the answer to that. It would have to be hypothetical. Are two million Cambodians worth ten thousand more Americans? As I said, I have concerns about the war, also."

"You can't deny that we were supporting a corrupt regime that oppressed its people." Thorn thrust a finger at him

"Why should I deny that. When we fought the Korean war, South Korea and North Korea were ruled by despots. Syngman Rhee was a dictator and so was Chiang Kai-shek in Taiwan. It was our bad guys against the communist bad guys. There's one thing that you need to consider. Both Taiwan and South Korea are thriving countries now. How many elections have North Korea, China, and Vietnam had?"

"How can we in good conscience ally ourselves with despots when we are fighting to prevent the takeover of a country by another form of despotism?" Thorn sifted dirt in his hand. He yanked at the grass beside him. "Surely, that makes us as bad as the next guy."

"It's war, Thorn. You ally yourself with whoever is fighting your enemy. What about your beloved World War Two?"

"What about it?"

"We were allies of Joseph Stalin. Remember – the other mass murderer that invaded Poland as an ally of Hitler. Stalin butchered more people than Hitler. Was World War Two worth fighting with Stalin as an ally?"

Both were quiet.

"I hate arguing with historians." Thorn tossed aside the grass in his hand.

"Granddad, where are you?"

"Over here, Alex."

His grandson exploded into the clearing. "Grandpa, we saw an eagle! You can't believe how big they are."

"I need to get back to my son." Thorn placed his cap back on his head. "He went on the same hike." He held out his hand. "Don't think we're finished talking. We'll continue this some other time."

He placed his hand on Thorn's shoulder. "We'll be having this conversation until we're both dead."

"This was good. If I argue with you, I can stop arguing with Sarah. In those abortion debates, she makes me feel like the Gestapo. Arguing life, life, life while I'm saying death, death, death." Thorn held up his hands and made a 'V' with his fingers. "At least when I'm arguing with you, I'll be arguing peace, peace, peace and you'll be saying war, war, war."

* * *

The rain began again in earnest thirty minutes after the helicopter crash. The skies loosed a deluge of lightning, thunder, and water.

"A thunderstorm? How can you fight a war in a fucking tormenta?" Cochise shook his head in disbelief.

"This is great." Anderson forced his cleaning rod down the barrel of his rifle. "The rain will help hide us and get our asses out of this fucked-up mess of a snafu." He dismantled his cleaning rod, placing it in his rucksack. "I gotta go check our route with the captain. You guys get squared away and be ready to move when I get back."

"We seem to go from mess to mess. We get muddier and dirtier with every passing day." Duffy placed a radio battery in his rucksack. "It's hard to keep equipment clean in this crap, and I personally feel like a waterlogged raisin. My wrinkles are getting wrinkles."

Terry reached for a claymore mine. "It's not helping my feet." A medic had given him some powder. He, in turn, passed some to

Cochise. "Keep your socks dry and change them as often as you can. How the hell am I supposed to keep my feet dry?"

"We're gonna have to wait on our feet to dry out, Malloy," Cochise said. "I figure the way we're going, they'll be dry in about three months."

"I just want to get moving. I can't get that frigging medevac crash outa my mind." Brumsen settled a belt of well-oiled machine gun ammunition into his M-60.

Everyone paused to look up at the mountain as the booms of artillery came rolling down the hillside. Streaks of lightning crackled over the mountain and seconds later the thunder boomed across the valley, indistinguishable from the artillery bombardment.

Brumsen shook his dark head. The black mohawk streak of his hair sparkled with raindrops. "I know I don't want no part of that crap up there. This is a fuckin' nightmare. Those poor bastards gotta start moving up that hill sometime today. I wanta be outa here by then."

Anderson came back ten minutes later carrying more claymores, detonators, and ammunition. He distributed the material to each man. "They've delayed using the Fourth Battalion as a blocking force. This weather is screwing up everything."

Laying a plastic-covered map on the ground, Anderson pointed. "We've been assigned this sector of jungle to cover. Two more recon teams are on their way right now to their own sectors. The captain wants us to find trails the enemy could use. He wants us to do everything we can to slow down enemy movement that can help supply their forces on this mountain. That means booby traps, ambushes, and artillery strikes. We have two one-oh-five batteries, two one-five-five batteries, and maybe one one-seven-five battery to support us."

Cochise whistled. His face held his usual grim slit of a smile. His eyes did not smile. "Big-time payback."

"Yes, big-time payback – if we do our jobs." Anderson picked up a roll of tape and several rifle magazines, which he placed into his rucksack. "You guys are terrific. I couldn't ask for better men. You need good men." Everyone sat up a little straighter and circled closer.

"We head south one click. Then we turn west toward Cambodia for two clicks and head north. Any big troop concentrations, we call in artillery. Booby-trapping trails is horseshit. We're not going to waste our time doing that. The North Vietnamese have got to have some way of moving all of these fucking troops around this jungle. There's gotta be a couple of big speed trails.

"Once we go north," Anderson continued, "I think we'll find that trail. If we do, we can get some serious payback and perhaps slow down their troop movement as well. Cambodia is only a couple of miles west of here." Tapping the map with one finger, Anderson rubbed his chin with his other hand. "We may just find ourselves in another country. Any questions?" The squad was silent. "Okay, let's get the fuck outa here."

The men daubed their faces with black and green camouflage paint. Cochise brought out two small jars of red and yellow paint. The squad dipped their fingers into the jars. Terry streaked red paint from his left eye to his jaw line. A yellow streak ran down the right side of his face. Black and green splotches dotted his forehead, chin, and nose.

The men hurried through the jungle with Cochise on point. They stopped briefly at a listening post outside of the perimeter. The three men at the post slumped over their weapons. They stared at the squad with hollow-eyes in heads attached to tired shoulders. Like everyone else, they had not shaved, bathed, or slept in several days. Tattered jungle fatigues hung on each one of them. Still, the M-60 machine gun and their own personal weapons gleamed with oil. A helmet full of grenades sat between them.

"There's been nothing out in front of us," answered one to Anderson's query about enemy activity. "If they have probes out, then they're somewhere else along the perimeter. Nothing here," he reiterated.

One of the men at the listening post waved a halfhearted goodbye. On the trek south, small-arms fire and explosions rumbled from the mountain. No sunshine penetrated the cloud cover. The monsoon torrents let up somewhat, but the rain continued.

The men paused around 2 in the afternoon when the squad turned west toward Cambodia. Anderson's floppy jungle hat hid his mohawk haircut. He wiped water from his unshaven jaw line, covered with green, black, and yellow paint. "I want to get at least a mile west of where we are right now, if possible. Then I want to turn north before we stop for the night. With the cloud cover, it'll get dark sooner, so we may be moving through the jungle at night. If the gooks can do it, so can we."

They moved west for three hours with no contact. After breaking for a quick meal, Cochise took a compass heading for north. They had been lucky in not encountering enemy troops. After asking Terry for the count, Duffy radioed the battalion to say the squad was in Indian country and moving north. They crossed many small paths, but did not stop.

At a stream, Terry lowered himself chest deep into water, holding his weapon above his head, and waded to the other side. He thought about the leeches in the water and knew, as the rest of the men did, that he would have some on him when he climbed onto the opposite bank. He imagined the slimy creatures slithering over his body and realized he didn't care. No time for that now. The leeches, like everything else not affecting him at the moment, could wait. He reached for a hand.

"Keep moving."

They turned north. It grew darker by the minute. The men did not slacken their pace. Anderson was determined to push as far north as possible. The squad stumbled and tripped over vines, tree roots, and plants. They kept moving. The slippery, rain-soaked ground caused treacherous footing. Terry brushed vegetation aside and almost stumbled over the rest of the men. Brumsen reached out to steady him.

"We stop here for the night," Anderson whispered. "Cochise is having trouble reading his compass."

Taking out his poncho, Anderson pulled it over him. "Malloy, what's the count?" Terry told Anderson, who knelt down with the poncho covering him. He flicked on his flashlight to study his map.

Duffy unharnessed his equipment, took off his shirt, and lowered his pants to his ankles. He slowly ran his hands over his body. He held up his left arm and stuck a leech with his bayonet. The slug shape, outlined against Duffy's skin, fell to the ground. Next, Duffy turned around to face the jungle. His exposed back revealed two three-inch black shapes hanging from his shoulders and one in the middle of his back. Cochise stabbed the slugs. He placed them on the ground and stepped on them.

The soft patter of the rain struck the upturned fronds and leaves of the trees. Brumsen and Duffy checked Cochise. Anderson motioned for Terry to turn around. He did so while taking off his fatigue jacket. Terry found one on his groin that he himself removed. Anderson, who had taken off three, whispered for him to hold still.

"Hurry, let's take care of these bloodsuckers first, and then we eat and rest." Anderson unbuttoned his shirt.

So many damn leeches. The entire squad was covered with them. No one cared.

By eight o'clock they had arranged themselves for the night in the order they would awake for watch. Duffy contacted Battalion and gave the radio to Anderson who whispered a situation report as silently as possible and then listened to the radio. Anderson sagged noticeably and listlessly replaced the receiver.

"We fought further up the fucking mountain today. One of our jets dropped a bomb on the medical evacuation point. It killed at least ten people, most of them were already wounded."

"We're insane." Everyone looked at Duffy, who shook his head. "We're fucking insane. What are we doing out here trying to kill people?"

"*Hijos de puta!* If the gooks don't kill us, our own side will." Cochise plunged his knife into the ground.

"Come on, Bros. Let's get a grip." Brumsen stuck out his big black hand, palm toward the ground. "We have to depend on each other." The men reached toward Brumsen's hand, stacking them one upon the other. "We all we got, and we all we need."

Terry already knew when he would be awakened for watch. He leaned back on his rucksack and fell asleep. The last thing he saw in the dim shadows was Anderson kneeling, staring off into the jungle.

Someone touched Terry's shoulder. A vise-like grip pressed his flesh. He came awake instantly, making no noise. Anderson's eyes were six inches from his own. He nodded, and Anderson moved on to Duffy, the last person to be awakened. Then Terry heard it, the sound of men speaking Vietnamese. Instinctively, his hand tightened around his M-16 on his lap. The muffled clatter of equipment being handled and tossed about floated through the jungle. These guys are noisy as hell.

Everyone awake, Cochise, next to Terry, cocked his head, listening. Anderson tapped Terry and Cochise. When they turned, they saw Anderson, kneeling with his rucksack in front of him, holding out a claymore with one hand. The other hand was still in his rucksack. Terry took the first claymore. Anderson gave a second claymore to Cochise. He brought out another, placed it on the ground for himself, and withdrew several strands of detonator wire with the blasting caps attached to them. He handed one roll each to Terry and Cochise, again taking one for himself. He pointed to Duffy and Brumsen, gesturing for them to stay.

The Vietnamese voices sounded indistinct, muffled by the rain and damp jungle. Whoever spoke did not attempt to lower his voice. Terry could not tell how far away the voices were. He guessed thirty to fifty yards.

Holding the claymore in one hand and the wire in another, Anderson lowered himself to his hands and knees and crawled through the jungle toward the voices. Cochise, carrying his own claymore and wire, followed. Neither carried a weapon. Terry lay down his rifle and got on his knees, following behind Cochise.

He lowered his chest to the ground. He had never crawled so slowly. As he pulled himself along the jungle floor, mold, mildew, and rotting vegetation assailed his senses. Whenever he felt Cochise's boot, he backed away a foot or so and waited for Cochise to move. The Vietnamese voices were silent.

The three men crawled for what seemed like hours. Lying immobile on the ground, he felt something slither across his legs. Terry remained absolutely still, a claymore in one hand and cord in the other, watching Cochise's two booted feet.

The Vietnamese voices began again. Several men laughed. Less than two miles from the battle, and these assholes were laughing. Pretty fucking confident. These bastards didn't have a clue. He estimated the voices at no more than ten feet from them. Cochise began crawling again. The voices grew loud. His heart pounded against the floor of the jungle. Blood coursed through his head. Every movement of his hands, feet and body was made in inches. He licked his lips; his mouth held no moisture. He felt an urge, a primordial urge, to be anywhere but there. How close were we going to get?

His muscles strained not only to move, but to move fast. Every ounce of energy, he mustered to remain on the ground. Tension coursed through muscles. Another urge to jump up and run through the jungle screaming, passed through him.

Cochise motioned Terry to come forward, Anderson's camouflaged face barely visible over Cochise's shoulder. He crawled around Cochise, and the three of them lay on the ground facing each other. Anderson placed his blasting cap into his claymore. Terry and Cochise did the same. The Vietnamese talked, but more subdued. Anderson made a spreading motion with both hands, parting Cochise and Terry. Both moved five yards to each side of Anderson, who was down on the ground again and crawling forward in line with them.

Terry sensed, rather than saw, movement in front of him. The Vietnamese chattered, no more than five feet away. The rain hitting the jungle foliage and the Vietnamese voices were the only sounds. Thank God for this rain and the wet ground soaking up noise. He smiled as he pushed the supporting legs of the claymore into the ground. He was thinking like Anderson. Moving backward, trailing out the wire attached to the claymore, taxed his energy more than crawling forward. Go slow. Go slower. He crawled backward by inches until he felt a hand on his boot.

CHAPTER FIFTEEN

Terry lay on his back, his hands clasped behind his head. He was fully clothed, except for his shoes. A contented and exhausted Alex snuggled in his sleeping bag. A chorus of crickets serenaded the camp. A screech owl howled in the distance.

What was he doing? He was going crazy, that's what he was doing. Was he actually waiting for dead men to come and looking forward to talking to them?

He turned on his side and pulled the sleeping bag around his shoulders. Closing his eyes for what seemed like the thousandth time, he willed sleep to come.

"You're nuts, Duffy."

"It's what I believe, Anderson. You don't have faith. So, you'll never understand the argument I'm making."

Throwing the sleeping bag off, he rubbed his eyes. The sound of metal clinking on metal came through the tent. Anderson and Duffy sat on the ground facing each other. Cochise lay on his side, his hand propping up his head. Brumsen's knees were drawn up to his chin. Muscled arms encircled his knees.

"Oh, I have faith. I have faith in this. Everyone understands this argument." Anderson lifted his M-16

Duffy sat cross-legged, hands in his lap. A floppy hat perched at a precarious angle on the back of his head. "There's nothing wrong with being merciful. If there's a forgiving God who is merciful to us, how much more should we show mercy to each other."

"That's a *big* if." Anderson snorted.

"What's the alternative, Anderson?" Terry interrupted. "Are we to live in the jungle and fight like animals for every little advantage? Isn't there something more to our nature?"

Duffy, legs still crossed, leaned forward. "Yes, there is. You have to have faith, Malloy."

"We're not always at war," Brumsen said.

"We have our country's laws that we live by most of the time." Anderson stretched out a slender hand for emphasis. "That's why we have countries. When we're in the jungle, there are no laws. There are no rights. There are no rules."

"That only pushes the problem to another level, guys." Cochise shook a pack of cigarettes until one tumbled out. "Nations become proxies for individuals. There's a constant struggle in the world for dominance." The glow of a match revealed Cochise's face. "As nations, we're right back in the jungle, struggling to climb out of the pit. We're talking about *la guerra*. There are no rules in war, Malloy. You know that. We had every right in the world to do what we did."

"Nations have a right to do what they have to do to protect themselves." Brumsen added. "We did what we had to do."

"That's just it!" Duffy pointed his floppy hat at Brumsen. "Having a right to do something doesn't mean that we have to do it or that we *should* do it."

"That's your opinion, Duffy. Our job was to kill the enemy." Anderson shifted his weight, bending a knee. "A nation's job is to protect itself from its enemies. What happens when we don't strike because of your so-called ideals and it comes back to haunt us."

Terry threw his arms out, shrugging. "I'm not in that world anymore, guys. I'm not nineteen and full of hate. I'm fifty-eight. I have a grandson. I don't want him to grow up in a jungle, or ever have to fight in a jungle."

"War is something that we, as people, as nations, created. It's not natural." Duffy uncrossed his legs, drawing his knees to his chest. "We don't have to live in a jungle with everyone, or every nation, out for themselves."

"That's some kind of art you're talking about. Are there any rules to art?" Anderson asked, borrowing Cochise's cigarette and lighting his own.

"It *is* an art." Duffy pointed toward Anderson. "You guys want me to accept the art, something that we've created, as reality."

"Granddad, is it time to get up?"

"No son, not yet." Beyond the group, the sun crept over the horizon. "That little voice in the tent belongs to my work of art, a living being that I helped to create. To have children, you have to have hope, hope that the future will be better. I have to work to make the world a better place, not only for him, but for all children. You can survive with a jungle mentality. But is that the only prospect for the future – mere survival, every man or group, or nation, for himself?"

Rose-pedaled streaks shot across the sky.

"Granddad, who are you talking to?" Alex's head poked out of the tent.

"Alex, come out here. I want to tell you about some dear friends of mine, whom I love as much as you and your mom."

The camp turned out en masse for the Sunday meditation service. When it was over, Thorn gave a speech on the environment.

"This morning, I've chosen the topic of the environment, because of our luck in participating in this first campout of universal brotherhood out here where we see the ultimate victim, the world and nature. This is one victim who definitely cannot speak for herself. I choose the gender of the environment with care. The earth is our mother, *Gaia*, who nurtures all of us. Western nations have been raping our mother for centuries. If that sounds obscene to you, I meant it to be.

"While we've been doing this, we've also been oppressing and raping our fellow brethren and victims in the second and third worlds. It's only when we redistribute the wealth that we industrial nations have achieved, not only to our own oppressed, but to other victims all over the world, we can at the same time, achieve a balance in the ecology.

"It's the greed of the industrial societies of the western world who have caused this crises. Only when every victim gets an equal share, only when societies all over the world are remade so that we are all brother environmentalists, working for the same vision of universal solidarity with our mother, *Gaia*, will we achieve our goal. This can only happen when we cast off the societal rules and standards that we've become accustomed to as inheritors of our culture.

"This may sound a little harsh to some of you. I want to end this by telling you that you can't both be an environmental warrior in solidarity with our brothers, and fellow victims, all over the world and expect to maintain your middle-class, bourgeois life. Our materialist's life has to end. Are you willing to sacrifice your materialistic lifestyle, which is what caused this problem to begin with. Once the means of production are in the hands of the environmental proletariat, we'll rest. Are you willing to fight for environmental solidarity with workers all over the world? Are you on the side of our brothers and sisters in all parts of the earth who are toiling in the trenches? Are you willing to sacrifice your mutual funds and your IRA? America is a land of individuals. We need to establish a new paradigm, one that promotes solidarity, negates individuality like China, and moves us closer together as a community."

The fathers and sons went back to their campsites and tore down the tents. Men and children, breaking camp, bustled everywhere. Boys and girls ran hither and thither with bundles tucked under their arms. A few expletives exploded from several fathers trying to roll tents, tent poles, and tent stakes into some kind of recognizable, orderly mass easy enough to carry. Terry stomped on the billowing tent, chasing the last vestiges of air from its folds.

A shadow appeared, falling across Terry's back, casting itself in front of him. "May I sit down?" someone asked.

He glanced over his shoulder. "Certainly." The man had a round face, attached to an equally plump body. Most of his short-cropped hair was gray. The most striking feature about his face was a pair of eyebrows that formed a continuous black and gray streak across his brow. He introduced himself as Homer.

Homer scratched his eyebrows. "I know who you are because of the papers. I arrived late yesterday and didn't get a chance to meet anyone. Then I went to find my son and didn't get a chance to introduce myself. So, here I am. I especially wanted to meet you, because I was in Vietnam, too. Where were you stationed?"

Gathering the tent stakes, Terry began to tie them together. "My unit's base was *Bien Hoa* and then we moved to *Dak To*. Most of the time, though, we were in the jungle."

"*Dak To* was not a pleasant place to be, was it?" Homer wrinkled his brow.

"You could probably say that about Vietnam in general." Terry finished tying the cord.

Homer's eyebrows rose perceptibly. "I was in the Signal Corps. I used to go down to the airfield where I was stationed and watch guys like you, the ones in the infantry, come in from the field. Their fatigues would be ripped and torn. They were dirty, unshaven, and smelled to high heaven. When they got off the helicopters, they had a look of utter exhaustion on their faces. Their sunken eyes had a worried, distant stare. I can remember it just like it was yesterday. When I was first in country, I used to take pictures of them as they got off the choppers and walked past me. They didn't even notice me. Eventually, I stopped taking pictures and would just stand there watching them."

Homer stared at the woods. "We'd hear the fights, sometimes, on our radio net. They were so confusing. We could hear the sounds of guns firing and orders being yelled. After every battle and fight I'd try especially to get down there and watch the guys unload from the helicopters. I don't see how you guys could stand it."

"We were all afraid."

"You were all afraid, but you went. I wanted to volunteer for combat, but I was too scared."

Homer's eyebrows dipped. His cheeks quivered. "When I got back from Vietnam, everyone assumed that I had been in combat. I didn't discourage it."

"You can be forgiven for that."

"You don't understand. I even made up stories about what I saw and did." Homer looked down at the ground and then at Terry. "I was a hero, twenty years old and a hero. People paid attention to me. There was no way that anyone could check it out, so I lied about my service. It was incredible. You could tell people anything, and they would believe it. There was even a guy who said he was in combat, who confessed to me that he was a supply clerk. He never left California. I never told him that I wasn't in combat. It got to where I was almost believing the things I was saying. I even went to counseling sessions for delayed stress syndrome. Looking back now, it was hilarious and depressing at the same time. I made up some real bad stories, Terry. Children were killed. Villages were napalmed and wiped out. The worst of it was that people believed me."

"Why did you say those things?"

Homer's shoulders held the weight of his lies. "Because people seemed to expect it. Plus, I had to have a reason for the delayed stress. They wanted to believe all the bad stuff. The worse I made it, the more they ate it up. I was respected. I was even interviewed and quoted by the newspapers a couple of times. They could never check out my stories. They wanted to believe every bad thing I said. Eventually, after some soul searching, I stopped telling people that I was in combat."

"What made you stop?"

"It's crazy, but I was in a 'delayed stress' counseling session, and some of the guys were talking about the money, you know, the benefits, I could receive. I knew I had to stop. No one was going to question me, not even the government." Homer sighed. "It was especially hard to give up that heroic persona and all those adventures. But I was living a lie, and I grew ashamed of myself. I had created a reality that everyone wanted to believe. My shame is finally what forced me to confront my lies. I know you think I'm crazy, but I had to tell you this to get it off my chest. Thanks for listening to me."

After shaking hands, Homer walked away. Terry watched him wind his way through the tents.

"You got any more like him around?" Cochise asked.

The men sat or squatted behind Terry, waiting expectantly for him to reply.

"Unfortunately," Terry said, "there are a lot more like him. It's a shame. People listened to him when he lied, but no one cares now that he wants to tell the truth."

"Hey, come on, guys," Duffy said, "he was apologizing."

"That's true, he did say he was sorry." Brumsen pulled a blade of grass and stuck it in his mouth.

"You got that right," Anderson said. "What kind of man would steal another man's valor? He's about as sorry as a man can get."

Terry looked down the hill, then back at the squad. "I want to ask you guys something. What did you guys die for? I'm really having a hard time figuring it all out. I understand geopolitics and systems of government. I can throw that bullshit out with the best of them. You're all good men. Why did you have to die?"

A silence followed, then Cochise spoke. "You said it earlier, Terry. I want my son to grow up in a country where he won't have to swim across a river, like one set of his grandparents did, to find work and better himself. Like all immigrants, my family wanted a better life here. I was willing to fight for it."

"I wanted the opportunity to better myself with the GI Bill." Brumsen eased the blade of grass out of his mouth. "It was the only way I'd be able to go to college. My mother dreamed of a house to live in, instead of an apartment to rent. She's never going to get one as a maid working for a janitorial service."

"I'm an American," Duffy said. "My country was at war. I felt an obligation to do my share."

"I felt the same way, Duffy," Terry said.

"Why don't you tell us, Malloy. Did we win in Vietnam?" Anderson asked.

"No, we didn't win in Vietnam. We won eventually. But not in Vietnam."

"What do you mean? Did we finally fight Russia?"

"We managed to avoid World War Three. We never fought Russia. Despite all the protests over Vietnam, the limited-war scenario partially worked. The last half of the twentieth century was a long struggle for the U.S. against Communism. After Hitler and World War II, Vietnam and Korea were battles that we fought as a nation against Russia, China, and their proxies. Vietnam was our biggest and the only real defeat. After Vietnam, Russian dominance was at its height in the late '70s and early '80s. Communists expanded into Africa and South America. Cuba sent troops to Africa. The Russians invaded Afghanistan. The Communists slaughtered two million people in Cambodia."

"How did that happen?" Cochise asked.

"We left Vietnam," Terry said. "There was no one to stop the Communists. Our citizens wanted us out of Vietnam and Southeast Asia. They felt the cost was too high to justify our continuing presence there. After the demonstrations and protests got us out of Southeast Asia, the Communists took it. Cambodia fell, and the Cambodian Reds slaughtered two million of their own people."

"So, the Vietnamese are free?" Duffy asked.

"No, there're still pockets of totalitarian Communist regimes. The Vietnamese aren't free. People are still trying to escape from North Korea and China. Cubans are still floating sixty miles to Florida and being eaten by sharks."

"We won," Anderson said. "What a kick in the ass that is. I can't believe those dumb bastards that planned the Vietnam strategy could do anything right."

The men laughed.

"The U.S. became the most dominant military and economic power that the world has ever seen," Terry continued. "You guys, you and your sacrifices, the guys who fought and died in Korea, Vietnam, and all over the globe, put us there. World War II was, unfortunately, just a prelude. We defeated one form of tyrannical socialism, only to be faced with a more insidious, dangerous form."

"Why was it more dangerous?" Brumsen asked.

"Communism disguised itself as a struggle for workers and the poor. The Nazis were trying to build a master race. It was easy to see their goals of world domination. The Communists used the plight of poor people in every country to gain a foothold. Once they were in power, they always ruled by tyranny and the tools of tyranny, just like the Nazis. The Free World's long struggle against the Communists will eventually be viewed like the Greeks' struggle against the Persians. Just as the Greek ideal of democracy spread to Europe, you guys helped save and spread democracy all over the world. You helped defeat an empire and system of government that was responsible for the deaths of over one hundred million of their own people. There has never been a more brutal empire or ideology in the history of the world."

"What kind of community do we have at home?" Duffy asked.

"Yeah," Brumsen said, "is my mom being taken care of? She didn't make a lot of money."

"Did my boy get a fair chance?" Cochise asked.

Patting Terry's shoulder, Duffy smiled. "The death and dying don't mean anything, Malloy, if we don't have a community of people who support each other."

"I'm ashamed to tell you that I don't know how your families are, but I'm going to find out, beginning tomorrow. As for our country, we're still struggling, still trying to work things out."

Terry switched his gaze when he heard Alex yelling good-bye to several boys. When he turned back, the squad was gone.

Finished with the packing, Terry and Alex made two trips, loaded down with camping gear, to their car. All of the children and fathers made a line at one end of the camp site and walked across it, picking up small pieces of paper and the usual detritus of an active camp.

His grandson stooped to pick up a chewing-gum wrapper. "Granddad, how old were you when you got your first gun?"

"Your great-grandfather bought me a small rifle called a twenty-two when I was ten." Terry took the wrapper from Alex and put it in his pocket. "I could only shoot it on Grandfather Terrence's farm. I hunted rabbits and squirrels. I also did target practice with it."

"Grandfather Terrence is who you're named after, isn't he?"

"Yes, I have his name. He's your great-great-grandfather; he gave me the first real gun that was all my own. Your great-grandfather and his brothers gave Grandfather Terrence a twelve-gauge automatic shotgun for his seventy-fifth birthday. He took his own shotgun, a twenty-gauge pump, off the wall, and gave it to me. Then we, my brothers, your great-grandfather, and his brothers and their sons, and Grandad Terrence, all went hunting that afternoon on Papa's farm. Remember, Papa is your great-great-great-grandfather, the one who barked squirrels. I was twelve years old. Papa couldn't go with us, because he had fallen and broken a hip. Papa must have been around ninety-five or six by then and walking was hard for him."

The line had reached the other side of the camp. Everyone shook hands and said good-byes.

"Can you take me hunting, Grandad?"

Terry put his arm around Alex and hugged him. "When you're a bit older, if you still want to go hunting, I'll take you.

* * *

The screams and groans of the wounded Vietnamese continued for what seemed hours. Terry had no idea how long they had waited for the North Vietnamese to send someone to help the men they had ambushed. One of the wounded kept saying the same thing over and over. Finally, either through exhaustion or death, silence settled over the Vietnamese lying on the speed trail. As the jungle grew lighter, an occasional groan filtered through the foliage.

The men, too, maintained their discipline and silence. Terry estimated them to be at least one hundred feet from the Vietnamese and ten feet from the speed trail. The jungle wrapped itself around the squad like a warm blanket. The NVA would never find them in this green fog. Trackers, if such existed, would find nothing but a cold trail.

Rain continued to fall and plop through the trees and foliage. Soggy ground absorbed not only water, but also noise, pain, and fatigue of the men, both Vietnamese and American. The squad squatted like Vietnamese. Mud and grime clung to them. Around them hovered the moldy, fungal smell of the jungle.

They squatted in a circle facing out. Brumsen, his M-60 on the ground in front of him, studied the ammunition belt that fed into his machine-gun. He used a small oil cloth to wipe the belt. Occasionally, he used the rag to swat at mosquitoes. Cochise squatted and peered through the jungle, toying with his knife, glancing up whenever one of the wounded Vietnamese groaned. Duffy, his hands over his protruding ears, seemed to be pondering something. He grimaced over his radio every time a cry of pain echoed through the jungle. Anderson continually looked at his watch.

Cochise lifted his head, then cocked it to one side, listening. Brumsen paused, watching Cochise, as did Terry. Anderson stood, moving a frond aside, and stepped toward the speed trail. The muffled sound came of men running on wet ground. Duffy crouched down even lower, swinging the radio and rucksack onto his back in a quick, practiced, easy motion. The North Vietnamese ran by the squad's position. Terry estimated the number to be no more than ten or twelve.

A cascade of spoken Vietnamese burst from the trail. The voices and sounds were like cannon shots after the comfortable silence of the groaning jungle. Every cry of pain was a justifiably sweet vengeance for the deaths of the men he had seen in the past few days. A vision of the burning helicopter extinguished any thought of mercy. The rest of the men surely felt the same way.

Anderson emerged from the foliage, smiled, and gave a thumbs-up.

Terry's thoughts raced back to when they had returned from placing the claymore mines. Anderson counted to three, and they pushed their respective detonator handles at the same time. The blast sent a shock wave through the jungle. The leaves and trees around them recoiled. Smoke and the pungent aroma of cordite hung over the jungle like a storm. Then the moaning, groaning, and screaming of the wounded broke over them like a wave. All the men, except for Anderson, were on their feet quickly, ready to move. Anderson knelt on the ground, motionless. He signaled everyone to kneel around him.

"Come on, Anderson." Cochise flicked a thumb toward the moaning Vietnamese. "Let's shoot these assholes and get the fuck outa here."

"Yeah, let's do it." Brumsen placed the stock of the M-60 on the ground.

A primordial cry of pain sliced through the jungle night, high pitched and continuous. The Vietnamese soldier screamed until he ran out of breath, ending in sobs. He then screamed again after he had drawn another breath.

"We're not going to kill those guys, and we're not going to run." Anderson paused as another scream interrupted him.

The squad glanced toward the screaming. Cochise smiled.

"Die in pain, you sonofabitch," Brumsen whispered.

"No mercy," Terry said.

"We do have to move though," Anderson said. "I'm hoping that these guys will get some help from someone. When they do, we'll follow them back to wherever they're taken."

Anderson unhooked the detonator from the wire. "That's got to be some kind of speed trail. First, let's move a couple of hundred yards away from here to lose any trackers that may come after us. With this rain, I seriously doubt anyone could follow our trail. They ain't goin' to send any trackers with a party to pick up the wounded. So, we'll circle back and get close enough to watch and listen to see if help comes for those guys. We wait. If no one comes by daybreak and any of them are still alive, we kill them and keep moving."

Vietnamese talking and the thwack of machetes cutting wood brought Terry back to the present. Must be cutting poles for stretchers.

Twenty minutes passed. The Vietnamese trotted down the trail, carrying the wounded men. A sharp bark of orders came from a man no more than ten feet from the squad. The footsteps of the Vietnamese diminished, swallowed by the jungle. Terry's hands turned white from clutching his M-16. They must think they owned this jungle, the way they were chattering. The squad stood quietly. With Cochise leading, they stayed slightly off of the main trail and hurried west toward Cambodia after the Vietnamese.

His breathing slowed as they walked. When Terry heard the groans of the Vietnamese, a deep feeling of satisfaction and deliberateness came over him. You asked for it, you bastards! When the squad of Vietnamese thudded down the path, his heart started pounding again. His hands were clammy. He broke into a sweat. Recognizing the symptoms, he realized with a sense of satisfaction that he was in control of his emotions and his actions.

Occasionally, as they crouched following the Vietnamese west, the squad came upon small trails. They stopped and crossed them cautiously. Many times Vietnamese voices came from the speed trail and moved eastward toward the battle, not westward as they were moving. Once, the soft voices of several women sounded over the patter of the rain. At these times they halted, waiting no more than a minute, then moving again. He continued the count.

The unabated rain muffled any sounds they made. But the possibility existed that a chance occurrence of someone seeing them by accident could happen.

He walked backward for a short distance. Then he stopped completely and squatted. The squad went on without him as he counted fifteen seconds off. He rose and glided through the jungle in a crouch. Brumsen, on one knee, held his fist in the air. Terry stopped.

The squad moved as fast as the Vietnamese stretcher bearers, having followed them at least a mile. The voices of Vietnamese floated on the air. Brumsen, without warning, crept at a right angle away from the speed trail, deeper into the jungle. Terry followed.

After a hundred yards, Anderson stopped the squad. "There's an intersecting north-south speed trail crossing the east-west trail we've been following. The men we followed turned up the north-south trail. We're going to set up two teams. Cochise, you and Terry go back and watch the east-west trail. I'll watch the north-south trail with Duffy. I want to get an idea of the volume of traffic. Brumsen, stay here. Set up the machine gun and put out claymores in case we bring back bad guys.

"This will be our fall-back position, if you guys hear any gunshots or explosions. I'll come here immediately, if I hear the same. Shoot an azimuth before you leave and establish a reciprocal heading to come back on. I repeat, any shots or explosions, and you guys get your asses back here."

Cochise gave Brumsen two claymores. Brumsen set the machine gun on the ground, removing his rucksack.

"Once back here and together, we move." Anderson dropped his rucksack to the ground. "You guys watch your step and meet back here in one hour." He looked at his watch. "That will be eleven o'clock. We're deep in Indian country, up to our assholes and elbows in Vietnamese. What's more, I think we're in Cambodia now."

CHAPTER SIXTEEN

His cellmate, a young college student named George, hugging the commode, could not stop gagging and heaving. Small pieces of food and stale beer soaked his brown beard. The smell of vomit permeated the air. "They told me if I ate something, I wouldn't get so drunk."

Terry sat on his bunk, elbows resting on knees. He held his head in his hands. Glancing up, he shook his aching head. "That depends on what you drink, George, and how much."

George, still on his knees, pushed himself away from the commode. "I guess I shouldn't have mixed the rum and the beer."

"No, that's not a good idea." Terry rested his chin on his hand. "Next time mix margaritas with scotch, or wine with bourbon, or tequila. Those are much better combinations than rum and beer."

"Thanks, dude. Why're you in here?" George switched positions, supporting himself on one elbow, his head leaning against the commode.

"I got in a fight with two guys who were fighting each other."

"You tried to break up a fight?"

"No. There were two guys in my yard when I got home from a camping trip this morning. They both started yelling at me when I pulled up. One guy wanted my autograph and the other guy was waving a sign that said I hated America. The guy who wanted my autograph grabbed the signed and hit the man who was carrying it."

"What happened then?" George picked what looked like a piece of pepperoni out of his beard.

"I grabbed the sign from the guy who wanted my autograph and hit him with it."

George crawled over to his cot. "Why?"

"I thought it was because the autograph man called the sign man a 'Nazi Bastard' before he hit him. But, thinking about it now, I might have just wanted to hit someone. Sometimes you just get tired of the bullshit."

"Boy, you can say that again," George said, leaning on his cot. "I said that to my girlfriend just the other night. She told me to go fuck myself. That's why I got drunk. You got in a fight with both guys? What happened to the sign man?"

"The sign man called the autograph man a 'communist sonofabitch' who hated America." Terry helped the groaning George onto his bed. "So, I figured that he deserved to have the shit beat out of him, too. If I had just hit them once it would have been okay. The sign was stapled to a broomstick. Anyway, I popped them each with the broomstick several more times and then I went inside and fixed me a drink. Five minutes later the police and an ambulance showed up. I saw them through what used to be my living room window. The sign guy and the autograph guy go to the hospital. The police took my whiskey away and here I am. They both pressed charges against me."

A clang of gears and locks shifting made Terry turn his head toward the cell door. Someone tramped down the cell block, footsteps echoing around the cells.

George lay on his back, one hand behind his head, the other picking regurgitated food out of his beard. "Lemme get this straight. You wacked a couple of guys in your yard for calling each other names?"

"Essentially, that covers it. There's just no civil discourse anymore. I'm tired of it. Everyone wants to label everyone they disagree with. Whoever makes the labels stick, wins. It's not a good way to discuss issues."

A balding police sergeant, eating a donut, opened the cell door. "Malloy, someone posted bail for you. Your free to go."

Sarah, sitting with her long legs crossed, waited for him. "Do you have any idea what is going on?"

Terry yawned and scratched his whiskered face. "Yeah, I just found out you don't drink rum and beer and eat pepperoni pizza when your girl tells you to go fuck yourself."

Wrinkling her brow, a cloud of puzzlement shadowed Sarah's face. "What in God's name are you talking about."

"Nevermind. What's up?" Terry waved her off with a weary hand.

"We've got another teach-in tonight and everyone is expecting you to be there."

"No way." He stared across the parking lot with tired, bleary eyes.

Taking Terry's arm, Sarah guided him toward her car. "You have to. You're a hero to the left now. Everyone admires the way you spoke out against the Greatest Generation. This is your chance to get back at them."

"Why would I want to get back at them. I don't give a shit what they or anyone else thinks." Terry eased himself into Sarah's car.

She leaned over and kissed his lips. "Okay, then it's your chance to clarify any previous statements. Would you like to do that."

"No."

"Terry, please! You're the one who has a little bit of celebrity now. You've been written about in the *Daily Rant*. We've put out a release that you'll be on the panel. Do it as a favor to me. The press will be there and it'll be a lot of publicity for the school."

He clutched her warm hand. "I'm tired. Take me home so I can get a drink. What's the subject?"

Sarah, making a left hand turn, let go of Terry's hand and grasped the steering wheel. "Gay rights."

"What the hell do I know about gay rights? You're not going to talk about raping lesbian cows are you?"

Laughing, she shook her head. "No, we just don't want to be accused of having a completely biased panel. Rich, Barbara and I thought you would give the panel an air of objectivity. Plus, the students love you. No one has ever generated this much excitement on our campus."

Duffy's voice came from the back seat. "So, people don't have a right to be 'gay' in this country?"

His arms began to itch. He crossed them and began scratching with both hands. Weariness suffused his entire body like a drug coming from an IV. "The word doesn't mean the same thing it did when we were in Vietnam. Now, it refers to men who love men, women who love women."

Duffy rubbed his chin. "That's a sin."

Weights pushed Terry down in the seat. He couldn't breathe. "We've separated religion and morality from public life now." He closed his eyes. Images of Ella floated into his consciousness. "I don't know anymore."

Sarah glanced in the rearview mirror, frowning. "Who are you talking to?"

* * *

He sniffed the single malt scotch then drank, the smokey liquid glided down his throat. The melodious sounds of Ted Weems' orchestra floated around the room.

Sarah cocked an ear, her blond hair falling over one shoulder. "Who is that?"

Terry took another drink. "Ted Weems, it's titled 'A Girlfriend of a Boyfriend of Mine'."

Reaching under Terry's arms, she pressed her breasts against his back and kissed his neck. "Where do you come up with these recordings?"

He sipped his scotch, enjoying Sarah's tongue flicking over the back of his neck. "My father loved big band music. I've been listening to this stuff since I was a child."

She nibbled his ear. "Let's go to bed. It seems like I haven't seen you in about two weeks."

Going up the stairs, the strains of "Oh! Monah" came from the speakers in the bedroom.

* * *

He smeared shaving cream over his chin.

"What kind of pizza do you want me to order?"

"Make one ingredient hamburger." He re-wrapped his towel around his lower body. "I don't care what else you add." He glanced into the mirror. A Vietnamese man, eyes bulging in terror, stared back at him. Blood dribbled from his open mouth.

Knees buckling, he closed his eyes and grabbed the sink. The glass of whiskey shattered on the bathroom floor. The towel slid down his legs and began to soak up the scotch.

When he opened his eyes, Sarah knelt at his feet using the towel to pick up the broken glass. "Terry, what is it? What happened?"

Using another towel, he wiped shaving cream from his face with shaking hands. "It's a nightmare, a man I killed in Vietnam. I need a drink."

Cochise patted his back. "You had every right to kill the *hombre, mi cuate*. That guy was in the wrong place at the wrong time."

"I know, I know." He lifted an exhausted hand toward Cochise, reflected in the mirror.

"Terry, who are you talking to? You did it in the car and you're doing it now."

"I'm talking to memories," he said, running shaking hands over his grizzled face.

"Watch where you step. I'm sure there's still some broken glass on the floor. Let's get you dressed first." She led him from the bathroom and brought a shirt and a pair of pants from his closet.

"I need to get out of this house."

"You need to eat something first."

He raised his leg as Sarah slipped on his pants. "I need to be able to look at myself in the mirror."

Finished tying his shoestrings, Sarah rubbed her chin. "We'll order the pizza here and give them my address. So, we'll eat there and that'll give me a chance to change my clothes."

"Okay," Terry said. "But let's go downstairs and get a bottle."

* * *

He placed the slice of hamburger and mushroom pizza back on his plate. "This stuff is tasteless."

"Why don't you put the scotch down and try to eat it while drinking water." Sarah, arms folded across her chest, rolled her eyes. "I want you sober tonight. There's going to be a lot of press there because of all the publicity you've gotten over the internet. If you don't mind me saying so, you look like crap."

He didn't want to hear anyone telling him he looked like shit, that he was drinking too much, or that he was a star on internet blogs. "Have you talked to Rich?"

"On the telephone. He thinks we've been fucking for a while."

"He started that crap with me at the camp. What did you say?"

"I told him that you and I had been fucking for years. That whenever we got a chance, we fucked like wild animals. Most of the time it was in between classes in our offices. Sometimes you liked to walk on the wild side. That's when you fucked me in the woods out beside our department building."

"Are you talking about the big azaleas and those maple and pine trees?"

Sarah nodded. "I told him that whenever you fucked me in the woods you would bury my panties out there as a trophy."

"What did he say?"

"It's hard to say anything when you're screaming hysterically into the phone." Sarah reached across the table and took Terry's hand. "Terry, tell me about Vietnam. What was it like?"

"How many years have I known you? You've never asked me that before. Why start now?" He squeezed her proferred hand

Wrinkling her brow, Sarah used her other hand to sweep back her hair. "After everything that's happened, I just want to try to understand you a little better."

How could anyone understand who didn't go through it? What should he say? He could tell her about the majesty of the jungle. What about the squad? The fear? The death?

"Understanding's got little to do with it. You could never understand. When you're in that jungle, it's staying alive in a full-tilt boogie environment twenty-four hours a day, seven days a week. You have to give yourself up. You know, realize that you're probably going to die. The pressure is relentless."

"How old were you?"

"Nineteen in physical years. The oldest guy in my squad was twenty-one." He held his head in his hands. "Nineteen-year-olds with guns, it's insane. You have to trust each other and be ready to give it up. I've never known men like that since. Now we've progressed so far as a society that we're sacrificing our daughters in the name of equality. When I think about Vietnam and how it was, my life now seems so hollow and empty, all bullshit. But at least I had a chance to see my child and grandchild. A lot of men lost a lot of tomorrows. I often think that I don't deserve the tomorrows that I've had."

He walked to the kitchen counter, grabbed a Kleenex, and dabbed at his eyes. He sat back down and laughed. "Thanks for asking. Sometimes I've felt a need to talk, but no one asks. Then other times, I don't want to talk and people ask."

"You were wounded, weren't you?"

He let go of Sarah's hand, fingers drumming the table. "I was in a field hospital watching over a friend. The NVA hit it with rockets."

"They shelled a hospital?"

"It's war. War is killing people. Everyone dies in war, even the living. It turns the world upside down. You're not thinking rationally. Rather, you're thinking rationally, but it's a perverted reasoning, exactly the opposite from the way you would think in the civilized world. You heard me the other night. War is killing the enemy. If you don't kill, you lose.

* * *

"Lima, Lima, this is Lima Victor, over," Anderson, cross-legged, whispered into the radio receiver. He brushed an insect from the plastic-covered map on his lap. He gave the coordinates of the intersecting high-speed trails and the traffic.

"Roger, Lima Lima, there were many wounded, walking and being carried on stretchers. Troops are heading east toward your position. There's a lot of traffic also going north." Anderson, his ear to the receiver, swatted a fly. "I repeat. Some traffic is moving east toward you and wounded moving west. The wounded are moving north at the crossing, over."

The men knelt around Anderson, facing outward, weapons across their knees. With Anderson not talking, faint booms and rumbles of explosions could still be heard. The battle for Hill 1036 continued unabated.

Cochise leaned on his rifle. "Wish I could have a cig."

The small group had ventured five hundred yards farther into the jungle to eat their first meal since the night before. They were taking a chance of the Vietnamese smelling the C-rations, but they needed something in their stomachs besides water. The cold food offered little in amenities.

"Roger, I think the wounded are being moved to a base camp located along the north-south trail. Roger, we'll scout north and fix the location of the base camp. It has to be a big one. What is the sitrep for 1036, over?" Anderson held the phone to his ear with his shoulder and opened a can of C-rations. "Roger, this is Lima Victor, out.

"They'll take the hill today. The battle is still going on, but the fighting is less intense. We inserted two companies from another battalion yesterday evening about a thousand yards from the western side of the hill. They've been heading east toward 1036 since this morning. One company encountered some pretty stiff resistance. It seems to be lessening now. Both of them are advancing, and I repeat, the resistance on the hill itself is pretty light compared to what it was. Helicopters are still grounded because of the rain, clouds, and fog.

"They want us to scout around and get a fix on the base camp, if we can." Anderson handed the receiver to Duffy. "This sonofabitch's got to be huge. With the traffic we've seen, there's no telling how big it is."

"They're trying to get our asses killed, Bro." Brumsen adjusted his machine gun, balancing it across his knee.

"They'll sacrifice us in a skinny minute." Duffy hooked the receiver on his webbing. "We're just part of the never-ending supply coming through the pipeline."

"This is going to be a tough nut to crack," Cochise said. "Even if we get in and spot the camp for the artie, we don't stand a snowball's chance in hell of getting outa here. What about you, Malloy."

"On my granddaddy's farm, this would be what he would call 'nut-cuttin' time. It's dirty work, but it has to be done."

Duffy leaned forward. "I feel the same way."

"Hillbilly, you definitely got a way with words." Brumsen chuck-led quietly. "My momma's gonna love you."

"I didn't say we wouldn't do it or couldn't do it." Cochise's black eyes blazed out of his camouflaged face. "I just said we don't stand a chance in hell of getting out of this mess in one piece. We have sev-eral hundred, maybe a thousand-who-knows-how-many Vietnamese around us. As soon as the artillery starts dropping on the base camp, whoever's in charge will know that there's a recon team out here somewhere."

"Cochise is right." Anderson examined his compass. "They'll do everything they can to find us. Let's do the job and get our asses out of here pronto. Cochise, I want you and Malloy to cross the east-west trail a little further down from where you set up this morning. Move about five hundred yards north then turn west. Find the north-south trail and cross it, if you can. We need to get a fix on how big this camp is. Duffy and I will go west across the north-south trail and then north.

"Brumsen, you stay here with the radio and machine gun. In case we don't get back, you have to call in artie for us." He grabbed Brumsen's broad shoulder. "Don't let us die for nothing."

"I'm there, Bro. I'm there."

Duffy held Cochise and Terry with his gaze. "You guys get your asses back here, and don't try to be heroes."

"After you cross the north-south trail and turn back west, look for a fairly large stream," Anderson continued. "There's one on our map, but who knows how accurate it is. There has to be water around their base camp, or they wouldn't be here.

"Leave everything here. Don't carry anything with you except ammo, water, and your map and compass. You're going to have to shoot azimuths to know how to get back here. If everything gets fucked up and one group doesn't get back before we leave, we'll fall back to tomorrow's rendezvous coordinates."

Cochise and Anderson marked the coordinates on their maps.

"There's a hill there, at least a little elevation in altitude," Anderson said. "Cochise, Malloy, if one of you doesn't make it, make sure the other doesn't forget the map or the compass. Brumsen, if none of us make it back, then you're on your own. Call in the artie, then haul ass. They know our coordinates from what I've told them. You can adjust the fire further north. I'm leaving you my map. Duffy and I will use my compass. You'll have the radio and the map. That should help you get out of this jungle shithole."

Anderson held out his hand and the members of the squad placed theirs on top. "Be back here in three hours, four hours max, because whoever is here is going to call in some heavy shit on you. Good luck."

Kneeling in the rain, water dripping from their mohawk haircuts, they shook hands. Black and green camouflage paint, mixed with the red and yellow stripes, covered their faces. They stared at each other with tired, determined eyes.

Cochise brought out his compass and shot an azimuth to the east-west trail. "It's payback time, *compadres*." Looking over his shoulder at them, with the feline grace that accentuated all of his movements, he crept into the green fog of the rain-sodden jungle. Terry, not looking back, hurried behind him.

Terry tallied facts in his head. No Vietnamese knew they were where they were. The ambush this morning had alerted the NVA of enemy activity. So, they needed to be alert for trackers. However, the jungle was incredibly big. Small units were hard, if not impossible, to find in the wilderness of mountains and valleys. Despite the dangers, he felt relatively safe for the moment. Stay alert! Stay alert!

They waited beside the east-west trail for ten minutes. Hearing nothing, Cochise bolted across first. Terry followed thirty seconds later.

Squatting on the ground, Cochise shot an azimuth. He pointed to his compass and held up three fingers. Then he held up five fingers twice. He headed on an azimuth of three-five-five. It would be important to know, because they would have to shoot a reciprocal azimuth on the return trip. Cochise held up five fingers and made a fist twice. Okay, they were going five hundred yards on 355.

He counted his footsteps. One hundred thirty paces equaled one hundred meters. At one hundred thirty paces, he tied a knot in his scarf. When he had five knots in his scarf, he would let Cochise know that the five hundred meters had been reached.

Terry counted, watched the swaying jungle and listened. His gaze moved everywhere. Any sound might be an advance warning. Sometimes he walked backward, still counting. At other times, he stopped and counted off a fast fifteen seconds, watching toward their rear for any sign of activity. Stepping off, he resumed his count.

They stopped at a trail. Terry knelt beside his partner five seconds later. The rain started again. The clouds touched the treetops. A few birds called to one another as the water pattered through the fronds.

He held up four fingers, balling his fist twice. Four hundred yards. One hundred more to go.

Terry ducked instinctively. Voices came toward them on the trail. Crouching, they took five steps backward into jungle. Cochise yanked his knife from its sheath. Terry took his bayonet from the scabbard taped to his boot. Both crouched on one knee. The voices grew nearer.

Inhale shallow quiet breaths! Don't hold your breath!

The voice of a man drifted down the trail. The unmistakable lilt of a young woman followed. The couple stopped ten feet from them. The Vietnamese whispered to each other. The woman/girl giggled. Holy shit, lovers!

Cochise pointed to his watch, holding up his outspread hand. Five minutes. Terry tightened his grip on the bayonet, knuckles white. He couldn't kill a woman! Breathe slowly, relax. Cochise glanced at his watch and held up three fingers. Come on, you stupid kids, move your asses. Movement?

"*O them mot chut nua di.*"

"*Tao khong the*," said the girl. She began walking down the trail, away from them.

The young Vietnamese man watched the girl move away. The two of them held their crouch. Slowly, the young man walked down the trail toward his girlfriend.

They darted across the trail. Studying his compass, Cochise stalked off into the jungle. Terry tracked behind him, counting. The pace was slow. Within ten minutes, they had travelled the last hundred yards of the northern leg of their journey. Cochise squatted with his compass out. Terry knelt beside him.

Although it was relatively cool compared to some of the jungle heat, their fatigues clung to them drenched with sweat. Small red birds twittered and fluttered in the branches. Yellow butterflies danced around the birds. Leeches, sensing their body heat, crawled toward them across the jungle floor.

Cochise pondered the jungle. Drops of rain and sweat rolled down his chiseled face. "'Nut-cuttin' time."

Disappearing into the green, holding a westward direction, Terry followed, counting.

Cochise, crouching, crept cautiously, the stock of his rifle tucked under his wiry arm. The barrel of his M-16 pointed straight ahead, ready to fire. Terry inched forward. Where was the north-south trail?

They stopped. Terry squatted next to Cochise. Vietnamese voices drifted through the jungle. Kneeling, they crawled forward. The voices came from their left, several yards away. The crawl was agonizingly slow. *Patience*!

One of Cochise's canteen caught on a vine. Without a sound, he edged backward. Terry did the same. Finally, the vine came free. Pushing it aside, Cochise moved forward. After crawling ten yards farther, he beckoned Terry. The voices were gone.

Terry crawled up on Cochise's right side. The north-south trail was two feet away. Foliage kept them from being seen by someone walking; however, hugging the ground as they were, they saw the trail and beyond it clearly. Hooches, with roofs and no walls, stood on the other side. The undergrowth had been cleared, but the taller trees provided a canopy that kept them hidden.

Touching Terry's shoulder, Cochise crabbed backward. He took out his map. "How far west have we come?" he whispered.

"Around a hundred and seventy-five meters."

"We gotta be in this general area." Cochise made an X on the map. "Let's move south and see just how big the camp is. We're going to stay five yards off the trail. I'll move to the speed trail at twenty-five-yard intervals."

Crawling south, Terry heard Vietnamese talking to his right toward the speed trail. They hesitated, listening, a minute later, halting again. Cochise motioned Terry to stay as he inched west toward the trail. Terry looked at his watch. They had been gone for an hour and forty-five minutes. Cochise crawled back through the undergrowth. He nodded. The camp was still there.

Without looking back, Cochise crouched and sidled his way through the jungle. He stopped two more times. Each time he crawled toward the speed trail and then back to Terry. Each time he nodded to let Terry know that the base camp was still there.

This is one big sonofabitch.

The fourth time Cochise disappeared, Terry crouched with a tree at his back. His rifle lay across his lap, one hand on the trigger and handle and the other hand on the barrel. A rustle came from behind him. He tensed. Someone began humming.

Inching up, Terry pressed his back against the tree. He turned his head to the left and peered cautiously around the trunk. A kneeling man, clad in green with a pouch at his side, rummaged through the undergrowth. He held purple flowers with the root systems still attached. He turned toward Terry and stood. Terry hit him with the rifle stock. The man's jaw cracked. He crumpled to the ground grabbing his jaw, and tried to get back up.

Don't shoot. No sound. He jerked the booted bayonet free, swinging it to meet the man rising to his feet. The bayonet caught the weakened man in his throat. The force of his thrust drove it out the back of his neck. The Vietnamese instinctively reached for the bayonet with one hand and grabbed Terry's wrist with the other, yanking at the bayonet.

Warm blood oozed over Terry's hand and ran down his arm. He let go of his rifle and grabbed the man's hair. With the bayonet still in the struggling man's throat, Terry slammed him against the tree trunk. The point of the bayonet embedded in the trunk.

The wounded man's eyes, locked on Terry, enlarged with terror. He continued to jerk at Terry's hand, attempting to yank the knife out of his throat. Blood spilled more freely. He kicked. Blood gushed from the man's mouth. Gurgling sounds escaped from him. His tongue bulged from his mouth.

No sound! No sound, goddammit!

Blood streamed down Terry's arm and the man's shirt. His grasp on Terry's wrist lessened. Still gripping the man's hair, he pushed the bayonet into the tree and yanked the head forward, sliding it up, then pushing it back down the blade, twisting the bayonet. The Vietnamese kicked feebly. Incensed that the man still fought, Terry jerked the blade out of his neck, plunging it back into the neck again and again. *Die, you sonofabitch!*

"Malloy, let him go. He's dead."

Terry moved in a fog. He gripped a handful of hair. His other hand held the bayonet, which was plunged into the man's neck. The neck was almost completely severed.

"Let go, Malloy. Let go." Cochise pried Terry's hand from the man's hair. "We gotta haul ass! I heard your rifle hit the ground. Someone else might have heard it, too."

Finally, as if waking from a dream, Terry let go of the dead Vietnamese, who slumped to the ground. The bayonet slid from the neck. Kneeling, Cochise took the bayonet and slipped it into the scabbard on Terry's calf. He handed Terry's rifle to him. Cochise lifted the pouch from around the man's shoulders. "Grab that shoulder."

Terry stared at the dead man.

Cochise's eyes were two diamonds staring at Terry. His lips barely opened as he whispered, "Malloy, snap out of it. Help me pull this guy away from here."

They pulled the dead man another fifteen yards through the jungle and dropped him. While Terry stared at the man, Cochise went back to cover up the blood and tracks.

Cochise hurried back. "That should give us a little more time."

A black stain covered Terry's fatigues.

"Holy shit, Malloy. What a mess."

Terry rubbed his hands. The blood smeared. He wiped his hands on his fatigues.

Shooting an azimuth to the east, Cochise grabbed Terry's shoulders and shook him. "No mercy, Malloy. Start counting. Tell me when we get to 175 meters. We're not outta this crap yet."

CHAPTER SEVENTEEN

On the way to the auditorium, Sarah had insisted that they stop at a coffee shop. At the auditorium, he had gone to the bathroom, poured out the coffee, and replaced it with whiskey from a flask. What the hell was he going to say to this crowd about gay and lesbian rights? Several reporters sat on the front row of the auditorium. Several other men that he didn't recognize stood in the back of the fast-filling auditorium. A waving hand drew his attention to Laura Boatwright. He waved back. He wished all of his students were as conscientious as she was. Images of Ella popped into his head.

Ella sat across from him at their dining room table, her reddish blond hair swept back in a pony tail. "They're human beings, Dad. They have a right to love who they want to as adults."

"I understand all that." Terry spooned gravy onto his rice. "It's just hard to get my head around two men or two women being together. I'm not as flexible as your generation. So, give me some time. Besides, when is it ever going to affect me?"

"They're Americans." Ella speared green beans, shoveling them into her mouth. "They have the same rights as all other Americans. They can marry whomever they want."

Scooping up a portion of the rice and gravy, Terry let the fork hover between his mouth and the plate. "To tell you the truth, I don't care what people do to or with each other behind closed doors. That's no one's business but theirs."

A microphone squealed. Rich, standing at the podium, fiddled with it. He ran his fingers through his hair. "Okay, as we are just about to start I have several announcements. The first one is about a meeting that The Unitarian Church of Universal Victimology is holding on the PWNA Act, otherwise known as the 'People With No Abilities Act'."

Was Rich going to tell them that he was a member of that church? He felt a gentle touch on his shoulder. Sarah sat down. The fingers of her hand drummed a rhythm on his shoulder. "Are you ready to kick off 'Diversity Celebration Week'?"

Rich's voice resonated through the speakers. "As you all know, there is severe discrimination against people who have no abilities whatsoever. This discrimination crosses all boundaries of race, color, and gender. How can we as members of the human race allow persons of inability to be scorned and ridiculed and discriminated against? This happens not only with jobs, but housing. Plus, our court system and jails are filled with people with inabilities. There is little chance of upward mobility and there is every chance of a lifetime of drudgery. So, if you want to stop employers from asking for references and job skills and allow non-abled people to compete in the market place, come to The Unitarian Church of Universal Victimology next Thursday night at seven o'clock. If you're a person with no ability and are struggling with performance-based raises and promotions, come to this meeting and let's begin to stop this type of discrimination."

"How did I let you talk me into this?"

"Because you wanted to get into my panties this afternoon." Sarah's white teeth flashed against her dark red lipstick. "You figured you better do what I asked."

He threw his head back, laughing.

Glancing at them, Rich grimaced. His eyes flashed daggers. He swiveled his head toward the audience when the microphone squealed. "Okay, we've several more announcements. Upcoming events at the school to celebrate diversity are the following. You can all pick up a flyer about this outside in the hallway.

"This Wednesday, Dr. Jazzbo will lecture on 'Hip Hop and Video Games: The artistic evolution of a rap star.' This will be at 1:30 P.M. in room 305 of the Fine Arts Building. After the lecture, Dr. Jazzbo will be autographing each CD that you buy.

"On Friday, also in room 305 of the Fine Arts Building, Dr. Shaba al-Sucdeq al-Salam will lecture on 'Islam: The Path to Spirituality and Peace'."

Another hand touched Terry's shoulder. Laura Boatwright stood next to him. Her smooth almond colored-skin reflected pools of light. Small, yellow bows were sprinkled around her head, attached to her corn-rows. Terry smiled and gestured her toward a seat beside him.

"Hi, Laura. How are you?" Sarah asked.

"I'm fine, Dr. Stableford. Dr. Malloy, would it be all right if I see you tomorrow? I've finished my outline for my senior thesis and want you to look at it."

"There are just a couple of more things." Rich cleared his throat. "This week's multi-cultural movie is Bad Country. Missy Gilbert is a western woman whose life is turned upside down when her husband, the local sheriff, is killed by a gang of roughneck cowboys. When no man steps up to take her husband's job, Missy pins on the badge. A woman in a man's world, Missy tames the town with her six-guns blazing and also opens herself up to new experiences with Miss Kitty, the owner of the local saloon. This movie was the winner of the prestigious 'Sappho Award' at the Montana Moondance Film Festival."

"Laura, it would be pleasure to see you. How about 9:30?" Terry placed both elbows on the table. "We'll have a cup of coffee and talk about your thesis."

"Finally, next Tuesday, and every Tuesday after that for the next month, is the beginning of a series of talks on 'Sexual Identity and Spirituality: New avenues of approach for the Queer-of-Color.'" Rich settled the microphone into its cradle. "Now, there have been some questions raised, and confusion, about this. Let me point out that the theme is 'Queer-of-Color' and not 'Colorful Queers.'"

Laura returned to her seat.

"Are you moderating tonight?" Terry asked.

"No, I'm on the panel."

"Who's running this shindig?" He reached for the coffee cup.

"What are you drinking? I smell whiskey." Her lips compressed, she rose. "What am I going to do with you? To answer your question, Thorn is the moderator."

Rich hustled back to the microphone. "I apologize. I have one more announcement. The History Department will hold a meeting for non-readers tomorrow at 4 in Room 238 of the History Building. The topic will be 'Multi-Media Approaches to Achieving your BA Degree: History on TV and Film: A deconstruction of the learning-through-books myth'."

Acknowledging Sarah and Terry, Thorn walked past them and shook Rich's hand. He sat down beside a man that Terry had not noticed. Lean and in his late thirties or early forties, the man had a Van Dyke beard and wore a neat gray pin stripe suit with no tie.

Terry unscrewed the cap of the bottle of water in front of him. "Who is that sitting beside Thornton?"

"That's Oliver Smyth-Wickham." Sarah reached for Terry's water bottle. "He's from the University of Georgia. He's doing a lot of good work in Queer Theory, Sexual Orientation and Gender Identity."

"Is he on the panel?"

"It's you, me, Rich, and Oliver."

"Now I would like to introduce a good friend, Greg Thornton, who will be our moderator tonight," Rich said, adjusting his coat. "In addition to being a great reporter, Greg is the town liaison for the Town and Gown Transgender Committee. He's done a lot of good work bringing the concerns of the College's transgendered community to the city council." Rich began to clap. The audience followed suit.

Taking the microphone, Thorn smiled at the students. "I would like to get started right away by introducing our very distinguished guest panelist. Dr. Oliver Smyth-Wickham is the head of the Queer Studies Department at the University of Georgia. His work has been published internationally. His last book, which was a best seller among the homosexual and transgendered communities around the world, was entitled, *Transgendered Like Me: A bearded man's pilgrimage in women's clothes; biased America in the 21st century*. He is also the co-chairman of the Athens Gaybutante Ball. Dr. Smyth-Wickham is an avid fighter for environmental justice around the world. Further, he has written several books for young adults. His last is entitled, *Roaming the Wild Plains: A tale of two stallions*. Would you please give a big hand to Dr. Smyth-Wickham."

Terry tuned out the applause. What the *hell* was he doing here?

The squad stood before him below the stage. Brumsen, cradling his M-60 machine-gun, made a sweeping gesture with his huge hand, shrugging. "You tell us. We don't have a clue."

Terry toyed with his bottle cap. "I'm witnessing the unfolding of the American Dream. Some people would call it a nightmare, possibilities that you could not imagine."

Sarah nudged him. Applauding students cheered him. Sarah motioned for him to stand. Terry, baffled, raised partly out of his chair and bowed. The audience erupted. A man and a woman with cameras stood in front of him and took his picture. Bulbs flashed around the auditorium.

Thorn waited for the crowd noise to die down. "Okay, we'll start with Dr. Smyth-Wickham. Would you please tell us what you think of gay marriage and why you feel that way."

* * *

When they returned to the rendezvous sight, they found Brumsen in wait lying upon his poncho. After studying Terry and the front of his bloodstained jungle fatigues for a moment, Brumsen threw a questioning glance at Cochise, who shook his head.

"Everything okay?"

Kneeling down, Cochise removed the Vietnamese pouch he carried. "Everything's fine. We had a little trouble, but we're here in one piece."

"I killed a man." Terry hesitated. "With my bayonet. The stupid bastard was walking through the jungle picking flowers."

Holding up the bag of the dead Vietnamese, Cochise opened it, dumping the contents on the ground. "He was carrying this." Cochise lifted three small bottles, a green liquid swirled in one. Two bottles contained pills. He placed the bottles on the ground and brought out a clear glass jar that held roots of some kind.

Raising a bottle, Brumsen examined it. "These look like aspirin."

Silently, Cochise turned the bag over and shook it. A smaller bag, tied with a string, fell out. A pungent smell arose. Reaching in, he sniffed the leaves, drawing back his head quickly and wiping his nose. "That's it. There's nothing else."

"This guy must've been a medic, or maybe a doctor." Brumsen studied the small bag.

The soft rustle of leaves and branches filtered through the jungle. Terry and Cochise grabbed their rifles and whirled in the direction of the noise. Anderson and Duffy emerged out of the vegetation.

Anderson glanced at the men, then focused on the spilled contents of the satchel. "What's this?"

"Malloy killed a guy who was carrying this. We think he was a doctor or a medic," Cochise said, handing a jar to Anderson.

Duffy cradled his M-16. "That makes sense, considering what we saw."

"What did you guys see?" Brumsen asked, handing Anderson his map.

"I didn't hear any gunshots." Anderson held up his hand to stop Duffy, then looked at Terry.

"I killed him with my bayonet."

Anderson's gaze wandered over the men. "We gotta get the fuck outta here. How long ago was this? Did anyone else see you?"

Cochise shook his head. "No, no one saw us and no one heard us."

"You sure?"

"Absolutely," Terry said.

"Okay, what did you guys find?"

"This is one big mother of a base." Cochise unfolded his map and tapped with his slender index finger. "We hit the north-south trail about here. Right across the trail, there's a big camp with seven or eight hooches that we could see. We headed south along the trail to see just how big the sonofabitch was. We went about a hundred yards south, and still no end to the base, when Malloy killed the gook. I decided it was time to haul ass."

"We had no trouble crossing the north-south trail." Anderson knelt and spread his own map beside Cochise's. "About a hundred yards into the jungle on the other side of the north-south trail, we found a stream and followed it. When we came to the east-west trail, we waited about twenty minutes. There was all kinds of traffic on it. One hundred yards north of the east-west trail, we found the base camp." He studied the map. "We got us one hell of a base here, guys. It's a big supply base, I think."

Picking up his gear, Duffy fitted himself into the harness. "Tell 'em the rest."

Anderson asked, weariness and resignation in his voice, "Why don't you tell it Duffy?"

"There's a pretty big hospital there. They have all kinds of wounded lying on the ground, and a couple of operating hooches, too."

Brumsen pointed to the bottles. "That explains this crap. The guy must've been a doctor."

Terry responded, "That explains the women we've been hearing along the trails, too. They're nurses."

"They could just as well be armed soldiers." Anderson slapped his thigh, shaking his head in disgust.

"That's true, *mi cuate*."

Duffy picked up a bottle. "I don't know if we should call this in, guys. There are women and doctors there."

"Who gives a fuck?" Gripping the telephone, Anderson spit on the ground. "They're in a fucking war zone, right in the middle of the goddamn jungle. Our guys are getting their asses shot off no more than two miles from here. They're going to get exactly what they deserve."

"Yeah, but there're doctors and nurses, guys, and we would be calling in artie on wounded men in a hospital."

"You gotta be kidding, Bro. That just means they're patching up people to send back at us."

Terry asked, "What about the wounded men that we shot? You know, when we set that ambush up after the recon team had been wiped out? We killed wounded then, and you didn't say a word. You even helped me kill that guy we found off the trail."

Taking of his helmet, Duffy looked skyward. The hand not holding the helmet moved up and down with his voice. "I know, but this is different. It just feels different."

"You saw them shoot down that Red Cross helicopter." Cochise shook the satchel at Duffy. "These people don't give a damn whether it's hospitals or what. If they get a chance, they're going to kill us."

"Cochise is right, Bro. You know those guys would do it in a minute. Besides, they store supplies there and those supplies are going to kill Americans. We didn't tell them to put a fucking hospital next to a supply dump."

"They're fucking animals," Anderson said. "Sometimes you gotta think like an animal to kill an animal."

"I'm not an animal, Anderson; I was created in God's image." Duffy leaned against a tree for support. "These people are human beings. Just because they would do it to us, does that mean we have to do the same things to them?"

"Yes, goddammit." Anderson shook his fist at Duffy. "I'm going to take some payback for every dead soldier, for every wound, for every ounce of blood that they've gotten from me and my men."

"Why do we always choose death? I want to choose life. We're going to be punished for this."

Anderson lifted the radio receiver to his ear. "God might have created you, but take a gander at where he put you. This is some world that he made. I think being in this fucking war is punishment enough. We're not in the world."

"He may have created the world, but he didn't create this situation." Duffy adjusted the straps of his rucksack. "We did; I mean men did. Men created this war, Anderson, not God."

"I'm too tired for this shit. You have to lose that religious, ethical crap, Duffy."

"We're still in Indian country." Cochise placed a hand on Anderson's shoulder. "Whatever we're going to do, let's do it and get the fuck outta here."

"I'm the one calling it in, Duffy. That should ease your gentle conscience about your guilt or innocence. Anyone else got a problem with this? What about you, Brumsen?"

"Do it. We need to haul ass."

Anderson turned to Cochise. Cochise nodded. "It's payback time."

"What world do you live in, Malloy, Duffy's or mine?"

Terry lifted his rucksack to his back. "Payback. No mercy."

"Everyone get packed. Let's move." Anderson gazed at the cloud-covered, fog-shrouded treetops. "No air support today. Lima Lima, this is Lima Victor, over. Roger, Lima Lima, this is Lima Victor. Stand by for a fire-mission, over. It's gonna be fine, Duffy. We have to move now.

"Start from the northern-most coordinate and walk it in, firing for effect. We're south of the camp, and that will give us time to get further south.

"This is Lima Victor, out." Anderson picked up his M-16 and his rucksack. "Hill 1036's been taken. They've grounded all helicopters in this area because of this friggin' fog and cloud cover. A helicopter is going to meet us tomorrow morning at the rendezvous point. We've got some traveling to do." A crack of thunder and lightning exploded above.

The first shells whooshed overhead. The detonations were too near to sound like booms and crumps of distant explosions. Every man winced from the thunderous sounds of the shells hitting the camp.

Anderson passed Duffy the radio receiver. "Let's get outta here. It would be just our luck to get hit with a short round just when we're almost home. Cochise, take the point. We have the usual order. Malloy, start counting."

The shells slamming into the base camp provided the impetus to hurry. At 4 o'clock in the afternoon, they should have at least two to three hours of daylight before darkness made movement impossible. Heading southwest for about forty-five minutes, Terry heard Duffy yell. Automatic rifle fire erupted. Terry crouched and ran toward the firing. More fire burst out of the jungle, including Brumsen's M-60.

"Cease fire," Anderson said, in a normal voice.

Pushing his way through the vegetation, Terry reached the squad kneeling over Duffy. Cochise bandaged Duffy's left arm. Brumsen picked up Duffy's radio and handed it to Anderson. Two bullet holes pierced the side of the radio. Two dead Vietnamese lay beyond him, weapons lying beside them.

"Fucking luck is no good. These two guys," Brumsen pointed to the dead Vietnamese, "came up on Duffy crossing the trail. Duffy saw them at about the same time they saw him. He shot one, and the other one got him. Cochise and Anderson got the other."

"The radio is useless." Anderson dropped it. "Duffy, you gonna be okay?"

"Yeah, he's going to be fine." Cochise finished tying off the bandage. "The bullet took out some meat along the bone, but he isn't bleeding much." Cochise held out two fingers. "Grip my fingers, Duffy."

"My whole arm and fingers are numb, but I can move everything."

"We have to move it, guys. We don't know who these men are. But, I don't want to wait around and find out."

Cochise gestured at the radio. "We can't talk to the battalion with this piece of shit."

"We're going to hustle our asses to the fallback position," replied Anderson. "It's elevated. It'll provide some defense, if anyone searching for these guys comes looking for us. Terry, you're going to have to watch the rear carefully. Don't let anyone get on us. Duffy, you gotta carry the radio. I don't want the gooks to find it and know we don't have one.

"Let's set up some booby traps. Brumsen and I'll booby trap these bodies. Cochise, you and Malloy, one of you go ten yards up the trail and rig a grenade, the other go ten yards down the other way and do the same. Work fast."

CHAPTER EIGHTEEN

Dr. Smyth-Wickham sauntered back to his seat to polite applause.

Terry had stopped listening. He pounded the table with his fist. What in God's name was he doing here? He didn't care about these issues.

The audience looked at him expectantly. Holding their breath, they were all expecting him to say something outrageous. Disappoint them very slowly.

"I don't really care if people get married or not, or who they marry for that matter. You can marry monkeys as far as I'm concerned." Laughter trickled through the audience. Everyone relaxed a little.

"Professor Malloy, can you please maintain a proper sense of decorum at this assembly?" Rich said, wagging his finger at him. "A lot of us are tired of your theatrics. We're discussing serious issues here that are important to the country as a whole."

"Serious issues my ass! The guy roamed through America with a dress and a beard for God's sake. So, what happened? Some people thought it was strange for a man with a beard to go around in a dress? It is strange! What do you think would have happened if he had gone into a Muslim country wearing a dress?"

Students applauded and cheered. Several whistled.

"If he wants to be a brave fighter for the rights of gays, go to Saudia Arabia and protest the beheading of homosexual men.

"If you want to discuss serious issues, why don't you discuss the fact that a lot of Islamic Governments are chopping the heads of off homosexuals? They stone women to death who're caught in adultery, but not the men. A lot of women who're raped in various Moslem countries are held responsible by their immediate family and are sometimes killed by their families in what's called an honor killing, for God's sake. Let's discuss how insane those actions are. Where are the fighters for equal rights when it comes to the victims of Islamic oppression!

"Where is Professor al-Suqdec al-Salam? Get him up here to talk about these cultural issues in the religion of peace. What a bunch of shit."

The audience whooped and clapped. A male voice yelled from the back of the auditorium, "Tell 'em Professor Malloy. Tell 'em like it is."

The students chanted. "Tell 'em! Tell 'em! Tell 'em like it is!"

Rich jumped to his feet. "Thorn, for God's sake, shut him up. Get control of this crowd. He's completely changed the subject!"

Facing the crowd, Thorn held up his hands. The students clapped in time with the chant. "Tell 'em! Tell 'em! Tell 'em like it is!"

Sarah walked to the center of the stage. With one hand on her hip, she put a finger to her lips and held it there. The clapping and chanting subsided. She lowered her finger. "Let's show all of our visitors, and our guest speaker, that we're not a mob." She turned to Thorn, nodded, and walked back to her chair.

Thorn said, "Dr. Smyth-Wickham has indicated that he wants to respond to Dr. Malloy."

"These views are not unexpected from Professor Malloy. I would like to say here and now that I've no hostility to the Professor. I've been doing some research in a new field called Genopolitics. Professor Malloy can't help the way he feels because he's inherited genes which propel him toward a conservative point of view. These types always live in fear of change, fear of everything. He's a victim, not of his nurturing, but of his genes."

Unfolding his arms, Rich gave a thumbs up.

Terry shook his head and tried to tune Smyth-Wickham out. Sarah, eyes twinkling, attempted to keep a straight face. He rolled his eyes at her. Sarah, turning her head away, put a hand to her mouth to keep from laughing.

"Professor Malloy, would you like to respond?"

Terry rubbed his dimpled chin. "It sounds like Professor Smyth-Wickham is telling me that I'm not thinking about the subject in a rational manner and I'm not making rational conclusions. I believe the way I do because I was born this way? Is that what you're saying, Professor? I was born with a certain set of genes."

Smyth-Wickham nodded.

Terry scratched forehead. "I assume that you feel the same way about your activities. You're not responsible for what you do, but were born that way."

Still standing at the podium, Smyth-Wickham agreed. "Of course, we're all products of nature, of our genetic make-up."

Smirking, Rich once again gave the thumbs up sign.

"If you're a product of nature, how do you procreate?" Terry drank from his coffee cup.

Rich shut his eyes and slapped his forehead.

Puzzled, Smyth-Wickham leaned toward the microphone. "I'm not sure I understand what you're asking."

The audience held its breath.

"I'm not sure I know what I'm saying myself. Since we're talking about my gene pool, let's talk about yours. I guess I'm wondering how homosexuals pass their genes along so they can create more homosexuals. If Darwin is right, it would seem that you would breed – or not breed – yourself out of existence. Were you born to a homosexual couple?

"Actually, I don't know if I've ever seen any animal in nature have sex with another animal of the same gender. I'm talking about elephants, giraffes, cows, or horses. Wasn't there a reference to horses a while ago?"

An avalanche of whispering cascaded through the auditorium.

Shaking his head, Smyth-Wickham clucked. "Let's keep this on an academic level and not stoop to gutter crawling, Professor."

"I actually think you'd be better off demanding equality as a citizen of this country entitled to the same rights of other citizens. Of course, I don't know if the right to marriage is in the constitution. But, I'm sure you can find judges somewhere who will find the right to homosexual marriages in the penumbras and emanations of the Bill of Rights."

Smyth-Wickham leaned on the table facing the audience. "Here you see a good example of what we're up against. This man is telling me that my love for my companion isn't natural. He obviously doesn't know what it's like to love another man. This type of discrimination is what we constantly have to battle against."

"No. That's not true. I've loved very good men, who I've begun to think of constantly. I just never wanted to have sex with them. And I think that's a natural feeling."

Pulling at his mustache, Rich leaped to his feet. "Thorn, stop this. I'm not going to stand here and let our guest panelist be insulted."

"I'm not insulting anyone. I'm telling you I don't care who you marry. I'm not concerned how two people feel about each other.

What I am concerned about is the cultural divide between ourselves and over a billion Moslems in the world. I'm not saying that either culture is right or wrong. People believe what they believe. So, I want you to ask yourself what culture you would rather live in: a culture that allows people to express their diversity and difference; or a culture that represses fifty percent of its population and I'm talking about women here. Do you want to live in a world where women are forced to wear burkas, where they're forced into marriages, and even in some countries, have female circumcision performed when they're nine or ten years old. And if they get raped, they're the ones who are guilty. Would you like to live in a culture where Mr. Smyth-Wickham would have his head cut off? You students have choices to make. We will still be at war with this culture when you have grandchildren. They will use our freedoms to defeat us. So, just ask yourself what culture you would choose, theirs or ours."

The audience erupted in cheers, chanting and clapping. Tell it! Tell it! Tell it like it is!

Rich spoke desperately to Thorn.

Thorn studied the panel and the audible audience. "Can I have your attention." The chanting slowly subsided. "It's close to intermission time. This is good time for a break." He gestured toward a long-haired young man with a guitar sitting on the front row. "I think we have some musical entertainment here tonight. Let's get this young man on the stage while we all relax during the intermission." Thorn clapped and gestured for the guitar player to come up.

Smyth-Wickham strolled down the steps of the stage, shaking his head at several reporters who gathered around him.

The guitar player stood in front of the microphone. "I'd like to dedicate this song to all those who are no longer with us. I've changed the lyrics a little but I'm sure you'll recognize the tune. If you want to sing along, feel welcome."

Rich stood with Thorn, gesturing at Terry. "You've got to get control of him. He's destroying what could be a great learning opportunity for these kids."

The guitar player strummed and sang:

Where have all the flowers gone
Long time passing?
Where have all the flowers gone
Long time ago?
Where have all the flowers gone?
Gone to Gay men every one.
When will they ever learn?
When will they ever learn?

Terry threw out his arms, bewildered. "But he started talking about my genes. Why can't I talk about his?"

"You've gotten this entire dialogue off the mark by talking about Arabs, genes, and male elephants fucking each other." Rich slapped his thigh. "And what the hell are penumbras and emanations? You're not making any sense. All I'm asking is to stay on the subject at hand. Thorn, you're the moderator. Keep control of this panel."

Smyth-Wickham grabbed Rich by the arm. "Do something to stop him, for heaven's sake!"

With questioning eyes, Rich studied Smyth-Wickham. "Stop who?"

"The goddamn singer!" Smyth-Wickham jerked a thumb over his shoulder.

The young man plucked his guitar.

Where have all the Gay men gone?
Gone to graveyards every one.
When will they ever learn?

The guitarist clapped his hands. "Come on everyone, join in."

When will they ever learn?

Several rows of the audience swayed together in their seats, holding lit matches and lighters in the air.

Blood veins bulging on his forehead, Smyth-Wickham shook Rich back and forth. "Shut that stupid bastard up! Shut him up!"

"Well, you've certainly made a commotion tonight." Sarah said, holding her chin in her hands and smiling.

"Me? What the hell did I do?"

On one side of the stage, Rich jerked the plug on the microphone.

"I just want to go home." Terry leaned back in his chair, threw his head back, and sighed.

"You can't go home. We have to go out and drink beer and pretend that we're all friends." Sarah leaned over and patted his hand.

Clapping, Rich walked toward the guitarist standing in the middle of the stage thumping the microphone. "Hey, let's give it up for Steve. He did a great job. We have some technical difficulties with the mics and won't be able to continue the performance."

Steve, grinning, held his guitar over his head, shaking it as he walked from the stage. The audience snuffed out their matches.

Smyth-Wickham shook his head and turned to Thorn. "This place is a nut house. I'm out of here. Tell them I'm not feeling good. Do me a favor. Take the guitar away from that Steve guy and shove it up his ass."

"In a gesture of collegiality, I must say that it's been a pleasure," Terry said, stretching out a hand. "You're welcome to come out and drink beer with us."

Smyth-Wickham sneered, pulling his goatee. "Fuck you and your collegiality. This is a revolution, Asshole. We're overthrowing your old-style way of thinking and old-style values that have been oppressing people for hundreds of years." Turning, he hurried off the stage.

"If he can leave, I can leave. Tell them I'm not feeling well either." Terry left the stage, carrying his coffee cup.

* * *

Conway Twitty's melodious voice drifted through the bar, singing hello to his darlin'. Terry moved his foaming beer mug in circles on the table.

"Rich said he would join us." Sarah pulled a chair from under the table and sat down. "I figured Thorn would too. They both should have been here by now. We canceled the program after you and Oliver left."

He wiped beer from his mouth with his shirtsleeve. "That's fine with me. That's the last time I let you corral me into anything, panties or no panties."

Sarah, laughing, ordered a beer from a gum-popping waitress. "Let's go to my place tonight. I don't want any rocks thrown at me and I certainly don't want to talk to any reporters hanging out at your house." She glanced at her watch. ""I guess we've been stood up."

"You guess?" Terry snorted. "Rich can barely stand to look at me, much less talk to me. He and Thorn are sitting in some bar, planning their next assault on what used to be a community. Let's get outta here."

* * *

The distant crumps and booms of the shells hitting the NVA base continued as the men hurried through the jungle. They hustled east for about five minutes when a closer explosion detonated. Terry glanced backward. That had to be one of the grenade booby traps. He scrambled through the jungle. The squad came into view.

"We have to assume they'll be tracking us." Anderson gulped from his canteen. "We're gonna have to hightail it. It'll be just like this morning. They didn't find us then and they won't find us now, if we're careful. Duffy, how's your arm?"

"There's no bleeding. I feel good. Let's go. We're wasting time."

Putting his canteen back in its pouch, Anderson tucked his rifle under his arm. He scratched his unshaven face. "They'll send out teams in different directions and crisscross the jungle to find us. The NVA know these trails. They know where the booby traps are and can move quicker than us. Whatever happens, we have to keep going. We can't let them fix us in one spot. If they do, we can kiss our asses good-bye." Anderson slapped his hip. "Goddammit, why did they have to hit the fucking radio? Malloy, let us know when we've gone 1500 meters. Same heading, Cochise."

Cochise slipped into the jungle. The squad followed. Although the pace quickened, Terry counted and maintained his usual routine and rhythm as "tail-end Charlie."

Occasionally, a trail slowed them down. Each man cautiously stepped over the trail then moved on. Terry halted several times and waited fifteen seconds, counting deliberately. He always delayed at trails. Each time he and the squad crossed one, Terry squatted five feet from it and waited, listening and counting. Fifteen seconds later, he moved in the direction of the squad. The same scenario played itself out again and again.

Stopped at a trail, Terry moved to tell Anderson that they had traveled 1500 meters. Brumsen's machine gun fired several short bursts. The sharp, heavy retort of a thirty caliber AK-47 responded.

Thirty yards maximum!

The M-60 roared again. Followed by two AK- 47 bursts from two different guns.

Move, Terry. Hustle, goddammit!

Hurrying through the jungle, Terry thumbed the safety, making sure it was off. He crept forward in a crouch. An M-16 fired a short burst.

Focus on the AKs! Focus on the AKs!

He brushed a frond aside with his hand. Another burst of firing penetrated the jungle. He isolated the heavier Vietnamese weapons. The AKs fired in an alternating pattern. Another burst. Closer. He crept toward the fire. To your right! Stay down! Stay down! A hollowness developed in the pit of his stomach. He breathed slowly, deliberately. An AK roared. Bullets broke the sound barrier over his head with a sharp pop, whistling through the leaves around him. An M-16 opened up in response to the AK. He winced, scurrying through the foliage. The distant AK fired again. Terry, crouching, saw a sandled foot appear in the vegetation.

Directly in front, the AK-47's roar deafened him. The foot shook when the gun fired. He moved behind the foot and saw the khaki-clad Vietnamese in a prone position. Got you, you bastard! His first two rounds went through the man's head. It disintegrated. An AK-47 fired further to the right. Terry stepped to the side of the dead Vietnamese and kicked him in the side.

"This sonofabitch is dead," he yelled. "Don't shoot."

Two grenades exploded simultaneously, drowning out any response. Leaves fell from the detonations.

"All clear over here," Cochise said.

"Malloy, we're over here."

He reached the squad at the same time as Duffy and Cochise.

Cochise ejected a magazine from his rifle. He patted Terry's shoulder. "When you spoke, I knew we could throw the grenades."

Anderson knelt over Brumsen, who was sitting on the jungle floor with a bandage around his left thigh. His left trouser leg had been cut open from his thigh down. The bandage was bloody.

"What happened?" Terry asked.

"I heard the guy moving through the jungle. I didn't fire because I thought it might be you." Brumsen clenched his teeth. "We saw each other at the same time. I fired and he dropped to the ground firing.

He got me good. I should've known you wouldn't make that much noise."

"I thought you would come from that direction." Anderson checked his magazine and slammed it into his rifle. "I was afraid to let anyone throw grenades. We had to keep his head down by firing at him, though. I hope we didn't come too close. Good work, but we've lost time. Every fuckin' Vietnamese in the country knows where we are now. Let's move."

Everyone braced and adjusted their rucksacks. Vietnamese voices filtered through and around the leaves and fronds. As if they were one man, every head swiveled in the direction of the voices. Terry and Duffy placed a hand under one of Brumsen's shoulders and lifted.

"We've come 1500 meters,"Terry whispered.

Looking at his compass, Anderson pointed. "The hill we're trying to reach is about three to four hundred meters in that direction. It will be dark in an hour. Thank god we still have this rain and cloud cover."

Brumsen walked a couple of steps, limping.

"Can you put weight on it?" Anderson asked.

He took more steps, grimacing. He clenched his teeth. "No bones broken. I can do it."

The sing-song pattern of Vietnamese percolated through the leaves once again.

Anderson lifted Brumsen's rucksack. "Duffy, stay with Brumsen and help him if he needs it. Terry, you're still tail-end Charlie. Stay close to us, no stopping. We only go as fast as Brumsen."

Crouching forward, compass in hand, Cochise pushed a banana plant aside and disappeared. Anderson stepped off behind Cochise, carrying the extra rucksack. Terry, carrying Brumsen's machine-gun, heart pounding, stepped off behind Duffy and Brumsen.

The blanket of fog descended like a shroud through the treetops. Soft, vaporous tendrils of white crept through the branches. Monkeys chattered and shrieked. A cacophony of birds, insects, and lizards created a ululating counterpoint to the monkeys.

After two hundred yards, the ground rose sharply. Duffy supported Brumsen. Terry was about to ask Duffy if he needed relief, when a thunderous burst of an M-16 broke the silence. Everyone crouched. Brumsen groaned. Terry, two or three yards behind searched to the sides and rear. The jungle, silent, held its breath.

Anderson ran back to them in a crouch. "Cochise just shot a gook. We have to keep moving and get to the top of the hill."

Brumsen's dark forehead wrinkled with pain and the strained effort of standing.

"You can make it?" Anderson asked.

"Yeah, but it hurts like hell." He pulled a bloody hand away from the bandage on his leg.

Cochise appeared, wiping his knife on his pants. His eyes burned feverishly. He drew a line across his throat.

"How's the arm, Duffy?" Anderson asked.

"It aches. I'm all right."

"These guys have got to be trackers. Let's hope that's all of them and we can lose ourselves in this jungle. We're going straight up the hill. It can't be more than two hundred yards. Cochise, you and Malloy move with us about fifty yards. Stop and wait ten minutes or so. Then come on up. We'll rest a while on the hilltop until it gets dark and then relocate." Anderson shouldered Brumsen's rucksack. He gave the M-60 to Duffy.

The grays slowly settled over the jungle with the descending fog. Terry searched the darkening vegetation. Less than thirty minutes of daylight.

Duffy supported Brumsen as he stood up. He had trouble steadying the big machine-gunner, slipping on the soggy slope. He breathed heavily. Terry reached to support him. When Brumsen slid and almost fell, Anderson and Cochise both returned to help.

The fog enveloped the jungle. Mist rolled along the ground and coalesced on Terry's face and hands. After they had gone fifty yards, Cochise knelt on one knee and propped himself against his M-16. Terry squatted beside him. Monkeys ranted. Soft tendrils of gray fog inundated the branches and fronds. Cochise, knife handle sticking out of its scabberd, was a visible shadow. Beyond him were outlines of vegetation. Outside of a five-foot perimeter, opaqueness.

They heard the whispering Vietnamese at the same moment. Two men talked quietly, but aggressively. The shadowy shape of a standing man appeared no more than six feet from them. The outline of a pith helmet topped the man's head. The blurry shape of a rifle barrel stuck out from his chest. The man disappeared, and another man took his place, then another and another. The men made little noise as they went by. Terry nor Cochise, kneeling in the vegetation, moved.

Terry counted fourteen men when the last walked by. He had not shifted his position since he saw the first Vietnamese. His calves hurt and his back ached. He wanted to stand. Cochise's grip on his shoulder restrained him. They waited for several minutes, then both stood.

Night had finally fallen. "At least they're not going toward the top of the hill," Cochise whispered, gesturing the direction they should go. "Hold on to my rucksack." He stepped into the night.

Both men crept, inching and feeling the ground with their boots for roots and growth along the jungle floor. Cochise halted every few steps to listen. Their rucksacks and equipment caught on vines. They moved patiently to undo the tangle.

Would they be able to find the squad?

The fog and mist did not lessen as they trudged up the hill. A fuck-you lizard began its mournful wail on their left. Further off, screeching monkeys quarreled.

They neared the top of the hill. "Cochise, Malloy, over here." Cochise ventured in the direction of Anderson's voice. A hand clutched Terry's shoulder.

"Wait here. I'll go get Duffy," Anderson said, relieved.

Seeing Duffy, Terry broke into a big grin. Duffy patted Cochise and Terry on their arms. "Good to see you guys."

"Duffy and I came back down the hill and spread out, hoping we might find you or that you might run into us." Anderson spoke in a subdued voice. "We left Brumsen up at the top. His leg isn't doing well. I'm hoping the bleeding's stopped. We'll talk more when we reach him."

The four men trekked up the hill and found Brumsen leaning against a tree. Terry and Cochise both moved to him, knelt on each side of him, and touched his arms.

"All right! Anderson was worried about you two assholes. I told 'em that the Bros would be all right."

After they shed their rucksacks, Cochise reported the NVA he and Terry encountered. "It's at least a reinforced squad, maybe two squads."

"I counted fourteen men," Terry added. "There could be more."

The men knelt in a circle around Brumsen facing each other. Anderson, fumbling with a twig, pondered the fog-shrouded jungle. Scratching his stubbled face, he balled his fist and thumped his knee with it. "Guy Edmond, how do you feel?"

"Weak."

Duffy touched Brumsen's shoulder. "He's lost a lot of blood."

"That may be one of the ways they're tracking us, because of my blood."

There was a momentary silence. Cochise adjusted his scabbered. "Who cares why?"

Pushing his helmet back on his head, Anderson rubbed the scar on his forehead. "If they know we have wounded, they know we can't move very fast. We have to assume that they know we're somewhere around here. We've killed several of them. They're not stupid, and they've tracked us for the last three hours. They were tracking us before you were wounded, Brumsen. They've probably been searching for us since Malloy killed that guy or since we called in the arty. Maybe it's been since we ambushed that squad last night. I don't think the first two guys we killed were there by accident." He rubbed his stubbled chin. "Let's not worry about it. This fog and the night is ideal to escape from these bastards. Brumsen, can you move at all?"

"I'm pretty screwed up. But, I'll try anything. My leg's gonna get stiff if we don't move. If we wait much longer, I don't know if I can."

Examining the bandage around Brumsen's leg, Duffy lifted his hands and let them fall in frustration. "The bleeding's stopped. If he puts weight on it, he'll bleed. Even if we devise a stretcher, he's going to bleed."

"Why don't you guys go? Leave me here with some ammo and come back and get me."

"I'll stay with him," Duffy offered.

"Me, too," Terry and Cochise said at the same time.

"No one is leaving anyone behind." Anderson sliced the air dismissively with his hand. "So far, no one knows we're here. They're sending a chopper tomorrow morning to pick us up. Let's just sit tight.

"Cochise, you and Malloy said the NVA were moving east, didn't you? I want you and Malloy to go east down the hill about thirty yards or so. If I were the NVA commander, I would put men on line and march them up the hill, either now or early tomorrow morning.

They like to attack early in the morning." Anderson took off his web gear. "But, putting men on line now would be very dangerous. They might shoot each other in this darkness and fog. They could send out one or two troops to probe up the hill to find out if we are where they think we are. That's what I would do, and that's why I want you two to go east down the hill. Don't shoot or do anything unless it's absolutely necessary. Even if we kill 'em without noise, their absence will tell their commander exactly what he wants to know. I have a hunch, he'll probe for us tomorrow morning."

The five men stared at each other with vacant eyes. Fog and mist oozed through the jungle, caressing the hillside. Precipitation coalesced on their dirt-covered faces and ran in rivulets down their necks into already soaked shirts. A chill gripped Terry. He shuddered.

A high-pitched voice shouted, "GI, you die!" The jungle waited. "GI, you die."

CHAPTER NINETEEN

The frustrated tone of Clarissa's email depressed him.

I can't believe you spoke out against homosexuals and their right to marriage. Porter is so upset. He says he is never coming back to the States.

Why do you have to embarrass me like this? The Atlanta papers are ripping you to pieces, calling you a Nazi and a homophobe. Please Terry, quiet down. Let it go.

What the hell was wrong with what he said? It was a straightforward talk. Different views were exchanged. Ideas were thrown around. He didn't hate Smyth-Wickham or homosexuals. He put forward arguments. Why couldn't they discuss the ideas? He thought they were interesting. Why should they hate him?

He relaxed, collapsing into the chair. It wasn't what he said. It was what they said he said. He opened a drawer on the desk and reached for the flask of scotch. Looking at his watch, he reasoned that 8:40 A.M. was a good time for a drink

A knock came on the door. He placed the flask back in the drawer. Laura and another young lady entered the office.

"Sit down, ladies." His face brightened.

Laura held the hand of a girl with long, black hair. Her big blue eyes were her prettiest feature. "Dr. Malloy, this is Becky."

Becky pulled at her pale, gray skirt. Placing both hands on her lap, she pulled at her skirt again. She ran her fingers through her hair.

Laura leaned forward. She didn't have her usual bright smile. "Dr. Malloy, Becky has a problem. I told her she should talk to you and maybe you can give her some advice."

Watching Becky fidget, he deliberately kept his voice quiet, attempting a soothing tone. "Talk to me, Becky. Tell me what's on your mind. If I can help, I will."

No longer running her fingers through her hair, Becky sighed. "Dr. Malloy, I'm pregnant. I thought my boyfriend loved me. But, he won't talk to me."

"Why won't he talk to you, sweetheart?" Terry, frowning, folded his arms across his chest.

"Isaac told me that it was my choice not to use birth control. I almost threw my purse at him. I told him it was his choice not to use a condom. I wasn't going to take that crap." A tear rolled down Becky's flushed cheek. "He told me I could get rid of the baby or keep it. It was my choice. He said he learned in a course on Constitutional Law, that women can do what they want with the baby and the father has no say so. Then he said if that's the way the Supreme Court wants it, then so be it.

"I asked him how he could be so mean. I can't believe I thought Isaac loved me. He just kept on telling me that it was a pro-choice society. I was the one who had to make the choice. He had no choice in the matter. So, he didn't have any responsibility." Becky's voice broke. Laura squeezed and held her hand.

"Becky, he may have no choice in whether you keep the baby." Terry clasped his hands and put both elbows on the table. "But he has legal responsibilities."

"I think that's why he took off to New Mexico to live with his father." Becky paused. "Both his mom and dad are lawyers."

Picking up the phone, Terry dialed Sarah's office number. "I'm going to ask a friend of mine to join us. Do you mind?"

As Sarah listened to Becky's story, Terry saw Ella, across the kitchen table, stuffing macaroni and cheese into her mouth. "Guys, I'm pregnant."

Clarissa dropped her fork. "What!"

Terry took Ella's hand. "How far along are you?"

"Just a month. Gus and I talked it over and we decided that we're going to get married."

"Ella, how could you do this to me?" Clarissa banged the table. "After all the conversations I've had with you."

"Calm down." He stroked Clarissa's arm.

Clarissa threw her blue cloth napkin down on the table. "Goddammit, don't tell me to calm down. If you'd been a little more demanding as a father and let her know what kind of expectations you had..." Clarissa buried her face in her hands.

Walking around the table, Ella hugged her mother. "Mom, Mom, it's not Dad's fault or yours. I want you guys to be happy for me. I'm going to be married."

"Abort it! You have no idea of the responsibilities you'll be taking on. Neither you nor Gus know when to keep your pants and panties on. How do you expect to know how to raise a child?"

"Clarissa, don't tell her that. Let her make the decision. Gus is stepping up to the plate. They're both taking responsibility for it. It's not just Ella's fault."

Clarissa stood, green eyes flashing. She picked up her plate. "I'm giving advice, discussing options. All the hopes and dreams I had for you, Ella, and you just poured them down the drain."

Sarah's voice snapped Terry out of his reverie. "Let's meet later on today and we can discuss this in private."

The two girls stood.

Terry said, "Becky, you came here for my advice. I can offer you little. You'll have to make the ultimate decision. Be merciful."

Her head down, Becky wiped a tear from her eye.

"That's all I've got to say. Mercy is a virtue of the powerful. It takes a strong person to show it."

After the two girls left, neither Terry or Sarah spoke for several minutes.

Eyebrows moving at a rapid pace, Jake Horowitz knocked on the open door. "You guys busy?" Coming into the room, he stood looking down at them. "I just got a call from Rich. It seems he was arrested last night around 3 in the morning. Do either one of you know about it?"

They shook their heads.

"For what?" Sarah asked.

Jake shrugged and took his pipe out of his mouth. "It seems he was out here in the little pine grove digging up the azaleas. The police gave him a sobriety test, which he failed. They charged him with public drunkeness, attempting to steal public property, and threatening a police officer with his shovel. Do you guys know anything that could provoke Rich to do something like this?"

They looked at each other and smiled. Both shook their heads.

Jake gently tapped his forehead with his pipe. He pointed it at them. "There's something going on here that I don't know about. Anyway, from your lips to God's ears. I need you two to get him out of jail. He asked me to help. But, I'm waiting on a call about my mother."

* * *

Rich rubbed at the dirt stains covering his knees. "Crap! I'll never get these stains out. They're brand new... the pants I mean."

"Rich, what happened?" Sarah asked, smoothing her napkin.

Throwing his napkin on the table, Rich shrugged. "I was out in my yard last night when the police pulled up. It seems some neighbors heard me or saw me. I don't know what the they were doing up at 3 in the morning. Anyway, I had been drinking and I locked myself out of the house."

Terry placed his coffee mug on the table. "Cut the shit, Rich. Jake told us what you did. How could you believe a silly story like that, Sarah and I fucking in the azaleas, for Christ sake! You didn't leave Diversity alone in that house did you?"

Hanging his head, Rich fiddled with the napkin. He looked at Sarah, who with unblinking, hard eyes, stared back. "No, she's with her mother this week. I just had too much to drink. All right, I've been thinking too much about this. I mean you two."

"You have to get over it, Rich." Not smiling, Sarah cupped her coffee in both hands. "You and I never had a relationship. We haven't tried to hide anything. It just happened."

Grimacing and shaking his head, Rich crossed his arms. "I've been a victim of catastrophes all my life. Nothing has ever gone right for me. My little whorehound mother sent me up for adoption as soon as I was born. I always imagine her fucking some college frat stud who hardly knew her. I can see her fucking her brains out in the frat brat's old Chevy at some drive-in movie. Then what happens? She put me up for adoption and I'm swept away by two die-hard Republicans. My name is Richard N. Breedlove. You want to know what the 'N' stands for? Nixon. Richard fucking Nixon Breedlove. What a crock of shit. I get screwed by that little bitch of a mother and then I get screwed by my fucking Republican step-parents. Do you know how hard it's been to go through life as Richard Nixon Breedlove, especially when you're progressive and on the cutting edge like me. I started leaving the Nixon out of my name when I turned twenty-one.

"And now what do I do? I spend my life in an endless pyramid scheme trying to convince journals to publish my papers. Then other professors can write about them. I can write about theirs and we encourage and help each other in a giant rip off. It's nothing but a huge pyramid of academic bullshit. We all sell to each other and nobody outside of the pyramid gives a rat's ass about any of it. No one reads it but people in on the scheme. States pour out millions of dollars to pay us. All we do is sell to each other. How different are we from Amway?"

Sighing, Rich shifted in his chair. "That's my shitty life.

"When I die, Diversity will take all those papers that no one has read and toss them, throwing my whole life in the trash."

"You need to stop whining and get on with your life,"Sarah said.

God, a glass of scotch would be great right now. He had to remember to bring the flask from now on. "I wouldn't be too harsh on your birth mother either."

Scowling, an arrogant tone entered Rich's voice. "Oh, yeah. What would you know about it?"

Terry adjusted his glasses. "Your mom must have had some strength. She carried you for nine months and gave birth to you. Can you imagine the shame and ridicule she must have endured four decades ago? Count your blessings. Abortion would have been a lot easier, I'm sure. Instead of having a life, you could have been an inconvenient footnote to someone else's."

"Okay, guys, I need to accomplish some chores before I see a young girl named Becky." Sarah gulped her coffee. She touched Terry's shoulder. "We're going to a charity performance tonight. Don't drink too much before you pick me up around 7 or I'll kick your ass."

Terry placed both hands on the table and pushed himself up. "Come on, Rich. I'll take you to your car."

When Terry stopped the car behind Rich's, he held out his hand. "No hard feelings, okay?"

Rich shook hands. "Tell me one thing. What does a woman like Sarah see in a geezer like you?"

"You want to know the truth?" Terry placed both hands on the steering wheel.

"Of course."

"When I spank her, I make her say, 'Thank you, Daddy.'"

Rich grabbed the door handle with one hand while tugging on his moustache with the other. "Sonofabitch! I want be able to get that out of my mind. Goddamnit!"

As Rich walked to his car, Terry heard him.

"Goddamnit! Goddamnit!"

* * *

Tugging on his tie, Terry held the door open for Sarah. People waved to them. Sarah waved back. "Leave your tie and collar alone. You look terrific. Don't spoil it."

Terry nodded as Sarah sauntered over to a couple. She wore a black dress with a big red belt that matched her lipstick. Her hair hung loose around her shoulders. High heels made her almost as tall as Terry, who admired her as she walked away from him.

Waving Terry to follow her, Sarah introduced him to a couple at the same time that an announcement came over the loud speaker. Lights started blinking. The concert was about to start.

Terry held Sarah's hand. He didn't even know what this event was for. He needed a drink, but had kept his word, only having two shots of scotch before Sarah came. Her smile was reward enough. If Clarissa had been just a little more lenient in her beliefs and opinions... Terry realized that he was looking around for the squad. He had ignored several gestures of recognition and good-fellowship. The men were nowhere to be seen.

The lights dimmed. Sarah reached for his hand.

"What is this concert for?" Terry whispered.

A young lady wearing blue jeans and a tee-shirt and carrying a guitar walked onto the stage. Sitting on a stool behind a microphone, she cradled her guitar. "Hi, I'm Susan Mitchell."

Sarah held a finger to her lips. "You'll discover soon enough. This young lady is a pretty well-known songwriter, very original."

Pushing the hair over her shoulders, the guitarist began to sing:

How many years will it be before
men will ever understand?
How many years will it be before
men will stretch a helping hand?
Cocksucker!!

Eyes wide, Terry turned to Sarah questioning? "What the hell was that?" he whispered and mouthed at the same time.

Someone two rows behind him began to bark in short burst.

He turned his head to look for the barker.

Sarah squeezed his hand, whispering in turn, "Don't look around!"

Shaking his head and frowning, he turned back to the singer, who sounded mysteriously like Dylan.

How many years must the bombers fly
before they're buried in the sand
The answer my friend...
Shithead!!

Across the auditorium someone shouted, "*Fuck it!*"

He raised his hands in perplexity, eyes wide and questioning. He turned in his seat once again.

Sarah yanked on his arm and lowered her head, indicating that he should do the same. "This is a charity benefit for Tourette's syndrome. Susan is a Tourette's Therapy specialist.

"Sonofabitch!"

His head snapped up. The person who had yelled the last epithet sat four seats down from them. "Sarah, that was Dean Smithson who yelled that."

Sarah violently shushed him. "Don't look at anyone or turn around. I'll explain."

Singing her song, the guitarist seemed oblivious to the shouts from the auditorium. Throughout her performance the auditorium percolated with the sounds of barking dogs and mewling cats. "Communist bastards!" came from a man wearing a priest's collar. "Asshole rednecks!" came from somewhere behind Terry.

Wiping his forehead with a handkerchief, Terry hunkered down in his seat. What in the hell had he gotten himself into now?

At the intermission everyone filed out dutifully to play at being collegial. Sarah held Terry's arm. They remained seated.

She fumbled through her purse and took out a cosmetic kit. "An article, called 'Inner Turmoil and Tourette's' went around the campus about three months ago. It was written by Professor Sacagewea. You missed it. Anyway, the article was a result of her studying the idea of normalcy. Who sets the standards for what's normal? Instead of trying to change the way people with Tourette's syndrome behave, why can't we shout and yell what we want, when we want. In other words, we should be more like the people who have Tourette's. They say what they feel. They're more in touch with their inner psyches. We so-called normal people, on the other hand, hold our feelings in and that causes anxieties and neurosis. So, Rich, who's on the Campus Entertainment Committee, asked the committee to host a Tourette's syndrome charity concert. Shoshonnah found a Tourette's Therapy touring group. There're several, that travel around the country to try to show everyone that it's okay for people to say what they think. They tour the country raising awareness and encouraging people to open up."

Terry slapped his forehead. "I should have known. So, do any of these therapists have Tourette's?"

Checking her forehead and pulling her hair while looking into a mirror, Sarah continued, "Of course not. This group is from Harvard. So, anyway, at the first concert, the first entertainer- therapist, invited everyone to say whatever they wanted. You know, let it all hang out, so to speak. We all closed our eyes and he began to sing. No one tried to see who was saying what and nobody mentioned it the next day except to say what a great evening they'd had. Imagine everyone saying exactly what they want to, Terry, and no one caring. It was amazing."

"Where was the first group of therapists from and did they really have Tourette's?"

Sarah put away her cosmetic kit. "Terry, they're Therapists. It's like asking if a psychiatrist is insane. I'm not sure where the first group was from, either Yale or Oberlin. You have to remember that we're doing this for charity."

Closing his eyes, Terry breathed deeply. He was in a fucking nut house. "Can I say something?"

"Of course."

"I want to go home and wake myself up. This is a fucking nightmare. If I'm not at home sleeping, then I'll have a glass of scotch and blow my brains out."

Sarah took out her lipstick. "Terry, don't talk like that. Just try to get in touch with your foundations. You might actually discover that you like the person you find. I know I do...like you I mean." A smile played around the corners of Sarah's mouth. Her eyes were gay and bright.

"You don't believe any of this shit do you?" Terry asked.

"Well, Mr. Terry, I have to say that life is interesting when you look at it as a Confederate infiltrator. Remember, I am a part of a vast conspiracy."

Perplexed at her humor and the secrets hidden in her smile and eyes, Terry sat back in his seat to endure the rest of the concert.

People filed back into the auditorium. A general buzz of gaiety bubbled up from the crowd. The lights dimmed. Three men walked on stage carrying two guitars and a fiddle. The fiddle player hopped across the stage.

As they began to sing a cacophony of voices erupted from the audience, ricocheting off the walls. "Fuck it!" "Eat me!" A man in the balcony yelled, "Spank me!" Someone barked. Another mooed. A woman behind Terry erupted with several snorts. The fiddle player hopped up and down with no rhythm. Around the auditorium, about twenty people hopped up and down in sync with him.

Shutting his eyes, Terry groaned. He had been saying exactly what he wanted to say for the last five days or so, and people had tried to crucify him. God. Lesbian vegetarians stealing cattle, the Unitarian Church of Universal Victimology, children shooting their parents with paint ball guns, college classes for non-readers, was he really an active participant in this insanity? But, how sane was he? He spent his days talking to ghosts, for God's sake. Did he live in this world? No, he was just trying to survive. What about the other world he lived in? The one he longed for. Anderson, Brumsen, Duffy, Cochise and, of course, darling Ella. All dead. Was that world any saner than this one? What were his foundations? How sane was he, one foot among the living and one foot among the dead. Where do you live, Daddy? What world did he want to live in? Which was real? Were they both true? Were they both false?

* * *

After the NVA stopped yelling, the squad took all of their grenades and claymores out of their rucksacks. Anderson counted fifteen grenades and eight claymores. "Cochise, I still want you and Malloy to go down the east slope about thirty yards. Booby-trap some grenades. I'm going to set up two claymores on the same side about five yards out."

Anderson's hand went to his thin neck. Jerking his hand away, he dropped a leech to the ground in front of him and crushed it with his boot. "Duffy and I will set up grenade booby-traps all around the sides of the hill, except on the east side. They'll be about fifteen yards out. I'm hoping they'll give us some warning of where and when we can expect attacks. After we do that, we'll try to dig some kind of a hole here to protect us a little. Those guys still don't know where we are. The chopper is supposed to be here at 7:30 sharp. If we can make it till then, we should be fine."

Terry's stomach growled. He had not thought of food in hours. Sharp lines of pain shot up his calves from his feet. Think of the jungle rot later.

"Let's check ourselves for leeches and then let's eat." Anderson took off his shirt.

"I definitely don't want any fucking leeches sucking my blood." Brumsen unbuttoned his shirt. "Right now, I need it all."

"Eat something that's good cold," Cochise said, leaning his rifle against a tree. "I don't think we better be lighting any fires."

"Maybe we can eat the leeches." Duffy's bare back exposed several.

Terry bayoneted the leeches on Duffy's back.

"Would one of you help me move this damn leg? It's stiffened up on me." Brumsen tried to shift his wounded leg.

They adjusted it.

Duffy pulled a leech off of Brumsen. "Don't fidget too much. You might start bleeding again."

The rain fell steadily. Through eating, Cochise placed the empty can to the side. "Anderson, Terry and I will start digging a hole while you and Duffy set up the grenades and claymores. Then you two can expand it, after we leave. At least we can get it started."

Anderson stood and took two grenades from the pile. He checked the pins and handed one grenade to Duffy. "We need a pit, Cochise , not a foxhole or a trench. I want it wide enough to let Brumsen stretch out and deep enough that we can all keep our heads down when we kneel and still be able to fire." Anderson knelt beside Brumsen. "Don't move too much, big guy. I don't want you bleeding to death on us. We're going to need you and that machine gun."

Grabbing entrenching tools, Cochise and Terry began to dig a square pit. They worked silently. Their shovels slipped into the mud easily. They threw the dirt along the top of the hole, to make it deeper. Anderson and Duffy returned and picked up more grenades and claymores.

Brumsen complained that his leg was hurting. Cochise removed his poncho from his rucksack. Terry held it over Brumsen like a tent while Cochise crawled underneath. Under the poncho, Cochise's cigarette lighter illumined Brumsen's wound. With his knife, Cochise cut the muddy bandage from Brumsen's leg and wrapped a new bandage around it, adjusting the leg.

"That feels better, Bros."

After Anderson and Duffy returned, the men all took turns digging. The deeper they dug, the muddier it became from the continuing rain. Each person digging lost his footing and slipped several times. Finally, covered with the muck and goo, they stopped.

Duffy's boots squished in the mud and made sucking sounds when he maneuvered. "This place is a swamp."

"Let's get some rest now." Anderson said. "They won't be coming tonight. If they come at all, it'll be around 5 or so tomorrow morning. Cochise, I'll wake you and Malloy around 12."

An arm gripped his shoulder and shook Terry awake. He looked at his watch. *Twelve o'clock midnight.*

Anderson plopped a grenade into Terry's hand. He handed Cochise two grenades. "It's time for you two to head out. There are no grenades on the eastern slope. You guys have to take care of that."

"Let Malloy stay here. There's no sense in both of us going." Cochise put his arm around Terry's shoulders.

Anderson shook his head. "If two of you go, one can sleep while the other watches and listens. That way you both get rest. I want you to go, because I expect they will attack from the east. The earlier we know they're coming, the better it is for us."

Cochise hefted his grenades. "I can't argue with that. I'm one tired *hijo de puta*."

"I want both of you back here by 5:30." Anderson lifted a shovel. "Duffy and I will tidy up this hole while you two are gone." He slid the spade into the earth before Cochise and Terry crawled out of the pit.

In less than a minute they scurried down the east side of the hill, stopping beneath a tall teak tree. They rested within the gnarled roots.

"I'll set up the booby-traps."

Terry gave his grenade to Cochise.

Cochise returned, sat down, and sighed. "That's it. We have a grenade on each side of us, twenty yards out. The one in front of the tree is out about five yards, because the tree will protect us from the blast."

Terry listened for any moving bushes or stumbles that would signify the sound of men, loaded with equipment, trying to navigate through thick vegetation and fog. The jungle reflected nothing but the clicks and buzzings of insects and the ever-constant drip and fall of rain. A bird whistled a melodic tune. Leaning against the teak tree, his damp, mud-spattered jungle fatigues clinging to his exhausted body, Terry understood the majesty and eternity of the jungle. *We will die and this jungle will remain. Am I really this trivial to nature?*

"Malloy," Cochise whispered, "I've something to ask you. I don't think I'm going to make it."

Terry attempted to say something, but Cochise held up his hand. "Listen to me. I want you to tell my son what kind of man his father was."

"What makes you think I'm going to make it out of this mess?"

"I just have a feeling about you, Malloy. You don't say a lot, but you're always watching. You seem to be in the right place at the right time. I can tell. You're a survivor. If anyone makes it, it'll be you. So shut up and listen to me. Believe me, I won't go down without a fight. But if I don't make it, you have to tell my son who I was. You have our addresses. We all wrote them down for each other."

"Of course I'll do it, Cochise. You can depend on me."

Silence. Cochise sighed. "You get some sleep. I'll keep the first watch."

Cochise woke Terry at 3, then fell asleep. The rain lessened. The fog remained. Terry, peering through the trees and foliage, saw a star.

By 5 in the morning the rain had stopped. The fog receded further down the hill. Terry woke Cochise. The black jungle changed to its usual grayness that preceded the day.

The explosion rocked both of them backward. Dust and leaves swirled around both sides of the teak tree. Someone screamed in Vietnamese. Cochise and Terry both jumped up and backed against the tree, weapons ready to fire. A tornado of leaves and smoke swirled to their right with another detonation and more yelling. Cochise and Terry ran up the hill. Gunfire erupted on each side of them. Bullets cut through the leaves and fronds around Terry. Both men fell, rather than jumped, into the crater.

Brumsen, sitting upright, leaned against the western side of the pit. He rested on his good leg, his wounded leg stretched out in front him. His machine gun pointed through a V-shaped aperture cut into the dirt berm around the edge of the pit.

Cochise cradled his gun, crawling to the north side. "Where's Duffy and Anderson?"

Brumsen pointed behind him in the direction from which the two men had come. "Down the hill. I'm covering this way in case they try to get behind us."

M-16s erupted on the eastern side of the slope. AK-47s roared in response. Duffy and Anderson both ran through the foliage and jumped into the pit.

Duffy gulped air. "I got one."

Anderson shoved a magazine into his rifle. "Good to see you guys. Malloy, you cover that side." Anderson pointed to another V-shaped aperture. "Cochise, you take the remaining side. Duffy and I'll cover this slope."

The bottom of each gun aperture touched the original jungle floor. Detonators lay on the ground with cords attached to them. The cords trailed through the apertures of the pit and out into the jungle.

AK-47s fired along the eastern side of the hill. Several rounds snapped through the leaves and branches.

"They still don't know where we are," Duffy said, rubbing his wounded arm.

"They're reconning by fire," Anderson added.

Duffy crossed himself. *"Credo in unum Deum."*

A line of fire erupted up and down the eastern slope and grew louder as the NVA approached the top of the hill. The firing increased. Bullets sliced through the jungle, shattering branches over them. Two men in pith helmets pushed fronds aside and emerged out of the jungle from the eastern slope. The Vietnamese soldiers, five feet apart, fired sporadically in two to three second bursts. They had no chance to catch sight of the men kneeling behind the berm.

Duffy shot one through the head and chest. He staggered backward, down the slope and disappeared into the jungle. Anderson shot the other man as he was stepping on the dirt mound surrounding the hole. The man slumped into a kneeling position, staring at Anderson, as if he were about to pray. The NVA soldier released his grip on his smoking rifle as he knelt. Looking at Anderson with wide open eyes and a quizzical expression, he attempted to grab the gun again. Anderson shot him twice in the chest. The bullets knocked him backward. His eyes still questioning as he fell.

"Patrem omnipotentem, factorem coeli et terrae, visibilium omnium et invisibilium."

More rifles fired on Terry's side. Bullets passed through the foliage over his head and kicked up dirt and mud on the berm. Cochise ducked from rifle fire coming from his side. The jungle to Terry's front ripped apart. The air expanded and contracted with the explosion. Smoke roiled up the slope. Men bellowed.

"Booby trap," Terry said.

"Et in unum Dominum, Iesum Christum, Filium Dei unigenitum,"

Another explosion, accompanied with screams, burst behind Terry.

Men fired from the slopes in front of Terry and Cochise.

"et ex Patre natum ante omnia saecula."

Cochise rested his rifle on the berm aperture. "Booby trap here, too! They're on three sides, now."

"Deum de Deo, lumen de lumine, Deum verum de Deo vero..."

The firing extended around the men, nearer and louder. Terry, peering through his aperture, saw muzzle flashes.

Anderson spoke calmly. "Malloy, Cochise, use the claymores, one each. They know where we are, now."

Cochise grabbed a detonator. "Everyone get down."

The jungle vibrated. Glimmering fireflies of tracer rounds sailed through the foliage, increasing in intensity from three different sides of the pit. Terry pressed a detonator as Cochise said, "Three."

"Crucifixus etiam pro nobis sub Pontio Pilato; passus et sepultus est."

The two explosions tore the fabric of the jungle apart. Shock waves rolled over the squad. Dust boiled up from both sides. Terry's ears rang. His body tingled with nerves and numbness. Pieces of leaves, fronds, and branches fell earthward. Vegetation and dust swirled from every direction. A tree limb tumbled to the ground in slow motion. The men, heads covered, returned to kneeling positions. Complete silence ensued as the debris continued to fall. Terry could hear nothing.

The squad stirred as the leaves and dust cascaded around them. Terry put a hand to an ear. It came back with blood. He stood up, then knelt again as a khaki-clad figure stumbled out of the blizzard of vegetation. The man held a weapon in one hand and attempted to lift it. His other arm, a bloody, shredded stump, waved at Terry. Tattered fatigues hung from the stump. Two inches of jagged, white bone jutted from the cloth. With a slight movement from the left, Duffy fired at the one-armed soldier. When Terry turned back, the one-armed man was gone.

Another soldier ran out of the smoke and jungle, firing. Terry shot the man in the stomach and chest. Momentum propelled him to the edge of the pit. The man's body seemed to have all of the chords of life cut at once. He collapsed, rather than sagged, to the ground. His upper torso draped across the berm.

Smoke began to dissipate. The bitter smell of cordite hung in the air. Ears still ringing, his hearing returned. The buzzing, tingling sensation continued in his body. Everyone in the squad fired short bursts into the jungle. Mushrooms of dirt flared up all around the berm.

"Firing from this side," Brumsen said. "We're surrounded."

"Et resurrexit tertia die, secundum scripturas;"

Terry glanced back at Anderson kneeling and firing beside the prone Brumsen. Brumsen's head rocked to and fro. He swivelled the M-60 back and forth, smoke pouring from its barrel.

"et ascendit in coelum, sedet ad dextram Patris."

Duffy knelt beside Cochise. Flickering tracer rounds shot from their weapons and rippled through the jungle. Two grenades careened through the air and rolled behind Cochise and Duffy. Terry, dropping his rifle, took two steps, grabbed a grenade in each hand, throwing them back over the berm.

"Et iterum venturus est cum gloria iudicare vivos et mortuos,"

As the two grenades exploded, two more sailed into the pit. One hit Terry in the arm and another landed at his feet. Terry tossed them back into the jungle. Duffy pressed a detonator. The blast of the claymore and grenades slammed Terry to the ground.

"cuius regni non erit finis."

Snowing leaves, branches, and fronds created a fog around the squad. Dirt, smoke, and plants swirled into the sky from the force of the detonations.

"Confiteor unum baptisma in remissionem peccatorum."

Anderson reached for one of the detonators near Brumsen and squeezed it. The jungle trees reeled, and recoiled again. The shockwave and shrapnel sliced through them, sending up more detritus to enter the moiling chaos.

"Et expecto resurrectionem mortuorum et vitam venturi saeculi. Amen."

An NVA soldier appeared above Cochise, on top of the berm, firing wildly. Terry reached for his rifle. Cochise shot the man. Duffy slumped to the ground. Another soldier hurtled through the choking smoke over the mound. Terry and Cochise both shot the man as his momentum carried him to where Anderson was firing with

Brumsen. The soldier collapsed upon Brumsen, who screamed in pain. Anderson yanked the man off Brumsen, heaving the limp body up on the berm. Cochise, a bandage in his hand, checked Duffy.

Three grenades skidded on the ground toward Anderson and Brumsen. Terry dove for one grenade, grabbed it, and threw it. Anderson threw another over the berm wall. Terry frantically searched for the other grenade. Brumsen's massive arm stretched across the pit. His arm arced through the air, releasing the grenade. His torso and arm exploded. An invisible sledge hammer struck Terry's chest, knocking him backward and down against a wall of the pit. Anderson, who had been standing between Brumsen and Terry, lay on his back, arms thrown over his head. Blood and shreds of Brumsen's flesh covered Anderson's face. Cochise, covering Duffy with his body, raised himself to a kneeling position. Glancing around, Terry lurched toward the detonator near Brumsen. He squeezed it. The concussion waves of the blast swept over him.

Get moving, get moving. How many claymores left?

Terry staggered to his original side of the pit. Hearing a distant noise, he turned and saw Cochise, screaming, take the pin out of a grenade and toss it into the jungle. Terry squeezed the detonator. Another concussion ripped through the area. As Terry crawled toward the third detonator, Cochise, still screaming, hurled another grenade into the jungle.

Cochise's second grenade exploded as Terry pressed the third detonator. Furious, numbing blasts rent the air. Anderson lay unconscious on the ground. Brumsen's torn, blood-soaked body lay crumpled against the wall. Terry clutched the last detonator and set it off as Cochise threw yet another grenade into the jungle. Terry pushed himself into the side of the pit.

As the last claymore detonated, two shapes hurtled into the hole. Both jumped over Terry, who lay against a wall, and smashed with grunts into a standing Cochise. Cochise hit one man with his fist. He dropped to the earth. The other Vietnamese swung his rifle like a club, which glanced off Cochise's ducking head. Terry lurched from the ground onto the back of Cochise's assailant. Both Terry and the Vietnamese stumbled past Cochise, who reached for his M-16. The first man Cochise had hit grabbed Cochise's legs, tumbling with him to the ground.

Terry and his opponent fell across the mound and rolled. Terry partially blocked a painful blow to the side of his head, reaching for the weapon that had caused it. With both hands on the rifle, he attempted to knee his adversary. Still holding on to the man's gun, he fell backward, jerking the rifle away from the grasping, kicking Vietnamese soldier. The Vietnamese shoved the gun aside and grabbed Terry's face and throat, scratching and clawing. Hands tightening around his neck, thumbs crushed his windpipe. Terry pushed the man's chin up with the rifle. His other hand tried to lessen the choking vice-like grip. Gasping and choking for air, he continued to push the man's chin back, back, and up.

The man's neck and head sagged. The grip on Terry's throat lessened. A warm wetness oozed between Terry's fingers. The hilt of Cochise's knife stuck from the Vietnamese face. The blade, buried to the hilt, had penetrated the man's left eye. Terry shoved the Vietnamese aside, twirled around, and saw a smiling Cochise, standing on the mound, straddling a dead soldier.

As Terry stood, he saw a blur behind Cochise and managed to scream before the soldier on the berm fired several rounds into Cochise's back. A red spray came out of Cochise's chest as he fell forward, staring at Terry. He could do nothing but watch as the Vietnamese's rifle swung toward him. The soldier's finger tensed, squeezing the trigger, when his chest ballooned with red splotches. A bloody mist enveloped the man. Anderson, kneeling, gripped a smoking pistol. He collapsed. Terry scrambled to him, helping him sit up.

Anderson's hand made a feeble, sweeping motion. "Check everyone."

Terry walked over to Brumsen's mangled body. Unseeing eyes gazed skyward. He bent down and gently closed both of them. He staggered to Duffy. The bloody, muddy bandage Cochise had tried desperately to place on him lay across Duffy's chest, covering a hole with shards of bone sticking out of it. Duffy's eyes were both closed.

Terry, legs weakening, sagged to the ground. He dragged himself through the mud and gore to the still body of Cochise. He rolled Cochise over onto his back and closed his friend's eyes.

Terry reached for a rifle. He walked over to Anderson and knelt beside him. Anderson, grimacing in pain, looked at Terry, his eyes knowing, yet questioning. Terry shook his head.

Anderson shut his eyes and lay back on the muddy ground. Tears and sweat streaked his face.

Terry examined a magazine pouch. It contained two magazines. He checked the magazine in the rifle. "I need to make sure."

Anderson, watching him, nodded.

Terry gazed around the pit. He pointed his rifle at a Vietnamese lying across the mound and shot him twice. He did the same to each Vietnamese soldier in the area. After he pulled Cochise's knife out of the dead man's face, Terry slowly moved away. He saw the one-armed Vietnamese that Duffy had shot and snapped off two quick rounds. The man's body twitched when the bullets hit.

The claymores and grenades had cleared a large area. Trees were down. Someone groaned. Terry lifted the branch of a felled tree. A man struggled to stand on bloody legs. The flesh around one of his knees had been shredded. A kneecap dangled from a shard of skin. Terry shot the soldier in his side and back as he leaned against a tree trunk. Without stopping, Terry continued to search for more wounded. He lost count of how many men he shot, not knowing or caring if they were alive or dead.

Terry found Anderson unconscious. After securing several bandages, he cut Anderson's fatigues from his arms and legs with Cochise's knife. He wrapped the bandages around Anderson's wounds. Terry picked up two grenades lying on the ground. One at a time, he pulled the pins and threw them into the jungle. After they exploded, he stared into the silence. Beating on his chest with one hand, he yelled as loud as he could until his voice grew hoarse. Terry stood in the middle of the pit until he heard Anderson's voice calling for him to pop a smoke grenade. The whump-whump of the helicopter descending drowned out all other noises.

Standing in a wire stretcher, a crewman lowered himself from the helicopter and helped Terry place Anderson in it.

As they lifted him into the hovering helicopter, the crewman turned, inspecting their hole and the carnage. He shook his head.

Terry slipped a poncho under Brumsen's battered body, motioning the man to help him prepare Brumsen for lifting.

The crewman examined Brumsen, Cochise, and Duffy. "These guys are dead. Let's get the fuck outta here. We'll pick them up later." He signaled the chopper to lower a harness.

Terry pressed a gun barrel against the crewman's head. Terry's cold voice could be heard over the roar of the helicopter. "I'll shoot your dumb ass here and now. Help me get these men aboard the chopper."

No one on the helicopter looked at or talked to Terry, sitting among his dead friends with an M-16 lying across his lap.

The field hospital where they took the squad was composed of several large tents and quonset huts. The hospital bulged with wounded, both American and North Vietnamese, from the battle for the hill.

Terry sat beside the bed watching Anderson, whose breathing, labored at first, grew easier. Anderson tossed and turned for an entire day. Once he tried to pull the tubes from his nose, mouth, and arms. Terry helped a nurse tie Anderson's wrists to the bed frame, leaving play, but preventing him from grabbing the tubes. Delirious, Anderson called out the names of his men. Occasionally, Terry, sitting beside him, took the wet cloth from Anderson's forehead, soaking it in cool water.

Anderson moaned and opened his eyes. He grasped Terry's hand. "I've had a dream, a very bad dream. Tell the squad to saddle up and get ready to go."

As Anderson drifted off to sleep, Terry held his hand without speaking.

When the rockets struck, Terry slept in a chair beside Anderson, holding his hand. A rushing wind lifted him from his chair. Blackness descended.

EPILOGUE

Terry stared at his watch. He had wanted to be early and here he was. He hoped that Alex was not too cold. Shivering, Terry hugged himself.

"What is this place, Grandpa?"

"It's called the Vietnam Memorial."

He stared down the ramp. It was a valley of death. The names on the stark, black granite overwhelmed him. Fifty-eight thousand dead.

The taxi had dropped them off at the World War II Memorial. The flags waved. The Washington Monument towered majestically in the background. The Lincoln Memorial sat serenely at the other end of the reflecting pool. This was not just a memorial. It was a celebration of patriots who fought for their country against foreign enemies. It was a pat on the shoulder saying, "Job well done. Welcome home, heroes." Those who grieved loved ones could find solace in a victorious outcome.

A tour guide had been speaking to a group, pointing to the Lincoln Memorial. "One of the concerns was not to spoil the sight-line from the Washington Monument to the Lincoln Memorial."

Terry peered down the reflecting pool toward the Lincoln Memorial. The Vietnam Memorial was to the right of the reflecting pool, 58,000 men buried in the ground. There was nothing there to spoil the sight-line.

His grandson was at the apex of the two ramps descending into the valley. What was this monstrosity of dead men's names? It was a wailing wall where people poured ashes over their head, a place for grieving, regretting, mourning, and gnashing of teeth. This wall was the last political slap at Vietnam veterans, a graveyard of names. There was no celebration here, no pat on the shoulder, no solace. What kind of monument would they build for the soldiers, for Ella, from Iraq and Afghanistan?

He stepped down the ramp into the pit. In ten minutes he was meeting Brumsen's sister, Alicia. He had spent a month finding everyone's family. The list helped place them in locations. Sarah had helped him. Shame flushed his cheeks. Why had he waited so long? Cochise's wife and son. There was no excuse.

When Alicia answered the phone he had asked for Mrs. Brumsen.

"I'm sorry, but she's not feeling too well. Can I help you? I'm her daughter, Alicia."

"My name is Terry Malloy. I was with your brother when he died. I just wanted a chance to perhaps say hello to Mrs. Brumsen and try to arrange a meeting."

"I thought everyone with Guy Edmond was killed. It's true, he died in Vietnam, but maybe you have the wrong Brumsen."

"No, I have the right person. Did Brumsen ever write to you about a kid they called Hillbilly?"

"Mom gets Guy Edmond's letters out at least once a year. We read them together." There was a note of tenderness in her voice. "So, you're Hillbilly, the boy from Tennessee, if I remember correctly. Guy Edmond was crazy about you. He spoke of you often."

Choking down a sob, Terry tried to talk.

"Hello, are you still there?"

"Yes, I'm still here trying to get control of my emotions. Trust me when I say the feeling was mutual. Brumsen was a wonderful man. I'm coming to Washington for a conference soon. Do you think we could meet? You probably have a lot of questions you want answered and I have a lot things to tell you about your brother."

Terry had reached the apex of the walls. Alex ran to him, taking his hand. He turned right and went to the numbered block of granite that had the names of his squad. There they were: Vernon Allen Anderson, Guy Edmond Brumsen, Joseph David McDuff, Jorge Valentine Montoya.

Closing his eyes, wiping tears away, Terry ran his fingers over the granite, feeling the grooves of the letters one by one. "These are men that I love, Alex. They're all gone now. Good friends. Good men. I miss them."

A familiar voice spoke from behind him. "Hey, *amigo,* What the hell is this place?"

Opening his eyes, Terry saw the squad standing behind him, reflected in the wall. "This is a piece of black granite with dead men's names on it."

Brumsen cradled his machine gun in one hand, removing a toothpick from his mouth with the other. "Sounds like a gravestone to me."

Terry closed his eyes and leaned his head against the granite. "That's exactly what it is, a tombstone."

Eyes still closed, Terry heard the movement of equipment and men shuffling. Then he heard Duffy's gentle voice.

"Malloy, we've someone with us."

Terry opened his eyes. The squad still stood, reflected in the granite. At the end, Ella stood with a helmet hanging from her hand.

An MP arm badge hung from her shoulder, A forty-five holstered on her hip.

Terry moaned and sagged against the wall.

"Grandpa, are you okay?"

Visions of Ella danced in his head: skipping down the stairs in a pink, Easter dress with white socks and shiny shoes; kicking a soccer ball down the field, her reddish golden hair trailing behind her, sparkling in the sun; sitting on the couch in blue jeans waiting, for two hours, on her first date. My daughter! God, my daughter! He would never hug her again.

Wiping away tears, he patted Alex on the shoulder. "I'm fine."

Take me with you. I don't belong here. I'm not at home here anymore. This is not my world.

Ella's voice chimed in his head. "Someone has to show Alex how to be a man, take him hunting and fishing, encourage him in sports, help him with his homework. Dad, you're alive. Stay with the living, not the dead. Remember us."

Terry looked into the shiny granite. Ella was no longer there.

Anderson shifted his M-16 from one arm to another. "Whose that woman waving at you, the one in the blue dress?"

Terry, holding Alex's hand, turned his head. "I think that's Brumsen's sister, Alicia. I'm supposed to meet her."

Anderson adjusted the shoulder straps. "Okay, guys, saddle up. Malloy, you take the point."

5753589R00192

Made in the USA
San Bernardino, CA
20 November 2013